Getting Blue

PETER GETHERS

"Gethers' story is, again like life, punctuated with moments of magic, perfect meaning, of harmony when things come together and life shines with the promise it once held for a young centerfielder enjoying his first love affair and making plans 'to do the greatest thing anyone's ever done'."
—*Spitball, The Literary Baseball Magazine*

"Provocative . . . Gethers pulls you into the center of Alex's world and makes you root for him to achieve his life's ambition. . . . It's the kind of novel you'll want to lend to a friend."
—*The Tampa Tribune*

"Although Peter Gethers has framed his story knowledgeably and colorfully around the national pastime, he is more interested in the dreams of men and women, those who seek perfection and recognition—as he called it, 'getting blue'—and those who shy away from it."
—*The New York Times Book Review*

"A perceptive, compelling narrative . . . populated by memorable characters."
—*Publishers Weekly*

"GETTING BLUE has everything . . . a marvelous, warm, witty, happy, sad, comedic, dramatic, masterfully told story as American as *Tom Sawyer*."
—William Diehl

Getting Blue

Getting Blue

PETER GETHERS

LAUREL

A LAUREL TRADE PAPERBACK

Published by
Dell Publishing
a division of
Bantam Doubleday Dell Publishing Group, Inc.
666 Fifth Avenue
New York, New York 10103

ISBN: 0-440-50185-7
Reprinted by arrangement with Delacorte Press
Printed in the United States of America
Published simultaneously in Canada
June 1989

10 9 8 7 6 5 4 3 2 1
W

To Marc Jaffe: Boss, Mentor, Friend. Forever.

and to

The Pie, for all the years
Maura, for all the love
Janis, for all the aggravation

ACKNOWLEDGMENTS

I would like to thank the following people, all of whom either read, edited, encouraged, or sold: Esther Newberg, Roberta Pryor, Jackie Farber, Judith Riven, David Handler, Laura Godfrey, Peter Kortner, and, as always, my parents.

To get that elusive beat, a jazzman
will do anything. Without it, he
cannot do anything.

—Barry Ulanov
A History of Jazz in America

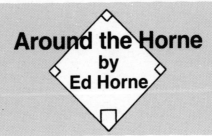

Around the Horne
by
Ed Horne

THE PLAY

He waited a long time for this moment. An entire career. An entire lifetime. That's a long time for one moment of perfection.

Most players never achieve it, though they understand it. Understand it? Hell, they *long* for it, dream about it. It's what makes them get up in the morning, what makes them sweat; it's what keeps them young in an aging world. Most people never even get to imagine such a moment, much less achieve it. It's why professional sports exists— because at least they, *we*, get to see it, hear it, dream it, live through it.

Rarely does it all come together like this: the player, the dream, the situation. But it came together yesterday here in New York, in Yankee Stadium, in right field, on the warning track. With millions of people watching, just such a moment occurred.

Alex Justin achieved perfection. . . .

PART ONE
1950s

Gold dust at my feet
On the sunny side of the street.

—"On the Sunny Side of the Street"

1

Ever since Alex Justin could remember, he'd had a secret world.

He didn't really think about it that much and when he did, as he was doing now lying in the cool Central Park grass, he never considered it a very big deal. What harm could be done? He simply liked to think things sometimes, and feel things, and he liked to keep them all to himself. Somehow it gave him a certain strength, this world. These secrets.

They were not dark thoughts, spirited away and hidden, locked inside—Alex did not have a lot of dark thoughts. Nor was he afraid of sharing these secret feelings—Alex did not have many fears either. What he did have was a very great skill, an ability, a talent. He could play baseball better than anybody in New York City, as far as he knew better than anybody in the world. He had never met anyone who could play baseball better than he could. And he had never, ever, met anybody else who understood this ability or the feelings he had about it. Never met anyone to whom he could explain it. Alex was *born* with an unsharable secret and somewhere, deep down at the core, he believed the very fact it was a secret to be part of the ability. So he added to the core, in bits and pieces. An observation here, that he tucked away, a perception there; an experience, a flash of an emotion. They then simply became part of his secret world. Part of him.

There didn't seem to be a real pattern to the things he buried within. Often it was just a sensation. Like when he got his haircut at Sal's, the same place his dad went, and Sal would prepare him—wash his hair, hot towel his face, snap the sheet-like apron in the air, then tie it around his neck—it always gave him these shivers of pleasure. When Sal would begin cutting, snipping away at the hair above his ears, he would actually feel this electric tingling up and down his spine, along his arms, and his eyes would close and lights would be dancing inside his eyelids. Or once when he went with his mom to a department store and he wandered off; he stood by the lingerie department and watched this saleswoman, a short, spindly woman who looked like the perfect aunt, he watched her sort through and refold a tableful of satin and silk nightgowns. It got suddenly quiet except for the soft Muzak in the background and the rustling of the clothing and the woman's soft breathing. There was this faint aroma of perfume, not one woman's but a scent of universal perfume. Alex felt lightheaded; he actually had to go sit down. It was nice, this dizziness, and soothing, and somehow it all tied in with Sal the barber and the feeling he got playing baseball on a sweaty, scorching hot day in a sandlot field by the stinking East River.

No, there was no pattern to his secrets. Lately they'd had a lot to do with sex, which surprised him because he did not really think about sex all that much. He liked it, that was for sure. He'd never actually had it, but he knew he *would* like it. While he had not yet slept with his first woman, he had seen some breasts and he liked those a lot.

About a year before, he had dated Mary Riley several times and had kissed her huge melonlike breasts with their tiny rubber-thimble nipples. For a while, once a week—Thursday nights from seven to nine when Mary's parents were out at the local ban-the-bomb headquarters, stuffing envelopes and manning the special Fallout Phones—Mary had let him lick his tongue over her breasts and moan urgently while she ground her teeth and kept her fingers taut against his temples and forehead, making sure his lips went no farther than she planned. After six weeks of such erotic enticement Alex suspected he'd gotten as far as he was going to get past Mary's unbelievably strong fingers. He didn't quite know how to cope with this feeling of helplessness and was sort of happy when she'd abandoned him for summer camp. Her long nails had left a tiny scar on his left temple.

Danny Cappollo, his best friend, knew about the kissing part and how, a few times, he'd come right in his pants and Mary had gotten completely grossed out, but even Danny didn't know about Mary's nipples or her sharp nails. They were part of Alex's secret world.

And he had a hunch the girl he'd just seen had become a part of it too.

He was lying on a sloping hill, under a tree, head south, feet north. His shirt was off, spread out under his back; his legs were bent, sneakers firmly planted on the ground, knees raised to the white drifting clouds. He was still wearing his baseball pants, having just come from a game. Grass stained, old and faded, they looked like pants that belonged to somebody who'd *done* something, and he liked wearing them. He'd also kept his thick gray sweatsocks on—they felt comfortable under the stretch bands of his pants. He'd had a great game earlier that morning against the Pirates, who were largely a bunch of turds and faggots but were good enough to be only two games behind Alex's team, the Tigers. Until he ran onto the field, Alex thought the weight of the flannel uniform would melt his whole body away on this, the hottest weekend of the summer. But when play started, the shirt was his skin, the pants part of his legs, and once again he was surprised how totally he was sucked into his game. He almost forgot who he was or what he did when he wasn't chasing fly balls and swinging the bat and stealing bases.

The scouts were out in droves. Everyone knew who they were there to watch, and Alex didn't disappoint a soul. His first time at bat he doubled, a vicious line drive pulled past the third baseman. Alex thought he had a triple, maybe an inside-the-parker, but the left fielder, Luis Hernandez, made a terrific play and Alex had to hold at second. His next time up the score was tied 2–2 and both pitchers were throwing beautifully. There was a runner on first and nobody out, so Alex laid down a perfect sacrifice; a show-off move without question, pure hot dog, but he did it sweetly. He knew those tough bastards in the stands with their hip flasks and notepads and memories of Wee Willie Keeler were impressed. In the fifth he made a great catch, robbing Teddy Birnbaum of an extra baser. Alex had to run to his left, toward the right fielder, who was unbelievably slow, into the middle of right field, and dive. He slid on his belly for three feet and when he stopped skidding he put his glove up and the ball slammed into the pocket as if it had eyes. Alex wasn't surprised at his success, but a gasp seemed to circulate around the bleachers.

His third time at bat Alex connected. The ball sailed out of the lot, just kept going and going, flying out into the sun. He went around the bases, so cool, so in control, that he got an extra round of applause just for his home run trot.

By the time he got to bat in the seventh inning, the Tigers were ahead of the Pirates seven to three and it was clear they were the better team. To clinch it, Alex hit a second home run, with two men on. When the game ended he was drenched in sweat, his hair matted to his forehead, his chest heaving with exhaustion, pride, and nerves. The scouts descended on the locker room, but he wasn't even supposed to talk to them unless his father or high school coach was present, so he beat it out of there the second the game was over. He ducked out behind the bleachers as soon as Paul Eagle hit into the game-ending double play, and hightailed it to his favorite relaxing spot in Central Park. He'd replaced his spikes with black high-topped Keds, his uniform shirt with a light blue T-shirt. And now, lying on that shirt, through half-closed eyes he saw a crown of dark, dark hair bob by over the rim of a hill. Delicate strands of silk floating belligerently, slithering elegantly, in the wind.

He braced himself and sat up attentively. The hair disappeared behind a bush and Alex scrambled the few feet to the top of the incline. The girl reappeared.

It was her.

He didn't know her name. He didn't even know what she

truly looked like, since he'd never gotten all that close to her; he couldn't tell if she had bad teeth or a crooked nose. He'd never heard her voice, didn't know what color her eyes were, didn't have any idea what she thought or felt. But she was a part of him.

He'd seen her before, maybe four or five times. He'd sit in the park, in his favorite spot, and she'd stroll by. Maybe she lived nearby. Maybe she just liked to walk. She never saw him or, if she did, didn't pay any particular notice. It didn't matter. Alex was content to watch unobserved.

He'd never seen anyone quite like her.

She, too, must have been a teenager, around his age. This day her frilly dress was cream colored—every time he'd seen her she was in some kind of white—full and flowery, yet it clung to her body, alive in its sexuality. He was able to see the shape of her breasts—they were small, firm, strong. She strolled along, ambled, strutted, as the sun played tricks with the color of her hair. Her movements seemed to summon everything around her, as though nothing less was her due.

The breeze swirled her dress, billowed it above her knees. She made no move to pull it down and her thighs beckoned, tan flashing contrasts to the clothing. They looked muscular; she could grip whatever she needed in those thighs. There were no hairs, no marring bumps, no scrapes or scabs or bruises. They were in perfect proportion to her calves and, in turn, to her tapered, nicely bony ankles. Barefoot, her arch was perfectly curved, her toes narrow but not too long. She had delicious-looking feet and she seemed barely to part the grass when she stepped.

The dark-brown hair was thick and straight, with the slightest wave. It came only to her shoulders but looked longer. It moved wonderfully, swinging back and forth with her strides, mistress of the wind. The face was sculpted. A marvelous knowledge shone from the eyes, a lusty sensuality in the slant of the lips. Her forehead was small and unfurrowed, her chin was rounder than it was square, with a tiny cleft.

She looked in his direction once, took more steps, headed nowhere in particular, glanced over his way again. He stared, never wavering, and thought she noticed him, but he wouldn't swear to it. The girl was hidden momentarily behind two fat people, then reemerged and was swept into a crowd of hot dog vendors, Negroes swilling beer, mothers leading their children in the direction of the zoo. Alexander Justin watched her until he had to run after her to watch some more.

He saw her buy a Good Humor, then leave the park. The last view was much like the first: the very top of her head bobbing up and down and eventually disappearing on the other side of a stone wall. His eyes stayed on the street long after she was gone, then he gazed at the park path she had wandered, retracing her steps. She was now a secret part of Alex Justin. He didn't know what he would do with her but he knew, somehow, he wanted to keep her.

"I heard you were good today."

Alex was eased out of his reverie by the soothing, soft, and familiar voice of Patty Farber. For some reason, even if it was totally unexpected, as it was now, he was never completely startled to hear Patty's voice. It always sounded natural, it belonged whatever the surroundings, whatever the situation. It was a gentle voice, soft, without shrillness. It had a slight tremor in it which sometimes meant nervousness or fear, sometimes delight and sometimes love. It was part of her mystery, part of her alluring vulnerability, part of the reason he cared for her so much, that sometimes it meant all four, all mixed together in one confusing, exhilarating moment. He no longer remembered if he'd felt this way about her voice—or liked it so very much—when he first heard it or whether this was the result of all the time they'd spent together.

"Where'd you hear that from?"

They spoke in a lilting singsong tone to each other, especially when they were casually teasing, which was much of the time. It was a tone of affection and had somehow become the way they talked to each other. He felt it was as if they were touching each other with their voices; it was like holding hands or gently placing palm to cheek. When other people were around, Danny or Alex's parents, he tried to speak to her in more normal tones.

Sometimes, though, he forgot and would turn red at Danny's silent mocking stare.

"It's *awwllll* over town," she said. "Scouts were there to watch you and you hit a home run and a triple and knocked in the winning run."

"You saw Beanie."

"Rats. Found out."

Beanie was her brother. An asshole but a pretty good pitcher. He'd pitched and won earlier that day.

"How'd you know I'd be here?"

Her voice deepened and took on the trace of a husky, bad foreign accent. "I know *evvverything,*" Patty said.

"It's weird, you know that?"

"What is?"

"You can sort of sense where I'll be, can't you?"

"I can, sometimes." She smiled as if that made her feel secure.

"I mean you *knew* I'd be here, didn't you? Right at this spot."

"You come here a lot after a game. Right at this spot."

"Yeah, but I could've gone to a movie or I coulda gotten hungry and gone to eat or . . ."

"I like that I can sense where you're going to be."

"I like it too," he said. "A lot. A *lot.* But it makes me kind of nervous."

She went back to the foreign accent. "Vherever you are, I'll find you." Patty grinned, went over to him, and kissed him lightly on the lips. Then she crinkled up her nose. *"Anybody'd* be able to find you."

"Yeah," he said. "I didn't shower after the game."

"Have you showered in the last *year?*"

He nodded, after thinking it over. "Once or twice. No, wait. Maybe that was last year."

"You know what Beanie said today?" she asked, dropping the teasing tone.

"Tell me."

"He said you were a sure bet."

"He did?"

"A sure bet."

Alex liked that, it made him smile with satisfied pleasure, but he said, "There's no such thing as a sure bet."

"Do you really think that?"

"No," he said. "I don't. Will you kiss me again, please?"

She made another face but stepped closer to him. Her hint of a smile told him that she didn't really care what he smelled like.

Their eyes met and lingered. Hers were brown and revealing, a little too nice, too clear. Too trusting. They showed she was still a very young girl. Alex decided, as if this were the first time he'd ever met her, as he did almost every single time he saw her, that he liked her a lot. He was suddenly very glad it was Saturday and he was standing in Central Park with his shirt off, smelling awful.

Patty Farber was not a part of Alex's secret world. She was not someone to tuck away and hide. She was someone to share with other people. She was someone to take into a crowded room and say, "Here, talk to her, she'll make you feel good, she'll understand you and she'll like you." She was a very special girl who, when he met her nine months, two weeks, and four days before, he'd known instantly he had to get to know better.

He'd seen her talking to Beanie before a game and he couldn't believe that anyone so pretty would even talk to Beanie Farber. She was little. Not short; she was taller than normal, although that always surprised him because she looked so fragile. Her hair was a medium-dark brown and very straight; bangs covered her forehead. Her skin was very white, her lips a little too big, and her chin was a tiny bit pudgy, the only part of her that had anything extra on it at all. Her eyes were shy and her arms were bare and so delicate-looking, even with the thin fuzz of dark hair that ran up to just below her elbow. Her face was serious, too serious; she looked as if she were trying to understand everything in the whole world all at once. And that trying to understand frightened her a little. Alex was about to turn away, to head to the outfield, when he saw her grin. It was clearly something that didn't appear on her face all the time—he wasn't sure how he could tell that but he definitely could—and it knocked him out. Something had pleased her, and that grin reflected more pleasure than Alex had seen in a long time. Her teeth seemed to sparkle and her eyes turned so peaceful and her whole face relaxed and it made him want to *make* her grin again. So he did something he'd never done before. As soon as Beanie turned to go to the pitcher's mound, Alex ran over to the girl. He had to shout, "Hey!" when he was still a few yards from her so she wouldn't move too far away for him to talk to her. She stopped when he yelled, looked curiously at him, waiting. But when he got close to her he realized he didn't have anything to say.

"I'm Alex Justin" was the best he came up with.

"I know," she said. Then with the faintest smile, not at all mocking, "You're the one they all talk about."

"Who?"

She waved her hand vaguely toward the crowd.

"Them."

"Who are you?"

"Patty Farber."

"Beanie's sister?" She nodded. "How come I never see you around? At school, I mean."

"I go to Hunter."

"Oh," he said, impressed. "A brain."

"That's me." She grinned and started to head back to the bleacher seats.

"Or on the playground," he said quickly.

"What?"

"I never saw you on the playground either."

"You just never noticed. I've seen you."

"Listen," Alex said, deciding that small talk was not his forte, "would you like to do something tonight?"

"You mean a date?"

"Well, uh, yeah. Kind of."

Her silence went on long enough that he became completely embarrassed and said, "Well, what are you thinking?"

Patty cocked her head, squinting at him. "I'm thinking that here it is Saturday afternoon and if I just say okay, you'll either think I'm unpopular or that I'm going to cancel my plans because I can't resist you. Maybe I should say no and then you'll be impressed and you'll have to come around again to try a second time."

"You have plans?" he asked.

"No," she said. "I'm unpopular."

They went to a movie that night, then had a Chinese dinner at the Hong Kong Gardens. They talked nonstop and Alex realized he'd never met anyone before whom he'd wanted to talk to so much. They talked about school, the future, her previous boyfriend, and how much she already wanted to go to college, even though she was a year behind him. They talked about baseball and friendship and the advantages of pepperoni versus just plain cheese pizza. Then, as they were about to break open their fortune cookies, she asked, "What do you want to do more than anything in the whole world?"

He didn't even think about that one. He just said, "Be the greatest baseball player who ever lived!"

"No," Patty said. "That's what you want to be. What do you want to *do?*"

He thought, but not for long. "Do the greatest thing anyone's ever done on a baseball field."

"What?"

"I don't know. Doesn't really matter. Something that's never been done. Something important. Something great and perfect."

"You can *do* something perfect, can't you?"

Her voice had this strange sense of detached wonderment, but he understood what she meant and felt that she understood him when all he said was "Yeah," and pointed in the general direction of where he'd played ball earlier in the day. "Out there I can."

He kissed her on their third date.

They went to another movie. He'd already seen it on a date with Gail Schneckenbert, but Patty hadn't, so he pretended it was his first time too. Afterward they were walking home, east for a few blocks, then up First Avenue. They lived just a few blocks from each other, in Stuyvesant Town in the twenties. The air was hot and thick, the sky threatening rain, but they were taking their time, not talking much, just enjoying being together.

"It's nice walking with you," Alex mumbled when they hit Fourteenth Street and he had decided the silence was lasting too long.

"We walk well together."

"Everyone tells me I walk too fast."

"Me too."

"Am I walking too fast for you?"

"No."

"Oh. Good."

"We're walking slowly."

"Yeah," he said.

"Even shuffling, you might say."

"I guess we are."

"Tell me about your brother."

Alex missed a step, twisting his ankle slightly. "Why do you, uh, what made you think of that?"

"I don't know. Talking about walking, shuffling."

"Oh. Yeah."

"When did he get polio?"

Alex took a deep breath.

"Do you not want to talk about it?" she asked.

"I don't usually."

"Okay."

"But I'll talk about it with you. I mean, whaddya wanna know?"

"When did he get it? The polio?"

"It got really bad about a year ago. When he was eleven, almost twelve. That's when he got the brace. Why do you wanna know?"

She smiled warmly and reassuringly. "I'm just nosy. I like to know everything. When I have a friend, I mean like you, I try to know every single thing there is to know about them. Him. You." She lowered her eyes.

"So you don't really wanna know about him. You wanna know about me."

"He's part of you, isn't he?" Then, when Alex nodded, she said, "It's the parts that make up the whole."

"Yeah," he said, but he didn't really know what the hell she was talking about. Parts. The whole. There was only just *you,* that's what he'd always thought. There was you and then there were all those other things that touched you. Made you happy or sad as long as they were touching you. They felt good or hurt but then they went away and you were still you.

"I'm sorry if I've upset you," she apologized.

"You haven't," he told her.

"Yes, I have."

"No, you haven't."

"I can tell."

"I swear."

"I'm always right about stuff like this."

"I'm not upset!"

"Okay," she said.

"You don't believe me."

"Sure I do."

"You don't."

"I do."

"I can tell."

"I believe you!"

"Swear?"

"No."

Now she grinned that grin at him, showing her teeth, which were perfectly straight and white. The grin was to cheer him up, to end their silly exchange, to let him know she wanted him to like her and not to ever let her upset him. Watching her grin, he wanted to tell her he was starting to think she was beautiful. It came out as "You have really amazing teeth."

"I bet you say that to all the girls."

He made a face at her, a get-outta-here face, but in case she didn't get it, he said, "Get outta here," and shook his head.

"I have an award-winning bite." She stuck her nose high up into the air. "As a matter of fact."

"Say what?"

Her nose came down and she shrugged. "My dentist made a

mold of my teeth and took it to a convention in St. Louis. My bite won an award." He laughed. "Don't knock it," she told him. "It's my claim to fame."

They walked another half a block before he started to laugh again. It began as a chuckle, eased into a snicker, and was getting ready to turn into a real belly laugh, tears and all, when he propped himself up against a building.

"Are you still on my teeth?"

"Most Valuable Gums."

"What?"

"Wouldn't that be a great award? Next year in St. Louis? The MVG Award?"

"I don't get it."

He cleared his throat deliberately, throwing his head back and pounding his chest, trying to stop his giggling. He sniffed and wiped his eyes. He let his fingers rest on his closed eyelids before he turned to face her. "You don't get what?" he asked.

"MVG."

"Like MVP." No reaction on her part. None. A total blank stare. He cleared his throat again. "Most Valuable Player?"

"Ohhhhhhhhhh."

"Get it?"

"Not really."

"You're not really known for your sense of humor, are you?"

Patty bared her teeth, chomping them together three times. "My bite. That's what I'm known for."

She grinned at him again and he didn't grin back, only stared at her with his eyes wide open, eyes that asked all sorts of questions, eyes that demanded all kinds of answers, and that was when he kissed her. He put his hand in the middle of her back and pulled her toward him. Her hip banged against his and her eyes widened in surprise at his sudden yank but she didn't resist so he bent down and put his face up against hers. Hesitating, he started to say something, but then had nothing to say. They were too close together for him to back off. He could actually feel her breath in gentle puffs on his face, warming the exact same spot on his cheek over and over again. He kept his eyes open and moved the extra few inches so their lips grazed awkwardly. The skin against skin made a slight noise, a tiny pop that made his head spin. Now he could smell her breath, the faint odor of 7-Up and mint mouthwash. He also smelled her perfume, which was a little too sweet. And there was something else too. Powder, maybe. Or shampoo. Or maybe it was just her, some special scent that made her Patty Farber, a mixture of cosmetics, chemicals, and soul. He drew away, only an inch, but there was, all of a sudden, an unmistakable gap to overcome. Patty didn't move, didn't change expression, only stared back at him, and her eyes told him it was all right. He came back in to her slowly and they kissed again, their bodies hugging, two separate puzzle pieces fitted together. The kiss stayed, lingered endlessly. He tasted the inside of her upper lip, a new sensation. It was smooth and wet. It tasted *shiny*. He grabbed the back of her head, seizing the ends of her hair, and slowly lowered her face onto his chest, importantly and solemnly. Patty rested against him, arms wrapped tightly around his body, and she chomped her teeth together three more times.

After that Alex entered into his first relationship. He liked it. He and Patty studied in tandem most weeknights—he was actually going to wind up with a B average for the semester thanks to her tutoring—and on clear weekends they dived gleefully into mounds of Central Park leaves. On rainy ones they drank hot chocolates and listened to music, sometimes Duke Ellington, sometimes Elvis. They talked on the phone forever, usually until Carl, Alex's father, threw up his hands in disgust and started yelling. Alex taught Patty the fine rules of baseball—she would never, *ever* bunt with two strikes on her, she promised, no, she *swore*—and he touched her constantly and reassuringly. He gave her his senior ring, a turquoise stone in a silver setting, and also his letterman's sweater. She knit him a long scarf in blue and orange—her class colors—to let other girls know he was hers, and which, as a side effect, kept him warm. They were like sexual magnets, making out in empty apartments, balconies of movie theaters, backseats of buses. They discovered the joys of tongues and hated every moment theirs were not intertwined. She was thrilled and got dizzy when he kissed her breasts and she loved to grab the top of his head and throw his bristly hair in every direction. She tickled him till he cried, he cracked his knuckles to drive her crazy. He dragged her everywhere, showing her off, delighting in her acceptance and approval of his favorite haunts. Alex's friends grew to like Patty's quiet ways, her timidity, they laughed when she slipped some of her own spirit into their rowdy camaraderie; her friends were surprised and a little jealous that she had snagged a hero. But, as a couple, they were too nice for anyone to hold anything against them for too long.

Watching her as they stood in Central Park, Alex for some reason remembered a conversation they'd had one evening sitting on "their" bench in Stuyvesant Town as the sun was going down.

"It's getting too cold to keep meeting on the bench," she had said.

"Whaddya mean, too cold?"

"I mean I'm too cold. Look, my hands are a strange bluish color."

"They're not so blue."

She reached over lovingly, but instead of playing with his hair, which he thought was her intent, she held her hand against his neck.

"Aaaauugghhh!" he said.

"See what I mean? Cold."

"Okay, okay. I admit they're cold."

"I'd say we have another week of the bench, tops."

"I'll miss it."

"That's nice. You're very romantic."

"Oh, yeah."

"You *are*. Much more than I am. It's because you're more . . . more *passionate* than I am."

Alex rolled his eyes lewdly.

"I mean it. But I know I've got the same kind of passion in me. I *know* it. I just don't know how to . . . show it."

"What are you talking about, Patty?"

"Oh!" she said, and clapped her hands together excitedly. "I've got an assignment for you!"

"Yes?"

She jumped to her feet. "Your assignment is, while we're young and in love, to take my passion and drag it out of me. Make me understand it, or at least recognize it and not be afraid of it."

"Uh . . ."

"I realize this is a lot of responsibility. Especially for a center fielder. But . . ."

"But what?" he said.

"But I trust you," she told him very seriously. "You're a star."

The park suddenly seemed crowded. Softball games and jump-ropers and baby carriages had materialized, as if out of thin air. A rubber kickball rolled to a stop in a thick patch of grass, inches in front of Alex. He bent down and tossed it back to a little boy whose playmates were hooting and hollering over the errant kick.

"I finished a great book last night," Patty said suddenly as Alex pulled his blue T-shirt on over his head, still wondering about trust and stardom and girls.

"Oh, yeah? What?" The shirt kept sticking to the sweat on his back.

"Lady Chatterley's Lover. Mrs. Young, my English teacher, told us that it was great but we weren't allowed to read it officially 'cause the school board thought it was dirty."

"That's all you had to hear, huh?"

"Yup. Right to the library for some smut."

"Good dirt?"

"It's not really dirty at all. It's a real beautiful love story. Very sad."

"I never understood how a love story could be sad. I mean, if two people are in love, then they're in love and it's not sad."

"Well what about if they break up?"

"Then they're not in love."

"What if events force them apart?"

Alex shook his head. "Love's love. If it's real, it holds you together."

"Wanna hear the opening line of the book?" He nodded and

she quoted, " 'Ours is essentially a tragic age, so we refuse to take it tragically.' I've been thinking about this all day."

"And?"

"Well, I don't think these *are* tragic times. They just seem fairly ordinary."

"Maybe D. H. Lawrence is smarter than you are."

"Maybe life was tragic *then*. Maybe now it's ordinary."

"I don't think I believe in tragedy," Alex said.

"I'm glad," Patty said. "Me either. *Now!* What are the plans for tonight?"

"How many times do we have to go over this?" Alex tried to pretend he was annoyed, but he knew she could tell he was pretending.

"Come on. I'm excited. Aren't you excited?"

He shrugged and looked extremely nonchalant. "Eh."

"You're lying! You're just as excited as I am!"

"Maybe a little."

She ran to him, almost jumped into his arms, ramming against him and hugging him, looking up into his eyes.

"I'm excited," Patty said again.

"I know." He grinned. "Me, too, me too."

"So what are we doing exactly? Let's go over it again. I don't want to blow my first prom."

"My folks want us to both be at the apartment around six-thirty."

"*Around* six-thirty?"

"*At* six-thirty."

"Okay." Patty's grin was lighting up Central Park. "What time is it now?"

"Around three." Before she could say anything, he said, "Ten after three."

"We better get going."

"How long does it take to get dressed?"

"Well it'll take you about two hours to tie your bow tie."

"That's not a bad point."

"Then what? What next?"

"Hold it. Just hold your horses. I think my dad's gonna open a bottle of champagne."

"Really? No!"

"I think so. I saw that he bought a bottle. He sorta hid it in the back of the fridge this morning."

"You know what?"

"Uh-uh."

"I've never had champagne. Never. Not even a taste."

"I had it once. I don't like it too much."

"I don't care. That'll be fun."

"Yeah. Then, the dinner starts at eight o'clock."

"Wait. We've gotta see my mom before we go. She wants a picture of you in a tuxedo. Are you getting me a corsage?"

"Am I supposed to just tell you? Shouldn't it be a surprise or something?"

"Okay. It'll be a surprise. So we'll see my mom for a minute or two, then what?"

"We'll meet Danny and the girl he's bringing."

"Who's he bringing again?"

"Diana."

"She kinda dumb?"

"That's the one." He knew she was going to go on about Danny and he really didn't want to hear it. He held up his hand, knowing that would stop her. It did.

"I'm sorry I don't like Danny more," she said, and he knew she meant it. She *was* sorry. "I mean, I kind of like him. There's something there I like. And I keep trying, I really do."

"I know."

The subject of Danny Cappollo briefly stopped the flow of the conversation. They stood there, awkward for a moment, until Patty touched his hand, once, lightly on the back, and went on.

"So then we're at the dinner . . ."

"And that's pretty much it. We eat, we dance. We'll probably have to watch Dominick Verner vomit when he drinks too much."

"Alex . . ."

"Danny's parents are out of town and I thought we might go back there afterward. You know, just to talk."

"That sounds good."

"And my dad is playing tonight," he said slowly. "A special

sort of thing. He thought we might want to come down there late."

"That'd be fun."

"I told him we'd see what happens."

"Let's do it, okay, Alex?" She touched his arm.

"Why?"

" 'Cause he'd like it a lot. And I've hardly ever heard him."

"Okay." He looked away from her.

"I mean, not if you don't want to."

"No. It sounds good. Let's just see what happens."

Alex wasn't a hundred percent sure why he was being so evasive about going to hear his dad play. He used to love it, but lately he'd felt, well, uneasy when he'd dropped in.

Carl Justin was a pretty average grade-school teacher. He didn't make much money and Alex also knew his father gambled away a helluva lot of whatever he made at the track. He had once taken Alex with him on a visit to his bookie, an awful guy who squinted and lisped and worked out of a toystore storeroom. Alex never asked his dad why he'd wanted him to see all this; at some point he thought it was his dad's way of saying, *See, boy, this is me. You're old enough now to see my life.* Alex didn't want to see this part of his dad's life. He much preferred the Carl Justin who could do crossword puzzles in ink, and who liked coming home after work, making them all drop any plans and taking the whole family out for a big Chinese dinner at a special dive under the El in The Bronx. He took his boys to football games and let them eat too much. He treated his wife to movies during the summer so they could escape the heat in air-conditioned comfort. He was wonderfully gentle with Elliot. He always bought an extra afternoon paper so Alex could pore over the sports pages. But best of all was every Monday night. It was Mondays when Carl Justin played the clarinet in Bell's, a tiny club on Grove Street. He played with a bunch of other guys who worked all week—one in the garment center, another as a dentist, and one with his very own mortuary—but who, on Monday nights, all took off their Clark Kent glasses and picked up their instruments to stomp out powerful Dixieland, coax out sweet blues, cry out real-life bebop jazz.

They were great, these guys. They called themselves Bell's Stars, and Alex loved to drop into the club, casually wave a hand at Johnny, the bartender, and carry his ginger ale over to a table where his dad could see him from the stage. Those were the moments when his father was at peace: when he was playing for beer and his son's satisfaction. The only moments.

That was something Alex did not understand. To Alex, life was easy and it confused him that his father, when not making music, made things so complicated. Carl struggled—against traffic, against politicians, against his students, against anything that offered resistance. He had a rigid moral code, not better than anyone else's, but different, and it was inflexible and forever. It was constantly making him new enemies and losing him old friends. Alex figured he was too young to understand his father, so he didn't really try. He assumed that, like everything else, it would all just fall into place one day.

Things usually fell into place at Bell's. But lately the music had started to have a funny effect on him. One night, a few months earlier, he was in listening to his dad's band and they were really wailing, really into it. Alex was alone; his mom had decided not to come. All of a sudden the music just grabbed him. Latched onto his stomach and wouldn't let go. It shook up his insides and made him go hot then cold then horny then violent then peaceful. He felt as if he were going crazy for a while, until the music stopped. Then he saw his dad heading over toward his table. He saw people milling around; a woman, a little drunk, wobble on her barstool. He shook his head to clear it; slowly the room came back into focus. His dad was smiling at him.

"Good set, huh?"

"Great, Dad. Great." His voice sounded okay. Natural. He was relieved. No one could tell what had happened to him. It had passed unnoticed.

Since then, Alex had become much more conscious of music. He started to believe it was behind everything that moved. It was always there: blatantly filling up a kitchen as it poured from a radio; sneakily slipping in and out of streets and shops as it was passed along by happy whistlers and unconscious hummers; it even permeated your brain and repeated itself silently over and over again, moving millions to an individual rhythm. He began to see music as more than a part of the background. It intruded, battered you. It could tell you what to feel. Sometimes music toyed with you, sweeping you along playfully, but sometimes, without warning, it made you burst. Sneaked inside you, shook you, shaped you. Left you whole, sure, but . . . changed.

Alex wasn't sure what to do with these realizations. The images were too jumbled for him to explain to anyone, even Patty. They were images he himself did not yet understand, could not yet deal with. So he tucked them away in his secret world and waited for something to spark their reemergence. He did not want them to reemerge tonight, however. Tonight he wanted things to be as wonderful as possible because tonight he was going to have to tell Patty that he was leaving in three days to go to Wilson, North Carolina, home of the Wilson Tobs, a Class B farm club of the Philadelphia Phillies. Tonight he was pretty sure he was going to break Patty's heart.

He'd gotten a decent offer from the Phils, a few days after Ewett Crane, their ancient scout, had come to their apartment. Forty-five hundred dollars a year salary, a $250 bonus for signing. They even paid for him and his father to take a train to Philadelphia, where Crane met them at the station and drove them to Connie Mack Stadium at the corner of Twenty-first and Lehigh. Alex was shown around the executive offices filled with expensive leather furniture that was starting to crack and scratch with age. He was introduced to the general manager, H. Roy Haney, and to Eugene J. Martin, the director of minor league clubs. Alex got a special treat when Richie Ashburn popped into the office to straighten something out about a deal he'd made with a sporting goods company.

Then Alex was taken down to the field, where he stood on the pitcher's mound and gawked at the 33,359 empty seats.

"I know what you're doin', boy," Ewett Crane called over to him from the first-base line. "You're hearin' the applause." When Alex nodded, awestruck, the scout muttered, "That's all right, that's all right. That's why we brought ya here."

Alex took a windup and threw an invisible ball toward home

plate. "Steee*rike!*" he hollered over to Crane, a big grin on his face. Crane did not grin back.

"What do you believe in, boy?"

Alex didn't say anything. He didn't know what to say.

"Do you believe in God? You can tell me the truth. I just wanna know."

Alex shrugged. "Not really, I guess. No." He didn't move off the mound.

"So whaddya believe in?"

Alex shrugged again, a little embarrassed that he didn't have an answer, at least not one he knew how to put into words.

"I'll tell you what you believe in," Crane said. "You believe in *yourself,* sonny boy, am I right?"

"You're right." Now Alex cocked his head, curious, and spoke more forcefully. "You're right."

"You're goddamn right I'm right. I'm not doin' this for thirty years so I don't know what I'm talkin' about. I can see with my own eyes. And when I see the way you walk and the way you hit and field and the way you wanna come up to the plate or get the ball hit to you when the game's on the line, I can tell you make your own luck! And you make your own luck, you don't need nothin' else."

"I see what you mean," Alex said. "Sort of."

"You wanna play baseball real bad, don't you?"

"Yes, sir. I do."

Ewett Crane leaned over, bent forward, practically touching his chin to his knees. He *sssssed* a drop of tobacco juice through his teeth.

"When you're good at something and you want it bad enough, bad enough to do what you're doin' . . . you *got* it! That's life in a nutshell, boy. I believe that all the way, heart and soul. Life's a game, one big game, and when you're playin' a game the best team always wins. Always! That's known as justice. And when you ain't got nothin' else, you can always count on justice. You work harder'n the other guy, you get better. You get better'n the other guy, you win. Then, when you win, you start makin' yer own luck. And when you're lucky you don't need nothin' else. That's what's *right* and right makes this here world spin. That's all there is to it."

Alex agreed with the old scout. And it felt right to play with the Phillies. But just in case, he also talked to a few other teams.

He had a firm offer from Cleveland and one from the Braves, both respectable. His favorite team, the Giants, had ignored him, much to his pain and regret, and the Dodgers had insulted him. They made him a flat offer of a four-thousand-dollar contract with no bonus. When Alex offered to come to Ebbetts Field to negotiate, the Brooklyn scout told him the deal was nonnegotiable.

"But I've already been offered more than that. The Phillies'll give me a bonus."

"Your bonus," the scout told him over the phone, "is getting the chance to play with the Brooklyn Dodgers."

So he decided to sign with the Phils and go with Ewett Crane and his luck. They upped the bonus to four hundred dollars and in three more days Alex was off to play for his first professional team. All he had left to do was tell Patty Farber, who picked that exact moment to say, "Come on, we'd better go. We've got to get ready for our perfect evening."

2

Stuyvesant Town began at Fourteenth Street, running up six blocks to Twentieth. It covered all the area from First Avenue to Avenue C, a huge housing project set up after the Second World War to help satisfy the apartment needs of the burgeoning middle class. There were thirty-five buildings, each thirteen or fourteen stories, holding 8,736 apartments.

The Justins' apartment was on the second floor of one of the monster red brick buildings. It was a three-bedroom place, one bathroom, nine-foot-high ceilings. There was wall-to-wall carpeting on the living-room floor, blond wood on the dining-room floor, and shiny tile in the bathroom. It cost $108 dollars a month. Dogs and air conditioners were forbidden.

Alex stood in front of his building, staring up at it, one foot resting on the chain links that were supposed to keep everybody out of the decorative grassy areas that dotted the complex. He could see inside his apartment, able to make out the figure of his mother, Virginia Justin—Ginny—through the flimsy beige curtains drawn across the front windows. She was moving around, bending over, straightening back up. She looked like she was setting the dinner table. Over to Alex's chair. Bend. Elliot's chair. Bend. Napkin, fork, spoon, knife. Up. Move.

It was the beginning of September, still hot as hell, and, watching his mother's shadow disappear into the kitchen, Alex was just deciding that, one, he should go in and change into his rented monkey suit, and, two, as soon as he got rich he'd make sure she had an air conditioner, when Danny Cappollo sidled up to him and jabbed a finger into his ribs.

"What's goin' on?" Danny asked.

"Nothin'."

Danny followed Alex's stare and saw the shadow of Ginny Justin. Danny smiled, the smile of a longtime best friend who understood unspoken sentiment.

"You wanna hear somethin' weird?" Alex asked.

"Sure."

"My mom's never had a vacation."

"Whaddya mean?"

"I mean she's never been anywhere. She says there's only one place in the whole world she wants to go."

"What's that?"

"Hawaii. And since they don't have the money to go there, she doesn't wanna spend money goin' to other places. She'd rather just save up until they can afford Hawaii."

"That is pretty weird."

"One night my dad surprised her and had a . . . a . . . a luau, that's what it was, for dinner. All this Hawaiian kind of stuff?"

"Yeah?"

"And he made her some Hawaiian drink. A mai tai. Yeah, he made her a mai tai in the blender. But you know what?"

"What?"

"She wouldn't drink it. She said she'd have the perfect mai tai when she got to Hawaii and she could wait."

They didn't say anything for a while.

"Your mom told me I could come over anytime for dinner while you're away," Danny said after a spell.

"Yeah? That's nice."

"I told her I'd be over once a week if she'd throw in your collection of *Mad*s."

Alex laughed. No surprise. He'd been laughing at Danny for most of his life. That was what Danny *did,* make people laugh, the way playing baseball was what Alex did.

Danny was short and unbelievably skinny, maybe weighing a hundred and ten pounds at most. Alex thought he was kind of funny-looking with his horn-rimmed glasses and hair that wouldn't come close to staying combed. But Danny had a string of girls, had already gotten as far as third base with two different ones. Danny's girls were never really great-looking—they were always just a little too fat or had bad skin—but they were never the real dogs or retards. "Never go after the great-looking girls." That was Danny's theory. "Go after the slightly ugly ones. They're grateful. They're so happy you're goin' out with them, they don't even care that you dump 'em after you get what you wanted." Alex admired Danny; he was smart. He was different. Not the most popular guy in school, but he didn't really care to be. Danny was friends with the people he liked, never paid any attention to the bullies who picked on him or the cheerleaders who giggled at him. Eventually his indifference stopped the bullying and the giggling. The cheerleaders, confused by their lack of power, decided he had to be cute in his own strange way and thus distantly desirable. The bullies, thrown by their failure to intimidate—Danny was impervious to books being snatched and dropped in puddles, oblivious even to flashes of sharp steel under his too-large nose—started to defend him, getting into fights with Puerto Ricans who thought Danny was a twerp.

Danny always told Alex: "People are assholes. Keep that in mind at all times and you'll be all right."

"I know," Alex once replied. "You've told me. Never let anyone know you too well."

"No, no!" Danny cried. "Never get to *know* anyone too well! That's the key! You know someone too well, then you think you know what they're really like. When ya think you know that, you start to trust 'em. And when you do that, that's when you get screwed. That's when they take your trust and shove it down your throat. You know what it means when someone looks at you and says, 'Trust me'? It means they want to squeeze your balls off."

Alex didn't agree. He liked people, felt comfortable getting close to them. Danny, philosopher of the twelfth grade, would look at his best pal and tell him, "Face it. You're an asshole too. We're all assholes. I'm an asshole and proud of it. Know thyself."

Danny Cappollo had a plan. He was going to go to college, learn everything there was to know about business, go into advertising, sell every product he could to every single asshole in the United States, and then retire at age forty.

"The other thing you gotta realize," Danny was always saying to Alex, "is that everybody's a salesman. You just gotta figure out what it is they're sellin'."

"What am I selling?" Alex once made the mistake of asking.

"You, you're lucky!" Danny raved. "You're sellin' *yourself.* Me, when I hit Madison Ave, I'll sell dreams, hopes, love! And if that doesn't go, I'll settle for toasters, cereal, and dietary products."

Alex and Danny were special: though they both knew they were to move off into separate worlds, they understood theirs was a bond that would stretch forever. Danny was by far the more cynical of the two. He went through life questioning, and as he got older and learned more, his questions got harder for Alex to answer. He stayed funny—got funnier, in fact. His humor now unveiled itself in unique patterns, routines which Alex sensed served not only as commentary but as protection. Against what, Alex was not sure. If their friendship had any boundaries, that was it. There was something that prevented Alex from ever delving into that part of Danny which was well screened by joke after joke. Sometimes Alex believed that Danny's jokes were impenetrable, other times he worried that there was something within himself that refused to drill. Danny, who tried not to worry about anything, was waiting to get into Columbia and three small schools, one in Massachusetts, one in New Hampshire, and one in upstate New York. He was excited that he was one year closer to retirement.

"So," Danny said.

"So," Alex said back.

"I thought we should have our serious talk before things get goin' tonight. You know, away from the girls and stuff."

Alex nodded. "I agree." He nodded again. "*What* serious talk?"

"Don't you have any serious shit to talk about before we go our separate ways? You know, crises of confidence or questions about VD or anything like that?"

"No. Do you?"

"You honestly aren't worried about a goddamn thing, are you?"

Alex shook his head and shrugged, almost apologetically.

"I'd like to be like you," Danny said.

"I thought you were."

"No. All you have to do is go ahead and be what you are. Me, I have to outsmart all the other suckers in the world."

Alex felt like he should say something wise, but nothing came to mind. There was really nothing to say. Their paths were chosen, their separate worlds were ready to be conquered. Now all they had to do was conquer them.

"I'm glad we had this little chat," Danny said. "I'll see ya on First and Twentieth at quarter to eight."

But as Danny took one jaunty step toward home, Beanie Farber came tearing up to them from the direction of the playground.

"Alex! Hey, Alex!"

"What?" Alex said calmly.

Beanie ran up to them, stopped, panting, waited to catch his breath before speaking. "Chuckie Frohman and Goober are about to beat the shit out of Elliot the Cripple!"

"Don't call him that."

"Okay, okay! But you better do somethin'!"

"Where are they?"

"By the oval."

Alex didn't move.

"Aren't you gonna help him?" Beanie asked.

Alex looked at Danny, but Danny was expressionless.

"Look, Alex," Beanie said, a little disappointed that his timely message didn't generate a lot more gratitude, "personally I think your brother's a shmuck and deserves whatever he gets. But I'm tellin' you, you don't get over there, they're gonna beat the living shit out of him!"

Alex sighed. He scratched his head with his left hand, then ran the hand through his hair, pulling it until it hurt.

"Okay," he said. "Show me."

Elliot Justin had been born four and a half years after Alex. Nine years later he contracted polio. Two years after that, Elliot the Cripple was born.

Alex and Elliot—the second son so named because their mother idolized Franklin Delano Roosevelt but thought it was too presumptuous to name someone after him so she opted for FDR's son's name—had been close from the moment the younger Justin bounced into the world. Alex liked to take care of Elliot when the smaller boy was a baby—*loved* to push his brother's stroller along the sidewalk and feed him and dress him. He was always the first to point out how clever Elliot was when the boy would do something cute or smart. Elliot *was* smart; Alex sensed, right from the beginning, that his brother was smarter than he was. The boy was more verbal. He was instantly attracted to books and, unlike Alex, who tended to trust only what he himself experienced, to learning from *things*. "What's that? What's that?" Those were Elliot's words when he was a baby.

As they grew older, their relationship became closer, based on all the real and true essentials of life. They both liked to heat up Pepperidge Farm frozen blueberry turnovers and, when their parents were out, eat all six in the package, topped with vanilla ice cream. They invented a game called "sock basketball" where they rigged up a backboard on a wastepaper basket and made incredible shots, way after Elliot was supposed to be in bed, with a pair of rolled-up sweatsocks swathed in masking tape. Alex even enjoyed taking his little brother along on dates. He liked when the girls he dated shared secrets with Elliot, had their own private jokes with him. Most of them realized that they didn't have to talk to him like he was a kid—he seemed to see things clearly, see through to the core of things, in a way that belied his young age. Alex loved it when people "got" just how smart Elliot was, when they realized how perceptive and sharp he could be. He was so damn sweet and innocent about his own intelligence, too, that it made Alex howl when he pulled it out of nowhere to top an adult. Alex felt no jealousy toward his brother. Mostly just pride and love.

Just before Elliot's ninth birthday he developed a fever. A high fever. And horrible pains below his waist. When his leg began to twist, to shrivel, they had to accept that it was indeed polio. Alex went to the doctor with him when it was time to put the brace on. It was a huge, heavy, and awkward monster, and when it was locked in place, Alex watched his brother's eyes change. The clanging of the metal seemed to reverberate throughout the doctor's office, and Alex saw Elliot change from a little boy who could have fun, who could laugh, be afraid, tease, and cry, to someone who would feel little else but bitterness and pain and hate. Alex saw the lip curl and the eye squint and he felt his brother's little hand turn cold. He knew that he had, at that moment, lost someone and something important.

Alex was not mistaken. Elliot was bitter about his fate and his bitterness turned him nasty. His nastiness, in turn, made him extremely cruel.

People had liked Elliot Justin. They felt sorry for him when he was struck down by disease. But when the neighborhood kids tried to help him get around on his new crutches, Elliot the Cripple spit at them. When that didn't keep them away he bit them, and after that he hit them. First he punched, a short jab aimed at the chest or chin; then, as he got stronger, Elliot developed a very impressive technique of leaning on one crutch, raising the other, and smashing across the head anyone who so much as talked to him. Soon the kids left him alone. But even that wasn't good enough for Elliot the Cripple. He started going *after* them. He could move swiftly, silently, swinging his braced legs along with the wooden crutches, and he began swooping on unsuspecting Stuyvesant Towners, belting them from behind. Hard. As his reputation spread, he started the Elliot the Cripple Patrol. Every night around eight-thirty or nine he'd go outside to exercise his rapidly deteriorating leg muscles. He'd catapult himself around the playground for half an hour, doing his damndest to inflict pain on any kid who got in his way. It didn't take long for the Counter Patrol to spring up.

The Counter Patrol was usually made up of three or four recent victims of crutch-induced concussions who would do their best to knock Elliot the Cripple to the ground and in the process, if possible, hurt and humiliate him. That was what Chuckie and Goober were doing as Alex made his way over to them. They were dancing around Elliot, just out of reach of his crutches, taunting him, waiting for an opening when they could dart in and kick him down to the pavement.

Elliot Justin had been about the most enjoyable and best kid Alex had ever met. Elliot the Cripple was, without doubt, the meanest asshole cocksucker in Stuyvesant Town. He had no friends, no future, no redeeming features. Elliot Justin emerged rarely these days. His parents loved him and treated him well, but that never seemed to be enough for the boy. At times it was as if little Elliot delighted in their guilt—their guilt over having brought a child into the world only to see him suffer. Sometimes Alex could break through, occasionally there would be a flash, a moment of tenderness, of vulnerability, of fun. Rarely, though. And getting rarer. Elliot was resentful. Spiteful. Sometimes *afraid* of dealing with Alex because he was a whole person. But none of that mattered to Alex Justin, not at this moment anyway.

Beanie had pulled up short, panting again, maybe twenty feet from where Chuckie and Goober were taunting Elliot. Alex stopped too. And a second later Danny caught up with them. Chuckie and Goober turned, aware of the three of them. They hesitated.

"I'll take Goober," Danny said.

"I'll do it," Alex told him.

"I'll help," Danny said.

"No. Lemme just do it, okay?"

Seeing these boys tormenting his brother brought a gush of emotions that he couldn't, wouldn't, try to stop. Elliot was in pain, in need of help, and Alex felt he could ride to the rescue. Danny saw the expression on Alex's face.

"Okay," he said. "Yell if you want me."

But Alex was already walking forward. He thought, *Maybe*

*this will help, maybe we'll be friends again. Maybe he'll know
how much I want him to be whole again.*

So Alex went forward to save Elliot.

"Cut it out, Chuckie," Alex said, his voice particularly deep and
growling. Chuckie was a nasty kid—fat, pimpled, unpopular.
His idea of a good practical joke was unwrapping a piece of
gum, urinating on it, rewrapping it, and giving it to some poor,
unsuspecting shmoe.

"Fuck off," Goober replied, hoping he wasn't offending Alex,
whom he liked. Goober wasn't a bad kid, only dumb. He'd just
flunked the eleventh grade.

"I mean it. Leave him alone." Alex suddenly became mildly
uncomfortable. He felt a little too Alan Laddy.

"Hold it, Goob," Chuckie said. And there were the four of
them, Elliot in the middle, his back to Alex, Goober and
Chuckie standing in front of him. "I think you should leave,"
Chuckie said to the would-be hero. "We're gonna get him
sooner or later, so it might as well be now."

Elliot swung a crutch resentfully at Chuckie's head, but
Chuckie jumped back and laughed when it sailed wide by two
feet.

"Jerk-off!" Elliot spat at Chuckie.

"Gimp!" Chuckie returned with a smug smile. He didn't
mind being called a jerk-off nearly as much as Elliot hated
hearing any word in the "cripple" family.

"Chuck," Alex said menacingly.

"Do you know what this guy did to Freddie Parks, Alex?"
Goober asked. "Fourteen fuckin' stitches. Right here!" Goober
jabbed his thumb over his right ear. "Almost spilled his brains
onto the fuckin' playground."

"Leave him alone and get outta here."

"Alex." Chuckie was pleading.

"If anything happens to him, now or ever, I'll hold you responsible."

"Alex. Aaaallleex!" But Alex shook his head and that was it.

"Shit," Chuckie said. "You're really turnin' into a faggot." He
turned to Goober. "Let's forget it," he said.

"What?"

"Let's just forget it, okay?" Chuckie put his hand on Goober's wrist and nodded. Goober was not happy, but he threw his hands in a what-the-hell way. They each took two steps away, Elliot glanced at Alex, then Chuckie and Goober charged, yanking one crutch and throwing it into the grass, punching Elliot in the stomach, and kicking his other crutch out from under him. Elliot went down, scraping skin off his forehead, smearing both palms with dirt and blood, stinging all over with tiny pebbles of pain inside patches of rawness. His tormenters ran. When Alex had made sure that Elliot was reasonably okay, he took off after Chuckie and Goober, chased them till they split up on the other side of the playground. Alex, never hesitating, went straight after Chuckie, who cut through the grass, jumped over drooping chain barriers, grabbed at rocks, and threw them back at his pursuer. Alex finally had him trapped, panting and cornered in a building lobby, but, remarkably quickly for such a fat kid, Chuckie sneaked around a young mother with a child, dashed into an elevator, and farted defiantly as he watched the door swing closed on Alex, who was tangled up with the three-month-old baby, her hooded perambulator, and her angry parent.

When Alex got back to his brother, the boy was standing again, holding on to one crutch. They stared at each other, Elliot defeated, Alex humble.

"Get me my other crutch, please," Elliot said meekly to Alex, who nodded apologetically. He wanted to hug the boy, to carry him home, but Elliot would never allow it, he knew. Elliot had never allowed Alex to touch him after the brace had been put on. So he just bent down and retrieved the crutch.

As soon as the heavy crutch was handed over, Elliot drew it back in a well-rehearsed motion and emotionlessly whipped it directly into the side of Alex's head, gouging out a chunk of skin above the left eye, making a sickening crunching noise when the wood followed through to connect with the skull. Elliot stayed to watch his victim flop to the ground, before propelling his way into their apartment building, so quickly that he was safely through the heavy glass door before Danny Cappollo could even race to his friend, who by then was twisting on the pavement, clutching his hands to his head, moaning and bleeding as if he would never stop.

It wasn't nearly as bad as it looked. The doctor came promptly, cleaned off the last drops of blood that hadn't been cleaned away by Alex's mother, swabbed the wound with cotton balls soaked in stuff that stung beyond belief, sewed sixteen stitches, wrapped a bandage tightly around the top of Alex's head, told him he was a perfect patient, and said there was no reason he couldn't go to the prom and have a good time as long as he promised not to drink or get into another fight and as long as he didn't mind the headache he was sure to have for a day or two.

So Alex was only running a half hour or so behind schedule. He'd bathed instead of showered so the bandage wouldn't get wet and now he was in his tux, standing in the bathroom as his father tied his bow tie for him and his mother leaned in the doorway, a wonderful mixture of pride and pleasure and sadness on her face.

His dad was done. He smiled at Alex, stepped around him, and went into the living room. As Alex peered into the mirror, straightening his tie and his bandage, patting down his hair, his mom made no move to leave. If anything, she settled even more comfortably against the door frame, staring at him, pursing then unpursing her lips.

"We haven't talked about Elliot yet," she said finally.

"Yeah," Alex agreed.

"He didn't realize. If he'd known how badly he was going to hurt you, he wouldn't have done it."

"You're just saying that 'cause you're his mother and that's the way you have to feel. But you didn't see his face. He *wanted* to hurt me."

"Alex, oh, Alex. Do you have any idea how hard it is for him? I mean to see you play baseball and go out on dates and walk."

"Yes. I guess I do."

"And can you understand how much rage he has?"

"I guess so."

"I don't think you can. I don't think you know much about rage yet."

His mother looked so sad now. Alex liked his mother a lot, and didn't like to see her sad. He liked her prematurely gray hair, liked the fact that she was nice and enjoyed singing old songs slightly off key and got along with everybody, liked her dreams. He wasn't afraid of his mother; he wanted her approval but he also knew that basically he'd have it no matter what he did. He wished he knew what he could do now to please her. He wished he knew the right thing to say.

"Are you gonna punish him, Mom?"

"Your dad and I are talking about it. We don't know what to do exactly. Do you want us to punish him?"

"Yeah. Yeah, I do."

"How?"

"I don't know. Allowance?"

"You think that'll do it? Taking away some money?"

"No."

"So what do you suggest?"

Alex waited a long time before answering. Then, staring into the mirror, he said, "Make him talk to me."

"What?"

"Make him come in here and talk to me. He won't like that."

"No, he won't."

"Mom, I really love him."

"I know. We all do."

"Why doesn't he love us?"

"He does, Alex. He does. But it's hard for him to show now."

"Yeah. This was a funny way to show it."

"I told you, he's full of rage. And sometimes love and rage, they can get all mixed up. They can get confused. Sometimes it's easy to hate the people you know love you because it's pretty safe. Elliot has to get that hate out somewhere, on someone. I think he knows you're strong enough to take it."

"I guess I am."

"Good."

"How long'll he be like this? How long'll I have to be so strong?"

"I don't know. Until he gets over it."

"He does other stuff too. To other guys."

"We know what he does, sweetheart."

"Well, what am I supposed to do, then?"

"About what?"

"About him. About his love and hate."

"I'm not sure. I like your talking suggestion. Let me see what your dad thinks. Okay?"

"Okay."

She smiled at him, then turned and left. The smile made him feel good. It was a healing smile, it somehow made him less angry at his brother. He *was* strong enough to be hated, Alex decided. He'd make sure he was strong enough—to be hated *and* to be loved.

Everyone was in the living room: his folks, Patty, Danny, and Diana. Alex and Elliot faced each other in Alex's bedroom. Alex sat on his bed, his shoulders slumped forward, his hands clasped in his lap. His head was tilted down but his eyes shone up at his brother, who stood, weight shifted onto both crutches, which he held in front of him.

Elliot had come into the room without knocking. Standing in front of Alex, he'd said, "I'm sorry for what I did."

Alex didn't say anything at first. He didn't say, *That's okay. Forget it,* which was his instinct. Instead he broke Danny Cappollo's Law Number Three in the Philosophy of Assholism: Never ask why. Alex had asked Danny what the meaning was behind this particular theory. "I never want to know the reason for anything," Danny had said. "For one thing, you may start feeling sorry for someone who just took a dump on your face. For another, reasons are never as clear cut as people who've got 'em think they are, so you're never really gettin' the truth. Third, they don't really make any difference, do they? Someone may have the best reason in the world for why he just fucked you over, but it don't change the fact that you, pal, are still fucked. And then, finally, it violates my most rigid rule: Never get to know anyone too well. Reasons lead to understanding; understanding leads to friendship; friendship leads to all sorts of unpleasant things—trust, need, *expectations.*" Alex, sitting on his bed, remembered the way Danny had said the word *expectations.* As if it were the dirtiest word in the English language.

Anyway, he thought, he had just violated Law Number Three when he asked Elliot, "Why? Why'd you do it? I was just tryin' to help you."

"I don't want help."

"Why not?"

"Not your help."

"Elly . . ."

"You have everything."

"No, I don't."

"You're perfect."

"I'm not."

"If you give me too much, then maybe you won't be so perfect anymore."

Alex wanted to cry. But he had no answer.

"Don't do it," Elliot said again. "Ever."

"I'm going to miss you when I'm away," Alex said to his brother.

"You are?" Elliot was surprised. "How come?"

Alex was quiet for a moment, thinking, then he started to laugh. "I don't know," he said, and he laughed harder. Elliot almost laughed too; his lip twitched up and for a moment his eyes sparkled and his chest heaved, but he didn't let himself laugh. Alex stopped, laughed one more quick, one-syllable laugh which just escaped from inside, then said to Elliot, quite seriously, "No, I know why. It's because when I leave, things'll be different. Somehow I think if I stayed, things'd be okay here, with you, with Mom and Dad. I don't think that makes any sense, but I always have the feeling that if I'm around, everything'll be okay, eventually. But when I'm gone, who knows what'll happen?"

"Do you have to go?" Elliot said very softly. "I don't want you to go. I want everything to be okay here."

Alex blew out a deep breath, leaned back against the wall. "We haven't talked like this in a long time." Elliot nodded. "I used to like talking to you. Even when you were really a little kid, I mean, when you probably didn't understand what I was talking about."

"I tried to understand."

"I know. Maybe that's what I liked."

"So why are you going away? What's the reason?"

"There is no real reason, not way deep down, not the kind of reason you want, anyway. It's just that . . . this is what people *do*. They leave."

"But it makes other people unhappy."

"Only partly. Take Mom and Dad. They're unhappy to see me go, I mean at least I hope so, but they're also happy because they know it makes *me* happy."

"Is Patty happy too?"

"She doesn't know yet."

"Why?"

"I'll tell her tonight."

"Why didn't you tell her?"

"I don't know."

"Will she be angry?"

"That I didn't tell her?"

"That you're leavin'."

"No. Not angry."

"Will she be happy?"

"No, I don't think so."

"Then . . ."

"Listen, Elly. One day you're gonna do something that's gonna make one person happy, another person unhappy, you're gonna do something for *yourself*. For no other reason than it's the right thing for you to do. For *you*. It's a really great feeling. You don't have to worry about teachers or Mom or Dad or your girlfriend or *anybody*. All you gotta do is go follow your plan."

"What plan?"

"There's always a plan, isn't there? Like when you graduate from sixth grade you go to junior high. Then high school. Then college. And then college plans some sort of job for you. And the job plans a higher and higher salary. You know what I mean? A *plan*."

"I think so. What's your plan?"

"You wanna sit down?"

"No," Elliot said, not resentful.

"Well, my plan is to go off to North Carolina and play for a while and then go to the Phillies and play for real."

"What's the rest of your plan? After the Phillies?"

Alex laughed. "My plan doesn't go that far. That's too many years away."

"Tell me more about this plan."

"I don't know too much more. But I know there comes a time when you've gotta decide what the point of it all is. And right now, it seems to me that *I'm* the point. Just like in a few years you're gonna decide that *you're* the point. And then you'll have to decide what you're gonna do about it." Alex couldn't tell what Elliot was thinking. The boy's eyes were red from holding back a few tears. The meanness, the thing that had been in his face for years now, seemed to be gone. Alex thought he'd seen it ebb out of him as they'd talked. But something else seemed to have ebbed out of him as well. To replace that bitter belligerence there was . . . nothing. A strange void.

"You want some champagne with us?" Alex asked the boy.

Elliot shifted his crutches from front to either side, one under each arm. He shook his head at Alex's question and turned away.

"I'll miss you too," Elliot said before he swung out of the room.

Carl's champagne was cold and good and tasted very adult. He made a speech that went on a little too long about maturity and growth; Alex and Patty and Danny grinned at each other but they didn't mind, it was allowed, and Ginny actually started to cry, clucking at herself to stop, but cried anyway. Then they went to Patty's mother's house.

"A tuxedo," Mrs. Farber breathed to Alex. "I never thought I'd see the day. And a corsage."

"It was a surprise," Patty told her.

"Let me get my camera," Mrs. Farber said. She scurried into the hallway and was back in an instant. "Okay. Hold on a second. I've got to get this in focus. Beeyootiful," she said, fiddling with the camera. When she was ready, she cleared her throat and waved her hand. "Beeyootiful," Mrs. Farber declared. "You both look beeyootiful."

Patty grabbed Alex's arm. "You do," she said. "You really do." And for the first time in front of her mother, she kissed him.

A flashbulb went off and the kiss was recorded for posterity.

The cab—no bus tonight—took them to the prom at the Lexington Hotel in midtown. On the ride over Patty and Alex touched each other constantly on the arm and on the leg; twice Alex reached over and lovingly stroked her cheek with the back of his hand. All during dinner—creamed chicken, mixed peas and carrots, a soft roll, and lemon meringue pie served in the Penthouse dining room—they kept some part of their bodies touching. Danny and Diana sat to their right, and Danny, as previously agreed upon, spent the night fielding any questions directed toward Alex about his baseball future.

After dessert Alex and Patty danced friendly fox-trots and slow waltzes. They held each other very tight and periodically stared into each other's eyes with their zombielike gazes that could be created only by full moons and first love.

When the evening was officially over and the senior class had finished with their speeches, awards, crying good-byes, and yearbook signings, Alex and Patty and Danny and Diana walked home. They were loose and playful, they'd had nothing to drink but felt drunk. They ran a few blocks, sprinting madly and yelling; they skipped part of the way; Danny even crawled one whole block, thriving on the stares of those returning from dinner or a movie or a show. Alex's tie was loose, hanging open around his neck. The dancing and the emotion and the nerves had wrinkled his tuxedo and partially untucked his shirt. With his arm around Patty's shoulder, listening to Danny explain that his parents were in the mountains for the weekend and they all had to come over for a final celebration, Alex was pretty happy.

At Danny's apartment the first thing they did was open a bottle of bourbon.

"My father bought this for me," Danny said. "He told me never to tell my mother but he thought I deserved to get drunk for graduation." He laid out three shot glasses, one for him and two for the girls. He then disappeared into the kitchen and came back with a tall glass and a quart of milk for Alex.

"What is this?" Diana asked. "Bourbon and milk?"

"Just milk," Alex mumbled.

"Alex doesn't drink," Danny said, and when Diana stared at him incredulously, Danny felt the need to explain. "He's an asshole."

"Athlete!" Patty defended.

"Oh, yeah. I always confuse the two."

Diana elbowed Danny. "You mean," she asked Alex, "you don't drink at *all?*"

"Hey," he said, springing up quickly, pantherlike. "I am an ath-uh-lete. Definition: A gifted and superior member of the human race, pure in body, spirit, and mind. Able to leap tall buildings in a single bound, stop a bullet—"

"Oh, God." Patty groaned. "Can I have some of that bourbon?"

"Hey," Alex said, jumping over to her and sitting himself down on her lap, "I wasn't finished."

"Get off me, you big oaf. You're breaking my knees."

"Not even one sip?" Diana asked, still in somewhat of a state of shock.

Danny laughed and poured the bourbon into the shot glasses. He made sure he filled Alex's glass of milk to the very top so Alex would spill some when he tried to lift it.

"That will do you no good," Alex told him. "Because of my purity my hands are steady, my nerves are like . . . like . . . ."

"I'm sorry I corrected you," Patty told Danny. "Asshole was definitely the right description."

They each now raised their drinks in a toast.

"To your dad," Alex said, and they all drank. Alex gulped his milk down in one quick motion, wiped his mouth with the back of his hand, and said, "Aaahhhhh. Now that's a man's drink." Alex realized by the silence that he should move on to a new subject, so he picked up his yearbook and read: " 'When times are tough and you're in a trance,/Remember Lana's underpants.' "

"Now there's a beautiful memory," Danny said sadly.

"Lana Turnbull always sits like this in Geometry," Alex explained to Patty, turning his knees outward. "Everyone can see up her dress."

"Uh-huh. I think I could have figured that one out."

"Hold it," Danny said solemnly, and held his hand up for silence as he read from his book. " 'You may be small but you have a brain./I hope that we shall meet again' Mary Kay, KL5-6094."

"Mary Kay wrote that?"

"Yup."

"I don't believe it!"

"I swear!"

"She's cute!" Alex said to Danny, impressed. He turned to Patty. "She *is* cute"—hoping Patty would be as impressed with his best pal as he was.

"We studied English poetry together in a class. That's why she thought she could rhyme *brain* with *again.*"

"I'm jealous." Diana pouted.

Danny rolled his eyes and patted her on the head.

"Here's a classy one, Dan. 'Roses are red, violets are blue. You're good with a bat but in Spanish PU.' "

"Gotta be Larry."

"Nope. Hank."

"Close enough."

"Can I have another drink?" asked Diana.

"Me too," Patty said, and Alex looked over at her, surprised. "Well," she told him, "it's a celebration. And we're not all as pure as you."

"You said it," Danny yelled, and filled every glass to the brim.

" 'To Alex. Thanks for sitting next to me in English. You made the year a success. Good luck in whatever next year brings. Sincerely, Leslie McCawbar.' Shee-ittttt!"

"Definitely the first woman president," said Danny.

"I think we should have a real toast," Patty said.

"All right!"

"To Franklin High," Diana giggled, and raised her glass high.

"To the Philadelphia Phillies," Danny said, and then, banging himself in the head, he added, "Shit!"

"To us," Patty said quietly to Alex, but she put her glass down on the coffee table before she drank and walked into Danny's parents' bedroom.

"I'm sorry," Danny said. "I can't believe I did that. Shit."

"It's all right." Alex sighed.

"What's going on?" Diana asked.

Danny slithered next to her and bit her neck. "Why don't you come into my room, my dear, and I'll show you some of my racier Hardy Boys first editions."

Diana giggled but allowed Danny to lead her away. Alex sat alone, breathing in and out in exaggerated but slow, even gasps. He tapped on his thighs, a rat-a-tat drumbeat, then again, and again. Then he went in after Patty. She was sitting on the bed, her back to the door. He expected her to be crying, or at least furious, but she seemed quiet and relaxed.

"I'm here," he let her know. "I'm in the room and I'm closing the door." He did so, she didn't budge. "I just closed the door. I'm now moving so you can see me." He went around the side of the bed to stand in front of her. When she finally looked up at him, he shrugged. And shrugged again for not being able to come up with anything better than a shrug.

"The thing about apologizing," Alex said, "is that it never really does much good. I mean, I did something stupid and if I could do it all over again, I'd probably do the same thing because I *am* stupid. What I did was *me*, if you get what I mean. So I don't know if it'll mean much to say I'm sorry. I guess it won't. So I won't. Say it. 'Cause then you'll only be angrier because I'm saying things that don't mean anything. I better shut up."

"I'm not angry," she told him. "I'm really not. Although I don't know why."

"I'm sorry," he said. "I'm *real* sorry."

"I knew you'd have to go away. We've discussed it. I knew you'd have to go somewhere. Philadelphia isn't so far, even."

"I'm not going to Philly, exactly. I go to Wilson, North Carolina. It's for a minor league team. The Tobs. Great name, huh?" He tried a laugh, but it sounded hollow. To his annoyance the laugh and the self-conscious feeling that came with it hung in the air. "I'm leavin' in three days, Patty."

They didn't speak for a while. Gradually, they merged together. She slowly moved into his arms, sliding her body close, closer, until it seemed to melt into his. She buried her face in his chest and he just rocked her back and forth, listening to her delicate, rhythmic breathing. He inhaled deeply, amazed yet again that he knew someone well enough to recognize her smell. He liked that, especially when they stayed this close and he could simply breathe her in. She smelled the way she felt. Powdery. Smooth. Mysteriously intangible.

Patty stood up eventually and went to the bathroom, splashing some cold water on her face. When she came back to him, she took his hand in hers and brought it to her cheek.

"I didn't cry," she said. "That's good, huh?"

"I like holding you when you cry. It's nice in a way."

She laughed. "I knew this was coming."

"What?"

"This whole scene."

"You did?"

"Yes."

"How?"

"Alex. Alex, because I know you. I could tell you didn't want me to know something, or at least you weren't ready to tell me, and I know how you get. You make these things so private. And personal. I don't understand it exactly, but I can see when it's happening."

"Really?"

"It's like you have something to do or think or understand and everyone else is shut out, doesn't exist, until you've done it."

"Yeah," he said. "I guess I do kind of do that."

"When did you decide?"

"To go to Wilson?"

"Yes."

"Three weeks ago."

She made a clicking sound with her tongue. "I knew it," she said. "I could tell by the way you were acting."

"How was I acting?"

"Different."

"How?"

"Funny. Kind of removed. Nicer to me all of a sudden, but a little distant."

"I hope I never have to become a spy." Then he said, in a gush of honesty, "I was afraid to tell you."

"I was afraid to ask you."

They both smiled.

"What were *you* afraid of?" she asked.

Alex shrugged. "Dunno." Another shrug, along with a wince and a scratch and a tug at his nose. "I guess I didn't want to make you unhappy."

"No. You didn't want to *tell* me that you were going to make me unhappy."

He nodded glumly.

"I was afraid to ask, because I was afraid you wouldn't tell me. I didn't want to find out that I'm shut out of your private world." She smiled a sad, nervous little smile that was an invitation for reassurance. Alex swallowed, uncomfortably. He wished he had a stick of gum to chew or a drink to hold. He needed something to *do*. "Why are you like that?" Patty asked, when no sweet words came.

"Dunno."

"Why do you get so funny about . . . showing things?"

He chewed on the inside of his lip before answering, but he bit down too hard and his head jerked up in surprise at the sudden prick of pain. Once his head was up he had to look her in the eye.

"I guess I kind of figure nobody's too interested," he said slowly. "I just don't wanna let anyone know . . . well, this is gonna sound dumb."

"It won't."

"I don't want people to see me when I'm tryin' to figure somethin' out, when I'm in motion, if you know what I mean. When I'm not . . . uh . . . not . . ."

"When you're not a star?"

He didn't respond. Not a nod or a shake. He was thinking about it.

"I want to be inside you when you're like that," Patty said, and there was a very sweet and young urgency to her voice.

"Maybe I don't like what's inside me. When I'm not bein' a star."

"Then I want you to share that with me. God, so much! I don't only want to know you when you're perfect. I want to know you always."

"I think I was wrong," he said, and the way he was staring at nothing made her think he hadn't been listening to her. "It's not that I don't like what's inside me. I think it's just that I don't know yet what it all adds up to. Maybe I know what's there, I just don't know what it means."

"Then I want to find out with you."

"Do you?"

"I want us to be one."

Now he stayed quiet.

"So what does this do?" she asked. "Your going off to become a Wilson Tob."

"It doesn't do anything. From Monday to September something I'll be down South. And then I'll be back."

"And then?"

He scratched at the back of his elbow. "And then I guess we'll try to be one." She smiled. It started small but worked its way up to become a real dazzler. "I don't know what it means, exactly, but it *sounds* right."

"Will you write me?" she asked.

"Of course!"

"How often?"

"I dunno. Once a week?"

"I'll write every day."

"Really?"

She nodded. "What will you call me in the letters?"

"Huh?"

"The salutation. What will you call me?"

"I don't know," he said. "Dear Patty?"

"How about 'darling'?"

"Forget it!"

" 'Sweetheart'?"

"Too mushy."

"Maybe."

"I'll work on it."

"It better be good."

"It will be."

"Good."

"I don't like writing letters, though."

"Why not?"

"Somehow, the things that I see and feel, they're just never the same when I try to describe or explain them. They are what they are when they are. To tell about them later always seems to turn them into something different. Plus, if I ask you a question in a letter, it's like a week later before I can know the answer. If you even remember to answer it!"

"Are you nervous?" Patty asked.

"About leaving?"

"Uh-huh."

"You promise you won't tell anybody what I'm about to tell you?"

"Promise."

"Swear?"

"Swear."

"Well, the last few nights I haven't slept at all. I lie there in bed and I keep thinking how I don't know anyone in Wilson, I don't know if I'll have a phone, I don't even know where my new home is. I don't even know where *Wilson* is."

"I showed it to you on the map once. When you went for your Phillies interview."

"I know, I know. But maps aren't all that real for me either. Like letters. It's just paper. It can't really show you where something *is*."

They didn't say anything for a few minutes. Patty seemed to be absorbing this new information. Then, suddenly, she said, "I'm not very pretty, I don't think. I'm smart, but I'm not really *that* smart; I mean, I'm not a genius or anything and I don't have any real talent."

"Come on, what are—"

"Alex. Let me say this."

"But—"

"Please." Confused, he nodded and she went on. "I don't have any real talent. Not like you. I can't do anything special and I don't have these great goals either. I'd kind of like to go to college—in fact, I want that more than anything, to go to school. I really want that. Then, I don't know . . . you know, just the husband and the kids and I guess a nice house. A job, 'cause I'd like to be *something*. That's nice. It's *nice* but it's not . . . much."

"Uh," Alex said, hoping she would just continue because his "uh" was only a punctuation. He didn't have any idea what to say. She continued.

"I've never thought about anyone or anything the way I've thought about you," Patty Farber said. "And I think about you all the time. It scares me. Sometimes at school, all during math class I just think about you. And, Alex, I miss you when I don't see you, isn't that funny, I mean even for an hour or two. And, and now, sometimes things happen and I think, *Wait'll I tell Alex* or *I wonder what Alex'll think about this.* I've started doing that a lot."

She was getting excited but was careful not to rock the bed, as if movement would shatter the mood.

"What I'm trying to do," she went on, and he caught just a spark of how truly hard this was for her when her whole body seemed to twitch, an involuntary spasm, "is to explain something about me. I'm not exactly sure what it is, but I want to try to explain it."

Silence.

"My parents. That's the beginning. They, um, they split up when I was seven. I've told you all about that. How they fell in love 'cause they were both artists. My mom was a great violin player, believe it or not. And my father was a painter. A pretty good one. They got married. And I guess it took seven years for my mom to realize that pretty good painters don't make a really good living. She, um, put down the violin and learned to type. And she gave my father a choice: his painting or his family. Well, you know which one he chose. When I was nine, he left New York completely and moved to Washington. Seattle. I got my last letter from him when I was eleven. I don't have it anymore, though I wish I did." Patty swallowed, composed herself. "The letter said that he was a weak man. He couldn't act until he was pushed to the wall. He knew I hadn't done the pushing and he was sorry I got caught in the middle. He also said that he had a new wife who had a child of her own. The new wife didn't like him being in such close contact with his old family. Sooooo . . . he told me she was a whole bunch of things I didn't understand then—insecure, protective, jealous, you name it. She was pushing him to start fresh, he said. So he was. Again, he said, I was caught in the middle. I wish I remembered the letter better, Alex, but I don't because I burned it right away. I put it right down in the middle of my room and set it on fire. There's even a small carpet burn still there because I just sat and watched it burn until my mother came in and stamped it out." Patty forced a tiny laugh. "She spanked me afterward as hard as she ever had or has since. Oh, and one last thing the letter said was that he wouldn't be in touch with me anymore."

Alex shifted his hand just a bit. His fingers moved around her ankle.

"He also sent me something which I, um, still have and I brought it to show to you. I told you, I sorta knew something like this would happen tonight and, well, I just wanted you to see it. I've never showed it to anyone. Not to anyone. Even my mom doesn't know I have it. It's a charcoal sketch he did of me. The left side of it is my father's memory of what I looked like when he last saw me, when I was nine. The right side is his version of what I'll look like when I get to be a grown woman. And it's inscribed, uh . . ." She held the sketch up to read the writing on it, still not showing Alex the drawing. " 'My darling daughter,' " she read. " 'This represents the two things most precious to me: the past and the future. In years to come I shall always look for a beautiful young woman who matches my imagination. And when I find her I will tell her that I have always loved her and always will.' "

She turned the sketch around and showed it to Alex.

"He made you look beautiful," he said slowly.

"Did he?"

Alex nodded.

"I always thought it made me look ugly. Unwanted."

"No," he said. "It doesn't."

"My mom and I have a pretty strange relationship, as you've probably noticed." She forced another little laugh as she went on with her story. "Sometimes she blames me for ruining her marriage, sometimes for holding me back from marrying again. Sometimes I blame myself too. Sometimes I hate her, sometimes I love her. I don't really think about my father much anymore. I just cry sometimes. Or think about how my boyfriend tries to keep me separate. I think about how I'm caught in the middle again, between you and something I don't understand."

She was done. Her jaw moved, barely, but nothing came out, so he knew she was done. Patty shook her head in wonderment at all the things that were, somewhere, inside her. All the twisted passions. And much to his shock, she started to laugh.

"Alex," Patty said suddenly through her giggle, "I'm happy. I don't know why but I am. How could I be?"

"You're easy to please."

"Not so easy."

They kissed. A stored-up tear rolled down her cheek and onto his lip. He licked the dab of salt away and squeezed her. He could feel the muscles in his arm tighten and he knew she was enjoying his strength.

"What?" she said when he paused for air.

"What what?"

"There's something on your mind."

"We're not one *yet*, Patty."

"But there is, isn't there?"

"Yeah."

"So like I said—what?"

"Well, you know how you wanna be inside me?"

"Yes."

"I wanna be inside you too."

"What?"

"I wanna have sex."

She took a deep breath. Her head cocked to the right and her brown eyes blinked as if maybe she hadn't heard correctly.

"You asked," Alex said.

"I asked."

"You said, 'What?' and that's what."

Patty tried to grin and it almost worked, but the sudden pressure kept pushing her lips together. "I knew this was going to come up too. I tried to imagine how you'd do it. And how I'd react. I thought you'd kneel or something and it would be like a proposal."

"I was too blunt, huh?"

"Mmmmm."

"What were you gonna do? I mean, when I knelt and all that?"

"I was going to blush beautifully. Then get all warm and slip under the covers and you'd come in with me. And then it would be all over and I'd feel the happiest I ever felt in the world."

"Well, look. It still sounds good."

"Uh-huh."

"How do you feel now? Perfect?"

"Nauseous."

"Yeah."

"I *want* to make love with you, Alex."

"You do?"

"Of course I do."

"Great!"

"But why now?"

"Because I'm leaving."

"But you'll be back. You said you'll be back."

"Sure, but . . . this way . . . I mean, if we do it . . . there'll be a tie or something."

"I'm tied anyway."

His foot pawed at the ground. "Yeah, I am, too, Patty. But I'm gonna be with, you know, real people soon. And women. I'm gonna be with women and stuff."

"Would you sleep with someone else? If you're on the road?"

Alex twisted his neck to escape his chafing shirt collar. "I think I would. Yeah. I might. Maybe."

"But not if we sleep together now?"

"No. Then I wouldn't. I swear."

"I may be a virgin, but I know how it works. One time won't keep you from getting horny for six months."

"But I'll *have* something. That's how I feel about it. I mean, if you don't wanna I'm not gonna go out and look for some floozy or anything. But I can't make any promises. No promises."

"Okay. No promises."

"I *like* promises!" He stood up and sighed dramatically. Then he sat back down beside her. "I wanted this evening to be so perfect."

"It has been."

"Sure. You've been unhappy for three weeks and I'm makin' a jerk out of myself 'cause all I'm doing is tellin' you how I'm gonna sleep around with the first girl who likes the way I swing a bat."

She laughed and wanted to touch his face but held herself back because she knew he would shake her away. "It's been a perfect night for me, Alex. Really."

"You're very weird."

She raised her eyebrows and now knew it was safe to put two fingers gently on his arm. "We have an hour before I have to be home."

"Uh-huh."

"Can we take our clothes off and just lie together?"

"I don't know." Alex put his hand up to his forehead and rubbed his eyes. "Boy, I don't know."

"I'd like to very much." When he didn't answer, she kissed him. She took a long time to reach his lips, leaning into him an inch at a time, staring into his eyes the whole way. Her tongue reached out and grabbed him, sucking him toward her.

"Uh," he managed to breathe. "Uh."

In one motion they lay down together on the bed. Patty unbuttoned his shirt, kissing his chest after each button was undone. She bit his nipples, chewing on them and licking them, and when he writhed in pleasure she put her hand on his bulging penis and let it rest there. She'd never touched him there before.

"Can I, like, make one last plea for real sex?"

She shook her head but then she also removed her dress, proudly tossing it onto the floor. She slipped off her shoes, rolled her stockings off her legs, and ran her fingers around the top of her panties. In one quick courageous jerk she slid them down to her ankles and flipped them away with a kick.

"Now you," she said.

Alex had never seen her completely naked before, was not aware that she was so small, that her body looked so firm, that her white breasts looked so pretty against her tanned chest and stomach. It took him a moment to recover, then he jumped out of the rest of his clothes.

"Lie next to me and kiss me."

"Okay." He knew he would have said okay to anything.

They kissed. Her bare shoulders, moving up and down with each breath, were the sexiest things he'd ever seen. Her neck, like a swan's, arched to curl over his neck; her legs wrapped around his legs. He was so overwhelmed, he didn't think to kiss her again or touch her or anything. He was motionless. When she placed his hand on her breast and gently twisted his fingers around her nipple, Alex wanted to come so desperately he didn't think he could control himself. His penis was throbbing in such quick, hard spasms that he dropped his arms to his side, clenched his hands, and racked his brain to think of things that would hold him back. He went over the entire Giant roster, which he usually practiced when he masturbated to hold him off for the real thing, but that didn't help now. He flashed on Elliot, but that didn't sit right with him, then tried to imagine what North Carolina would be like. Next, he began listing as many vegetables as he could, ordering them alphabetically, and that seemed to slow things down.

"I love you, Alex."

"Wait! Don't talk. Hold it!" He closed his eyes and held his breath until he was sure he wasn't going to shoot his sperm up to the Cappollos' ceiling. When he finally felt in control, he took a deep breath, relaxed, opened his eyes to find Patty staring at

him, and put his arms around her, gently rubbing his hands up
and down her back. He had gotten up to "lettuce," though for *b*
he'd cheated and used a fruit and for *f* he'd used "fried zuc-
chini."

"Do you mind?" she asked, snuggling back into him.

"Not having sex?"

She nodded.

"No, I don't mind," he said.

"This is nice. Being close to you."

"It is. It's nice." His penis started to throb again. He noticed
the surprised look on her face when it banged against her thigh.
He had an image of it, like an out-of-control garden hose, ca-
reening madly around the room, knocking over lamps and tables, until he willed it to stay still.

"Will you tell me?" she asked, kissing his neck, one light,
sliding kiss.

"What?"

"Will you tell me when you sleep with the girl who likes the
way you swing?"

"No! Patty, what do you think I . . . I wouldn't do . . ."

"I want you to."

Alex shifted her weight to the other side because his right
arm was going to sleep. "You want me to tell you?"

She nodded. "I want to know. So we'll be one."

Alex said nothing, buried his face in her soft hair.

"Will you tell me?" she asked again.

He lifted his head and let his gaze cover her entire body from
head to toe. He stared into her eyes while she peered back
curiously, brushed her hair aside and softly kissed the side of her
cheek. He laid both hands on her breasts, put his mouth on one
nipple, then the other, sucking them gently, really just holding
them there inside his lips. His left hand moved to hover over
the mound of hair between her legs; he let his fingers slip into
her only until she gasped, then he gently removed them. He
moved his mouth to cover hers and pushed his tongue in past
her teeth, filling her mouth. When their kiss ended, he said that
he loved her.

She was satisfied with the answer.

"Welcome to Auntie Joy's Roomin' House at one thuhree-four Broderick Street. I'm Auntie Joy. That's what you must call me. My real name is Lillian, Lillian Joy, but everybody calls me Auntie. Auntie Joy. Got a nice ring to it. Say it, boy, you'll feel right at home."

Alex stared at the wonderfully friendly woman who carried around, with her huge grin and two-hundred-pound frame, an overwhelming aura of biscuits and fresh fruit pie and sizzling fried chicken. She was his new landlady and he liked her instantly, felt that nothing harmful could possibly penetrate her massive protective apron.

"Hello," he said, a little intimidated by the combination of his long train ride from New York, all the soggy pineapple danish he'd eaten along the way, Auntie Joy's thick southern accent, and the misty, humid air that seemed to be permanently settled into the cozy living room of the boardinghouse.

"Auntie Joy," she prompted.

"Hello, Auntie Joy," he said, feeling just a little silly.

"Goo-oood." She beamed and gave his cheek a good old squeeze. "Let's go upstairs now, honey, and I'll show you your room."

Lugging his two heavy Samsonite suitcases, he followed her up the carpeted stairs. Humming some made-up jolly tune, she led him along the upstairs hallway, past two rooms, until they reached the corner bedroom. She motioned him inside.

"You get acquainted with your new surroundings," Auntie Joy told him. "I'll be in the kitchen, so if you need me, just holler. I won't say I'll come runnin', but at least I'll hear ya."

The room was fairly large, with a few interesting twists and turns and slants and slopes. One of the two beds was tucked away in an L-extension off to one side and was barely visible from the other bed, which was close to the door. Alex assumed that the bed by the door was his since the other already had a lived-in look to it. Though recently made, and minus even a hidden bubble signaling human contact, there was a plaid cloth suitcase peeking out from under the metal frame. At the head, hanging a foot above the pillow, was an autographed photo of Jackie Robinson, and next to that was a nonautographed painting of Jesus Christ, peering down from his usual lofty perch. Alex shifted his gaze from his roommate's nook and took in the rest of the room's features. The furniture was old, used rather than antique, and didn't match too well, but it somehow looked fine when tossed all together. Thick screens on the four windows kept the buzzing flies out, but not the sweltering heat, which invaded mercilessly and overpoweringly, seemingly generating from the walls and ceiling and floor. The whole room smelled pleasantly like damp wood, like an attic. Everything was spotlessly clean. Each article belonging to his new roommate—hairbrush, shoes, baseball glove, a transistor radio—was laid out purposefully and exactly. There was little disturbance in the room and less personality, unless preciseness fit into either category. With walls and ceiling painted a glossy white, the only bits of color came from a blue-and-green-and-purple patchwork quilt tossed over the back of a wobbly chair, rough brown wooden beams, and remarkably shiny brass doorknobs on the two closet doors.

Alex walked over to a window, sweeping his eyes over his new hometown. Steam seemed to be rising from the sidewalks of Wilson, North Carolina. A few townspeople strolled along them in a sweaty, sleepwalking kind of trance. Alex made out a row of stores, protected by a line of rocking chairs, barricaded in by awnings and parking meters. He counted a butcher shop, a men's clothing store, another for women, a greengrocer, and two variety stores that looked as if they sold a lot of junk. The murmurings that filtered up had a mild southern twang, the stillness radiated a pleasing languor. He thought how strange it was, how exciting, to suddenly be in a whole new world.

"Hi," he heard from behind him. Actually, it was a sound more like "Hahy" and Alex swung around suddenly, wincing at the crick he caused in his neck. "Ah'm Scott Hunt. All right if I come in?"

"Sure. We're roomies, aren't we?"

"We are," Scott said, in what Alex was already recognizing as his painfully slow and thick hillbilly drawl. "But I know how these things are." He inched inside, easing the door shut behind him. "You're new here and your momma and poppa ain't here, and bein' in a big town an' all."

"It's not so bad," Alex tossed off, far more cavalierly than he felt. Then it registered. "A big town?"

"Yeah. I was the same way. Shoot, ya get bowled over by all these stores an' people an' noise. It was the noise that got me the worst."

"Where'd you grow up?" Alex wondered, not quite believing that there was someplace smaller than Wilson.

"Dunston, Alabama."

"Kind of a little place?"

"Shoot, yeah. I knew everybody in town. Heck, most of 'em was in my family."

"A townful of cousins, huh?"

"Not exactly. Most of 'em were my brothers and sisters."

Alex laughed and Scott grinned back at him. He had a very easy grin. Oddly enough, though, it conveyed no humor. In its place was a kind of benign acquiescence to circumstance. He was grinning because Alex was laughing, because it was an easier thing to do than *not* grin. It was an oddly reassuring expression, reflecting a remarkable lack of concern for life's obstacles.

"Where *you* from, Alex?"

"New York. The city."

"That's what Auntie Joy said, but I just didn't believe 'er. I'll be. I guess this place ain't so big to you."

"It sure ain't."

"It's a good place, though. I'll tell ya. People are *real* nice. Everybody's good to the players. *Real* good."

"Whaddya do here, mostly?" Alex wondered nervously. It was beginning to sink in that he was now actually transplanted into the middle of nowhere with nothing to do and no one to do it with.

"Do?"

"Yeah. At night. Or off days. Or just to . . . do something."

"Well, I'll tell ya, Alex. What I like to do mostly is eat."

"Eat?"

"Yup."

"You mean . . . *eat?*" Panic set in. Not only was he living on Mars, his roommate was a Martian. Alex's body sagged and his face scrunched up as if he had just swallowed a gallon of unsweetened lemonade. Scott seemed oblivious to his roomie's stuporously confused reaction and concentrated for a long thirty seconds on chewing off a cuticle from his thumb. When he looked back up, Alex was still not pulled together.

"What time is it?" Scott asked.

"Six-thirty."

"You're gonna see what I'm talkin' about in five minutes sharp. Auntie Joy is the best damn cook I ever saw, and I like to eat her cookin' more than maybe anythin' I ever done in my whole damn life. I shouldn't really say this, but I swear it's practically a ree-ligious experience."

Alex cleared his throat and twisted his neck, a sign that he was returning to life.

"Isn't there, like, a movie theater or somethin'?"

"We got a movie house. Sure. But you ain't gonna wanna be goin' to too many o' those."

"I'm not?" Scott shook his head. "How come?"

"You'll see tomorrow, when you meet Charlie."

"Lassiter?"

"Yup. He's not real big on his boys havin' enough of anythin' left to go on out at night. He likes you to play baseball, and if you're not playin' baseball he wants you to be *talkin'* baseball, and if you're not talkin' baseball, he'll allow you to eat, but if you're not doin' one o' those damn things he likes ya to be sleepin'."

"That sounds okay to me," Alex said dubiously, and thought, *Well, here I am in the pros.* "Nothin' I like better'n baseball."

"That's what I thought," said Scott. "Until I found myself Auntie Joy's cookin'."

As an athlete, even as only a budding professional, Alex's nature was to be compulsively competitive, to look at life as a continual competition, even if the contest was only between himself and his own past. He thought in terms of winning and losing—there was very little else that mattered and very few things in life that couldn't be won or lost. Alex, by skill and now by habit, was a winner, and a gracious one. When he was forced to assume the role of loser, he usually reacted in one of three ways.

His most frequent response was to devote himself, fiercely and single-mindedly, to reversing the result. He would not rest until he toppled the man, the team, the thing, that had bettered him. If it was a matter of getting a hit off a troublesome pitcher, he would study and be patient and when the time came he'd know what to do—wait for the inside fastball on an 0-and-2 count—and do what needed to be done—drive in a run or sacrifice or get on base and steal. If he decided his obstructively messy room needed cleaning, he would defeat the mess tirelessly, scrubbing the floor until it shone, vacuuming the corners until all traces of dust had disappeared. If something heavy needed carrying, his shoulders handled the load, refusing to bow to the strain, rejecting any thought of rest or assistance.

The rarest of responses for Alex, generally when it was a competition not of his own choosing—a pop geometry quiz, a political argument with his father, losing a date to another suitor—was simply to shrug it off as unimportant.

And then, if he couldn't reverse a loss or ignore it—when all other choice was ruled out—Alex had a third and most difficult response. He accepted his subservient role and admitted that second place was, at times, unavoidable, calming himself with his own superiority in a separate area or skill. These concessions were not common but when they occurred the victor earned, not Alex's wrath or jealous resentment, but rather his absolute and undying respect. He often entered into a bond with whoever was able to triumph over him, a strangely substantial bond and an oddly affectionate one. These competitions were sometimes dramatic and public, oftentimes unnoticed by any but the participants, beginning and ending as matter-of-fact occurrences; yet, for Alex, they contained the full power and emotional drain of performing in front of a bleacher full of fans.

That night, at Auntie Joy's dinner table, there was such a contest. It began in fun, stemming from earnest hunger, was called attention to by Auntie Joy as surely and perceptively as Red Barber, and when it was over Scott had earned not only Alex's respect but true awestruck acknowledgment of the southerner's superior talent and untouchable ability.

Alex had thought he could outeat anyone he'd ever met or ever would meet. He definitely could throw down more Sabretts, pizza, knishes, or egg rolls than anyone in Stuyvesant Town. So as they sat down before Auntie Joy's colorful spread, Alex thought nothing of it as he kept up with Scott through four biscuits covered with melting butter and fresh honey, eight chunky ribs dripping with barbecue sauce, and two helpings of sugar-glazed yams. They eyed each other warily over three thick slices of cold ham, two ears of corn, and four more ribs. Then slugged it out over two huge spoonfuls of collard greens, a pitcher of iced mint tea, one more slab of ham, three more biscuits, and two more dollops of yams. It seemed to Alex that all he did was stop once for a deep breath, but he then watched, paralyzed, as Scott put away another corn, a heaping of greens, two more slabs of ham, and six more ribs. And the amazing thing, perhaps even more overwhelming than Scott's actual appetite, was his perfected technique of eating and talking at the same time. It took all of Alex's concentration to keep pace, to prove his mettle trying to match the champ bite for bite. But Scott could gab away. Each time he opened his mouth to speak, Alex was positive that gravy was going to come dripping from Scott's lips or that corn would come spurting out onto the tablecloth, but no, never, not once. The fork would disappear into his mouth, withdraw, attack the plate anew; the mouth would re-open and, magically, the food was gone, a rambling sentence having replaced it. Scott was a Merlin at the dining table.

"There's other boys here, you know," he'd say, and the fork was in the yams, spearing a thick hunk with a blob of butter. "Walter and Chris've got the room on the second floor. And Jerry and Dave got the one next to us. They're all good ol' boys." Auntie Joy let out with a "Hummph," meaning she wasn't sure they were so good. Alex glanced at her, wondering at her disap-proval, and by the time he'd looked back at Scott, not only were the yams gone, but the fork was digging at the ham and he was already onto another bit of info.

"Walter's our catcher and Chris, he's a pitcher. Got great stuff, but he ain't doin' too well. I dunno why. Charlie thought it'd be good if they room together, you know, get to know the way the other thinks'n all."

Auntie Joy clucked again, the fork made two trips to the mouth, once with a previously dropped bit of rib, once with a combination of greens and yams.

"Jerry's our first baseman. Hits pretty well but can't field worth a lick. And Dave's a pitcher too. Our star pitcher. He's unbelievable."

Alex finally got a word in. "Don't they eat here?"

"Supposed to." Auntie Joy mumbled. "They sure are sup-posed to."

"Now, Auntie," Scott said sweetly, "you know they do most of the time." A rib was cleaned in a split second. "They're crazy when they don't, I'll tell ya that." That made Auntie Joy happy again.

Finally, by the time Scott pushed his plate away with a sigh, an indication, Alex thought, not of fullness but regret that he'd eaten all there was to eat, Alex had recovered enough to split a whole fresh blueberry pie, covered with thick cream, and drink down a quart of cold milk. Auntie Joy was beaming.

"You did right proud," she told Alex. "Right proud. You darn near put as much in your stomach as this'n. Didn't think you had it in you, bein' so skinny 'n all. But I ain't never seen no one eat like this boy. I don't know if it's even natch'l for a boy to eat like this'n does, but it sure does my heart good."

"Auntie Joy," Scott murmured, still chewing on a piece of crust, his mouth ringed in blueberry purple and milk white, "it's because you're the finest cook and the greatest person alive. An' I swear, that's the Lord's truth."

"Don't ya love him?" she asked Alex. "Don't you just love him?"

Scott grinned modestly, accepting Auntie Joy's affectionate praise and that special look from Alex, the look indicating that the friendship could now begin in earnest, on equal terms.

Upstairs, Alex stumbled into the room, took two wobbly steps, toppled over onto his bed, and made several weak, pathetic, gasping noises.

"Was I lyin'?" Scott asked.

"Uh," Alex said. His mouth fell open and stayed open. He couldn't close it. He hoped he wasn't going to drool all over his clean, fresh-smelling pillowcase.

"That woman is somethin', ain't she?"

Alex felt it coming, at long last, and then it poured out of him, a rich sonorous belch, from way deep down, that reverberated throughout the room.

"Ahhh," he heaved. "Ahhhhhhhhhh."

"I know what ya mean," Scott said.

"Uhhh," Alex snorted. "I don't know how you do it. I don't think I can breathe."

"I think Auntie made up some ice cream this mornin'. I'll get ya a dish if you think that might make you feel better."

"Ohhhh. Uhhhhh. Bleahhhhhh."

Scott stood over Alex, who was immobile and now clutching his bulging stomach, watching to make sure he wasn't going to die or anything. When he was sure his new room- and team-mate was safe, Scott went over to his own bed and plopped down. Alex groaned and forced himself to sit up with as much dignity as he could muster.

"Oh, God," he got out. "You do this every night?"

"Wait'll ya see breakfast. Oh, man!"

Scott grinned another one of those dumb smiles. Only Alex was beginning to suspect it wasn't any great revelation of stupidity, as he had judged earlier, but rather of something else, something as plain and unusual as the fact that Scott seemed to appreciate everything and everyone he came in contact with. He seemed to have no protective devices, to be one who waded right into the world with his chin thrust forward, his hands at his side. Alex could not decide whether this was a flaw or a strength, whether this was honesty or the self-destructive move of a retard. He knew what Danny would say, that here was the ultimate example of his philosophy, the Perfect Asshole. But Alex was not sure. He did have this mildly unnerving premonition that he would, one day, wind up laughing at this likably simple cracker. But he knew he would regret that laughter, regret it terribly. He shook that feeling away and another one, easier to take, replaced it. Alex suspected that Scott probably wouldn't mind being laughed at. He sensed that Scott understood that being laughed at was part of what he was supposed to do. It was part of the plan. Alex thought about that for a while, deciding there was a fifty-fifty shot that he'd hit on something, and waited for the swelling in his stomach to go down so they could talk more and explore each other further.

"That side of the room okay with you, Alex?"

"Sure."

"We can switch after a spell, if you wanna."

One more deep breath and Alex felt he was beginning to recover. "This seems okay. One side of a room's pretty much like another, I guess."

"That's very true, Alex," Scott said, quite somberly. "That's *very* true."

Alex shrugged. *Justin's the name,* he thought, *and wisdom's my game.*

"That's your closet there, Alex. It's a little bit bigger than mine. I thought that was fair, since I have this bed and the extra space."

"Okay. Thanks."

"And Auntie Joy don't mind what you do to the room, so long

as you don't destroy nothin'. You can put up pictures or whatever ya want."

"Okay."

"I put up a few myself."

"Yeah, I see. Robinson, huh?"

"It sure is. The best second baseman alive, in my opinion."

"Yup. I agree."

"A couple of the boys, they give me a hard time 'cause I like
him so much. 'Cause he's a nigger 'n all."

"Oh." The word took Alex by surprise and suddenly made
him tense, uncomfortable, left without a response. Alex was not
particularly racist, no more so than anyone living in a big city
where part of one's daily routine was being overpowered by
various sects, races, and religions. Ginny had talked to him
about the way Negroes were treated in the South. He was not to
get caught up in that, she'd explained. He was to ignore color
and stand up for what was right. His mother had a much clearer
vision of what was right than Alex did, along with a blinding
faith in that vision. Too blinding, his dad said. She couldn't
admit that a cause could go sour or a person corrupt. Carl called
her a passionately liberal person. But no, Alex had decided long
ago. She was a passionately *good* person. But what would she do
with another good person, which Scott so obviously was, who
called people niggers? Would she recategorize him, shifting him
from the good to the bad column? Would she change her opinion of him, going from like to dislike? Would she try to change
him? There were so many options and they had only just begun
their conversation. Alex didn't know which option to take, so he
did what he usually did in a pressure situation: he waited.
Waited for the whole hand to be played, until there was only
one right move to take.

"You don't mind, do ya? About the picture, I mean."

"I don't mind."

"We got a coupla nigras on the team this year. First time. You
mind *that?*"

"Nope. I don't even mind that."

"Good. Me neither. Some of the boys, though. They ain't
crazy about it."

"Well, I bet the niggers aren't too crazy about it either."

"I bet they ain't. But I bet if they play like Robinson, this damn town might elect their first nigger mayor."

Alex laughed and nodded. Relief relaxed the muscles that had tensed up and down his back. His first crisis had been easily diffused, had proved to be nonexistent. He wondered if that were the way with all crises. He hoped so.

"Willie Trotty, he's one of the colored guys. He's the best baseball player I ever saw."

"What position?"

"Center field."

Alex coughed and cleared his throat. "*I* play center field."

"Well, I hope you don't mind sittin' on the bench."

"I didn't come here to sit on the bench."

"Like I said, Willie's the best I ever saw. But I ain't ever saw you yet, right?"

"Right," Alex said. "That's right."

"Well, I just hope you can run like the wind and hit like the devil. 'Cause that's ol' Willie."

"I'll do my best."

"I'm a second baseman, myself, Alex," Scott told him, digging himself into his bed for long-term comfort. "Starting second baseman for the Tobs."

"Well, I got nothin' against infielders."

"I guess you might say I'm the best second baseman in the Carolina League. I hope that don't sound like braggin'."

"Not if it's true."

"That's right. That's *right*. I think we're gonna get along okay, you know. We seem to think the same."

Alex nodded in agreement and smiled. "And where's the other guy play?" he asked, pointing to the painting of Christ.

Scott was puzzled. "Who?" he asked, looking around to see if he was missing something.

"The guy with the long hair."

Scott turned around, saw the painting, turned back to Alex, staring, squinting at him. He started to say something and stopped, hesitated, tried to speak again, but it came out jumbled, so he stopped again, and stayed quiet until he had composed his speech.

"Why, that's the Lord, Alex," he explained very slowly and seriously.

"Lord?" Alex asked innocently. "Oh, yeah. Shortstop, right?"

"That's Jesus. The Lord!" Scott was not just confused now, he was shell-shocked. Alex was already starting to feel bad. He could tell that Scott was getting frustrated and Alex didn't know him well enough yet to tell how he'd handle that frustration, whether it would turn into anger or not.

"I was just kidding," Alex revealed. "Just kidding. I know who it is."

Scott said nothing. Alex figured he was trying to decide whether to believe this new statement.

"Honest. I know who it is. I swear."

The silence was long and frozen. Then came that same goddamn dumb grin.

"Ohhh," Scott said. No anger but no humor. Maybe a hint of understanding. "I guess I don't have a real good sense of humor, Alex," he said. "I usually don't pick up on jokes and stuff like that."

"That's okay. It wasn't much of a joke."

"No, no. I get it. I get it now. It was funny." Scott's grin widened, yellowish teeth moved up and down. "You sure took me in, I'll tell ya that. I get it. Why, I thought you were . . . I don't know what. Crazy!"

Alex shrugged, half apologetically, half reassuringly, hoping that the minor gesture convinced the southerner he was reasonably sane. Scott appeared to be deep in thought. His eyes were half closed and his forehead furrowed in wrinkles of effort to drag some thought out of his brain. He suddenly snapped his fingers and Alex sprang to attention.

"I know a joke."

Alex nodded eagerly, approvingly. He could tell that Scott thought this might be a breakthrough. "Let's hear it."

"I hope I get it right."

"I hope so."

"I think you'll like this one. It ain't dirty or anything. But it's funny."

"Okay."

Scott went right into his joke as determinedly as he might stroll up to the plate looking for a game-winning hit.

"Okay. There's this Indian named Shortcut. Uh, no. I mean Shortcake."

"Shortcake."

"Right. His name's Shortcake. No, wait a second. He wasn't an Indian. He was a cowboy. That's it. Hold it. Lemme start all over."

"Okay." Alex could see Scott mentally erase the false start.

"Right. There's this cowboy named Shortcake. And all the Indians loved him, even though he was a cowboy. He used to hunt an' all, and nobody bothered him or nothin'. But one day he was comin' into the tribe's, uh, campin' ground, and a new guy in the tribe didn't know who he was so he shot an arrow right through Shortcake and killed him dead. Well, everybody was cryin' an' all sad, y'know, an' nobody knew what to do when they found out ol' Shortcake had bought the farm."

"Bought the farm?"

"You know." Scott pointed up, indicating that ol' Shortcake was now in heaven, and Alex nodded that he was following.

"So, anyway, the big chief of the tribe decided that somebody had to bury Shortcake. So he went off to the bravest brave and he said, 'You're the number-one bravest brave. Will y'all bury our friend?' And this bravest brave says, 'No, I can't bury Shortcake, he was my dearest and truest friend.' So the chief goes off to the next bravest brave but he couldn't do it neither. And all the way down the line. None o' these brave braves could bury Shortcake. The chief didn't know what to do. So he went off to his wife an' told her the sad story. When suddenly he says to her, he says, 'Hey, I got an idea. Why don't *you* all bury Shortcake?' An' his wife, the squaw . . . are you listenin'?"

Alex nodded and waved him on impatiently.

"She turns to the chief, looks at him like he's plumb outta his gourd, and says, 'What? Squaw-bury-Shortcake?' "

There was a long silence. Long.

"Ya get it? It's a pun. Squaw-bury-Shortcake. Like strawberry shortcake. It's—"

"I get it."

Scott beamed, so proud that he'd managed to get a whole joke right. He waited nervously for a response, like a puppy who had fetched a ball for the first time. The silence lasted long enough to be awkward, for Alex to see the pride in the eyes begin to turn to confusion and embarrassment, and then Alex broke down and just laughed. He slapped the air and laughed and laughed, his laughter settling things down, opening the dam for that gush of energy that two eighteen-year-olds can generate when they unfurl and destroy any barriers between them. And that burst kept them up till one o'clock, even though Scott insisted on turning off the lights at eleven.

They talked about New York and Dunston, the other players in the team, the rules, Auntie Joy's ice cream, music, girlfriends, and life. As Alex's eyes closed, weighed down by an onrush of exhaustion, he felt fine. Fine. He couldn't wait till the next morning when he would get to put on his new uniform and play some ball. He thought of what Ewett Crane had said to him: "You make your own luck." Alex knew he was ready to make his. Oh, yeah. Oh, yeah.

And so he fell asleep, peacefully ecstatic, not even minding the subdued mumblings about sleep, Jesus, and protection from the bed across the room.

"Justin!" Charlie Lassiter thundered.

Charlie was the manager of the Tobs, a fiftyish-looking man, short, with too much of too many things stored away in his belly. He was red and meaty and the first thing that hit Alex was that the man who now controlled his life smelled like beer, tobacco, sweat, leather, and Brylcreem. Alex learned to trust both his nose and his first impressions from this premier session with Charlie. He was to discover that the beer was Bud, the tobacco Bull Durham; the sweat was a brutal desire to beat everything and everyone at anything; the leather was toughness and age, pure and simple. The Brylcreem was Brylcreem, and Charlie obviously didn't believe in doing anything in little dabs.

"Justin. I'd like you to come up here, please."

They were in what passed for the locker room, a tiny gray concrete room with a few hooks twisted into the walls as hangers and fewer benches jammed together on the floor around the tin lockers. The whole team was gathered, putting on their uniforms, lacing up their spikes, getting ready for battle. Alex and Scott had walked to the park—Scott said the stroll loosened him up, set his brain to working, got him in the mood to let the game take him over. Alex was glad to be in motion, ridding himself of extra nervous energy. They walked past the towns-people, some of whom knew Scott and waved good luck at him;

past a mile of scattered houses with swings in the front yard and
battered cars and plastic swimming pools in the back; past a
mile or so of open pasture, dotted with grazing cows and an
occasional horse. Alex tried his best to concentrate only on his
upcoming workout and possible participation in that night's
game, but never before had he lived in a place where he could
actually walk right over to a bunch of cows, hear noises like
wind rustling tall grass, smell scents other than exhaust fumes
and soggy garbage. He was overwhelmed by the quiet and the
calm and the fact that it stretched on ahead for miles and miles.
It took his mind off baseball, something the jamming electricity
of the city had never been able to do. He assumed he'd get used
to it, though. He assumed that the lack of energy emitted from
Wilson would eventually enable him to channel even more of
his own energy into baseball.

The two boys didn't talk much—they had talked themselves
out during the night—but halfway to the stadium Scott did
warn him: "Charlie'll prob'ly haul you up in the locker room
and give you a speech. Don't let it worry ya none. He talks
tough to scare ya—and it works, I'll tell ya, but he's a real good
guy and he'll treat you fair."

So, standing up in front of the team, wearing only his underwear and socks, Alex wasn't totally terrified. He felt like a complete, stupid one-hundred-percent asshole, but he wasn't
caught by surprise.

"Justin," Charlie Lassiter said, "this is the whole team right
here in front of you." He made a grand gesture to the athletes.
"And, boys, this is Alexander Justin."

The team made a collective noise that was supposed to be
hello. Alex made a weak flip of his right hand and said, "Alex,"
hoping that wasn't an impertinent correction.

"Justin," Charlie went on, "I just said this was the whole team.
But it's not. We're missing one player. We're missing Buddy
LaRue."

Alex felt Charlie Lassiter was waiting for him to say something about Buddy LaRue. But what? From the tone of the
conversation Alex assumed the poor guy had just been run over
by a truck. Should he offer his condolences?

"Do you know *why* Buddy LaRue isn't here, Justin?"

"No, sir."

"Do you even know who the fuck Buddy LaRue *is*, Justin?"

"No, sir."

The manager had gotten the answer he was looking for. He positioned himself perfectly behind Alex so he was, in fact, talking directly to the boy but, theatrically, was really speaking to the whole team. Except for Buddy LaRue.

"Buddy LaRue was cut from this team yesterday. He was told to pack his bags and get the hell out. *I* told him that, *I* was the one who called him into my office and said, 'Buddy, I'm afraid we ain't got no room for you no more. I'm afraid I'm gonna have to take the only fuckin' way you know how to make a livin' and throw it out the fuckin' window.' " The manager smiled, menacingly sweetly. "Do you know *why* I had to do that, Justin?"

"No, sir."

"Guess."

Alex hesitated. " 'Cause I was called up?"

"Ahh. A brain."

"That's right?"

"That's right."

"Oh."

"Now lemme tell you a little somethin' about Buddy LaRue, okay? He was twenny-seven years old. That's goddamn old to be playin' in this piss-poor league in this shit-ass town! You don't get outta here in two years, three years tops, you ain't *never* gettin' out, least nowheres you wanna go to, and that's the fuckin' truth. Most guys like Buddy, they quit. Can't take it, not worth it for 'em to stay. The money's shit, the traveling stinks, the other players are all a bunch of hotshot young assholes like you, and the women who fuck B League players may be the ugliest goddamn women in the whole goddamn world! Do you understand what I'm saying to you?"

"I don't think so. Uh . . . sir."

"What I'm tryin' to tell you, Justin, is that Buddy LaRue loved this goddamn game, that's why he stayed here. And more than he loved this game, he loved this team. When he left yesterday morning, he cried. Broke down and cried right here in this room, sobbed his fucking guts out for maybe an hour because he loved this team! And this team loved him. Is that right, boys?" Again, there was a slurred noise that sounded vaguely affirmative and either silently hostile or a little bit bored. "He was a leader, he kept us loose, he was a pro who knew what the fuck he was doing when he was busy doing it, not some fuzz face who don't know shit from fuckin' shinola. Buddy LaRue was like a son to me and an older brother to every man on this team and now, because you've got some talent and are ten years younger, you're here and he's already halfway to Palookaville!"

Lassiter came up in front of Alex, faced him nose to nose, or as close as the shorter man could get to that position.

"Now. What does all this make you want to do, Justin?"

"Sir?"

"I said, what is it you want to do, now that you've heard what I just told you?"

"It makes me want to kill myself, sir."

The whole team, minus Buddy LaRue, laughed. A strong current that vanished as immediately as it arose when they saw the look on their manager's face.

"That'll cost you five extra laps after practice," Charlie said very quietly.

"Yes, sir. I'm sorry."

"When I want a joke, I'll ask for a joke."

"Yes, sir. I'm sorry."

"When I want you to give me a straight answer, that's what I expect you to do."

"Yes, sir. I'm sorry."

"A good man's never sorry, Justin. He just never does it again."

"Yes, sir. I'm—" Alex stopped himself. He was a good man.

"Now. Should I tell you what it is you should want to do, now that you've heard me talk about Buddy LaRue?"

"Yes, sir. Please."

"You should want to go out there and play such fucking good ball that in three weeks I don't even remember who the fuck Buddy LaRue *is!* You should come up to me and say, *But, Skip, he was like a son to you,* and I'll say, *Justin, boy, you're battin'*

*three seventy-five and playin' the field like fuckin' DiMaggio
and I don't have no goddamn son!* Do you understand that?"

"Yes, sir. I sure do."

"Okay. Good." He paced back and forth behind Alex now,
and Alex was hoping it was almost time to sit back down and put
his pants on.

"We've got a few rules here, too, you should know about. Not
many, 'cause I don't think men should take too many rules. But
we've got a few. Johnson!"

A guy in the front row, with a horrendous complexion that
made his face look somewhat like a plaster-of-Paris relief map of
South America Alex had made in the sixth grade, jumped up
and hollered, "Be at the stadium three hours before a home
game, be at the bus one hour before we leave on a road trip!"

"That's for infield and batting practice, strategy sessions,
team prayers, and when I have to make a shit-ass speech like
this one," Lassiter embellished. "Butler!"

Another player, this one fat with bad teeth, leapt to his feet.
"Lights out at eleven except when there's an off day the next
day. Then it's one A.M.!"

"And I check up on you, so don't get lazy or careless. Many a
good player has fucked up 'cause he didn't get no sleep," the
manager explained. "I seen it happen too many times. Jones!"

"Stay in shape!"

"The key to success. Emory!"

"Don't drink nothin' harder than beer!"

"Whiskey's the downfall of an athlete. Stay away from it. You
wanna pound one, pound some beer. You wanna drink a brew
for breakfast, go ahead, it never did no one no harm. If I catch
you poundin' whiskey, you sit for a week and don't get paid.
Hunt!"

"Pray and trust in the Lord to take care of us."

"I put that one in mostly for Hunt's sake," Lassiter told Alex.
"But it can't do no harm. Manning!" There was no movement
from the troops. "Manning!"

A startlingly good-looking blond boy in the back row stood up
very slowly, as if resigned to upcoming punishment. His hair
was short and bristly, his eyes brown and half closed, hinting

defiance. His skin was very tan and healthy-looking, emitting a glow that crept into the boy's persona. He was really so hand-some that, for some reason, it embarrassed Alex and he looked away when the boy smiled ruefully at him.

"You gonna say something, Manning?"

Manning's hands went immediately into his pockets as he peered up at his manager. "There aren't any more rules, Char-lie."

"That's right, there ain't." Boy and man faced each other, Alex caught in the middle of the mysterious pull of their antago-nism. "Justin?"

"Sir?"

"You can call me Charlie. Or Skip."

"Okay."

"You ever seen this here gorgeous boy standing up in front of you?"

Alex, in need of guidance, glanced at Scott, who, barely per-ceptibly, nodded.

"Yes, sir, uh, Charlie. Skip."

"You've seen him?"

"Yes, sir."

"Where?"

"What?"

"Where have you seen him?"

Alex stared at Scott helplessly, moved his hands in a quick motion, indicating that Scott had better get him out of this or he'd kill him. Scott's response was nervously to shovel his hand toward his mouth. A clue. Alex frowned and blinked, meaning *Do it again.* Scott did it again, twice quickly.

"Eating?" Alex meant to say it to himself in the silent recesses of his confused brain, but it mistakenly shot out of his mouth.

"What?"

And then Alex got it. "Eating!" he practically shouted. "I saw him eating! Uh, I mean, at the dinner table." He composed himself and strung the whole thing together calmly. "I met him last night at the dinner table. At the boardinghouse."

Charlie was clearly disappointed, Scott equally relieved. Manning was harder to read. He looked up from the floor only once, flickered an expression of thanks at Alex, then looked back down at the gray cement under his feet. His second day here and Alex realized he was already playing, living, under a new set of rules. There were new sides to be chosen, unknown standards to live up to, personalities, morals, angles, and loyalties to be discovered, judged, and acted upon. He hoped he'd just made his first right move.

"Okay, boys," said Charlie Lassiter. "Now that this bullshit's over, let's get out there and pound that fuckin' field."

The game that evening—a six o'clock starting time—was against the Fayetteville Highlanders. Fayetteville was about a two-hour bus ride from Wilson, and the Highlanders were one notch above the Tobs in the standings for the eight-team Carolina League, two and a half games ahead, in second place. There was a particular rivalry between the two teams, one that stemmed from blood in addition to geography. The richest and most influential family in the area, the Potters, had suffered, several years previously, a serious internal rift. The two brothers and equal holders of the huge Potter cotton fortune, Frank and Bobby Ray, had a fight over a woman. She was Bobby Ray's mistress but she also happened to be Frank's wife. When the veil of ignorance was lifted from Frank's romantically clouded eyes, the rivalry turned into the equivalent of a turn-of-the-century bare-knuckle championship brawl—it was going to go on forever or until one fighter dropped and couldn't get up again. Frank finally and somewhat unwillingly called it a draw and relocated in Fayetteville. The only times he ever returned to Wilson were when the Tobs hosted the Highlanders. During those games Frank and a black limousine's worth of cronies sat behind the visitors' dugout cheering maniacally and viciously for his adopted home club. Bobby Ray and his new wife, Frank's ex, stayed behind the home team dugout along third base, eating picnic dinners, drinking from plastic pitchers of Bloody Marys, laughing lightheartedly, and casually, almost incidentally, rooting for the Tobs to crush the intruders and, if at all possible, induce a fatal heart attack in Frank.

While Alex, oblivious to the ritualistic tension, shagged

fungoes in center field during his first pregame warm-up, the true hardcore fanatics trickled into Fleming Stadium to watch their boys work their asses off. Alex played a medium center field, confident of his ability to go both backward and forward. For over half an hour he positioned himself directly facing the batter, coach Larry Kovnowski. He bent over slightly at the waist, glove hand resting on his left knee, right hand with a death grip on his right thigh, eyes focused on the spot where, every five seconds or so, the ball tossed up by the coach would float down to the point of impact with Kovnowski's swinging bat. Despite all the surrounding chatter and noisy movement, Alex always heard the clear crack that accompanied the hit. His favorite moment came as the ball flew toward him. He would wait for it to zero in on his glove and, a split second before it was trapped and conquered, he would jab the leather in the meat of the palm, signaling that the ball was his and that the out would be made. To Alex that slap, that awareness that everything was in its proper place, was all. He loved that sound and would even stand alone in his room, or stroll outside town, on a hill somewhere distant from observing eyes, and recreate it over and over again, slamming his fist expertly into the same precise spot, conjuring up the spirit and the vision of victory. Out in right field, when the ball was caught, he would fluidly scoop it out of the glove and throw it back to the coach on two perfect bounces. Then he'd immediately return to position to bide his time statuelike and wait for the ball to be sprayed his way again, wait for that moment when he could slap leather and be satisfied.

After forty-five minutes of that he took batting practice. One of the pitchers—Alex thought he heard someone refer to the guy as Duane—stood on the mound and mechanically threw easy-to-hit fastballs letter high, right down the middle of the plate. Alex had the feeling everyone was watching him, so, attempting to impress, he overswung repeatedly. Trying to take everything downtown, he kept grounding weakly to the shortstop. The worse his hitting got the angrier he grew and the more feeble was his luck and skill. After yet another infield out Alex slammed his bat down on the plate. Coach Kovnowski strolled over to him and said, "If you're horseshit enough to break a bat over batting practice, then you deserve the ten-buck fine it'll cost you." Alex took a deep breath, felt over-whelmingly dumb, and surprised himself realizing how quickly he had blown his famed cool. He stepped back up into the box and laced two solid line drives into the left-field alley and one into the right-field corner. The groove was there and he began stinging the ball, scattering hits all over the field, sending one tall can of corn way out into the dead-center bleachers. Scott replaced him in the batter's box, slapped him on the rear, and told him, "Good goin', roomie."

He didn't know exactly what to do next, so he stood awk-wardly, watching Scott take his first few swings. Alex felt a tap on the shoulder. He shifted his glance. One of the black players had tapped him. He was already several feet away from Alex, down the first-base line. The negro barely flexed his glove; he wanted Alex to have a catch with him.

Alex nodded. The black kid, now close to first base, lazily tossed the ball. Alex caught it in an easy, relaxed motion and threw it back to his teammate. The ball went back and forth as they found a rhythm. Alex no longer felt awkward or out of place. He felt himself becoming a part of a machine. It was the role he knew and liked best.

It was hot and he was sweaty. That was his only excuse for the next throw he uncorked. Alex felt the ball slide off his hand, directionless, out of control. *Shit,* he thought, embarrassed be-cause he knew instinctively he'd just thrown it into the stands. He turned away in disgust, angrily kicking the dirt with his right heel, but out of the corner of his eye he saw the black guy move. It was without effort, almost as if everyone else in the stadium were standing still, frozen, so he knew he had all the time in the world to do whatever needed to be done. And somehow the ball was caught. Just as if it had been a perfect throw. As if it had been what Alex had meant to do.

The black guy strolled back to his spot up the first-base line, smiled at Alex as if nothing out of the ordinary had happened, and tossed the ball back in a simple fluid motion. But before Alex could resume the back-and-forth throwing, the black kid was loping off to the outfield to talk to the only other two colored players Alex could spot on the field. He looked around for somebody who would tell him who this black guy was, but nobody seemed to be paying attention. Everybody was busy getting ready to play their own game, so Alex just stood and watched the guy lope along, gracefully and powerfully and silently.

Charlie Lassiter didn't start him when the game began, much to Alex's dismay. But during the first inning the manager motioned Alex to sit beside him.

"Learn for a few innings, son," Charlie said. "Watch and see how things are done, who does what. Always know two things before you enter into any sort of game at all: who you're playin' with and who you're playin' against. Don't worry about missing this one. You're gonna play lotsa baseball for the next few months."

The first thing Alex learned was that Willie Trotty was the teammate who'd tapped him on the back, the one who had made the miraculous catch on the sidelines. The second thing he learned was that Willie was, in fact, the greatest baseball player Alex had ever seen. The Negro center fielder looked like a god when he stepped onto the field. There was an arrogance to the bounce of his heel-toe walk, but it was a beautiful arrogance that perfectly fit his remarkably lithe and muscular body.

Alex couldn't take his eyes off the man as he dominated the outfield just by standing, unmoving, in center field. The first fly ball that came his way was simply gobbled up. Alex could swear that Willie never moved, that he just stared the ball into his vacuumlike glove. It was like a great magic trick: The ball is hit to center, ladies and gentlemen, and the Great Willie makes it disappear before your very eyes!

When Willie came to the plate in the bottom of the first, he golfed a single to left on a ball that Alex would have sworn was unhittable. Then, before anyone realized what was happening, Willie rounded first and just kept going. Once again, it was as if everyone else moved in slow motion because there, suddenly, was Willie standing on second base. He didn't grin with satisfaction, didn't acknowledge his stirring feat. He brushed off the one bead of sweat on his forehead and began stalking third base.

Alex felt a bit dazed.

It was the first time he'd ever seen someone who was as good as he was.

Maybe better.

He stared out at the center fielder as the second inning began and thought, *No. I'm better. I am better. I must be better. I know I'm better.* He thought that over and over again silently to himself for the rest of the inning, until he was sure he was right.

The third thing Alex learned, to his total shock, was that Scott Hunt was a maniac on the ball field. The instant his roommate appeared on the diamond he began talking, mumbling, hollering, twitching, dancing, bobbing. Like a man possessed he dived after impossible ground balls, ran full speed to first base on a walk, slid into second base with spikes aimed to dismember. When someone did something wrong, a missed sign or an error, he screamed at them. When they did something right, he raced from his position to hug them and laugh delightedly. *No wonder he can eat so much,* Alex thought, *he probably loses ten pounds every game.*

When Scott came to bat in the third inning, for the second time in the game, Charlie nudged Alex. "Watch this tough monkey," he said. "This guy is one tough monkey." And then he hollered out to the field, "Get on base, monkey!"

Scott stepped out of the batter's box and glanced over at the bench, acknowledging his manager's order. He took two practice swings, stepped back up to the plate. The first pitch was a fastball high and inside. Scott didn't flinch, he stood there fearlessly as the ball missed beaning him by two inches. The second pitch was a curve which he swung at and missed. On the third pitch, another fastball came in hard, inside, just off the strike zone. Scott leaned forward on the balls of his feet, twisting his body so he could take the throw right smack on his shoulder. The ball bounced off the fleshy part of his arm and rolled a few feet away into foul territory. Without hesitating or rubbing the wound Scott sprinted directly to first base, immediately taking a daring lead toward second before the pitcher even had the ball back in his hand.

"Gets hit more than anyone I've ever seen," Charlie told Alex. "He loves it. Loves to get hit with the ball. He'll do anything to win. Tough monkey."

Charlie put Alex into the game in the seventh inning as a defensive replacement for Willie Trotty. Before dashing onto the field Alex tried to freeze the moment, hold it in his mind. This was it, his first step toward what he had waited for ever since he was old enough to pretend the Spalding he was bouncing off a stoop was really a homer he was smashing out of the Polo Grounds. But as he trotted to center, the moment fizzled anticlimactically. He couldn't focus on the people in the stands, nor on the hazy blue of the background sky, not even on the encouraging jumble of encouragement Scott shot at him as he passed him by. Alex felt very much alone and isolated and he saw only his turf, his home in center field. He stood, trying to clear his head, as his teammates in the infield tossed the ball around. The fog began to lift only as he vaguely heard his name announced over the echoing PA, followed by a smattering of welcome applause.

Willie was moved to right field, but he waited for Alex before jogging over.

"You got my job, white boy, and it ain't fair."

"I don't have it yet."

"You got it. Check out all that clappin'."

"Maybe I deserve it, then. Maybe I'm a better ballplayer."

Willie looked him over head to toe. "You do got *po*-tential," he said, "but I am here and now."

"The best man'll win, I guess," Alex said naively.

Willie laughed. "Shit, man. White *po*-tential *always* wins over colored here and now. Hell, that's all you white people is, *po*-tential."

Willie ran off the field—gliding over the grass and dirt—and Alex found that, despite the confused thoughts racing through his brain, he had automatically fallen into his fielding stance. Suddenly the pitch was being thrown. The pounding of blood inside his head made him dizzy, but as the batter swung and missed, he was ready. His instincts had rejected any other reaction but the one telling him to do what it was he did and do it right.

He wound up making a perfectly ordinary catch in the eighth inning and coming to bat in the ninth, popping up in foul territory behind first. But the Tobs won and everyone was happy. Alex knew he had begun his membership in a new family.

In the locker room after the game Dave Manning tapped Alex on the shoulder. "Thanks," Manning said.

Alex shrugged at Manning and slipped his comb into the back pocket of his chinos.

"I mean it," the pitcher told him. "I owe you one."

"Forget it. And it's really Scott you owe. He's the one who—"

"Yeah. I saw."

They went through one of those moments where they both wanted to say more, but both were too young and too awkward to know where to begin. Finally, Alex just coughed and indicated he was on his way out.

"You goin'?" Manning asked.

"Guess so."

"We'll give you a lift."

"You got a car?"

"The Lump does." He raised his voice and threw out, "You ready, Lump?"

"Yeah," a player across the room, whom Alex recognized as the team's catcher, replied. And then Walter Lumpano yelled, "Hey, Preacher, you wanna ride?"

"I'll be ready in a minute," Scott drawled, having returned to his normal off-the-field slow-moving, easygoing incarnation. "An' I wish you wouldn't call me that, Walter."

Manning laughed. "Let's go," he said, and, meeting Charlie Lassiter's eyes from the opposite corner of the room, he slapped Alex on the shoulder, the noise echoing and lingering in the sweaty air of the room.

* * *

"Haw!" said Dave Manning, rolling his shoulders back in disbelief. It was quarter to eleven that night and they were all in Manning's room.

"Haw?" asked Alex Justin. *"Haw?* That's one dumb laugh you got there."

"It's just," Manning intoned as solemnly as he could muster, "that I am in a full-fledged state of shock."

"Likewise," Chris Cannon added. "Ditto and likewise."

"I just don't drink," Alex explained.

"Never? You never have?"

"Never have or will. Never even tasted a sip of beer."

That did it. The final straw. There was a roar from the corner, an unintelligible mixture of outrage, pain, and disgust.

"The Lump speaks," Manning said as Alex's eyes bulged.

With yet another roar Walter Lumpano opened another bottle of beer and sucked it down in one giant gulp.

"The Lump speaks again." Manning laughed.

"And speaks the truth," Jerry Bartkowski said, and he too picked up a bottle of cold beer and chugalugged it.

The Lump banged his fist on the table and he, Dave, Jerry, Chris, and Scott each grabbed a bottle and gulped, bending over backward to drain every last drop of alcohol, twisting their lips around the neck of the bottle, squeaking and slurping any remaining drops of moisture into their mouths.

"That's what we think of you, douche bag," the Lump told Alex.

"You better not tell the Skip you don't drink, Alex," Scott warned. "That may be it for your baseball career." And in an afterthought Scott shook his head, a confused punctuation to this strange turn of events. "Even *I* drink."

"Even you?"

"Translated," Manning cut in, "that means, 'I may be a religious fanatic but I ain't no saint.' "

"That's *co*-rrect," Scott agreed.

"Amen," Jerry tossed in.

"Hallay-fuckin'-looya," said the Lump.

"Uh-oh!" Jerry Bartkowski suddenly was struck by a horrible thought.

"What is it, Ski?" Chris asked.

"Uh-oh!" Jerry repeated.

"Uh-huh," Manning agreed, excited, getting what it was to be gotten. "You're right. Uh-oh!"

"What is it?" Scott asked nervously.

"I'll tell ya what it is!" the Lump bellowed. He returned to Alex and demanded, "What about sex?"

"What about it?"

"Y'ever get any?"

"Well . . ."

"We'll give ya the benefit of the doubt. You can count sniffin', dry humpin', tit fuckin'—"

"I got a girlfriend back home."

"Shit!" the Lump swore.

"That means the answer's no," Manning explained to anyone who didn't understand the Lump's response.

"Hey, fellas," Scott put in, defensively. "I've got a girlfriend too."

"But you're too dumb to fuck," the catcher told him.

"We've obviously gotta get Alex laid," Manning announced.

"You guys are fuckin' assholes," Alex said.

"Well." The Lump was clearly relieved. "At least he swears."

There was a knock at the door.

"It's five to eleven, boys," Auntie Joy called in. "Almost time for lights out."

"Wrinkled old cunt," the Lump mumbled.

"Hey!" Scott said, not amused.

"Okay, Auntie Joy," Manning sung out. "We'll break it up in two minutes."

They heard her clump down the stairs.

"I forgot," Lump told Alex. "The Preacher here has the hots for Auntie Twat."

"I do not," Scott said, annoyed. "I just think she's a nice lady."

"I guess we better get back to the room," Alex said to Scott.

"Forget it," Manning said. "We never actually listen to her." He turned the lights off as a decoy maneuver. "Stick around.

We've gotta figure out how to get you laid. And we gotta initiate you."

"Initiate?"

"We're gonna take you cow tipping."

"Say what?"

"Don't worry about it. All in good time. But first things first. Who'd fuck Alex?"

"What about Lump's sister?" Jerry asked.

"Eat my dick," the Lump growled wittily.

"How about your mother?" Chris asked the Lump.

"You can both chew on it."

"I've seen it," said Jerry. "It'll have to be one at a time."

"Dolores," Chris suggested. "She'll spread 'em."

The Lump was incredulous. "A jig? For the first time? Whaddya wanna do? Ruin the guy for the rest of his fuckin' life?"

"Louisa," Manning decided.

"Ahhhhh, Louisa."

"Oh, yeah."

"Good. Good choice."

"Hold it, hold it, hold it," Alex said. "I don't wanna get laid by Dolores or Louise or anybody."

"Louis*a*," Scott corrected.

"I don't care what her name is. I don't want her."

"You're lying," Manning spoke up calmly. "It's very clear you're lying through your teeth. Here we are, five happy-go-lucky guys, or rather, three happy-go-lucky guys, one crazed disciple of Christ, and one subhuman, if you'll excuse me, Lump, and we are all offering you a chance to have sex with an eighteen-year-old girl with giant tits you can rub all over your face and a box that smells like Chanel Number Five, and you say, 'I don't wanna get laid'? You're lying."

"Maybe," Alex admitted.

"No," Manning insisted. "You lied. Let's hear it."

"Uh . . . when you put it that way, I may have stretched the truth there."

"Come on. Out loud."

"Okay. I lied. *If* she's as great as you say!"

"She is."

"You can put your dick in her fuckin' ear, for Chrissake!" the Lump added.

They all nodded happily and settled back into their scattered positions. Manning and Jerry both sat on Manning's bed. Chris was lying down, stretched across the other bed, hands clasped behind his head, staring up at the ceiling. Scott was slouched down in the room's easy chair, Alex sprawled on the floor, head propped up by his hand. Walter Lumpano was squatting in the corner, bulging legs oblivious to the strain of holding up his enormous bulk, needing only a mask and shin guards to step right into a game. The room smelled of beer and the air was filled with the pleasant sense of camaraderie.

"Okay, boys," Auntie Joy said from outside their door. "I've given you fifteen minutes extra, so you all can be very happy that you've fooled me and pretended you're all grown up. Now get out of that room, brush your teeth, and y'all better be in bed in ten minutes. Y'all got that?"

"Got it," they all mumbled.

"Got it, got it, got it."

"Uh-huh, uh-huh, uh-huh."

"Yeah, yeah, yeah."

And Manning nodded, a signal to all of them, and whispered. "Fifteen minutes. Cow tipping."

Fifteen minutes later, teeth brushed, hands washed, and ears cleaned, Scott and Alex were shimmying down a rope that was tied securely to Scott's bedpost, hung out the window, and trailed down to the street below. When they hit ground, the others were already gathered.

"What are—" Alex began.

"Sshhhh!" Manning cut him off.

"Auntie Twat has ears like a fuckin' Indian!" the Lump whispered.

No one said a word until they were several blocks away from the house.

"Okay," Manning said to Alex. "You can ask questions now."

"What are we doing?"

"We're not gonna *answer* any of your questions, but you can ask 'em."

"I don't like this."

"What a pussy!" the Lump sneered.

"You got five minutes to wait, Justin. Just hold on."

When they hit the edge of town, Chris Cannon led the way back through a large field. It was dark, darker than Alex ever remembered the night being. He enjoyed the sound of their shoes tromping over grass and weeds; in the absolute stillness of the meadow the scuffling sounded like muffled thunder.

"Okay," Manning said, assuming the tone of a commando. "I see one."

"Hot fuckin' damn," the Lump said.

As they crept forward, Alex made out a shadowy figure several yards in front of them: a cow.

"Perfect," Scott said.

"I don't get this at all," Alex let them all know.

"Okay, Justin," Manning told him. "We are now gonna introduce you to one of North Carolina's major joys. You are gonna have your first cow-tipping lesson."

"Over here," Jerry said, as he tiptoed around behind the cow.

"How come he's so still?" Alex asked.

"A city boy if ever there was one."

"First of all, he's a she," Manning said. "Second of all, she's asleep."

"Standing up?"

"Whaddya expect?" the Lump wanted to know. "It's a fuckin' cow."

"They all sleep standin' up," Scott explained. "That's just a fact o' life."

"All right. Let's cut this gabbin' and get to work," Manning directed. "Alex, you get over there behind that hind leg."

Alex did as he was told.

"Bend down."

"Huh?"

"Bend down. On all fours."

"Why?"

"Because we're gonna tip 'er."

"I don't get it."

"You bend down behind her back leg. Then we'll get on this side and push. She falls over . . . and then you're gonna see somethin' you'll never forget."

"What?"

"You gonna do it or not?"

Alex sighed and got down on all fours. The next thing he knew, the others were screaming one long "Whhhoooaaa!" and pushing against the cow with all their might. Suddenly, hundreds of pounds were pressing down on his back; for an instant he was sure he was going to be crushed by this stupid-looking animal. Then the weight was off him and he was about to leap up and run. And then came the explosion, a roar, a whooosh, like a great airplane zooming by. Before Alex knew what had hit him, he was covered, from head to toe, in what felt like a hundred pounds of cow shit.

"Run, asshole," the Lump shouted, "or that bitch is gonna kick the fuckin' balls offa you."

And the others took off, laughing, running, while Alex struggled to his feet, aware that the animal was mooing and bellowing and thrashing; not fully believing that he was in the middle of nowhere and some cow had just taken a dump all over his entire body.

He chased after the others, not really angry, rather fulfilling his role as prank victim. By the time he caught up with them, he was laughing too. And as they pulled out towels and wiped him off, heading back toward town, Alex thought it had been quite a day. A beginning, a clear-cut beginning. And another thought already began to pound inside his head but he shoved it away. *No,* he decided. *Forget it. Don't touch it.* But it sneaked back in and he thought, over and over again: *Louisa.*

They were gathered in Manning's room. It was a rare off day. No game. No long, boring, dusty bus ride. No practice—a rare indication that Charlie Lassiter had a heart beating beneath his Tobs uniform. It was a sweaty day, and all they wanted to do was sit as still as possible and figure out ways to keep cool.

Chris Cannon was playing his guitar. His girlfriend had just written him a Dear John letter, and he was paying her back musically. This was about the seventy-second straight hour they'd all listened to Chris compose his masterpiece, and they were hoping he'd finish soon.

"Here's the new chorus," Chris said, and began to strum and sing again.

I don't like ya
I'd like to punch ya
I'd like to take a steamroller and crunch ya
I'd like to find ya
And then I'd blind ya
And then I'd sing my songs and not mind ya

Chris was stuck on the final stanza.

"I think I got it," Manning said. "I think I can help you out."

"Let's hear it," Chris said, and began to strum again.

"Oh, what you got that I don't have to win my luscious

Venus," Manning sang, imitating Chris's bluegrass twang.
"Have you got the millions she desires, have you got a two-foot penis?"

Chris immediately stopped strumming.

"Catchy," Alex said.

"You're all a bunch of very sensitive guys," Chris said.

Manning agreed. "Especially the Lump."

They all looked over at the Lump, who, oblivious to the racket, was having a real good time catching flies. In his constant squat in the corner he decoyed them by staying as statue-like as he could, just waiting for an unsuspecting fly to land on one of his hairy arms. He would give it a few moments of false security on its temporary perch, then lunge into action. His hand moved shockingly quickly, capturing the fly inside a clenched fist. He would listen to the frenzied buzzing and bumping from palm to finger, then he would squeeze once, open his hand, and proudly expose one crushed fly to his slightly nauseated teammates. He had tossed his seventh dead fly into the middle of the room before Manning decided to put a stop to it.

"Listen, you scum bag," Manning put it gently. "If you throw one more fuckin' dead fly on my side of the room, I'm gonna make you eat every fuckin' one of 'em."

"That won't work, Dave," Alex told Manning. "The Lump eats dead flies for breakfast. He likes 'em."

"Fuck you," the Lump retorted. *"Live* flies for breakfast. Dead flies for lunch."

Chris Cannon banged his hand down across his guitar.

"Dead flies for lunch," he sang. *"That's all my baby'll feed me."* He didn't have a decent rhyming line and it was too hot anyway, so he just dropped his guitar onto the floor with a thud.

Jerry Bartkowski came into the room, carrying a copy of *Time* magazine tucked under his arm. Scott followed right behind him, somewhat agitated.

"It's true, it's true!" he was saying, his voice squeaking with excitement.

"I think you're a nutcake."

"What goes on?" Manning asked.

Jerry rolled his eyes. "The Preacher's givin' me a lecture on the connection between baseball and that old-time religion."

"I speak the truth. You boys don't know it, but this here thing we do is close to God."

"I think you've gone off the deep end, Preach," Manning told Scott.

"I think I want a new roommate," Alex said.

"All baseball is *de*-rived from the religious rites of ancient times. Fertility rites, mostly."

There was a snort from the corner.

"Uh-oh," Manning said. "Lump thinks he heard a dirty word."

"It's true," Scott said. "Fertility rites."

"More!"

"Looks like the Lump wants to hear about this," Alex put in.

"Yeah," Manning added. "He just said something that sounded almost like English."

Although it was not yet noon, the Lump started on his second six-pack. After one long swallow a belch indicated that he was ready to hear more about fertility rites.

"Five thousand years ago in Egypt," Scott went on, "they had the first batting contest."

"I feel like I'm in school."

"This is worse than school. He doesn't even know what he's talking about."

"Worshipers of Osiris, the god of agriculture, would place his image—"

"Is that *His* or *his?*"

"—his image on a cart and try to rush it into the Temple of . . . the Temple of . . . shoot, I don't remember the name of the dang temple."

"Unimportant, professor."

"Yeah. Anyway, these guys had sticks. And an army of priests, with clubs, would line up outside the Temple of Whatever-it-is and try to fight them back. The idea was to hit the head off Osiris."

"Sounds like fun."

"Sounds pretty fuckin' stupid to me. Stu-fuckin'-pid!"

"Whaddya expect?" Scott asked. "It was five thousand years ago. Ya think they were as smart as we are? But the whole point was to have a sort of game that would help the crops grow."

"Why didn't they just hire niggers?"

"Shut up!"

"When does the fucking start?" the Lump wanted to know.

"What fucking?"

"I thought this was about fucking. Isn't that what he said before?"

"Ya know," Manning said to Alex, "maybe the Lump really is as stupid as we pretend he is."

"There's more," Scott said defensively.

"Oh, good. Here comes the fucking part."

"Egyptian high priests used a ball as a symbol for their spring-time ceremonies."

"How does he know all this stuff?" Alex wanted to know. "Seriously."

"The ball was a symbol of potency. And pictures have been found of nude women playin' ball carved into tombs built two thousand years B.C."

Scott paused dramatically, waiting for this astounding historical revelation to set in.

"See, asshole?" Lump gloated to Manning. "I told you we'd get around to this."

"I'm leaving," Alex said.

"There's gonna be a quiz later," Manning said.

Alex was out the door, but not before he heard, "The Christian church, in its wisdom, noticed how popular these pagan rites were and stuck 'em into their Easter ceremony." He took the steps two at a time down to the parlor, opened the front door, squinted at the bright sunlight, stepped out onto the streets of Wilson.

Walking slowly, enjoying the peace and silence of being alone, he thought about Patty. He missed her, even though he was getting about three letters a week. Nothing important. Chatter. Little insights. Gossip. A few jokes. A lot of tenderness. He could feel her love for him through her words, her phrasing, her choices of what to tell him and what not to tell him. When he read her letters he could just see her thinking and thinking and thinking before putting pen to paper, straining to please him, to sound interesting, to make him laugh. He could see her mailing it and then, as soon as it dropped to the bottom of the blue-and-red mailbox, deciding that it was a lousy letter, wanting to take it back, thinking that he'd hate it. And he could see her delight when she opened his return letter which told her, truthfully, how much he loved hearing from her, how her last bits of news had thrilled him. She would shake her head and think, *What's* wrong *with him that he likes me so much?* He could see it all, and, shuffling along the dusty main street of Wilson, North Carolina, he grinned, warmed by the thought of the girl back home.

He had been a little concerned lately that he hadn't been thinking about her enough. He found that many hours went by where he thought about a lot of other things: baseball, his friends, this girl Louisa whom he still hadn't met, the South, the quiet of the fields, his weekly paycheck . . . There were so many damn things to discover, to appreciate. And then he'd remember Patty. He *liked* thinking about her. He wished he would do it more often as he was now. There was just so damn much that got in the way.

"Hey!"

Alex looked up, turned from side to side, didn't see who'd called him. For a moment he felt a little silly because he'd just assumed he was the one being called. It wasn't as if he were still on the Stuyvesant Town playgrounds. He tried to return to his thoughts, couldn't quite return to the mental path he'd been following.

"Hey, Pote."

Alex looked up again. Turned. Across the street was Willie Trotty. It took Alex a second to realize that Willie was walking, keeping pace with Alex. Willie's steps were so smooth, so casual, it seemed as if he were lounging against a lamppost. But no, now he was crossing the street, coming over to Alex.

"Hiya, Pote."

Alex nodded, smiled, stopped walking. "What'd you call me?"

"Sorry. It's the little nickname we colored boys on the team made up for you."

"Pote?"

"Potential."

"Very cute."

"We coloreds have to work twice as hard and be twice as good as you whiteys just so we be seen half as worthy. Luckily, that ain't really too hard."

"You're startin', aren't you?"

"I'm startin'. But I won't be soon. Least not in my position. *You* gonna be in my position. They can't sit me down, but they sure as hell can move me round."

Alex started strolling again. Not fast, not to get away from Willie, just to keep moving. Willie strolled along with him.

"I'm good," Alex said. "That's why I'm gonna be in center field."

"You good," Willie agreed. "You real good. But not as good as me." Alex said nothing. "Potential," Willie muttered after a few more steps. "White boys got potential. Black boys got whatever they did the game before."

"I'm good," Alex said again quietly.

"You good," Willie agreed again. "There's three good boys on this team, boys gonna go up. You an' Manning an' Lump."

"And you," Alex said.

Willie smiled. Alex saw he was missing a couple of teeth. "An' me," he said. "If I can learn to reach my *po*-tential."

"How old're you?" Alex asked.

"Twenty. And I ain't learned much in those twenty years."

"How's that?"

"Son, what you're lookin' at is one strong, stupid, southern buck nigger. I like to fish, I like to play ball, I like to fuck, and I don't like to take no shit from nobody."

"That sounds all right to me."

"That," Willie Trotty said, "is my definition of a big, fat loser."

"So what is it you haven't learned?" Alex asked.

"How to lose," Willie said. And then, very slowly, again, "How . . . to . . . lose."

Alex stopped walking. Willie kept going. Three, four steps

ahead, the black kid glanced back. "You been to the nigger part a town yet?" he asked.

"Uh-uh."

"You wanna go?"

Willie didn't slow down. Alex hesitated, then started walking. He had to do a quick little hop and skip to catch up to Willie and start walking with him, stride for stride.

Willie Trotty—and Ben Ellerbee and Donnie Lawrence, the other two black guys on the team—lived in a rooming house not too dissimilar from Auntie Joy's. The smells were the same—everything in the house, including the furniture, smelled as if it had just come out of the oven—and so were the hazy lighting that filtered through all the rooms and the couches that sagged in all the right places. Donnie and Ben were pretty surprised when Willie brought Alex upstairs.

"You all been formally introduced to Pote?"

They tried not to show their surprise, simply nodded, cool as could be.

"I brought Pote up here to listen to some music. Teach him 'bout southern life. That kinda thing."

"Nigger," Donnie said to Willie without looking up, "I don't want no shit in this town. I don't want no shit in my *life*. This boy seem like a nice boy. But we start hangin' round with nice white boys and there gonna be so much shit on the ground there ain't gonna be no place to walk."

"You like music?" Willie asked Alex. Alex nodded. Willie turned to Ben and Donnie. "You gents like to come into my room and hear the sounds?"

"Fuck, fuck, *fuck*," Donnie said.

"He good," Willie said, pointing to Alex. "Ask him. He tell you himself."

The four of them sat in Willie's room and listened to a scratchy recording of Mingus's "Chazz Fingers." When the song was over, Willie said, "See that? That ain't potential. That is god-damn music from heaven."

They listened to the rest of the album. No one spoke. Alex

eventually closed his eyes, relaxed, and began to be whisked away by the wondrous sounds, sweetly lifted and carried to another place, much as he had been that one time in his dad's club. Listening, he thought of his dad, of his mom and Elliot, of Patty. Briefly he wished she could be there with him, leaning back, quiet, feeling this incredible surge of peaceful energy. Then she was out of his thoughts and it was just him and the sax and the piano and the crackling skips of the needle. He'd had no idea anything could sound like this.

By the time the album was over, Alex had begun to think that Willie Trotty might just be right. Music from heaven.

Slowly, gradually, Alex became a full-fledged member of the Tobs, absorbed into the bloodstream of the seventeen-member team. As the season progressed and the summer rolled inexorably toward its conclusion, his life gradually began to reshape and redefine itself, keeping many elements of the past, rejecting some, and inventing new traits, ingredients, and directions.

His play on the field was exemplary and, as always, brought him respect along with a certain command. By the end of July, Alex was hitting .320, playing a brilliant center field, and establishing himself around the league as a clutch player, a force to be reckoned with, one who was leading the Tobs into second place and a legit shot at the B League pennant.

Alex's easy confidence spread to others, kept things loose. He responded best when a response was needed most. He loved those situations where it was do or die: men on base, two outs; a screaming line drive diving in front of him in the late innings and a tiring relief pitcher on the mound; a hit to the right side needed to keep a key rally going. The outside world slipped into a blur. He saw nothing, heard nothing, felt nothing but a pure desire to do battle. And to win. Charlie Lassiter talked a lot about being a professional, about what it meant to do your job day in and day out, to fill a role within a larger structure. To do what was expected, make few errors, and, simply, to last and survive as someone who got the job done. But to Alex that was for other people. He was there to do great things.

He tried to share this with Patty, knowing how important it was to her to "be one." But he could never really do it, not in his letters, not in their once-every-two-weeks phone conversations. Alex told this once to Manning, told him a little bit about his world apart from Patty, said it bothered him that he didn't know how to bring her into it.

"I think," Manning said with a raised eyebrow, "that everybody needs secrets. That if you take someone's secrets away from him, you can take away his whole life."

"It's not secrets exactly," Alex replied. "I'm not hiding anything."

"Everybody hides something. And I think that's okay. That's the only interesting thing about knowing people—trying to find out what they're hiding."

Alex wanted Patty to know what he was hiding. But in his letters he only told her what he did on the field—the hits, the RBIs, the catches. He could never share with her how he felt. He could never tell her about what it really meant to him. He could never tell her about the dreams he had. The luck and the greatness. His potential. The moment.

The moment.

That was his secret.

That one instant, that one split second, when he knew it would all come together, when it would at last *mean* something. Alex knew he would reach that moment and he knew he would reach it on the ball field. He knew it would change his life.

But that was separate from Patty. That was all his. And somehow the fact that it was separate gave him freedom, a freedom he wasn't ready to give up. He would one day, he was sure. But not yet.

Maybe one of these guys would understand. It was possible they knew what he knew, felt what he felt. Manning, maybe. Or Willie. They both had their secrets, secrets that gave them strength. Secrets he hoped one day they could share.

Much to his relief he didn't have all that much time to wonder about secrets or sharing or being one or, for that matter, anything else. His new professional life was enveloping him. It dominated his mind, his actions. Much of his time was taken up now with long bus rides. From Wilson to Durham for a game with the Bulls. From Durham back to Wilson then on to Kingston. From Kingston to Highpoint-Thomasville. Back to Wilson. Back into the bus. Out to a stadium, back home. Then out on the road again. He played endless rounds of gin rummy with teammates, learned to read *The Sporting News* on bumpy, swerving country roads, trained himself to lean back on uncomfortable bus cushions, close his eyes, ignore the chattering insults and leering obscenities, the popping open of beer cans, and drift off into an exhaust-fumed sleep. But there was always a game to play, always something to prepare for, to wait for. Something was always going to happen, the plan was always being carried out. And for Alex that constant was as addictive as breathing, as eating. It kept him alive.

Teammates were becoming friends. Or if not friends, forces. Ties were forming, molding, bonds twisting themselves into new alliances. There was Henry, from Arizona, who chewed tobacco, but not well, and always had brown saliva dripping down his shirt. Lester, who liked nothing better than to pop his pimples on the dugout bench, splattering whoever was foolish enough to sit next to him. And Randy, who earned the baaing nickname Raaaaandy because of his proud proclamation that he had porked more sheep than any living white man. There was Doug Trent, who was unanimously voted into the All-Ugly Hall of Fame, Jackie Amalti, who swore he had Mafia ties and that the first pitcher who beaned him would get fitted for a pair of cement overshoes. There were the Chess Players, two infielders who were never seen apart and who would sit on the bench and say, "Knight to king four," and then keep quiet for twenty minutes before coming up with "Pawn to rook three," and no one knew whether they were really playing chess or just putting everyone on; the Flakes, two relief pitchers who had once nailed everyone's shoes to the floor of the locker room. Alex meandered his way through a new maze of relationships, bumping into hostile walls, changing directions, ploughing ahead. There were new layers and complexities to relationships that Alex could feel developing with age and maturity. He was growing. And attachments changed along with perceptions.

His one gnawing regret was over his relationship with Willie Trotty. At the ballpark Willie, Donnie, and Ben hardly ever acknowledged his presence. They kept apart from the rest of the team, quiet and separate. But Alex and Willie, away from the park, saw each other, were becoming important to each other. Willie had even begun hanging out at Auntie Joy's. Manning liked him, so that was enough to get Willie accepted by everyone except the Lump. He would come over and play records, teach Alex about jazz and the blues. He moved tentatively at first in their white world but soon became more comfortable, more aggressive. He made jokes now, spoke his mind, argued. Once Donnie and Ben came over, but they never came back. Willie explained that they were afraid.

"Of what?" Manning asked.

"Of anything they don't know," Willie said. "Of everything."

Alex liked Willie, but there was a constant tension between them. As Willie had predicted, Alex was given the center-field job and the black man—he was a man at twenty—was shifted to right field. When Willie would make a fine catch running into Alex's territory in center, Alex always felt that one instant of Willie's glare. It was not hate, not at all. It was more a display of strength. *They can give you everything but my talent* was what the glare said. *They can give my position, they can give you my awards, but I still got* me. *They can't take no part of* me! When Willie would get on base, Alex felt the glare into the dugout. *I'm here, I did my job. Let's see you do yours!* And so Alex felt himself rising to new heights. He met Willie's challenge and felt himself improving because of it. As he did, he was aware that Willie was recognizing Alex's ability, respecting it. The only thing that still bothered Alex, as the summer progressed, was that every so often, for a moment here, a moment there, a flash, a shimmering image or shadow, Alex saw Willie do something that Alex himself could not do. He saw it, knew it. Willie Trotty was a better ballplayer. It was the first time Alex had ever felt it. And for the first time he let Patty into his secret world. He needed to tell someone.

He wrote in one of his letters:

I have come up against something that can't be overcome by discipline or direction or practicality. Even if you're great there's still the overwhelming possibility that you're not great *enough*. When I see Willie play I can feel doubt. But I won't let myself feel it for long because I think I'm not even willing to settle for greatness. I want to be greater than great. I want perfection. The perfect throw, the perfect catch, the home run in the bottom of the ninth. That's the way I'm going to beat the Willie Trottys of the world. Perfection.

The Moment, he thought, when he put his pen down. *That's as close as I can get to telling her about the Moment.*

Most of Alex's free time was not spent worrying about Willie or being perfect. Most of it was spent with the boys in Auntie Joy's rooming house. They were beginning to jell as a unit— Dave Manning, Walter Lumpano, Jerry Bartkowski, Chris Cannon, Scott Hunt, and Alex. None of them seemed to go together as individuals. Yet they worked as a whole. As a team.

The strangest combination of roommates was Chris and Walter "the Lump" Lumpano.

Chris was the least dynamic but most pleasant force in the group. He was a lanky, easygoing sort who could throw a baseball harder than any other pitcher Alex had ever seen. His arm was like a rubber band the way it swiveled back and then snapped forward in one herky-jerky motion, rocketing an unhittable ball toward the plate. As often as not it sailed wildly to the backstop or skidded through the dirt. But in a game, when he had two strikes on a batter, the crowd would always tense and players in the dugout would start to pace and mutter, "Light the fuse, Cannon. Light that fuse." And the pitch would come, sometimes strike three, blown right by a swing from the heels. "Boom! Way to go, Cannon. He lit that fuse. Yeah! That fuse was lit!" The phrase caught on and Chris Cannon became Fuse, the new Bob Feller, the phenom with the great left arm; the boy with the brilliant fastball and terrifying lack of control. But as explosive as he was on the field, that's how quiet Chris was inside the protection of Auntie Joy's. He occasionally picked up his battered old guitar and sang some country music, but other than that Alex was never sure what Chris did or thought or felt. He rarely spoke, didn't seem to read, never made wise-cracks or played practical jokes.

Alex learned that Fuse was from Florida. Fort Lauderdale. His father was a disc jockey who used to tell his listening audience, every day, what a great athlete his son was. He'd started boasting about Chris's great arm over the airwaves when Chris was three years old. Then, when listener response was positive and more cute anecdotes were called for, Chris's father went out and bought a hardball. He started rolling it back and forth with his son, waiting for Chris to do something amusing or exciting enough to be repeated in the six-to-ten slot on WFLA. If the tot didn't come up with anything, the DJ would just make it up.

"Chrissie threw a curveball today, ladies and gentlemen. I swear to you-know-who. Five years old and the kid's got a better curve than Early Wynn. Now if I could just teach him to throw a spitter, we're takin' on the Yanks!"

By the time Chris got to high school, his left arm was a revered weapon in the Francis Drake High Sailors' arsenal and Chris Cannon became a local celebrity. He mowed them down on the ball field and his father rehashed every pitch to an audience of thousands. On the field Chris's left arm did the talking for him; off it his father took on the same responsibility. By the time he reached Wilson, Chris had lost the habit of speech. So he just shyly went about his business as the Fuse, sending all newspaper clippings dutifully back home to his Fort Lauderdale legions.

Chris's roommate, on the other hand, never did anything shyly.

Short, squat, burly, and hairy Walter Lumpano's personality matched his body. Walter was from Cleveland and had been called Lump ever since he could remember. That was his name. He didn't answer to Walter and would usually snarl viciously at anyone who insisted on calling him that. Alex wasn't sure how much of what made Walter "the Lump" was an act, a pose, and how much was real. The meanness was real, of that Alex was fairly certain. The Lump gleefully regaled the gang with tales of his Cleveland days: how he'd go down to the train yard and roll alcoholic bums, setting fire to their shoes while they slept in the winter, dropping dollar bills in the dirt to watch them fight each other and grovel for the money. That was the Lump's idea of a good time. That and fucking every woman in sight since he was twelve years old.

"My first pussy," he told Alex, beer dripping down his double chin, "was this Jewish girl. I was workin' in a market. She had me carry her groceries home and then she practically begged me to fuck her. Jews love to fuck, you know. They do anything. And they're weird. This one had all this hair under her arms. Jews are hairy, anyway. Big bushy fuckin' armpits, she had, and she wanted me to lick 'em. Can you see it? Twelve fuckin' years old and there I was eatin' all this Jew hair from her fuckin' armpits. Shit. It was great!"

Alex was repulsed by the Lump's sexual exploits, real or imaginary. He couldn't fathom the Lump having sex with anyone; it was impossible to visualize any sort of tenderness or compassion or love passed down along by this brutish nineteen-year-old. Alex tried to envision Patty with the Lump and it frightened him. *This Jew girl,* Alex imagined the Lump reporting back, *only get this, this one had straight hair on her pubes! No fuckin' curls!* Alex didn't like even to pretend that Patty might fall prey to the meaty tentacles of someone like Walter Lumpano, who read nothing but comic books, spoke of little but ugly, urgent sex, felt no need to do anything but satisfy his own immediate lusts. Alex was sure that Patty wasn't even aware that people like the Lump existed. Hunters, they were. Survivors, probably. Tough and unfeeling, of a different world. Alex wondered if Patty could survive in such a world. Probably not, he decided, for she had too few defenses and they were fragile ones; she was far too vulnerable. He, on the other hand, was learning to make his way. For better or worse he was wising up to the ways of reality. Again, his education on the ball field was standing him in good stead. He knew to go with his strengths, to use those skills which he could exploit rather than those which were exploitable by others. Power could defeat power, but when faced with finesse, his emerging philosophy of life was go with the pitch and hit to right if necessary. Take what's there. With the

Lump, Alex sensed his own key impulse was his willingness to accept the Lump for exactly what he was: the greatest catcher Alex had ever seen. The Lump could call a good game, block the plate like an immovable brick wall, rocket a ball to second base to throw out a runner. It was not possible to injure the Lump: he played with spike wounds, broken fingers, legs that were so black and blue they looked like they should be amputated. He hit for average, for power, he could even steal a base if necessary. Walter Lumpano was a superb athlete, talented and dedicated, and it was as such that Alex accepted him, no, more than that, was drawn to him. Liked him. They met on a common level where merger was not just legitimate but inevitable. Alex had no desire to expand those parameters or even to question them. That was what was there for him to hold, that's what was real, and so that was enough for Alex to use to establish a necessary bond, one that pushed them both forward. One that kept them both on the same side.

Alex thought he and Dave Manning might become friends, not just teammates. He sensed, in Manning, an equal—in judgment, in strength, in control. But Manning proved difficult to get close to. He pushed people away, and Alex was not the sort to push back for too long. There still was something special between them, though Manning insisted that whatever it was remain vague and undefined. They were equals in too many ways, that was part of the problem. They were both used to being leaders, and Alex, to his annoyance, found himself parrying and fencing with Manning over their respective roles. Manning played games; he delighted in confusing and obscuring patterns and established expectations. As he confessed to Alex after a particularly harsh run-in with Charlie, "Most ballplayers are so goddamn stupid the only way I can even stay in this game is to do some mind-fucking."

"But don't fuck with Charlie," Alex had said. "He'll just come down on you harder and harder."

"Charlie hates me. Doesn't matter what I do, he'll come down on me."

"Why?"

"Because he's stupid too. He's just smart enough to know how stupid he is and *all* of this is. Only, he can ignore it. He can ignore anything if it'll help with a baseball game."

"I still don't get it."

"Charlie thinks I'm a bad influence."

"You? Why?"

Manning laughed. "Brains are the curse of the working man. Charlie's Law."

Dave Manning had plenty of brains. He was the only one of the bunch who planned to finish college. He was enrolled at a school in Michigan, had gone there in the off season the year before, would start his second year when October rolled around again. Dave was from Michigan. His father was a doctor, his mother a housewife, more than content to divide her time between shopping and golf tournaments at the country club. Dave Manning, Sr., wanted Dave Manning, Jr., to be a doctor also, but Junior did not care much for the sight of internal organs. Nor of country clubs, nor of suburban Ann Arbor. Junior told Senior he preferred the sight of a curveball slicing across the plate for a called strike three. And the cheers of the crowd. And the beautiful cheerleaders who dated beautiful pitchers. Dave spent his first year in Wilson learning how to be a pro, and this year he was learning how to be a winner and perfect his craft. He did not have Chris Cannon's overpowering stuff, but he had brains and an uncanny repertoire of pitches for one so young. His fastball was acceptable, his curve was big league average. By the end of a year in Wilson he could throw a screwball for a strike with the count full and he could make a batter swing so early on a change-up that his outfielders could be back in the dugout before the pitch settled into Lump's waiting mitt. He came back to his parents after his rookie season and told his parents he was now to be considered a baseball player. He would go to college, finish if he could, but his slider was to be his scalpel and the dugout his hospital.

"You could be saving lives," his father had told him.

"Yeah," Manning replied, eyes unblinking. "I'm starting with my own."

One night after Manning had pitched a six-hit shutout, he and Alex sat on the lawn outside Auntie Joy's. It was dark, very black. The streetlights were dim, casting faint glows, murky balls of light that seemed to hide the sleeping town rather than expose it. Crickets rubbed their wings in the bushes, tree frogs croaked ragged tunes.

"You made it look easy tonight," Alex told Manning.

"That's what I'm trying to do."

"Is it?"

"What?"

Alex shifted his weight. He had been leaning against the trunk of a large oak tree; now he sat forward.

"Is it as easy as you make it look?"

Manning smiled and slowly peeled the skin off an apple, a delicate maneuver performed skillfully. "Is it for you?" he asked.

"Yes," Alex said. "It is easy for me. It always has been."

"And always will be, probably."

"I hope so."

"Yes," Manning said. "In answer to your question. For me also. It *is* as easy as I make it look."

"Is that the truth?"

"No." Manning smiled. "No, it's not as easy as I make it look."

The smile drove Alex crazy. There was some force that Manning was keeping bottled up within himself. Not hidden simply by quick-flying jokes like Danny Cappollo, *everything* seemed to be part of Manning's mask—his talent, his brilliant good looks, his cocky aura of adventurous leadership. The smile, which was perpetually plastered on Manning's face, made Alex feel he was always one step behind the pitcher, that Manning knew something important that Alex was not yet aware of. It wasn't a belligerent smirk, nor a seductive leer. It was not a confident gleam of power, certainly no revelation of weakness. It was, as Alex read it, a challenge. A dare. An athlete risking yet another competition. *There is a big secret, a huge and important one,* the expression on Manning's face said. *There is something to be discovered, there is a truth worth knowing. Find it,* that look dared. *Find it and you will have won.*

"You're the only person," Alex said with a sigh that night,

"who can make both yes *and* no sound like lies to the same question."

"What is truth, anyway?"

"Oh, please."

"I'll tell you, if you want to know." Alex shrugged and Manning went on. "Truth is whatever's convenient."

"I don't think that's my definition."

"Truth is whatever people want to hear. Truth is whatever people *think* is true."

"Uh-huh."

"No one's really interested in truth, anyway, are they?"

"I am."

Manning raised his eyebrows skeptically and bit into his skinless apple, taking almost half of the fruit in one bite. Alex thought there was more to come. But Manning stood and walked lazily back to the house, leaving Alex on the lawn with the rumbling sounds of the night.

Ski, Jerry Bartkowski, was the housemate Alex was becoming most comfortable with. He was a surprising person and Alex was constantly underestimating him. Ski's father was a steelworker in Pittsburgh, and that's exactly what Ski looked as if he should be doing. He was a huge guy, so muscular he looked too stiff to be an athlete. Alex had never seen a neck like Ski's except once, caged in the Bronx Zoo. It went from his head straight out to his shoulders in one muscular mass. But despite his immense size and impressive appearance, his position on the team was precarious. Ski just didn't seem to do anything quite well enough. He hit .265 when he needed to hit .280. He doubled instead of putting the ball out of the park. And his work around the bag was competent at best, rather than smooth and graceful. His size probably worked against Jerry, because he gave the appearance of superhuman potential. The all-too-human results were gravely disappointing.

Ski had a surprisingly docile personality. He was very easygoing, never raised his voice, rarely used his physical superiority to intimidate. Alex noticed that Jerry Bartkowski was someone who backed away from his own physical nature, fought against his own strength, his own essence, was warring to break out of that imposing shell. He was not a leader. In fact, he so idolized Manning that he followed him nearly blindly. Ski warmed slowly to Alex, partly, Alex thought, because he felt that somehow Alex threatened Manning's role as leader. But that barrier soon faded and Alex and Ski spent much time together. Of all the guys, Ski was the only one he really talked to about Patty. Jerry was a gentle sort and liked the idea of love.

"I think that's all that matters in life," Jerry said when Alex told him that the concept of love confused him.

"I don't know where it fits," Alex said.

"It don't fit nowhere," the big guy said. "Don't fit nowhere. It's all around, things fit into it."

Alex considered that and thought it possible.

"But what about you?" Alex wanted to know.

"Oh, I got someone."

"You never talk about her."

"Yeah. I know."

"How come?"

"I tell ya, Alex. Maybe this ain't normal, but it's the way I am. When I'm here, she ain't a part of my life. I'm someone else when I'm not around her. And she is too. And when I get back there, who knows? Maybe she'll be a different person altogether. Maybe she'll have to wear glasses or somethin' and maybe I won't like her in glasses. Or maybe I'll meet someone here and she won't like that. I just figure there's too many things can go wrong when you're not together."

"Have you met someone else here?"

Ski shrugged. "There's a few. It's hard to know what's right or not when all ya do is ride smelly buses and dig out ground balls all day. I mean, it's hard to tell whether you're likin' someone 'cause you like 'em or whether you like 'em 'cause they're there and there ain't no hassle. I don't really know. I dunno. I guess I'm one of those guys, too, who don't like bein' alone. I'd rather be with someone, don't matter much who."

"Huh. I'm not like that, I don't think. That's kinda weird."

"Yeah, well. There are so many damn confusin' things."

The one person who was never in the least confused was Alex's roommate. Scott had God, a girl back home, and a starting job, so there was nothing to confuse him. He wrote home every day and prayed every night and his faith in himself and his routine was unshakable.

Off the baseball diamond Scott was friendly, relaxed, faithful, beguilingly innocent. He loved to chew the fat with shopkeepers. Whenever he had free time he could always be found in front of Wilbur James's grocery store playing checkers with whoever had time for a lengthy game, a friendly chaw, and good-natured gossip about locals, politicians, and sports. Alex could lie in bed and, if the windows were open, listen to the tall tales spun on the boardwalk below. Scott believed everything he heard, accepted fantasy as wondrous fact. Almost every night, as the two boys lay in the darkness awaiting sleep, Scott would toss in his day's learning. Bubba Bender had played baseball with Ty Cobb, rammed a ball right into Cobb's teeth when the Peach had slid into second with his spikes too damn high. Old Man Kraft had fought side by side with Teddy, the God-lovin' Roosevelt. Delilah, the crazy black woman who wore three jackets even in summer, she had twenty-three children— and would've had more except she'd started killin' 'em when they were born 'cause she didn't know what else to do. And each night Alex would murmur along with Scott's astonishment at what a great old town this was, what amazing people lived in this glorious ol' country.

Dotty was his girl back home, back home in Dunston, Alabama. Dotty was still in high school, she was fifteen. They were going to get married as soon as Scott made it to the majors.

"Will that be a life?" he asked Alex over and over again. "Me an' Dotty, we'll have a nice little house, a garden an' all. All the guys on the team'll come over for dinner. And I'll be gettin' all my money from doin' the one thing I love doin'!"

The only time Alex ever saw Scott sad was when he thought about leaving Auntie Joy's.

"I tell ya, I love that woman." And his face would elongate in a depressed projection of life without the wonderful woman's fruit pies and ribs. "I don't think Dotty can ever learn to make a meat loaf like Auntie's," he once confessed to Alex. But then he brightened. "Well, maybe we'll just have to come back here for vacations. Yup, that'll do it! Every vacation we get, we'll come right back here to Auntie Joy's for three good meals a day. Heaven on earth."

Alex was still amazed at the transformation that occurred when Scott stepped onto a ball field. He became a bundle of nervous energy, whirling like a tornado kicking up dust and dirt. Scott didn't have an overwhelming amount of natural talent, but he made up for that with hustle and sheer guts. He sprinted to first after a base on balls, took extra bases with daring running, crashed into fences chasing foul pops. And crowded the plate every single time he stepped up to bat, daring the pitcher to plunk him with a fastball, more than glad to accept the pain for a freebie to first base. That became his trademark. Almost every day the box score in the Wilson *Times* would have a small stat at the bottom: HBP (Hunt).

"Scott's crazy," Manning once said in the dugout when standing near Charlie Lassiter.

"He's a tough monkey," Lassiter said. "Disciplined."

"Yeah," Manning had said. And then to Alex, quietly, "Crazy's more like it. Out of his fuckin' mind."

Those were the main components of Alex's new world, a sphere into which he had slipped easily and successfully, establishing much the same position as in the world he'd left behind.

With no limits except, apparently, those which were self-imposed, Alex liked his first flush of freedom. And he was beginning to wonder just how far he could go. The one phrase that kept coming back to him was *all the way*. Over and over again.

All the way.

The first week in August, Alex was lying on his bed after another two-ton Auntie Joy dinner. He lay on his side so his cheek could soak in whatever coolness was still fresh in the pillow.

Ski stood by the door, looking like some sort of ancient bodyguard. Manning was on Scott's bed, on his back, hands locked behind his head, staring at the ceiling. Willie was by the hi-fi, lifting the needle off a record, about to put it back down on another song. The Lump wasn't there; he wouldn't stay when Willie came over. The Fuse's parents had come to visit and he was off with them. Scott was playing checkers down on the street with one of the storeowners.

"Okay, now listen up, children," Willie was saying. They all heard the click of the needle coming to rest on a groove for the next song. "This is Sarah doin' 'Lover Man.' "

Sarah Vaughan's deep voice began to sweep over Alex.

"That's Dizzy on trumpet," Willie went on. His voice was soft, almost as if it were recorded as the normal background for the song. "Bird on sax. This is one of the Three Deuces sessions. Can you boys even imagine what it was like to be there when this music emerged for the first time?"

"Like magic," Alex said.

"Like showin' an empty sleeve and then whippin' out miraculous sounds that could change people's souls."

Alex thought of his dad. Did his dad feel this way when he played at Bell's? Would his dad be proud that Alex was beginning to understand and appreciate this magic? Did his dad even know the magic existed? Alex wanted to know, to ask him. Maybe his dad had had this secret world, too, buried inside him all the time. Alex made a mental reminder to try to ask his dad when they saw each other next.

"Listen, listen. Oooh-eee, nice an' easy. That's Al Haig at piano. That's Curly, Curly Russell, makin' the bass sound pure as it can sound. Stan Levey playin' perfect drums."

Alex closed his eyes as Willie talked.

"Okay. Now, now, now. Everything blends together, in an' out an' around an' high an' low. Here it is. One perfect, final thing."

They had been in there for an hour, the others drinking beer after beer, listening to song after song. Alex could hear a rustling when they moved, could smell the stale alcohol wafting into the woodwork. But for Alex, for this moment, they didn't really exist. They didn't exist, Patty didn't exist, Auntie Joy was not on the planet, even baseball wasn't real. Nothing existed except his immersion in the sensuality of the jazz smoking out of the hi-fi speakers. For a brief moment he was frightened; he knew he was going too far, knew this music was doing things to him it shouldn't do. But then the fright passed and the pure pleasure was back. The pleasure of being overwhelmed by a great and powerful hum.

When the song ended his eyes opened gradually, as if awaking from a disorienting dream.

"Nice," Manning said slowly. "Very nice."

"Yeah," Ski agreed. "That was good."

"Aaahhh." Alex smiled. "Aaaaaahhhhhhh." He rubbed his eyes, stretching his legs and arms out as far as they could go in each direction. His bones cracked neatly, and despite the hundred-degree heat, he ran his finger along an armful of goose bumps.

"God-*damn,* I like that music," Alex said. "I don't know what it is exactly. It sure does get to me, though. Makes me think all sorts of things."

"Oh, yeah? Like what?" Manning wanted to know.

"It's hard to say, I guess. It drops little thoughts into my head but then it doesn't let me hold on to 'em. It never lets anything stay there long enough for me to really . . . *catch* 'em."

"Uh-huh."

"You don't know what I'm talkin' about, do you?"

"Uh-uh."

Alex sat up. "Do you?" he asked Willie. Willie just smiled. So Alex went on talking.

"It's like, just now I'm lyin' here and the music's goin' and I know you three are in the room but suddenly the music's tellin' me I'm all alone. And I felt I *was* alone. And then I felt happy, but not, Ya!-Whoopie!-Turn-cartwheels! happy. Quiet-and-peaceful happy. The music was sort of saying, *You're doin' okay. You've got things licked. Keep on this wavelength and you can feel like this all the time.* And so that lasts for a while, but I can't stay on this wavelength because the music changes and it's not Dizzy all of a sudden, it's Sarah singin' and that tells me somethin' different." Alex made a fist and drove his hand into his gut. "I just can't hold on to that yet, can't grab it and keep it." He shook his head. "I'll tell you what it's like, but you're gonna think this is crazy."

"You're gonna have to go some to sound crazy now," Manning said.

"Go ahead," Ski urged. "I wanna hear."

Willie said nothing.

"It's like when a ray of light shoots into your room, you know, sunlight comin' right through the window. And inside the beam there's all these little . . . *things* . . . floating around. It's dust, mostly; things in the air that come in through the window or get picked up off your desk. Well, sometimes, you should watch dust . . . trapped in this beam of light. Bopping back and forth, going up, zigzagging down. I can watch it for a long time, like twenty minutes. And then a shadow comes up, the sun gets blocked off, and then there's nothin' there. You can turn over and swat at the air and nothin' moves, nothing dances. This whole little . . . world . . . it's either moved to another light beam or it's just . . . gone." Alex cleared his throat and did his ballplayer tug at his nose. "So, anyway. That's what I think of sometimes when I'm listening to jazz, because that's the way my head feels. As if it's stuck in a separate beam of sunlight and all these things are dancing around in there. And then a shadow comes and"—he flexed his fingers outward—"everything disappears."

"I once got so drunk," Jerry Bartkowski announced, "that I climbed up this tree, the biggest tree in this park near my house. I climbed up to the top of this fuckin' thing and I jumped because I was so smashed I thought I could fly."

"What," Manning demanded, "are you talking about?"

"I swear, I thought for sure I could fly. Sssshhhwwoooo . . . right out over all the trees, straight back home."

"What happened?"

"Went straight down. I fell like thirty fuckin' feet or somethin' like that."

"Yeah?"

"And that's it. Nothin' happened. Didn't fly, didn't get hurt. Got up, walked home, never tried it again."

Alex and Manning looked at Ski suspiciously.

"I'm tellin' you this," he said to Alex, "only because that's the closest time I ever came to feelin' what it is you're talkin' about. It was like I had done somethin' perfect. I mean, it seemed like a fuckin' miracle to me, drunk as I was. Great feeling, *great* fucking feeling. But then by the next day, I didn't have it anymore. It had sorta disappeared. Like the dust, you know?"

"I have a secret," Willie said.

They waited.

"Music *is* a miracle. I know it. And these jokers?" He nodded at the record. "They know too. I mean, man, they *know*. They done it. They created the perfect blues. They kept moving their whole life, they started somewhere"—a finger waved at the record—"and got to here. You understand? And I'm gonna do that too. I'm here now but someday I'm gonna be there. I'm gonna get blue."

"Get blue?" Alex asked very softly.

"That's what I call it. You start here." Willie put his thumb and forefinger together and drew his hand across in front of his chest, a wire from nowhere to somewhere, "And you move slowly. You learn. You create. You get better an' better." He dropped his hand to his side. "You're gettin' blue. Like the folks on the record."

Willie took a deep breath. He looked somewhat embarrassed.

Alex sat up, not embarrassed at all. "Yeah," he said, excited. "The Moment."

"Say what?"

"The Moment. That's what I call it."

"No, man," Willie told him. "It ain't no moment. It's a lifetime. It takes a whole damn lifetime 'fore you get blue. But when you do . . . oh, momma."

"Dust. Flying. The Moment," Manning said. "Getting blue. That's all bullshit, if you ask me. Make-believe. You're lookin' for shit that's not there."

"So what do you want?" Alex asked suddenly.

Manning smiled and spoke slowly, laconically, as if he were a math teacher explaining for the tenth time a simple equation. "I wanna go out there and pitch one no-hitter after another. I wanna do something and *feel* it. Then I'll turn to every single person in the stands and say, *Fuck you. I'm not ever gonna be what you want me to be, not ever again.*" He laughed. "Gettin' blue. No such thing, pals. There is no such thing."

"You're drunk," Ski said slowly. "You've had too much to drink."

Manning shrugged, not concerned. "Alex," he said, "I have a question for you."

"Okay," Alex answered suspiciously.

"I wanna know why you never let me introduce you to old Louisa." There was no meanness in his voice, there was no *anything* in his voice. But he was leading somewhere and it seemed dangerous.

"I just decided it wasn't right," Alex said. " 'Cause of Patty an' all."

"Lay off him, Dave."

"I decided to be faithful."

"More rules."

"What?"

"I'm not saying this to get you angry, Alex," Manning said easily. "I just never saw a guy who followed so many goddamn rules."

"They're my *own* rules. Nobody else's."

"That doesn't change what they are. Goddamn rules." Manning's eyes closed, flitted open. "You know what the guys call you on the team?" he asked Alex.

"No."

"Tell him, Ski."

" 'Judge,' " Ski said.

"Huh?"

" 'Judge,' " Manning repeated. "They think you've got a good eye for balls and strikes. Never let a bad pitch fool you, always know when to go for a sure thing, that kind of stuff. You're a good judge. And you know what *I* think? I think it's more than that. I think it's more than just bein' on the ball field. I mean, let's face it, you understand the difference between right and wrong. Know when something's true. Or a lie. One of the fuckin' few."

"Listen," Ski said, "maybe I shouldn't've said anything about jumping out of that tree. Now that I think about it, it sounds nuts."

Willie was over by the record player, looking back and forth between Manning and Alex.

"You know the rules," Manning said, incredulous at such an achievement. "And follow 'em. Coach says run laps, you run laps. Auntie Joy wants you to eat home cookin', you eat home cookin'. You got a girl back home, you make up more rules than the fuckin' army so she doesn't get pissed off."

Alex flushed angrily, stung by the indifferent contempt disguised in the pleasant flow of Manning's voice.

"That's not—"

"You don't smoke, you don't drink." Manning tipped over one beer can and six others fell like dominos. "You go to bed by eleven. You never tell a lie, you probably salute the flag when you see it." Manning smiled, a wide smile, and, if possible, his voice got even calmer. "When the fuck do you let go?"

Alex was up and took one tense step toward Manning. But, so quickly, like a giant cat, Jerry was there, in between them. He didn't have to say anything to Alex, Alex understood there was no way he was going to rush Manning. So he took a deep breath and sat back down on his bed. Ski stayed where he was, not yet trusting Alex's acknowledged truce.

Manning didn't move, didn't flinch when Alex had started to come toward him. He looked down at the floor awhile, then looked back up at Alex.

"I apologize," he said. "I don't apologize to many people. But I'm sorry I said those things. There's nothin' wrong with bein' what you are."

"I don't think," Alex said, "you know what I am."

"No. You're probably right." He nodded toward Willie. "I guess your music just got to me too," Manning said.

"I got things I want," Alex said. "I got things I want *bad*. And I don't know any other way to get 'em than the way I got."

"Sometimes I see too many ways," Manning said. "Or no ways. Maybe that's *my* little secret."

Ski sat back down and Alex leaned back against the wall, grinning awkwardly. Willie turned the record over on the turntable. When the needle clicked onto the vinyl disc, Alex lay back down on the bed, cheek on the pillow, closed his eyes, and waited for Sarah Vaughan to come and whisk him away.

Getting blue, he thought. Yeah. *Yeah.*

The next night the Tobs lost to the Greensboro Patriots. Alex went one for four, striking out twice. After the defeat Charlie insisted on lecturing the team about intensity and concentration. Alex and his housemates fidgeted nervously while their Skipper droned on. They were all intensely concentrating on the clock, because they wanted to be at the Wilson Diner by nine o'clock.

At five to nine Alex was in front of the diner, patting his hair into place via the reflection in the restaurant's plate glass front.

"You look beautiful," the Lump told him. "A lover boy if ever I saw one. A real lover-fuckin'-boy."

"Did the Lump have to come tonight?" Alex asked Manning.

"It's his car."

"Well, keep him quiet, okay?"

"Do my best. Nervous?"

"No."

"Good."

"I haven't made my mind up, you know. I mean, this isn't a sure thing."

"I know."

"I gotta see her first. Then I gotta see if I'm in the mood. There're a lot of things that enter into it."

"Let's go inside."

There were only a few people still left in the dining room. One elderly couple sat in silence sipping tea. One young couple, seemingly just passing through town on their way elsewhere, munched on Sal's Coconut Custard Pie, the diner's specialty, although no one had ever been able to verify the existence of Sal. The young couple washed the local delicacy down with icy Coca-Colas.

Alex's eyes went right to the waitress behind the counter. She was very plain. Her skin was pale, dry-looking, her hair brown and thin. Her body seemed reasonably okay, certainly nothing spectacular. Alex was particularly disappointed with her breasts, which were small and uninviting.

"I don't think she's so great," Alex said sullenly. "I don't see what the big deal is."

"Don't jump the gun," Manning replied. "That's not Louisa."

"Shit, no," the Lump embellished. "Louisa's got tits the size of that one's head."

"There she is," Ski pointed out.

Alex swung around abruptly to take a look at the girl emerging from the kitchen.

"Impressive, ain't it?" The Lump looked at Alex, awed in the presence of such a great structure. "Greatest pig-fuck in the whole fuckin' world."

The teenage girl in the waitress uniform bearing down on their table was short, maybe five three or four. She had stocky legs, oversized thighs with plenty of inviting flesh rustling against a skintight skirt, calves that were leaner and muscularly firm, ankles that squirmed sexily in her high-heeled shoes as if they couldn't wait to be free and kicking amid a couple of rumpled sheets. Her arms were plump, her hands large and strong, fingernails long and pointy like a witch's red weapon. Lips that pouted, eyes that didn't do much of anything, fat cheeks with a touch of acne, too-blond hair that swirled all over the place, cheaply Medusa-like in effect. And then came her breasts. Only these weren't breasts, these were tits. Tits like gun turrets. Heavy mounds mightily exposed by an insanely low-cut white shirt. These were the things which wet dreams are made of.

Alex was experiencing what could best be labeled mixed emotions. On the one hand, his feelings were plain and simple and easy to cope with. He wanted to smother himself with her greasy body and never come up for air. Like a trained seal his dick had snapped rigidly to attention, and Alex felt like it would take a long, complicated surgical procedure ever to relax it again.

There was also, however, a complication. Something was not quite right. The girl was spectacularly slutty, no question about it. But he felt a curious detachment. Several thoughts flashed through his mind: *How many guys has she fucked? Will I tell Patty? Should I tell Patty? Why am I thinking of Patty now? Why do there have to be so many smirking assholes sitting at my table? Do I really want to do this? Is this what it's all about? Why am I thinking so much?*

And then there came a voice, seductively throaty and thick, higher pitched than expected, pleasantly vacant and curious. Alex had no more time for silent confusion.

"Hi, boys. What can I do for y'all?" Her searching gaze landed on Alex. She smiled very sweetly, if a bit automatically, at the new boy in town.

"Sit on my face, okay?"

"Lump!"

The waitress turned distainfully to the overweight catcher. "Walter." Her voice was slow; sound dripped out of her mouth like thick, milky syrup. "You are dees-*gus*tin'. A pee-eye-gee."

Manning interrupted before the Lump could do any more damage. "Louisa."

"Hi, David."

"Yeah. Hi. Louisa, this is Alex Justin. He's the one I told you is real anxious to meet you."

She turned to Alex. Her breasts seemed to move before the rest of her body.

"Hi," he said, and felt incredibly stupid.

"Hi," she said, and her smile widened. Moisture bubbled on her lips.

"Hi," he said again, and had to look over at Manning helplessly.

"Louisa," Dave spoke up, "you doin' anything after work tonight?"

"Not a thing, honey."

Manning kicked Alex under the table.

"Oh." Alex stirred in his chair. "Uh. Would you like to do something. After work. Uh, with me?"

"What?" she breathed.

"What?" he asked, confused.

"What?" she whispered, now also confused.

"Wait," he said, and needed help from Manning again.

"She wants to know what you want to do."

"Oh! Oh, uh, do. Yeah. Well." He coughed. "Well, I don't know. What to do. What do you wanna do?"

"Holy shit!" the Lump growled. "What a dumb asshole! An ass-fuckin'-hole."

"Walter," she reprimanded as her tongue moistened her upper lip. "Grrrr-osssss. Don't be naughty."

The Lump snorted and the old couple off to the side called Louisa, motioning for the check.

"I'll be right back," she said to Alex, and slithered off across the room.

"You're not doin' too good," Ski told Alex.

"I can sense that."

"I think she likes you," Scott said.

"You do?"

"Shit," the Lump added. "I'll be in the bathroom. Gotta take a giant dump."

When the Lump was a safe distance away, Alex leaned over the table and touched Manning on the arm.

"I think I'm gettin' cold feet."

"What's wrong?"

"Don't know."

"Why don't you go talk to her alone?"

"You think so?"

Manning nodded.

"I guess it can't hurt."

"That's for sure."

Alex shoved his chair away from the table and stood up. He

casually sauntered over toward the counter, not so casually slipping on a wet spot on the floor, falling, and knocking over a table and two chairs. From his prone position he looked over at the guys. Ski was laughing hysterically, as was Cannon. Scott looked concerned. Manning had his face buried in his hands. Alex righted the furniture, brushed himself off, and went over to lean on the counter top.

"Y'all all right?" Louisa asked.

"Fine." Alex nodded. "Fine." He nodded again. "Fine."

"I've seen you play ball," she drawled.

"You have?"

"I saw you hit a home run. It was *real* excitin'."

He wanted to say something but didn't know what he could possibly say, so he just kept nodding. Behind Louisa the other waitress, the plain one, was looking at them, listening to their sparkling conversation. When his eyes met hers, she shook her head, turned away, and slowly swung her nonexistent hips back to the kitchen.

"So what would you like to do tonight?" Alex asked Louisa.

"Whatever you want, honey."

"Oh."

"I get off in half an hour."

"Uh-huh."

"So why don't you just be here?"

"Uh-huh. Okay."

She smiled, put a fingernail in her mouth, and sucked on it. "See ya later." And as an afterthought: "Alligator."

Alex went back to the table.

"That was good," Manning said. "You made it all the way back without tripping."

Alex rolled his eyes.

"So," Ski asked. "How'd it go?"

"Great."

"Yeah. She's a terrific conversationalist, isn't she?" Manning said.

"She seems like a nice girl," Scott added.

"I gotta ask a question," Alex said.

"Shoot."

"Did the Lump ever fuck her?"

"Louisa?"

Alex nodded.

"Sure."

"We've all fucked her," Ski chimed in.

"Except the Preacher," Chris Cannon said, and Scott smiled shyly.

"Alex," Manning said, "even you don't think a piece of raw meat like that is gonna wait around for you to be the first one to pork her."

"No, no. Nothin' like that. I just . . ."

Ski put his hand on Manning's shoulder. He let it rest there and the size of it against Manning's thin arm startled Alex.

"I understand," Ski told Manning. "I understand what he's sayin'. Morals."

Manning shook his head. "Rules."

The Lump picked this moment to return. "Ah. That was one great dumpola!"

"We're all thrilled for you," Manning told him.

"So what'd I miss?"

"Nuthin'."

Louisa returned, smiling coyly at Alex her entire wiggling route across the room.

"I'm back," she announced.

"Listen," Alex said to her. "I can't make it tonight it turns out." He looked at Manning, who was absolutely impassive; his lips were pressed together, freezing his face into an impenetrable mask.

The Lump was incredulous. "What? And I didn't miss nuthin'?"

"I'm, uh, I'm, uh, feelin' sick. And tired. Real tired."

"Oh," Louisa pouted, her lips dripping sweet southern sugar. "And I won't make you feel better?"

"Well. You would. But not tonight. Not tonight."

She was confused. This was obviously a first.

"Well, shit, *I* ain't doin' nothin' tonight!" the Lump told Louisa. "I'll take ya on."

"Oh, Walter," she flung. "Dees-*gus*tin'." She looked back at

Alex, sadly, he thought, and for a moment he wavered, but then she turned back to the Lump. "What time?" she asked. And put a wet smile on her face.

Outside, Lump was hustling them all into the car.

"Let's go, let's go," he said. "I wanna get back here before she changes her fuckin' mind."

"I think I'm gonna walk," Alex said.

"It's three miles," Scott told him.

"I don't mind."

"What a fuckin' moron!"

"I'll go with you," Scott said loyally.

"No, that's okay. I feel like walkin' alone."

Manning stopped before getting in the backseat. He stood up, face to face with Alex.

"Will you do me a favor?" he asked quietly. "I don't ask for many favors."

"Sure," Alex said.

"Tell me what happened."

Alex's eyes narrowed curiously.

"In there," Manning said, and tapped the side of his head. "Inside."

"I just decided you were wrong. I suddenly didn't wanna do it and I don't even know why, but that didn't matter 'cause I just didn't wanna do it. I *do* follow my own rules. But that means I don't have to follow anyone else's. Even yours. Maybe especially yours."

"Well." Manning smiled, inscrutably as ever, let the smile linger too long. He patted Alex, strangely proud, on the shoulder. "Have a good walk, Judge."

The road ahead was flat. And dark. Even shadowy mysteries were few and not very intriguing: an imposing tree, a rickety fence, the dart of a dog or a rabbit. The landscape worked against imagination.

Alex walked slowly, carefully, and methodically. He was not upset about what had happened earlier. In fact, he was rather pleased, if a bit puzzled. In some vague way a barrier had been torn down between him and Manning. Somehow, that final pat on the back seemed to signal a letup, or at least a change in their competition. Alex was also not worried about his decision to pass on a roll in the hay with sweet Louisa. *When it's right,* he thought. *Trust your sense of timing.* He was not ready to release his more romantic notions, his ties to a nicer view of the consequences of such important actions as lovemaking.

The sound of a car engine filtered softly in from somewhere behind him. It came closer, got louder. The noise was surprisingly unobtrusive, rather soothing as it blended in with the country silence. The first flicker of lights rebounded now off the road ahead of him. He felt himself, for an instant, bathed in headlight white, then slipped back into the darkness as the car passed him by. He looked up, expecting to watch it disappear along the distant dividing line, but the car slowed, the driver looked back at him. The car pulled off to the side, then backed up the twenty-five feet or so to stop alongside Alex.

"Hey," the waitress from the diner, the plain one with thick ankles and small tits, said. "Wanna ride?"

"No, thanks," Alex replied. His voice surprised him. Because he hadn't been expecting to talk, it came out of his throat gravelly and rough.

"What happened to your buddies?"

"I just felt like walkin' is all."

"Yeah. One of 'em's back there havin' a go with little Louisa. The fat smelly one."

"The Lump."

"An' here I thought tonight was your turn."

"Yeah. Well."

"Well, indeedy," she said through the half-open window. "Sure y'all don't wanna ride?"

Alex nodded. "But thanks."

"Okay," she drawled. And the banged-up Chevy took off. It went about a quarter of a mile, then stopped. Alex watched the red taillights weave back toward him.

"Listen," the waitress said when she was back to being even with Alex. "Y'all wanna go for a drink or somethin'? A piece of pie? If you want, afterward I'll drop y'all back here and you can walk again."

Alex put his hands on the roof of the Chevy. He peered into the front seat, at the waitress, and laughed.

"Sure," he said. "What's open?" And he hopped in.

"What's open?" the waitress asked incredulously as she put the car in forward and began to drive. "You think you're in some hick town, ain't nothin' open past ten o'clock?"

"Oh, no," he said. "I'm sure there's lots of all-night places. After-theater spots and such."

"My, yes. Tons and tons. Why, we'll just head to the real hot spot."

"I thought we just *came* from the real hot spot."

"Just sit back and relax."

"What's your name?"

"Katie. Katie Gray."

"Is that short for Katherine or somethin'?"

"Nope. Not short for nothin'."

"Oh. Just long for Kate, huh?"

"My name's Katie. That's what it says on my birth certificate an' on my driver's license. What you see, honey, is what you get."

They pulled up to a small green house not too far from Auntie Joy's.

"This is the hot spot?"

"My apartment." He tilted his head. She shrugged. "Nothin' else open in a dump like this."

Katie opened the front door, which led into a long hall and stairway. Everything was quiet and clean; the only hint of seediness was the carpet running up the stairs. It was faded, way past its prime. Whatever design had once been stitched there, it now blended together to form a rust-colored muddle.

She lived on the second floor in a one-room apartment with a kitchenette built into the wall.

"Ta daaaa," she said, flicking on the light.

"Nice." He nodded.

"Oh, right," she said. *"Real* nice."

Bright sprays of flowers, bunched sporadically around the room, brightened the drab green walls. Two stuffed animals—a raggedy, fuzzy black dog and a large brown panda—softened the place, added a penetrating touch of single-womanhood. Magazines—one copy of *Look,* two months' worth of *Screen Star*—were arranged carefully on the coffee table, as proudly exposed as if they were fifty-dollar books on the art of Matisse.

"Sit down on the couch," Katie said. "I'll make us some coffee."

He sat gingerly and watched her stir two teaspoons of instant coffee into cups of steaming water. The cups slattered against the saucers as she carried them over to Alex. Her hands were unsteady.

"Well, now," she said, sitting on the floor, legs crossed under her.

"Mmm," he said, sipping the coffee. On the first sip he burned his tongue so badly, tears came to his eyes. He clamped his mouth shut, waiting for the pain to disappear, hiding his total idiocy.

"So you're the one from New York, huh?"

He had never heard anyone other than Scott accent the *New* rather than the *York.* There was something mildly annoying about Scott's interpretation, something wonderfully charming about Katie's version. He wondered if the fact that she was a girl was the only difference between annoying and charming.

"Yup," he admitted. "All my life."

"That must be exciting."

"I guess." He slurped the hot coffee, now burning the roof of his mouth. He was sure he'd be scarred for life. "What do you mean, 'the one' from New York?"

"Oh," she said, "this is a small town. Everybody keeps track of who comes in and who goes out. I'd heard about you. The one from *New* York."

"What'd you hear?"

She batted her eyes at him, letting him know that she knew he was fishing for compliments.

"Everybody said you were the big star. The big star from the big city." Alex sat back, a little smugly. "So how are you doin', big star? You the savior of the almighty Wilson Tobs?"

"Doin' all right, I guess." He looked down modestly. "Don't you go to any games?"

"I've been. But I don't like baseball much."

"You don't?"

"Do you?"

He laughed. "Well, sure. I mean, I play it."

"Lotsa folks play at things they don't like."

"They do?" he asked, and she laughed.

"Why, you sound genuinely surprised."

"I am, I guess," Alex said. "I can't imagine doing something I didn't like."

"Oooohh-eeee." She laughed. "How old are you, honey?"

"Twenty-three," Alex said quickly.

"Uh-huh," she said.

"Twenty-one," he came back with. "Really."

She said nothing.

"Eighteen," he told her, and looked down at the floor.

"Eighteen," Katie hooted. "My, what a nice age to be."

"How old are you?" Alex asked.

"Never ask a girl her age, honey, 'specially not a southern girl. It ain't proper."

"Oh. Sorry."

"But then neither am I—proper, I mean. I'm twenty. An *old* twenty, but twenty I am."

"You don't seem like such an old twenty to me."

"Oh, honey, don't even ask. I am old and wise beyond my years. Seen things I never shoulda seen, done things I shouldn'ta done. At least not yet."

Alex sipped his coffee, which was now blessedly lukewarm. The more Katie talked, the more attractive she became. She was skinny—scrawny, actually. Her arms were bony, with little scratches on them, as if she were used to being bumped around, bruised. Her nails were bitten to the quick, her hands were rough; they were working hands. She was gutsy, her face said, and confident, but she was also nervous and unsure of herself, in no way ready to drop her steady stream of chatter for more revealing silence.

She crossed her skinny legs and said, "Do you mind?" but

before he could even answer she had kicked off her shoes, stretched her toes out, and gone, "Aaaahhhhhhh."

"How long you been a waitress?"

"For-*ever!*"

"How long is that?"

"Goin' on four years now," she said a little less dramatically. "But it does seem like forever."

"You don't like it?"

She looked at him as if she couldn't believe he was serious. Then, when she saw that he was, she shook her head in wonder.

"No, honey. I don't like it."

"Why don't you quit?"

"Gimme your cup." She rattled both cups over to the kitchen and poured more coffee. She rattled back to the battered sofa. "Now, what was it you said?"

"Why don't you quit?"

"Little things like money, eatin', breathin', livin'."

"Aren't there other things you could do?"

"Sure. Except you gotta add self-respect to the above list. I don't have a lot of it, but I got *some.*"

Alex thought about that for a moment. Then he said, "Oh," when he got it.

"Yeah." Katie nodded. "Oh."

"Can I ask you a question?" Alex asked. He was suddenly timid, and as his eyes drooped and his muscles relaxed, he casually stretched his legs, arched his back, and comfortably laid his head back on the wood frame of the ratty couch.

"Shoot," Katie said.

"Why'd you stop and pick me up?"

She shrugged. "You looked lonely. It was a long walk back." She reached directly behind her, over her left shoulder, to scratch some place in the middle of her back. Her nose scrunched up with pleasure as she erased the itch. Alex could see the stubble of her shaved underarm hair. "Maybe I felt like talkin' to somebody who wasn't a slob or a jerk or . . ." Her voice trailed off as she concentrated on her itch again. He could hear her nails, rough against her skin. "Or whatever it is people

are around here," she finished. Then started again. "So tell me
'bout *New* York."

"It's okay."

"That's one of my dreams. To go to *New* York. Stay at the Puh-
laza *Ho*-tel."

"Oh, yeah?"

"Yeah," she said. Only it was more of a dreamy hiss than a
word, as if New York meant, to her, sparkling diamonds and
midnight suppers and glorious mink stoles. With one simple
yeah Katie had conjured up a world where there were no
sweaty waitresses with sore feet and no torn couches with wine
stains, no Pullman kitchenettes or fat, pimply farmers who
grabbed ass like it was bales of cotton.

"There's not much to tell you about New York."

"No?"

"Uh-uh."

"I know all about it, anyway. Through books and movies."

"What do you know about it?"

"That it ain't North Carolina. An' that's enough for me, I will
tell you that."

"I like it here."

She laughed a harsh laugh.

"No, I mean it. I do. It's quiet."

"It's quiet, all right."

"It's nice. You can think about what you're doin'."

"Yup. That's the problem. There's plenty o' time to think
about what you're doin', only there ain't no one here doin'
anything worth thinkin' about."

He shrugged, noncommitally, not ready to give up his defense of his summer home.

"And listen, honey," she said. "I been down here my whole
life, an' I'll tell you that when you do try to move on up, try to
get a little somethin' done, someone'll always come by and sure
as hell put a cripple in your getalong."

"Come again?" he said.

"A cripple in your getalong."

He shook his head.

"It means that people don't like nothin' to change."

"Ah," he said.

"You like things to change, don't ya, honey?"

"When it's for somethin' better."

"*All* change is for somethin' better. That's my whaddyacallit, my philosophy of life. Anything that changes, it's gotta be better. You want my other philosophy? My other words of wisdom? Durin' the day, keep the load off your feet; come nighttime, keep it off your mind. The gospel according to Katie."

"It's late," Alex said. The apartment had suddenly grown uncomfortably quiet. "Guess I should go."

"Want a ride?"

"Oh, no. I'll walk. It's just a few blocks."

"Y'all have a curfew or anything like that?"

"Yeah. I'm way past already. Way past."

"You won't get in trouble or anything?"

"Naaaah."

"Well," she said.

"Well."

"Well."

"Uh . . ." he started.

"Yes?"

"I got another question for you."

"Shoot again."

"Would it be all right if I maybe asked you out one night? Not like for a date or anything, but, you know, maybe dinner. Or somethin' like dinner. Maybe."

"Now, why would you wanna go out with someone like me when you coulda had a date with sweet little Louisa?"

"I don't know. Maybe I got no taste." He smiled. She said nothing. "So? Is that all right?"

"Why, I'd be flattered."

"You would?"

"I would."

"Okay, then. Okay."

"Wait," she said as he reached for the doorknob.

"What?" he said, freezing.

"You have a girl?"

"A girlfriend?"

She nodded. He waited, sighed, then he nodded too.

"What's her name?"

"Patty."

"It bother you, talkin' about her?"

"A little. Does it bother you? I mean, my havin' one?"

"Not at all. She's way up there in New York. And I'm all the way down here in little ol' Wilson. It can be our little secret." Katie's thin left leg, with her too-thick ankle, turned coyly inward. Her lips parted, and her demure smile showed crooked yellow teeth. "Besides," she said, "we're just havin' dinner. Or somethin' *like* dinner."

7

It was the middle of the night and Alex couldn't sleep. Active morning seemed eons away, restful dreams just as far. His body was tingling, his head was light, from the affront of undesired stimulus; heavy eyes refused to close. His mind was trying to put it all together, but that was useless. It was the middle of the night and he was thinking about Patty. He was thinking about how, in his last letter, he'd told her how much he loved her. He was thinking about the grin that had to be on her face when she read it because she knew how hard it must've been for him to put it down on paper. He smiled now and wanted to see her. He wanted to talk to her about love and about secrets. For he had a real secret now, and he liked it.

"Whatcha lookin' at?"

Alex looked down at Katie, startled that she was awake, yet not entirely surprised. He had wanted her—had been silently urging her awake, hoping she would share in his restlessness.

"Whatcha lookin' at?" she repeated. Her tongue licked sleepy film off her lips.

"Just lookin'."

"Come to bed. It's kinda creepy to wake up and there you are, starin' to beat the devil."

"I can't sleep."

The rustle of sheet against sheet. Not an angry sound, some-how a motherly one. The girl rubbed her eyes and yawned.

"I've never spent a whole night with a girl," Alex said.

"Oh," she said. Another tender rustle. "I get it. You're just takin' in all you can take in. That it?"

"I was just lookin' at you."

"Mmmmm," she purred and her eyes closed again as she turned over.

"Can I touch you?" he asked.

Her answer was muffled by the pillow, but it sounded pleas-antly inviting. Alex moved slowly. One leg glided over, propped itself up, then the other leg, and he was straddling her. His hands rested gently on her warm shoulders, his knees grazed the sides of her chest. He ran a fingernail up her neck, his hand unfurled to stroke, caress, her hair. Alex kissed the back of her head, then her neck, then each shoulder. The kisses were light, sweet, not sexual, not anymore. They had made love many times that night and each time was longer, more exhausting, than the last. He had gotten to know her body in ways he had not dreamed were possible. His kisses were now simply ac-knowledgments, fond approvals of the parts he had strained and sweated over and battered earlier. He kissed her shoulder blades now, let his lips linger on the bony points while his hands massaged over her visible vertebrae. Her skin was firm, as if it were pulled taut, as if there were barely enough to cover her bones and veins. She felt hard and firm to the touch, and Alex was somehow relaxed by the thought that it would be difficult to hurt her.

"Come to sleep," she murmured from somewhere distant. "Come lie down and sleep."

"I will," he whispered. "I'm just savorin'."

The night before, when he'd arrived home, Alex had sneaked into the house, up the stairs, thrown off his clothes, and quietly eased himself under the covers of his bed. He stayed tense for a minute, then relaxed toward sleep. And it was when he was about to drift off that Scott spoke.

"Alex?"

Alex didn't answer. Scott didn't repeat the word but his silence was not one of acquiescence; he would wait, Alex knew, all night if necessary, for an answer.

"Yeah," Alex said. "Hi."

"We were mighty worried."

"Worried?"

"Well, you just disappeared."

"I'm all right."

"Where were ya?"

For perhaps a minute there was only the noise of two boys breathing. It was as if, for a brief moment in time, the room was sealed off and the windy inhale and exhale of breath was all the sound in the world.

"Alex?" Scott broke the spell.

"I was talkin'," Alex said. "I was just talkin' with somebody."

"Yeah. That's what Dave said."

"How does that guy know so much?"

"It's 'cause he always thinks the worst of people."

"I didn't do anything bad. All I did was meet this girl and talk."

"No, that's not what I meant. Manning said you didn't wanna really be alone. He said that when someone says he wants ta be by himself, all that means is he wants ta be with someone *else*. He thinks that everything everybody says is a lie."

"That's bullshit."

"Yeah," Scott said, not sounding very convinced.

"So what was I lyin' about?"

" 'Bout why you didn't go ahead and get laid."

"Oh, yeah? Why didn't I?"

"He said you thought you was doin' somethin' better'n us, but that you were really just afraid."

"Afraid of what?"

"Well, here's what he said that bothered me so much, Alex. That people won't ever do stuff they think they're gonna like. 'Cause when they really find somethin' they like, it's too dangerous. They can't stop doin' it. Then everything is different, 'cause nothin's as important as whatever it is they like. And want. That's what David said."

"I mean, what would I do? Just keep fuckin' and fuckin' until I die? Is that what I'm afraid of?"

"I guess not."

"So forget it. I mean, we play baseball, don't we? We like that more than anything, and that's not dangerous."

"That's right," Scott said. "That's right."

"So?"

"So sometimes I am afraid. I mean, afraid of . . . shoot, I don't even know what."

"Forget it. There's nothin' to be afraid of. You do what you want because it's the right thing to do. And there's nothin' dangerous about doing the right thing. Is there?"

"I guess."

"Good night." Alex turned over on his side. "Okay?"

"Okay. 'Night."

And the room, once again, was filled with the sounds of gentle breathing.

The next day he sat through a breakfast of obscene jokes and hooting leers.

"So now we know why Louisa wasn't good enough for you."

"You had pussy waitin' for you all along, you bastard you."

"How long's this been goin' on, Alex?"

Alex was good-natured about it, but he wouldn't answer. He smiled all through the breakfast, nodding politely, raising his eyebrows at particularly disgusting comments, calmly ignoring everything else.

"Did her box smell?"

That was good for a raised eyebrow.

"Is she nice?"

A polite, if curt, nod.

"You gonna see her again?"

A flicker of a smile.

"Did she swallow it or spit it out? Louisa likes to put it all over her face."

Manning was strangely silent during the meal, uninterested, as if he already knew all the details of the evening that he needed, or wanted, to know.

As soon as he was finished eating, Alex went outside. He walked up Main Street, loitered in front of the window of Selma's Stout Shop, peered into the Wilson Seed and Feed Store, watched the lazy lines in the First National Bank of Wilson, N.C. Eventually he found himself, as he'd half known he would, in front of Katie's rooming house. From across the street he stared up at the curtains on her window. They fluttered and Alex wondered if she were watching the ripply movement from within.

The rest of the day vanished in a blur. He walked to the stadium, practiced, played, did his share to contribute to the victory. He rode home with the gang, raided Auntie Joy's fridge for leftovers. Joked with Manning, teased the Lump, listened to the Fuse twang out a few C&W tunes. Then he was walking again. Up and down the boardwalk on Main Street, kicking dirt along small side streets, sauntering without direction, watching the moon's smile, gradually zeroing in on the unavoidable target. The curtains were still rustling, a light was on. Alex swallowed hard twice, caught his breath, and went to the front door.

"Well," said Katie. "Is this dinner or something?"

Alex nodded and they went upstairs. He didn't have to do much, he let her lead him. They sat on the couch and she kissed him, rolling her tongue around his gums, sticking it deep down his throat until he thought he couldn't breathe. Her breath was slightly sour and it made him recoil when it would waft, periodically, through his entire body, taking over his senses. But he quickly grew to desire this strange, pungent odor, he wanted it always, and he kept his mouth against hers, pressing, trying to suck all her breath into him.

Katie smiled when they came up for air, smiled at his earnest urgency. She lifted off her dress and stepped out of her panties. She reached behind her back and unhooked her bra, taking it and flinging it across the room. She held him back, arms outstretched, until he was no longer moving ravenously toward her. Then her hands swiftly unbuttoned his shirt, pulled it off, barely touching his skin. Alex kicked his shoes and yanked his socks off. She reached for his belt and unbuckled it, drawing it from his pant loops as if unsheathing a sword. She undid his pants, unzipped them, then stripped them away firmly and slowly. He pulled off his own underwear, dropped it awkwardly onto the middle of the floor. He stood before her naked.

"Oh, honey," she said. "You got a lot goin' for you."

They made love.

Passionate, hot and sweaty love, gasping and yelling and scratching and hurting and laughing. Then slowly, gently; one lingering movement. And yet again, an exhausted sort of love, hard and straightforward. And one more time, this one a celebration, a summation of all they had done already.

She had grabbed him by the hair and pushed his head between her legs. "Uhh!" he moaned and jerked away, but she gripped his head and held him there. He thought, *Oh, Jesus, I'm gonna hate this!* But she kept him there and she taught him. "Use your tongue. Further inside. More. Lower. Kiss me there, yes, right there. Deeper." His mouth filled with hair and he began to enjoy it, the taste, the smell, the fact that he was obviously driving Katie wild with pleasure. She screamed when she came and licked all her own come off his proud lips.

Katie then told him it was his turn and she gave him his first blowjob. He was afraid of coming, afraid, somehow, this might damage her. But as her fingers massaged and her tongue tickled and her lips sucked, he lost all sense of anything other than desire for release. The pleasure overwhelmed him, shocked him. And as he was coming he tried to speak but couldn't. "Oh, my gah . . . oh . . . oh . . . holy sh . . . I don't . . . Geezahohgagah . . . ohhhhh" was the best he could manage, then he flopped backward on the bed, looking for all the world like a man just saved from drowning.

They talked. But not much. Pleasantries. Giggling. Understanding sighs.

Finally they slept. Touching. Smelling. Drained. Until Alex woke up in the middle of the night.

Savoring.

"All right, I got a question. I got an important question," Alex Justin said.

"Shoot."

They were on the team bus on their way to Durham to play the Bulls. "I know it gets hotter'n hell down here, but what *is* it with the South and cold beverages?"

"What are you talking about?" Manning asked.

"Okay. We just passed an old grocery store. The sign said: GROCERIES, CIGARETTES, COLD BEVERAGES."

"So?"

"Wait. Half a mile later we passed a bait store. What'd the sign say? BAIT AND COLD BEVERAGES." He jumped up and jammed his hand against the window. "Look! Look!" he said.

Several Tobs twisted their heads so they could see where Alex was pointing. He was pointing at a sign for a bar. The sign read: WE'VE GOT THE COLDEST BEVERAGES IN TOWN.

"How cold can one beverage get?"

"That's a very interesting concept," Manning told him. "It'd be more interesting, however, if I didn't think you were losing your mind completely."

"I'm starting to have dreams about signs. ALL OUR BEVERAGES BEEN FROZEN TWENTY-FIVE YEARS!"

"Is that mah accent y'all are tryin' to mimic?" Scott demanded.

Alex ignored him. "I swear to God, I have this new fantasy. I'm in a bar and this guy walks in. His name's Bubba. Bubba's six five, two hundred seventy pounds. He pounds the bar and says, 'Gimme the coldest beverage you got!' The barkeep brings out a dusty and icy bottle of Coke, carried on a pair of ice tongs. Bubba grabs it with his bare hands, drinks the whole thing in one gulp, and the bartender faints."

"What happens then?" Scott wanted to know, leaning forward.

"Bubba's elected sheriff by popular demand."

"Alex," Manning drawled, "I do believe the South is getting to you."

"The people are kinda slow, you gotta admit."

"Huh?" Scott asked.

"I went into the five-and-dime yesterday and gave the salesgirl a five-dollar bill for a stick of gum. 'Fahve cents,' she said. It took her an hour to gimme change. 'Tehhhnnnnn cents, *fif*teen, tweehhhnnnn-tttyyyy-fahhve.' Now she's on a roll. 'Fifftty, seventy-faahhhhve, one dollar!' Now she's hit the dollar mark in only half an hour and she's real proud. *Real* proud. 'Two dollah. Thuree dollahs. Fooouuurrrrrr dollahs. *Fahhve* dollahs.' I'm tellin' you, an hour!"

"Did she say, 'Y'all come back now, heah?' " Manning wanted to know.

"Yeah. That's when I went for her throat."

"There ain't nothin' wrong with the South," Scott said.

"People talk funny," Ski told him.

"I heard one yesterday," Alex said. "Put a feather to your tickle box."

"Use it in a sentence, please," Manning said.

In his best southern accent, Alex spoke. "Y'all gotta see this movie. It's *real* funny. It'll put a feather to your tickle box."

"Ah don' like this," Scott said.

"I want a pizza," Alex said a bit desperately. "I want a cannoli. Some Chinese food!"

"What about deep-frahd chicken livers!" Scott said vehemently.

"What?"

"You don't get those up your way."

"That's true," Alex admitted. "And they are tasty."

"What about hush puppies?" Scott was now getting belligerent.

"No hush puppies in New York. This is a good point."

"They're *real* good with a cold beverage," Manning said.

"The South is a strange place, all right."

The conversation stopped suddenly as Manning and Scott and Ski and Fuse and Alex stared at Willie Trotty, who had just told them that the South was a strange place.

"Strange for whites, strange for colored," Willie said. "Strange."

"Where you from, Willie?" Manning said. "You never talk about where you're from."

" 'Bama," Willie told them. "South as you can get."

A few guys on the team looked up, surprised that Willie had just come over and sat down with Alex and Manning. It was his first public acknowledgment that they were his friends.

"You wanna play some cards?" Alex asked.

"In the South, Judge"—it was the first time Willie had called him Judge; he usually still called him Pote—"coloreds and whites don't do stuff like that together."

"This is a bus, though, you know, Willie. It's like neutral territory."

Willie turned to the two other black players on the team. Ben and Donnie both shrugged. Willie grinned and turned back to Alex.

"I can outrun ya and outhit ya, no reason not to take your money playin' cards."

"Willie," Manning said.

"Yo."

"Not that I'm the suspicious type, but why is it that all of a sudden you're all bein' so friendly in public?"

"You don' like it?"

"I don't know you well enough to like it or dislike it. I'm just curious. I mean, usually I say hello to you on the street, you turn away."

Willie hesitated, then smiled a huge, ear-to-ear, shit-eating smile. He jerked his head at Alex. "It's the Judge here, boy. He's bringin' out the friendly side o' me."

"Why's that?"

" 'Cause he's hittin' ten points more than me an' if I don't watch mahself, he may catch me in home runs. This boy look like he may be gettin' blue an' I wanna be there to see it. I thought it was now time to start bein' friendly."

The Tobs beat the Bulls five to two at the Durham Athletic Park. Alex got two hits: a single to right and a double down the third-base line.

After the game the whole team went to the hotel, the Durham Inn.

"This is the worst fuckin' shithole on the whole fuckin' schedule," the Lump growled. "Why the fuck do we stay here?"

"It's the only place that lets niggers stay," Willie told them. "You can thank us later when the waterbugs crawl on your head in the middle of the night."

"Let's hang out," Scott said.

"Where the fuck we gonna hang out in Dur-fuckin'-ham?"

"I'm hungry. They got a restaurant in the hotel?"

"Yeah," Manning said. Then he turned to Willie and asked, "They let coons in the restaurant?"

"Long as we don't rape the waitresses."

"Comin'?"

Willie said yeah without hesitating. Donnie and Ben said nothing, but they came along.

There wasn't a booth big enough to seat nine, and rather than draw attention to themselves by moving tables together, Willie, Ben, and Donnie sat separately, one booth away from Alex, Manning, Scott, Lump, Ski, and Fuse.

Alex was halfway through a really rotten slab of meat loaf when four men walked into the restaurant. Four white men. They were pretty big, tough-looking, and everybody noticed them, but nobody thought too much about it. Alex watched

them, though, as he wiped some thick gravy off his chin. He had
a bad feeling about them, a feeling that got even worse as they
saw Willie, Ben, and Donnie and began talking. Loud. Saying
some nasty things. Alex's eyes got hot, but before he could even
think about moving, Ski grabbed his arm.

"They're used to it," Ski said. "Don't interfere. Those guys are
used to talk like that and they don't get angry like we would."

Neither Willie, Ben, nor Donnie even so much as glanced
over at the tough guys, so Alex relaxed. After a minute or so the
guys got up to leave, saying they wouldn't drink with niggers.
On the way out they stopped at Alex's table. They had seen the
way he'd been staring at them.

"How come *you* boys can keep food down with alligator bait
so close by?"

Manning didn't bother to look up. He just said, "Well, for one
thing, they smell better than you do."

The obvious ringleader sneered at the pitcher. He didn't
make a move—it would have been six against three—but the
sneer was so ugly that Alex had to stop eating. The hate that
surrounded the man's yellowed teeth turned the boy's stomach.

Ben or Donnie never let on that anything had happened. But
Willie, when he went to the bar, passed Manning and nodded a
thank-you. "I appreciate it," he said. "But don't do it again. If
people need talkin' to, I can do it myself."

"Okay," Manning said, not insulted. "If anybody else needs
talking to, I'll send 'em your way."

Willie smiled and ordered a round of beer for everyone and a
Coke—a cold Coke—for Alex. When the drinks came, he insisted on paying. They nursed the one drink for a good half
hour, except for the Lump, who went through four more. They
were all relaxed now, as fatigue combined with alcohol to make
them sleepy, satisfied with their day's work and play.

Then the tough guys came back.

The second they walked in the door, everyone knew there
was trouble. But no one had any idea how bad.

They went right over to Willie's table and told them to leave.

"Niggers ain't allowed to eat white food or drink white beer,"
the ringleader said calmly. The colored baseball players never

so much as moved, they never looked up; it was as if they didn't hear a word.

"Don't do nothin'," Scott said very quietly when he saw the look exchanged between Manning and Alex. "It's different down here, so don't do nothin' if you can help it."

"Didn't you hear, niggers? We said beat it."

"Outside, cocksuckers."

"Filthy, scummy, colored, cocksucking niggers."

Willie looked up, very briefly, but none of the three moved.

"Won't move, huh?"

Donnie and Ben didn't look up. Willie shook his head. "No," he said very quietly. "We won't move."

The door to the restaurant opened and about twenty men walked in. They all had sheets on, with white hoods. The only human part of them that was visible was their mean eyes, crazy eyes staring out. Alex looked at those eyes, and even though they were all he could see, he somehow knew what the men all looked like. He could clearly see their fat, jowly faces. He could see the thick hair all over their backs. He could see their soft beer bellies. He had to close his eyes so he wouldn't see any more.

Some of them had guns, holsters over their sheets. Scott started to shake. Alex knew that never, never, had he been that scared. And he knew he was scared not because he was afraid of getting hurt. He was scared because he knew that what he was seeing was just pure insane, wild, uncontrollable evil. It was not something that he had ever seen before, but it was something he recognized, and it made him go cold, dead cold, inside. He wanted to run to Willie, tell his friend to get the hell out, to run as if his life depended on it. But he did nothing. Because he knew Willie wasn't going anywhere. Sure as he knew Willie understood about the Moment, about what he called "getting blue," that's how sure he was that there was no way in the world Willie was going to leave the restaurant because these fat, mean, crazy white guys told him to go.

Everything that happened next happened so quickly it was more like a dream.

Only it was no dream.

Half of the KKK goons came over to Alex's table. They pulled their guns and clubs and told the white boys not to move. The other half circled the three black players. "Get out," they said. "We don't like niggers in white places. Get out of the restaurant, get out of the hotel, get out of town."

Then nothing. No sound. Nothing.

And then Willie stood up. Real slow. He turned to the leader, the one who had just told him to get out of town. Very calmly, Willie smiled; the same smile Alex had seen so many times after a graceful running catch. He smiled at Alex. Then he smiled at the men standing above him. And to them he said, "Fuck you up the ass."

Nobody could believe it. So Willie said it again, only now it seemed like he was saying it to everyone in the room. And he smiled directly at Alex as he spoke.

"A little poem for you white trash scum bags. 'I'm gettin' blue. So fuck you.'"

They didn't have a chance. Willie, Ben, and Donnie were kicked and hit and clubbed and beaten until Alex thought they were going to die. And none of the other teammates could move. Manning had a gun pointed right at his head. Scott was crying, blubbering. Ski and Fuse put their heads down on the table and refused to look. The Lump was biting his lip so hard, blood was oozing down his chin. Alex was twitching, shaking so he thought his veins would burst.

It seemed like forever, but the beatings only took fifteen minutes. When the room was totally silent, Ski lifted his head, sure it was all over. It wasn't.

Two guys picked Willie up off the floor. While they held him, arms behind his back, the leader went face to face with him.

"Here, nigger," the guy said. He said it so softly and unemotionally that it seemed almost nice, polite. "This'll teach you to speak back to white folks."

And he cut out Willie's tongue.

Alex heard it. Heard the knife whoosh through the skin. He saw it too. Saw the blood and the tongue, looking like it was breathing there on the floor, pulsating like a dying fish stranded on the beach. Alex went crazy for a second. Insane. He charged the man with the knife. But he only got about two steps because he was knocked down by a club. He didn't lose consciousness, it didn't even hurt. It slowed things down, made the room look and sound as if everyone were moving at half speed. And by the time he was up, everything was over, everything was done. A Negro doctor was with Willie and the others; the Klan was gone. Most of the team were back in their rooms.

Manning and Ski came into Alex and Scott's room. Scott was talking about the Bible and love. Ski paced up and down the room, grunting and groaning with the effort of holding all his violence inside. Manning never changed expression, never reacted, never moved or spoke. Alex just cried and cried and cried.

Cried and cried.

He desperately wanted to grab out for Patty so she could wipe out the stain of what he had just seen. He wanted to see her, let her hold him; he suddenly wanted to be with someone he knew would never hurt him, never lie to him, never let him down.

And even in his disgust and despair, even in the agony he was feeling for Willie Trotty, Alex Justin felt the slightest tingling of pleasure in his awareness that he had just felt his first urgent need for love.

The pitch to Jerry Bartkowski was a foot outside and tailing away. But there were runners on first and second and two outs and Ski was zero for his last twelve, so he was desperate. He swung as the entire bench groaned and swore. It was strike three and runners, yet again, were stranded forlornly.

"Pissfuckshit," Charlie Lassiter said to Alex.

"Yeah." Alex nodded in reply. "Know whatcha mean."

"Listen, boys," Charlie yelled, hoisting himself up off the bench. "We gotta win this pissfuckin' game, 'cause those shitfuckin' second-place Twins are comin' here in three days. Now, for those o' you who can't add, we got a two-game lead, and we got two games with the Twins. So we keep winnin', we're gonna win the whole fuckin' pennant. We lose, and I mean lose to these Hi-Tom bastards today, we go right down the ol' shit creek! So win this fuckin' game, you shithead assholes!"

"He's inspirational, I'll give him that," Manning said to Alex.

"Keep my seat warm," Alex said, and trotted out to center field.

It was the top of the seventh. The Fuse was having one of those rare days where he was living up to his potential. His curve was slashing over the plate, his fastball was humming, crackling with power. In six innings he'd given up one run on only three hits and two walks. He'd struck out eight Hi-Toms.

But Josh Dade of the Toms was holding the Tobs in check. The game was even: 1–1. Though the Tobs had seven hits and four walks, they couldn't seem to get any men across home plate. And Dade was known to get tougher the longer he lasted.

Alex watched Dade from right field as the pitcher came up to take his turn at the plate. He was one mean guy, Alex thought, a helluva competitor. Dade was the only successful black pitcher in the league; he probably was the best pitcher in the entire Carolina circuit, even better than Manning. He hated everybody, that was the secret to his success. He wouldn't so much as speak to any player on an opposing team, never wanting to risk friendship with someone he might have to strike out with men on base. He didn't even like developing bonds on his own team. "There's such a thing as trades," he'd said. "You might be my friend today but you're a potential enemy tomorrow. So stay away from me." That was the message that Dade advertised: *Stay away. Don't get too close, 'cause you're only gettin' in my way.*

Dade was a winner, Alex knew. He despised failure, so refused to let himself fail. And the guy was tough as nails. Alex had heard that the year before, Dade had been hit by a line drive right on his knee. He had refused to come out of the game, pitched the last two innings, won the game. Then they found out his kneecap had been fractured.

Tough, Alex thought, tough and mean, as Dade hit a sharp grounder to third. Bucky Williams fielded it smoothly and threw it over to first for the out. One away.

Alex glanced at his right, checking on Phil Mannetti in center. Mannetti was starting because Donnie Lawrence had quit the team. He hadn't said a word to anyone. But the day after the incident in Durham, Donnie disappeared. Everyone knew he was never coming back.

Ben stayed. Ben Ellerbee. He was in the hospital for two days then returned to the team, his face a swollen, bruised mess, his torso covered with ugly marks and swellings and hideous purple blotches. Ben never spoke of the incident. *"The incident,"* Alex thought. *That's what it's become, a moment already receding into the hazy past.* It was something not to think about, something that would soon have only a name, no reality. The incident. And no, Ben never spoke about it. But he never spoke about anything. He didn't say a word when he rejoined the team, total silence when Charlie kept him on the bench for a week, no response when he went back to his starting job in left field. He was as silent as Willie was going to be for the rest of his life.

Willie. Alex didn't know what had happened to Willie. Charlie made a brief announcement, said Willie had been sent to a hospital up North. Alex didn't know where. Just up North. He tried to find out. Asked Charlie. Asked the doctor. But all he was told was "up North."

He asked Ben but Ben wouldn't even talk to him, just stared straight ahead as if Alex weren't asking him a direct question. And then Alex didn't know who else to ask, so he stopped asking. There was no point. When Willie wanted to be found, Willie would let Alex find him.

From center to right to up North.

Alex shook his head, trying to chase these interfering thoughts away. They had no place out on the field. They should not exist out on the field.

There were two outs now. The Hi-Tom shortstop had popped up to Ski. Chris was pitching to their second baseman, a speedy Latin guy who Alex heard didn't speak one word of English other than "What room number?" The Latin guy got hold of one of Chris's fastballs but he didn't get enough of it and Ben was able to catch it, effortlessly, silently, on the warning track.

Bottom of the seventh. Scott was leading off, followed by Bucky. Then Alex. Alex wanted to hit with a man on base, in scoring position. All he was thinking about was golfing a fastball in the left-center gap. Everything was starting to blur, become background. All he cared about was putting a bat in his hands and winning the game.

"Get on base!" he shouted. "Get on, get on, get on!"

Scott stopped on his way to the plate and smiled over at Alex.

"On base, tough monkey!" Charlie yelled. "Do it, monkey!"

And Scott tapped the dirt off his spikes with his bat. He nodded.

The first pitch was a fastball, just outside. It missed by inches and Scott held up his swing to take ball one. But he moved several inches closer to the plate. If the next pitch was six inches outside, he'd hit it.

The second fastball was outside, but a few inches too far. Again, Scott was tempted but held up and the count was 2 and 0. He crowded the plate even closer, his upper body leaning away over into the strike zone. Josh Dade stepped off the mound.

"Move back," he hollered to Scott. "You in my territory!"

Scott didn't move. He wiggled his bat tauntingly at the pitcher. Dade moved halfway to the plate as the Tobs jeered at him from the dugout.

"Get back on the mound, Dade," the umpire threw in.

"He's in my territory, man," the black man complained. "That's a pitcher's pitch you takin' away, man," he said to Scott, almost pleadingly. "You takin' away my territory and I won't allow it."

"It's mah territory now," Scott said, and smiled.

Dade went back to the mound and threw a high hard one on the inside corner that miraculously missed plunking Scott in the ribs, and even more miraculously was a beautiful strike. Scott moved inside another inch.

"On base, monkey!"

Dade slowly, calmly, walked all the way to the plate and went face to face with Scott.

"Move back and give me what's mine or I'm gonna have to do somethin' about it. Gonna play some chin music."

"Get outta here, Dade," the umpire said. "You got ten seconds to get back to the mound or you're outta the game."

Dade stared at Scott, never turning away. "Listen, you white motherfucker," he practically whispered, a steely whisper, words that were solid iron. "Give me back my territory or I'm gonna hurt you."

Scott grinned. Dade whirled and returned to his proper position. His next fastball broke Scott Hunt's skull.

The ball went straight for the forehead and Scott never flinched, he stared at it all the way, welcomed the nauseating crunch with a martyr's smile. He dropped straight to the ground, no twisting, no sagging, no flopping; dead weight that refused to quiver.

All hell broke loose. People screaming for doctors, for an ambulance. For revenge. The Tobs bench attacked Josh Dade, who fought back like a wild animal trying to claw his way out of a swift death trap. The Hi-Toms fought for their pitcher, tackling and punching whoever got in the way.

Alex Justin screamed. Over and over again he yelled out, "No!" He screamed until he didn't recognize his own voice, until it sounded to him like some strange wail from the heavens, permeating the land. "No! No! No! No! No!"

He tried to reach his roommate, but he never got close. There were too many bodies, too much action. Alex threw his body against the crowd surrounding the fallen second baseman, but he could not push through. Once, when he was knocked to his knees, he looked up, was able to focus, and he saw Ben on the bench. Ben was standing, frozen. Silently he was waiting for the game to begin again. Silently he was saying that, perhaps, this was all part of the game.

And Alex screamed, "No! No, no, no, no, no, no, no!"

And Scott was driven away in a red-and-white ambulance.

And ten minutes later a relief pitcher was throwing to Bucky Williams with a pinch runner on first base. Alex was kneeling in the on-deck circle. Over and over he heard the sound, saw Scott fall, saw Willie's tongue, heard his own scream, watched silent Ben, felt the murderous hate from Josh Dade's eyes. He swung his bat, scattering the images. They returned, he swung, they vanished.

"Come on, Bucky!" he screamed, and then louder, "Bucky! Let's go! Let's go, Bucky!" His throat hurt, it felt raw. But then he heard the chants from the stands: *Let's go, Bucky! Let's go Bucky! Bucky, let's go! Let's go Bucky! Let's go Bucky! Bucky, let's go!* Alex swung again, felt the power in his arms and wrists, saw the spin on the ball as the new Tom pitcher put it outside and walked Bucky Williams. And now it was Alex's turn. He was up. The crowd went crazy, the team stood and hollered from the dugout, he felt only the calm he always felt when he was about to hit.

The game was back in progress.

10

The Tobs won the pennant the next weekend. Alex's two-run home run in the eighth inning beat the Winston-Salem Twins in the first game of the series, giving the Wilson team a three-game lead with one game left in the season. April seventeenth had finally become September third and the Tobs were the surprise champions of the Class B Carolina League. Immediately after the final game Alex Justin was unanimously voted by the players on the Tobs their MVP for the year.

Charlie arranged for the party at the Wilson Lodge. They had the Cotton Bowl Room for the night. Free beer till midnight, huge, juicy sirloin steaks with a baked potato on the side. All the important denizens of Wilson society were there to salute the team and share in the joy of victory: Carl Fromer, the president of the Wilson Savings and Loan; Bobby Joe Ritter, who owned Fleming Stadium; Charlotte Banks, the widow of Arthur Ray Banks, who had been Wilson's most decorated soldier in WWI. Everybody was there, even Mayor Clement W. Stinson, who was so happy for the Tobs he just couldn't help crying when he made the first of many official toasts praising and thanking the Lord, the manager, the players, and the good old U.S. of A., not necessarily in that order.

Alex didn't go to the banquet. He put on his blue blazer and gray cotton pants, his red-and-blue tie; he shined his shoes and snapped on his cuff links and walked straight to Katie's house. He rang the bell, waited for her to descend, heard her flip-flopping footsteps on the stairway, stood there impassively as she opened the door, surprised to see him this early, all dressed up, surprised to see him at all. He went upstairs, ignoring her "What are you doing? What are you doing here? Alex, talk to me. Say something!" He didn't talk to her. He didn't say anything. He waited until they were standing in the middle of her living room and then he kissed her, only it wasn't his usual kiss, soft, exploring, giving. It was barely a kiss at all, more like a savage attempt to rip something from within her. She gasped and started to step away from him, but he held her firm, wouldn't let her budge. She knew she would not be hurt, knew he would never hurt her, so she met him on equal terms. She kissed him back, grabbed his hair, yanked so the tension was unbelievably sexy, then harder till he grunted and the muscles in his face contorted in pain, then harder still until he yelled and squeezed, crushed her to make her let go, and when she finally released him, he tore at her, pulling the clothes off her body in one motion, splitting her dress down the middle as if it were made of paper, and for an instant she thought she had miscalculated, that he *was* going to hurt her, but when he released her he just stood there like a hulking animal and made no move to go after her again.

Alex sat down, shook his head to clear it, wondering for a moment where he was. He didn't have long to wonder, for she now wrapped her thighs around his head, his face was buried in the hair between her legs. She twisted him down to the floor. His tongue darted in and out, lapping, devouring the oozing taste of wet cunt, sucking, plunging in deeply with his lips. He ate till she came, wet spurts of come dripping onto his mouth and chin.

And then he was all over her. Sprawled on top of her, spreading her come over her face, licking it off. He bit into her shoulder, put his tongue under her arm and drank in her sweat. Her small breasts went to his face and he practically swallowed them.

He surprised her by suddenly thrusting himself inside her,

but once he was there she held him, squeezing, rotating her hips, moaning, screaming, mouth open, eyes rolled back. They were breathing as one until he came in brutal spasms. He closed his eyes and immediately collapsed. She tried to jerk every last moment out of the act, refusing to quit, panting and groaning even louder until she, too, was forced to admit it was over.

They lay on the floor, separated now. Silent.

They went into her bedroom and made love twice more. Each time was a little slower, a bit gentler. When he came the third time they were hardly moving, barely breathing.

When they were done, Alex spoke for the first time. He looked down at his watch and said, "I missed the thing tonight. The dinner."

"Well, I'm late for work, so we're even."

"Thank you."

"My pleasure, honey. Truly and truly."

He laughed, rubbing his fingers across his wet chest.

"I think I better take a shower."

"I think my whole damn apartment better shower after that."

Alex walked into the bathroom and turned the shower on, watching as the hot stream of water began to fog up the medicine-cabinet mirror.

He rubbed the mist away with his right hand and stared at his reflection. For a moment he thought a revelation or a special insight was about to burst upon him. The mood and atmosphere were right. But nothing came. All he saw was a good-looking kid with dirty-blond hair, a thick neck, and a chest that was heaving as he breathed in the hot steam.

He stepped into the bathtub and took great joy in the hammering of the sharp drops against his body. The violence washed out of him, the desperate desire too. He turned the water off.

"Why didn't you go to the dinner?" she asked. He realized she'd been watching him shower.

"Dunno."

" 'Cause o' your friend? Scott?"

"I guess. And Willie."

"Bad stuff happens to people all the time, honey chile. That don't mean you gotta stop celebrating."

Alex thrashed the towel over his hair, drying it.

"I saw him today," he said, his voice muffled by the towel.

"Scott?"

"Went to visit him at the hospital."

"How is he?"

"All right."

"He is?"

Alex shrugged. "He'll live."

"And be normal?"

Alex shrugged again and methodically began drying his shoulders, then his arms, then his torso. "They say he won't think so good. But he *never* really thought so good."

"Do you want somethin' to drink? I jes' bought some apple juice."

"An' they say he might walk kinda funny. But he always had kind of a funny walk."

"Baby, I want you to finish dryin' yourself and come here to sit yourself down on the bed. I wanna talk to you."

"We're talkin' now."

"Well, we're changin' the subject. And what I have in mind is definitely bed talk."

Alex dried and sat.

"Okay," he said.

"I been thinkin' " is the way Katie began.

"About what?"

"About goin' to New York with you."

It didn't really register at first. He thought he must have misunderstood.

"What?" he said.

Casually, she repeated, "I been thinkin' about goin' to New York with ya."

Then he realized it was a joke. He waved at her, signaling that he got it. "Katie." He grinned and shook his head.

Katie watched as he walked into the living room and put his pants on. He had to fix one leg, which was inside out, before pulling them on. She followed him into the room.

"Alex," she said. "Honey, I wanna go to *New* York. With you."

It began to dawn on him that she might be serious. It began to dawn on her that she was way out of line.

"When are you goin' back?" she asked.

"I guess tomorrow."

"You guess?"

"Tomorrow. Two o'clock train."

"Thanks for tellin' me."

"I didn't think."

"Well, what *did* you think about me?"

"What do you mean?"

"I mean, what'd you think was gonna happen? That I'd just wait around here till y'all came dancin' back next summer?"

Alex cleared his throat. "I prob'ly won't be here next summer. I'll prob'ly be in Schenectady. 'A' ball."

"Schenectady? What the hell . . . ?"

"Yeah. It's a town. In New York. That's where I go next."

"So what was tonight? Bye-bye, Katie?"

He didn't answer. Katie sat down on the couch.

"Well, I'll be goddamned!"

"Are you all right?" he asked.

"Sugah, I'm *always* all right. This just ain't what I was expectin'." She blinked. "Goddamn, I can't stay in this shithole forever." She looked up at him, saw how confused and pained he was. "I guess little ol' Katie convinced herself that you were her ticket outta here."

"But I told you."

"You did?"

"I *told* you."

"About what?" He just stared at her. "Oh. About your little girlfriend."

"I told you all about her. And that I was goin' back to her. I never lied or anything. I told you the truth just so—"

"So this wouldn't happen. Well, that's what bein' human is, boy . . . knowin' somethin's goddamn wrong and then goin' ahead and pretendin' that it just isn't so." She closed her eyes. "Let this be a valuable lesson to you."

"Katie . . ."

"I think you should go."

Katie stood up, still naked. He took one step toward her, saw in her eyes that he should back off.

"Okay," he said. "Okay."

"Before you go, though."

"What?"

"She prettier than me?"

Alex was embarrassed. "Patty?"

"That's the one."

"She is. I think. Prettier than you." He nodded. "Yeah."

"Smarter'n me?"

He nodded again. "Smarter."

"Well, shit goddamn."

He turned to go, but she had one last question.

"So why did you come here, tonight? I mean, other than to say good-bye to good ol' Katie. What were you lookin' for?"

He hesitated.

"You can be honest. You sure as hell can. What *were* you lookin' for?"

"Relief."

She laughed. It was a mean laugh, but there was a hint of tenderness in it.

"Honey," Katie's parting words began, "that's not what women are all about."

The streets were deserted. It was after one-thirty in the morning.

Alex shuffled aimlessly along Magnolia Way. His walk was careless, recklessly lazy. He was trying not to think about what had happened that night at Katie's. What had happened to Scott. And Willie. He was trying hard not to think.

Alex found himself a block from the Wilson Lodge. With nothing better to do he walked to it, thinking perhaps he might peer in at the remnants of the party.

A light was still on in the Cotton Bowl Room. Charlie Lassiter sat at a table, half asleep, head bowed toward ten or twelve empty beer bottles. His breathing was thick and heavy and his skin looked particularly loose and red. Alex went up to the table, stood over his manager in silence. Charlie didn't budge. Alex sat down, as if his mere presence would cause a stirring. It didn't. The restaurant was otherwise empty. The thorough postbash cleaning was obviously scheduled for the next day, for there were dirty plates and scraps of food scattered on various tables. Chairs were overturned and puddles of beer spread across the floor.

Alex poked Charlie in his meaty arm. His breathing got thicker, more mucousy. Alex poked him again, harder, and with a start and a snort Charlie Lassiter awoke.

"What? Huh? Wha—" He saw Alex, and his bloodshot eyes tried to focus. He coughed, gathered up phlegm in his throat. He was about to spit it out, realized he was in a hotel, then realized he was basically alone so he hocked a good one halfway across the room. That seemed to revive him and he sat up, groaning.

"Justin."

"Sir."

"What are you doin' here?"

"Just passing by."

"Holy shit, my tongue feels like a fuckin' sandbox. Why the hell weren't you here tonight?"

Alex didn't answer.

"I asked you a question. Is there any beer in that fuckin' thing?" Alex handed him a bottle half-filled with warm beer. Charlie drank it down, made a face, and coughed. "You missed the fuckin' banquet."

"Sorry."

"Sorry shit!"

"Was it a good party?"

Charlie belched in response. Then he seemed to notice something about the boy sitting before him. "You look like you seen a fuckin' ghost. Wanna drink?"

"No, thanks."

"Hey, Justin." Charlie propped himself up with his arms, wincing. "Steady there, big guy," he mumbled. Then turned back to Alex. "Is there somethin' wrong, kid?" Alex didn't respond. Charlie rubbed his eyes, grunted when he touched his head. "If there's somethin' wrong, tell me now, or else I'm goin' home to puke my fuckin' guts out and take about forty fuckin' aspirin."

Alex opened his mouth to speak. Nothing came out, his lips moved slowly back together.

"You look like you're gonna cry, son," Charlie Lassiter said. "Is it your pal Hunt? The colored thing? You was friendly with that Willie, right?"

Alex didn't know what the hell he was doing sitting at the table with a drunken slob; he felt like a total asshole and was just about to stand up when the manager said, "What, is it leavin' that little waitress?" and Alex jerked his head around, surprised.

"Yeah, I know about it," Charlie said. "I know a lotta shit'd surprise you." Charlie spat again, looked among the bottles for any remains of beer. He found three bottles that were each about one-quarter full.

"Why do you rag Dave Manning so much?" Alex asked.

"That's what's makin' you cry, with all this other shit goin' down? I yell at your buddy?"

Alex didn't respond. Charlie drank one of the quarter-full bottles.

"Kid. I don't wanna make it sound like I got one foot in the fuckin' grave, but I been around. There's certain things you can spot just from bein' old. You can tell when your wife is foolin' around on you, you can tell when some hotshot pitcher's got a sore arm and won't say nothin'! You can tell when some big-city kid ain't gettin' enough sleep 'cause he's bongin' away at some small-town waitress. You can tell when someone's gonna take a swing at somebody else 'cause they're too full o' booze or just plain shit. And troublemakers is somethin' else you can tell. Always, plain as day, every fuckin' time."

"Manning? He does his job. He wins you ball games."

Charlie reached across the table and put one of his meathooks on Alex's shoulder, gripping it tightly, too tightly.

"I'm drunk as a fuckin' skunk."

"Yes, sir."

"That's why I'm gonna tell you what I'm gonna tell you. If I

was sober, I'd just chew your ass out for missin' the best fuckin'
party in the world."

"Yes, sir."

"I know you think I'm a dumb shit and maybe you're right.
I've done a lot of dumb-shit things. But I love baseball. I mean, I
love baseball. Do you understand what I'm sayin'?"

Alex nodded.

"The fuck you do! I've given up a wife and two kids for this
game. I ain't seen my youngest kid in . . . Christ, I don't even
know how old she is. Ya travel, you're on the road . . . that
ain't no way to keep a family together. There ain't no way to
keep *nothin'* together. Except a team." The last sentence was
whispered reverentially. For emphasis Charlie pounded the
table with the palm of his hand and said, in anything but a
whisper, "Except a team! Except a fuckin' team!"

Alex nodded. He knew that was all that was expected of him.

"I been on the road a long time. It feels like my whole life
sometimes. I've fucked whores, I've fucked Annies, I've jacked
off in more goddamn rooms than you ever been in your whole
life." He took a deep breath, tilted backward in his chair, and
for one horrible moment Alex thought Charlie was going to pass
out before getting to the point. But the man was a pro. "See, one
thing you learn on the road, you gotta take whatever it is you
want wherever it is ya can find it. Love, or sex, or whatever you
wanna call it—you take it for a night, an hour or two. A drink. A
shower. Shit." Charlie's face was screwed up in thought. He was
lettin' loose. "It ain't easy, Judge, boy, it ain't easy. And the one
thing you don't wanna do, you don't wanna make it *harder.* You
don't wanna make nothin' harder than it has to be, 'cause that's
the surefirest fuckin' way to screw up your whole damn life. You
wanna get laid, fine! Plunk down twenny bucks and get yourself
some girl who washes your dick and puts the rubber on herself.
You wanna win a pennant, fine! Get yourself the best buncha
ballplayers you can and don't think about things like whether
they're nice guys you'd want your sister to marry! You find what
you want and you pick the easiest way to get it. That's why I
never said nothin' to ya 'bout this little hootchie ya got here.
She's easy. She don't charge ya. I figure you know enough not to

get the clap, so fine, go to it. She's easy." Charlie sighed, ran his fingers through his hair, wiped the extra grease off on the table-cloth. "Man, oh, man. What was I talkin' about?"

"Manning, Charlie. Dave Manning."

Charlie sighed again. "He's pickin' the hard way to go. The hardest way." He belched. "That boy has talent, whoooo, does he have talent. But you're gonna see that go right down the toilet, 'cause it's almost impossible to keep that kinda talent up even when you take the easy way!"

"I don't get it," Alex said. "I don't understand."

Charlie bit a chunk of skin off his thumb and twisted his neck first left, then right. "When I was first married, shit, maybe two years, our kid fell down a flight o' stairs. She was a year, year an' a half old, she went down the whole stairs, landed right on her fuckin' head. And for three days we thought she was a goner. High fever, couldn't eat nothin'. And so I thought a lot about what would happen, I mean if she died. And I knew not a helluva lot was gonna happen. I mean, we'da been sad, we woulda gotten over it. She wouldn'ta grown up to be a whatever it is she does now, a housewife or somethin'. It woulda been one o' those *little* tragedies, that's what I got to thinkin' of it as, a *little* tragedy. Didn't really affect no more than a few people, didn't seem to really *matter*. I mean, in the grand fuckin' scheme o' things. Like yer pal Hunt. A *little* tragedy. He wasn't goin' nowhere, now he knows it. An' that's what'll happen to your buddy Ski. He'll get cut, he'll become a fuckin' miner or some fuckin' thing. It don't really make no difference. In the grand fuckin' scheme o' things."

"And Manning?"

"Manning don't believe in nothing. So he pushes, he shoves, he tries too damn hard at everything he does so he can maybe *find* somethin' to believe in. I'll tell you somethin'. Your colored friend, Willie. When things quiet down, when Manning goes home and thinks about it, he's gonna be *glad* that godawful thing happened to that poor boy. He's gonna be glad, 'cause for a little while at least he can believe in somethin'. He can believe in bad people an' evil things. And he'll like that. For a while.

And then he'll stop believing and he'll have to find something else."

"Charlie . . ."

"And I'll tell you somethin' else about Dave Manning. Why I rag him so much. Why I don't want him playin' ball for me. Manning ain't never gonna find nothin' to believe in. Not really. He don't believe in teams, he don't believe in, shit, he don't believe in love, he don't believe in no little tragedies. Like Hunt or Willie. So you know what he's gonna do? He's gonna find things that other people believe in and he's gonna . . . ahh, shit. What's the point? I'm drunk and I'm not makin' no sense. Shit, fuck, and piss."

"So what do I do?" Alex wanted to know.

"About what?"

Alex waved his hand around the room, around the situation. "About everything."

"You go home tomorrow and you spend the off season tellin' all your friends how you won the MVP. You get a job, stay in shape. Then, next year you come back here. Or more likely you leave me in this shit-ass place and move on up to Schenectady or Florida. You hit three twenny, you go on to the pros, you get your fuckin' pension. What you *don't* do is worry about who you're playin' with or what they're doin'. You don't make too many friends, 'cause you're gonna be doin' a lotta movin' on. You don't worry about gettin' beaned, you don't try to find your coon friend . . . what you do now is whatever baseball tells you to do. 'Cause if you do, kid, 'cause if you do . . ."

Charlie, by this time, had stumbled almost to the door. He put a hand on the wall to steady himself. He didn't finish the thought about what Alex could do. He couldn't. He was too drunk and sick and tired. "I'm goin' home," he said.

"Me too."

"I ain't done this much talkin' since I was married."

"I'll see ya next year, maybe."

"Turn the light out, Judge. I promised some-fuckin'-body I'd do that."

*　*　*

Manning was in front of Auntie Joy's when Alex came home. He was just standing in the front yard, leaning against the large weeping willow tree.

"I waited for you," he told Alex.

"I'm glad. I wanted to say good-bye."

"Hell, this isn't good-bye. You, me and Lump, we'll be around each other a ways yet."

"I guess we will," Alex said. "And the other guys?"

Manning shook his head. "They ain't goin' nowhere."

"Where are *we* goin'?" Alex asked.

"Where you *been?*" Manning said in that familiar taunting but friendly tone.

Alex didn't answer.

"You look different," Manning said. "Something happen to you tonight?"

"What do you mean?"

"I mean did you learn anything tonight? Somethin' I should know?"

"About what?"

"You tell me."

Alex thought for a while. "No," he said eventually, "I didn't learn anything. I just got a lot more questions and a whole buncha new stuff I gotta watch out for."

Dave Manning grinned. "I already got enough questions, Judge. And I think I know most of the stuff I gotta watch out for."

Alex grinned back tentatively. "I think you're prob'ly right."

"But you tell me if you ever learn something you think I should know, okay?"

"Okay," Alex said, still grinning, the grin becoming more genuine.

"You promise?"

"Why, Dave. You sound almost serious."

"Helluva season, wasn't it?" Dave Manning said.

"Helluva season," Alex agreed, and never remembered meaning anything quite so much in his entire life.

11

Alex got a hero's welcome back home in the safe environs of Stuyvesant Town.

He lugged his trunk along the linoleum hallway, used his key to open the front door, was disappointed when the lights were off and he realized no one was home. When he flicked the light on, he was unprepared for the "Surprise!" that was yelled out by excited voices. He was pleased, but wearily so. Three months earlier he might have gotten red faced, embarrassed, and shocked almost to the point of anger at the fun trickery. Now, however, he was surprised—but was reluctantly embracing the idea that surprises were things to be constantly expected. So he nodded to show his pleasure at the warm response and grinned politely to show his general gratitude.

Elliot was first in line to hug him. His little brother rested on both crutches with his left hand and put his right arm limply around Alex's torso. Alex was shocked to see how thin the boy had gotten, how wan. Away from home, when Alex thought of Elliot he did not conjure up the picture of a cripple. But the boy in front of him clearly was one. Alex tried hugging Elliot tighter to him, but the boy pulled back. He didn't ask Alex any questions, but his eyes seemed curious to find out what had happened, what wonders had been discovered during the long absence. They stared at each other, Alex trying to smile. He didn't know what to do. Did he tell the boy about things he might never discover on his own? Did he feed into his imagination, stimulate it, upset it, or did he stay quiet, keep Elliot in the dark about the love, the fun, the violence, the hate, he had discovered? The moment seemed an eternity. Elliot's eyes then shut down. Alex's mouth opened, nothing came out. Elliot let his right arm fall to his side; he grabbed his crutches and propelled himself out of the way.

Danny was next. He sauntered over to his best pal, who was bobbing his head back and forth as if he already knew everything Alex was going to tell him. They hugged, Danny's head bobbing all the time as they slapped each other on the back.

"You look good," Danny said generously.

"Thanks. I think you got shorter."

"Yeah, short's in now."

"That right?"

"Where you been? All the best people are short now."

Patty hung back. She wasn't comfortable enough yet with the family to break the protocol and rush in front of his parents to kiss him and grab him. It was a supreme effort, but she waited for Carl to shake his hand and tell him how proud they all were, and she waited for Ginny to burst out crying and apologize for her tears and kiss him and beam with pure love and pride.

Alex hadn't even really looked at Patty, except for an instant's glance out of the corner of his eye. He hadn't reacted to her except for a slight upward shift of the edge of his lips. But that was all she needed, for it was a soft yet penetrating expression and told her what she wanted to know—how exhausted he was, how much he had to tell her, how very glad he was to see her.

It was her turn now to squeal exuberantly and run to him, and she did, a huge smile on her face. She kissed him right on the lips, a long wet one, her joy suddenly unencumbered by the presence of the family. Alex didn't say anything; he hadn't said much to anyone. Patty put her head against his shoulder and stood quietly, hugging him possessively. He leaned on her for support, arms draped over her shoulders. He looked around at his parents and his brother.

"Am I glad to be home," he said.

* * *

His mom had made all his favorites—roast beef, fried potatoes, salad with French dressing, and her special chocolate date cake. Everyone chattered all through the meal. It took Alex a few minutes to reaccustom himself to being part of the family, but soon his reserve melted away and everything was back to normal.

"Got a joke."

"Danny, just because you're a hotshot college kid now, don't think you can tell *dirty* jokes here."

"Mom!"

"Look at him. Look at that grin. I can tell he's about to tell a filthy joke."

"It's clean, I swear!"

"Let him tell the joke, Ginny."

"Elliot's at the table."

"Elliot's old enough to hear a dirty joke, Mom," Alex said. He winked at his little brother, man to man. Elliot, embarrassed, kept his eyes on his roast beef.

"I think I'll wait," Danny decided. "The timing seems a bit off now."

"No, go ahead."

"I don't think so."

"Mom . . ."

"Tell me more about the guy who was beaned, Alex," Danny said.

"I'll tell you later."

"How's your mom, Patty?"

"She's fine, thanks, Mrs. Justin."

"What about the fight? What about this guy Willie?"

"I don't know."

"Have more beef, Alex."

"No, thanks, Dad."

"C'mon. A little more beef!"

"I'm full."

"A little more beef. Come ooooonnnn!"

Alex loved his family and he was truly glad to be home with them. And before he even got to dessert they were driving him crazy. He couldn't wait to get out of there, to get somewhere, anywhere, where he could be alone with Patty. He wanted to hug her; he needed the comfort of her too-white skin. When the chocolate date cake came he wolfed it down, gulping a tall glass of milk with it.

"Alex. Slower. You'll choke."

"Right, Mom."

He finished gulping and stood up.

"We're gonna go," he said. He was the only one standing and all heads were turned toward him questioningly. Patty wasn't even done with her cake. Danny was just starting on seconds.

"Uh," he went on, "I . . . uh . . . we . . ."

Silence from the group. Alex felt an estrangement, as if he were an outsider who had swept in, grabbed for sustenance, and was now deserting the troops.

"I think," Carl Justin said, "the young people want to be alone."

Alex shrugged, Patty stared down at her fingers folded in her lap.

"Well, I'd like to stick around if there's any more cake," Danny said, and everyone laughed. "Besides, I think the love-birds want to be by themselves." Alex blushed, everyone laughed again, but then Alex and Patty were out the door. They were on the hot Stuyvesant Town pavement, staring foolishly at each other, grinning, embarrassed, wanting to touch but not knowing where to begin. And so he just grabbed her and kissed her, not even catching her full on the mouth, but the point was made. Their lips adjusted, fit together, their tongues did their best to braid, and two bodies merged under the glow of just-lighted streetlamps.

They went to "their bench" off behind the playground. He leaned back, arms stretched over the gravelly backrest. She snuggled in to him, let herself smell his familiar sweat, feel the strength in his chest.

And they talked.

She told him all about school. About Mr. Pierson from summer school Biology II who told her she should stay in the sciences, maybe even be a doctor. And that her guidance counselor thought she might be able to get a scholarship so she wouldn't have to go to a state school. She told him about how so many of the kids treated her differently now out on the streets, as if his specter followed her around demanding respect; she laughed about a boy who kept trying to date her all summer; she filled him in on movies she'd seen, books she'd read, new friends, old friends, laughs and cries. She told him how much she'd missed him, how glad she was, how very glad she was, that he was now back with her.

Alex interrupted occasionally, to ask questions or laugh or tell her to slow down or add that he knew what she meant because the same thing had happened to him. Mostly he listened, though, until it was his turn. Then it all gushed out. He waved his arms and stood up and paced and got excited and spoke tenderly. He talked about loneliness and friendship, about a new world, about treachery and violence. He did his best to explain the new levels of competition he had reached, the brand-new satisfactions and disillusionments. He spoke about Manning and Ski and Lump and Scott and Willie. He whispered when he spoke about fear. He glowed beautifully when he gave voice to pride. He recreated his summer, thought by thought, crucial event by crucial event, emotion by emotion. He held nothing back, not even about baseball. He told her everything.

Except about Katie.

He held that back, not knowing how she'd take it, but, more importantly, not knowing how he felt about it. He decided he'd never tell her. It would stay buried. Always. Forever.

And then she asked about it.

"Did you meet her?"

His right arm twitched. "Who?"

Patty shrugged. "Your floozy away from home."

He tugged at his nose. "Naahh."

She said nothing.

"Why are you staring at me?" he asked.

She still said nothing. One eye squinted shut, opened again. She did not look unhappy, only questioning.

"We were apart for a long time."

"I know."

"It seems *right* to me that you're back. I mean, it all feels natural, comfortable. I don't feel nervous or anything."

"Me too. Me either."

She smiled. He smiled. Silence.

"I had sex with a waitress," he said.

"Oh."

"I wish I didn't now. Have sex with her."

"Uh-huh."

"I mean, I wanted to then. So I did. But I wish I didn't now, now that I see you."

"More than once?"

"What?"

"More than once?"

"No," he lied. "No, no. Once. Only once."

"Oh."

"Three times," he said. It was still a lie but it sounded like less of one.

"Three times."

"You wanted to know," he said. "You said you definitely wanted to know."

"Uh-huh."

"I shouldn't have told you."

"Yes," Patty said. "Yes. You should've. This is right."

"It doesn't feel right."

"Things that are right don't have to feel good."

"Then how do you know they're right?"

"You just know. And this is right."

"Right that I slept with her or right that I told you?"

"I don't know."

He had really thought, somehow, she'd be glad for him, that she'd be happy he'd gone and done it. He thought she'd see that now he could teach her, as he had been taught. That it was meaningless, no, not meaningless, but that it had nothing to do with *them*. It was separate. She had wanted to know, he had told her. They were one. She should be glad. She wasn't. She was miserable. Alex was starting to hope that things would begin to go a little more according to the plan.

"I love you," Alex said.
"I love *you*," Patty said.
He smiled sadly. She matched it.
"What do we do now?"

12

It was not a perfect body. But it was perfect that night.

To the sound of the scratchy sax floating in the background, to the piano soothing as accompaniment. She still had a bit of baby fat on her arms and thighs; the softness thrilled him.

He recognized her smell, it was already a part of his permanent store of sensual awareness. Naked and sweaty, there was the added scent of her vagina. That strange, fishy smell excited him. It cut through the dreamlike state of the evening; it even cut through the lure of the music.

They kissed for a long time, eyes closed, eyes open, eyes closed again. The song had changed. And changed again.

They felt each other. First tongue against tongue, then tongue over lips, lips over forehead and cheeks and nose and neck. Hands caressed shoulders, arms, breasts. Thighs pressed together cautiously, stomach flattened against stomach. Arms wrapped around backs.

His fingers slipped inside her. She jerked away but he held her still and he put them in her again. She moaned, even at his awkward touch, and he marveled at the wetness and the surge of urgency that was now entering their lovemaking. His hand went in deeper and deeper; she was writhing on the bed with her mouth open. He gently removed the hand, slowly pulled it out so as not to disturb anything inside her. He spread her legs apart, twisted himself down to her, and kissed the inside of her thigh. He felt her tense, but, holding her legs, firmly but carefully he moved his tongue inside her, snaking deeper and deeper. She gasped nervously, reached for his hair, and held it, pulling it tight against his scalp. More sounds escaped from her, short noises, nervous and passionate punctuations.

"Now," she said. "Now."

He was not an expert at this, so he moved carefully. He slipped a pillow under her head, put a hand on her knee, and flattened the leg. Seeing that her eyes were closed, he kissed her forehead. Her eyes didn't open but her lips rearranged themselves into a smile.

With one hand he reached for the opening, waited till he was sure the positioning was right. The music took over his consciousness and he entered her, thrusting himself in in one strong movement. It was not easy, he met with tight resistance, but he didn't give up. He made himself push harder. Her nails dug into his back and she screamed, biting the scream off as soon as it had flung itself from her mouth. She nodded her head, over and over again, telling him it was all right.

He moved, his hands on the bed holding his weight off her. In and out, over and over again, his waist rotating his body ever so slightly. She said, "Oh!" She said, "Oh! Oh! Oh! Oh! Oh! Oh! Oh!"

He came and she pounded his back, slapping her palms, slamming her fists against his muscles.

He lowered himself onto her so once again skin covered skin. All movement stopped. Their breathing joined the rhythm of the slow wail of the clarinet.

She opened her eyes. Smiled.

They kissed.

"Was it better?"

Those were the first words spoken since they'd come into the room. He knew what she meant.

"Yes."

"Why?"

Clinical. A real question. She didn't want romantic drivel, she wanted to *know*.

"Because there was love."

"Are things always better with love?"

He nodded.

"And is love forever?"

"Forever."

Patty smiled. Alex reached for her.

The music spun its lovely web around them as they cradled each other.

"Forever," she said.

"Forever."

They kissed again.

Around the Horne
by
Ed Horne

... He must have had a premonition. Because
in the bottom of the ninth, two outs, the bases
loaded, and the Reds' best hitter ready to swing
away, to be the hero, the Yankee right fielder
moved.

He ran.

He jumped.

Alex Justin leapt toward the moment that
would make him a legend forevermore....

PART TWO
1960s

I walked upon a rainbow
I swung upon a star
You had me up in heaven
That's why I had to fall so far.

—"You Let Me Down"

13

"You're still upset, aren't you?"

He took another handful of popcorn and crunched down hard on an unpopped kernel before answering. "Yeah. Yeah, I'm still upset."

"The houses are really nice in L.A."

Despite everything he had to smile. He wanted to sulk. He didn't want her to know she had made him smile. Not yet. He turned away from the TV to stare out the window at the white blizzard. It was coming down so hard that he couldn't see the night, only the thick downfall of soft flakes. He turned back to his wife.

"How do you know the houses are nice in L.A.?"

"I've been checking. I talked to people."

"What people?"

"People."

"I love you."

"Thank you. I know you think I'm just saying this to cheer you up and be supportive. I know that's why you're smiling. But it's not. The houses *are* nice in L.A."

"How nice?"

"I think we'll be able to get a yard. Think how much Russ'll like that."

"He will."

"Sure."

"It'll be hot too. No more blizzards."

"I like blizzards."

"Me too. But hot'll be good."

"You don't care?"

"That we have to move? That you were traded?"

He nodded.

"No, I don't mind, I don't care."

"A second-year utility infielder and a kid from the minors. A relief pitcher. That's who I was traded for."

"I know."

"You don't care about that either. Traded for two . . . just two *guys.*"

"No, my love. I don't mind that either."

"I like when you call me 'my love.'"

She just smiled at that.

"This is worse than when the Phillies traded me."

"Why?"

"I don't know. Once, it happens. And they got a good player for me. Twice . . ." He shrugged. "I like Chicago too. I'm gonna be sorry to leave."

She didn't say anything. She knew he didn't want her to.

"Patty?"

"What?"

"He worries me a little bit."

"Why?"

"I don't know. He's a strange kid. He's a great kid, but I worry about him. He's angry. He's frightened of things."

"You just love him, that's all. You don't want anything bad to happen to him. That's why you worry."

"Yeah," he said. "I don't want anything bad to happen to any of us."

He jumped when the phone rang. It was so quiet, the whole world seemed to be whispering. The sudden ring sounded harsh and jarring. He picked it up. For a moment the room was silent again.

"Hello," Alex Justin said.

"Hey," the voice on the other end said back.

"Hey!" Alex said. "What's doin'?" He looked at Patty and quietly mouthed the words, "It's Danny." She nodded, a silent and agreeable greeting to the caller.

"Alex," Danny Cappollo said, "when did your parents leave for Hawaii?"

"I guess you heard about the trade, huh?"

"Trade?"

"Yeah. The Cubs just sent me to L.A. A couple of days ago. I thought that's why you were calling. What did you say about my folks?"

"I spoke to 'em last week, just checkin' in, and they said they were finally goin' to Hawaii."

"Yeah."

"When did they leave?"

"Today."

"Today." Danny's repetition was flat, dull. Defeated.

"Yeah." Alex looked quizzically over at Patty. "Why?" he asked. And then he realized he didn't have to ask why. He knew. He sat up very straight and snapped his fingers at Russell, his son, who had just walked into the room carrying a glass of milk and a piece of frozen chocolate cake.

"Turn off the TV."

"But, Dad—"

"Turn it off!"

Alex's tone scared Russell. It scared Patty. When the TV was off, the room was absolutely silent.

"Alex?" Danny said, the long-distance connection echoing ever so slightly. "Alex, what time was the flight?"

"What?"

"When was their flight?"

"Patty," Alex said, "go get my parents' whaddyacallit, their itinerary." When she hesitated, he spoke again, very quietly. Too quietly. "Go get it, would ya? Go find it, okay?"

Patty rushed out of the room. Alex didn't say one word to Danny. He just listened to his old friend breathing on the line.

"Here it is," Patty said, and handed a piece of lined yellow paper to her husband.

"Dan?"

"Yeah."

"They left at eleven o'clock."

"What airline?"

"Worldwide-American."

"Today."

"February ninth. Eleven A.M. Worldwide-American."

Alex heard a sound from a thousand miles away. It came from Danny's lips and it was the sound of finality defeating hope.

"Alex," Danny said, finally. "Their plane went down. It crashed." He sighed, deflating. "They were killed."

Alex Justin said nothing. One thought, one image, shot up through his brain: his parents on fire, screaming a silent scream, falling through the air. The image plummeted, crashed. Disappeared.

Patty, who had moved to kneel on the floor by Alex's legs, shivered with pain. She did not know what Danny was saying on the other end of the phone, but eight years of marriage, of love, made her cramp with whatever hurt her husband was feeling.

"Alex?"

"Yeah," Alex said into the phone.

"Listen. It's in the paper tonight. They list the names of the passengers. This is gonna sound crazy, but their names are spelled wrong. It says Carl and Virginia Just*ern*. So I wasn't sure. That's why I had to . . . but it's them. It's them. It says Carl and Virginia Justern from New York."

"They prob'ly couldn't read my dad's handwriting. He writes really terrible."

"You want me to come out there?"

"What?"

"You want me to come to Chicago? I'll be there tomorrow, if you want."

"Chicago?"

"Alex, is Patty there? Lemme speak to her."

"My mom writes perfect. Really beautiful. They couldn'ta read her writing or they woulda got it right."

"Alex . . ."

"I'm gonna hang up now, okay?"

"Yeah. Look—"

"I don't think I can talk anymore. I'm just gonna hang up."

"Alex . . ."

Alex gently clicked the receiver down and gingerly let the phone slip from his fingers. He turned to face his wife and son with death in his eyes.

The door to his son's room was open, as it always was at night. He heard Russell's eight-year-old snores, sweet rasps that now seemed very much an indication of life from within the shadows. Alex decided the boy was too young to have nightmares carried to him in the middle of the night, so he closed the door, perhaps an inch, but enough to make him feel he had somehow protected him as only a father could.

Taking one step back across the narrow hall to better peer through the crack in the door, Alex watched his son's chest rise and fall with each heavy breath of sleep. And suddenly Alex could tell Russell was only feigning peace. The fake motion, the overly dramatic noises—he recognized them from his own youth and knew that Russell was awake. There was something vulnerable in the boy's lie and Alex thought perhaps he'd let it stand; he'd let the boy have his night of peaceful dreams. But he stood watching too quietly, for Russell opened an eye, anticipating the success of his ruse. The eye blinked closed instantly and was followed by a turn imbued with the false nonchalance of this phony sleep. Alex slid into the room, moved to the single bed in the corner, and eased himself into a small space on top of the rumpled blanket.

"Russ," Alex whispered.

The boy didn't budge.

"Russ," Alex said again, louder than a whisper, not yet a normal tone of voice. He touched the boy on top of the head, gently shifting the head from side to side with his palm. Russell could pretend no more, so he yawned and looked up sleepy-eyed at his dad.

"You up, Russ?"

"I guess so." Stre-e-e-tch. An overdone look of little-boy innocence. "Is it morning?"

He's good, Alex thought. *He's a good pretender, better than I was at his age.* And he suddenly remembered one night, God, maybe twenty years before, when Ginny had come into his room. He was lying awake long past his bedtime, in the dark, going over and over and over again a play he'd blown in Little League. His mother looked beautiful, a queen in a cotton night-gown, the one that always rustled along the floor, an advance whisper of her presence. It was a Monday night; he remembered that because Mondays were when his dad played clarinet down in the Village. Usually his mom went to the small club, dutifully sat in the back of the room with friends or alone, sometimes with Alex, and sipped her two Scotch-and-waters on the rocks. This Monday night long ago, she came home early, which she had never done before. Something was wrong, he could tell; his dad was not with her. There was no whispering, no echo of footsteps. Everything was too still. He turned immediately, scrunched up into a sleeping position, began to snore and breathe through his mouth. She rustled into his room, he felt his bed dip under her weight, felt her hand stroke his hair.

He didn't move, never asked her what was wrong, never found out why she was home all alone, *never* found out what it was that made her sit with him, silently touching him. Now, twenty years later, he knew she must have seen through him, had only let him pretend to sleep. He wanted to cry out because somehow he felt he had hurt her then, had not done what he was supposed to do. Had not comforted her when now it was too late for him to ever comfort her or apologize or tell her that he loved her very much.

"Dad?"

Alex looked down at Russell.

"Why'd you wake me up?"

Alex didn't answer. He wiped a useless tear from his cheek.

"Dad?"

"Yeah," Alex said. "Yeah," and coughed away his grief. "I wanna talk to you."

"About Granny and Gramps?"

"Uh-huh." Smart. Kids are smart. They pick up.

"I know something bad happened."

"Yeah." He swallowed, but there was nothing to swallow. "Something bad did happen."

"Are they dead?"

Alex wiped his eyes again.

"Russ, do you know what that is? Death?"

Russell nodded unsurely. "It's when people get real sick and then they go away."

"You're right, in a way. People do go away when they're . . . when they . . ." *Say it!* ". . . when they're dead." Alex wiped the cold sweat from his forehead. "But there's all sorts of reasons. Sometimes things happen. Sometimes things just happen to people and then they're dead." What else could he say? He was a father and fathers were supposed to have answers. Only he didn't. He had questions, plenty of questions. He didn't understand what had happened either.

"What happened to Granny and Gramps? Why did they get dead?"

"They went on a plane ride. And the plane had an accident." And so they screamed but it wouldn't have done them any good because they were on fire and they couldn't breathe and they were dead!

"Did it hurt?"

"I don't know. No." Yeah, sure it hurt, it killed. It hurt bad, had ripped them apart, made them bleed, and burst, and die.

"Is death good, Daddy?"

"What?" Russell never called him Daddy.

"Does it make you feel better? Does it make the bad things go away?"

Alex could barely speak now. "No, Russ."

"What does make the bad things go away?"

Alex was startled by the question. And saddened. "Do you have bad things, things you want to go away?"

"Sometimes."

"Death doesn't make bad things go away, Russ. Death makes *all* things go away. When you have bad things, you tell me. You come to me. *I'll* make them go away."

"Do you promise?"

Alex nodded. "Will you go to sleep now?"

"I'll try."

Alex kissed his son good-night. He stood up.

"Where are they now?"

Alex stopped. "Who?"

"Granny and Gramps."

"I don't know, Russ."

"In heaven?"

"I hope so."

"Did they do something bad?"

Alex caught his breath and then eased it out.

"What makes you ask that?"

" 'Cause they were punished. They musta done something bad."

Alex said nothing.

"Dad, did they do something bad?"

Still nothing from Alex.

"Did they, Dad?"

"Maybe," he said very slowly. He realized that his son had asked the very question that he himself had been asking over and over. Nothing happened that didn't deserve to happen. Alex believed that above all else. The harder you worked, the better you got. The better you got, the more likely it was you were going to be the best. When you were the best, you won. His parents had not won. They had most definitely lost. "Maybe they did," he said out loud. "Maybe they did do something wrong."

"Alex!"

Patty had come up behind them. In her flannel robe and funny slippers. He had never quite heard that tone in her voice before. It was fierce, sharp like an animal's claws.

"Alex, God!" Patty hissed.

"Did they?" Russell asked again.

"No, darling," Patty said. "They never, never in their lives. That's not why it happened."

"Then why?" Alex demanded. "Why?" And it came out loud; his deep, anguished voice seemed to fill the house.

"Alex. Please," Patty said softly. "Please."

"Then why?" he screamed, the first time Russell had ever

heard his father lose control. The scream was so loud, it scared him. If this bad thing had happened, how could his dad make *other* bad things disappear? More than hearing about death, this scream scared Russell. It was the first time he had ever seen his father cry.

"Hello."

"Elliot? Shit. I've been tryin' to call you all night."

"I've been out."

Cold. Stiff. They were strangers.

"Did you get any of my messages?"

"Yes."

"Elliot, do you . . . I mean . . . Jesus, do you *know?*"

Yes, he knew. Of course he knew. Alex could hear his little brother controlling whatever turbulent emotions were swirling around inside him. And he remembered something. Today's deaths seemed inextricably tied to yesterday's memories. He remembered standing by his brother as the heavy metal brace was clasped over Elliot's leg, as the sweet face with the smart smile hardened into something as difficult to look at as the crippled leg.

"I know."

"Oh, Christ, Elliot, why didn't you call me?"

"Alex?"

"Yeah."

"I hear somebody else talking."

Elliot was right. Somewhere a crossed wire was letting in the faint drone of two women cackling in the background.

"He was gorgeous!" Alex heard one of the women say.

"Alex?"

"What?"

"I don't know exactly what I'm supposed to do."

"About what?"

"I don't know. Everything."

"Yeah."

"I'll be through with law school in the summer. Where am I supposed to go? That's what I've been thinking of. Where am I supposed to go when I'm supposed to go home?"

"I'm telling you, the fish was incredible!" one of the women burst in.

"Try not to worry about stuff like money or . . . home. I mean, I don't have that much, but you know wherever Patty and I are, or whatever we got . . ."

"Not only that," a shrill voice interrupted, *"I swear to God, Ellen, he wanted me to pay for my share! After that dinner!"*

". . . and there'll be lawyers or somethin'. I mean, I guess there's a will and all that."

"Listen, Alex. I'm not really thinking about that kind of stuff. I just don't want to think about . . . you know . . . about . . . about . . . them."

"I know, kid."

"They never even landed! They never even got there!"

"I know."

"Mom never even got to taste a . . . what is it? What did she want so bad?"

"A mai tai."

"Yeah. She wouldn't ever drink one in New York, remember? 'It can't be as good,' she said. 'I'll wait till we get to Hawaii.' "

"Yeah."

"She died without ever drinking a fucking mai tai."

"Did you kiss him?"

"Are you kidding?"

"He is cute."

"Cute but chuh-eeeeep!"

"Elliot, come on out here. Tomorrow."

Silence.

"Elliot. I want you to come out here. I . . . I think we should be together."

Only strained breathing, no answer. Now Alex desperately wanted to see his brother. He wanted to go back to the days when they were friends. He wanted to hug Elliot, to feel the flesh that he knew would still be familiar from the days when they slapped each other on the back and he gave the boy piggyback rides when they were supposed to be in bed. Alex wanted to see Elliot and to tell him that they were family and would be family forever. Teammates never to be traded.

"Get on a plane tomorrow morning, okay?"

"I can't get on a plane. No." Alex felt Elliot shiver all those miles away. "I couldn't."

"Okay. Then catch the first train, okay?"

"Syl, I think there's someone on the line!"

"Elliot, okay?"

Silence.

"Ellen?"

"Syl?"

Silence. Why wasn't he answering? What was wrong? What was happening? Where was his brother?

"Elliot?"

Click.

Silence.

"I'll call you back, Syl."

"Good-bye."

Silence.

Silence.

He listened to the buzz of the telephone. It was humming a warning that it was off the hook. He already knew that. He had done it hours ago to stop the calls.

He was awake. He had taken a sleeping pill for the first time in his life but he was awake and he knew he would be all night. He did not really want to fall asleep, he was not yet ready to relinquish his hold on the pain. It was as if his anguish was somehow a tenuous tie to his parents, keeping them flickeringly alive. But he was even more afraid of consciousness, his visions were scaring him. Over and over again he saw them, heard them. They were in that plane, quiet, waiting. And then their faces were giant, distorted, screaming images of agony. He tried desperately to imagine what they must have felt, thought, but he could not, even in his most desperate stretches, imagine that kind of fear. And so he lay awake, sweating, clammy, despite the cold and the sound of the frigid wind banging shutters against the old house.

Patty was quiet, but she was also awake. He knew she would lie there next to him all night if need be, prepared to give him whatever he needed, even silence. He took a deep breath and grazed his hand against her blanket-covered knee. He was comforted that, even under two layers of wool, the leg felt familiar to him.

"My darling," she said.

"What?"

"Nothing. I just wanted to call you 'my darling.'"

"Thank you."

She smiled.

"I keep seeing them," he said.

She said nothing.

"I just keep seeing them dying."

"I see them too," she said. He winced at the ugliness. "But maybe I'm seeing something different from you."

"I hope so," he said.

"I'm seeing them comforted because they're together. And I see them calm. Holding hands."

"You're right," he lied. "That's now what I'm seeing."

"Can I turn the TV off?"

"No. It's almost time."

"Alex. I don't know if I can watch this."

He said nothing and she stayed, unwillingly, but she stayed, and somehow time drifted and it was on. The newscaster was telling about the second largest air disaster ever in America. A hundred and thirty-three dead. Crashed into the mountains. Cause unknown. There were pictures of the wreckage, flames, bodies.

Finally, Patty jumped up out of bed and, with a shaking hand, switched off the television. She stood by the set, looking at her husband. Alex's eyes were closed. He had not moved for several minutes. He could have been asleep. Unhearing, uncaring. She quietly got back into bed with him, putting her arms around him, settling her head on his chest.

"Patty," Alex said finally.

"What?" she whispered.

"Russ is afraid. I'm sorry I scared him."

"You didn't scare him. He's just never felt anything like this before."

"Neither have I." She watched him chew on his lip. She didn't know what he was thinking. Without moving he said, "What'll happen to him?"

"To Russ?"

Alex nodded. "In California. And after that. When we're old. When we're dead. What's going to happen?"

She smiled sadly. "I don't know."

"What's going to happen to us?"

"We'll be all right."

"What's going to happen to me?"

"Go to sleep, Alex. Please."

"That's what'll happen to me. I'll go to sleep."

She kissed him on the forehead, slipped her arms around him, and gently rocked him all through the night.

Alex, Patty, and Russell flew back to New York for the funeral service. It was a small crowd. Ginny and Carl did not have a lot of friends. Their energy was spent on their family and on themselves. They had once told Alex they'd started as a world of two. Then, with Alex and Elliot, they became a world of four. When Alex and Patty got married, Carl and Ginny told them they were proud to become a world of five.

Danny was at the service, of course, and Alex was glad. They shook hands, then hugged. There was no need to say much. Words were unnecessary, would have been intrusive. There were several moments when Alex wanted to laugh to break the tension, and if, waiting for the funeral to begin, Danny had spoken, he would have. Instead, Danny would merely raise an eye—at an ugly sport jacket or a particularly fat relative—and they were able to share the moment silently, comfortingly.

Elliot was there too. Alex had not been sure he would come. He wore a suit, dark blue; Alex did not know that his little brother had even owned a suit.

Alex didn't go over to Elliot. He didn't know how to do it or even what to say. Danny tried to edge him over. Patty tried to tug him. But he passively resisted. He wouldn't let himself be led.

Danny went to Elliot. Alex watched them talk. They seemed

relaxed and friendly. Danny sympathetically put his arm around the boy's shoulder. It was then that Alex realized his brother was not on crutches.

Surprised, he watched Elliot move to talk to Patty. There was a bad limp, and the outline and bulk of the brace was evident under the suit pants, but there were no crutches.

Alex started to cry right then. Only for a moment. He stopped himself. And then when he looked up, Elliot was talking to Russell. He was smiling at Alex's son, nodding. Russ looked solemn; he was listening intently.

Alex took a deep breath and moved to them.

"Hello," he said to his brother.

Elliot nodded.

"Are you all right?" Alex asked.

Elliot nodded again.

Alex smiled at Russell. "What were you two talking about?"

Now Elliot smiled. The meanness behind the smile made Alex blink.

"I asked Uncle Elliot if you used to get rid of bad things for him."

"And what did Uncle Elliot say?"

"He said that you used to."

"Did I?" Alex asked his brother.

Elliot just smiled again.

"You look good," Alex told him.

"Thank you."

"You're walking better."

"No crutches."

"You don't look—" Alex stopped himself.

"Like a cripple?" Elliot finished.

"Yes."

"But I still think like one," Elliot said. "And that's the important thing."

"What have I done to you?" Alex asked suddenly. His voice was almost a whisper. "What have I done? Here, I'm askin' you. I don't get it. I don't understand. I've tried to . . . to love you. I've tried to . . ." He stopped. Coughed. Wiped a couple of drops of sweat off his forehead. "What can I do? What do I have to do to make things the way they were?"

"Maybe things were never the way you thought."

"Is that true? Is that *true?*"

"I don't know. I don't remember the way things were. I only know the way things are."

"That's sad."

"Maybe. I don't know. I think when you start finding stuff out, most of the stuff you find out is sad."

Neither brother spoke for several seconds. Alex took Russell's hand and held it tightly.

"You have a nice son," Elliot said. "Be careful."

"Of what?"

Elliot didn't answer. Instead, he turned away.

"Wait," Alex said. "I can—"

"No," Elliot said. "No, you can't. And please don't try." Alex's little brother looked over at the small crowd of people, now moving into an adjoining room. "Let's go," he said. "I think the funeral's about to begin."

14

The station wagon rattled as it turned into the driveway, scraping over the double bump meant to slow down to a crawl all cars turning into the gray parking lot. It was a dazzling, cheery, sunny day and the asbestos ground was streaked with patches of bright white; the painted green lines delineating parking spaces looked phosphorescent. Box boys in red-striped aprons politely loaded bulging paper bags into trunks and backseats; women in stretch pants briskly wheeled shopping carts and tiny toddlers. The glass building loomed over La Brea Avenue like a transparent dinosaur.

Patty Justin climbed out of the passenger's door, made sure her shopping list was in her purse, and locked the door.

"You don't have to lock it," the driver told Patty. "People don't steal in L.A. And besides," she said, jerking her head at the inside of the car, "there's nothin' worth stealin'."

Patty nodded, impressed, and unlocked the door with a grand flourish. Then they walked past the newspaper dispensers and mechanical rocking horse—one ride for one dime—stepped on the rubber mat that activated the electric sliding door, and walked into Ralph's Supermarket.

Patty waited until both their carts were planted firmly in front of the frozen food section before wondering aloud about the real reason Walter Lumpano's beautiful blond wife had insisted on her company for this little grocery excursion.

"What was so urgent," Patty asked with a smile, "that I had to leave my soaps and my Mr. Clean?"

Emmaline Lumpano picked out one frozen broccoli and one peas-and-carrots combo. She then removed her sunglasses to reveal an ugly wound, raw looking and purple.

"Lump's started to beat the shit out of me," she said.

"It happened once before. That's it," Emmy said, maneuvering toward the dry cereal. Her glasses were back in place, covering the spot where the Lump's fist had met her eye.

"My God," was all Patty could say. "Leave him."

Emmy laughed. "No, thank you. Where would I go?"

"Stay with us."

"Oh, sure. I'll bunk out with little Russell."

"Well, you've got to do something!" Patty realized she was on the verge of becoming hysterical. It was Emmy who'd been hit, why wasn't *she* upset?

"Ain't nothin' to be done," Emmy said, and shrugged. That was that.

"Was it an accident?"

"Hell, no."

"What happened?" Patty forced herself to be calm, as soothing as possible. She was scared by the proximity of this violence. But, she thought, Emmy had to be even more scared.

"Drink, drugs, and sex happened," Emmy said. "The usual Lump special. He took greenies to get up for the game, drank a half bottle of bourbon and a six-pack *after* the game, and then wanted to have sex."

"You didn't?"

"There was no way that lug was goin' muff divin' in his condition."

"What'd he do?"

Emmy tapped the left side of her glasses in case Patty had forgotten the results of the battle.

They rolled down the aisle together in silence.

"You're a lucky woman," Emmy told Patty when they hit Pet Food.

"I know."

"Do you?"

"Yes," Patty said. "Oh, yes."

"Good."

"Only . . ."

"Only?"

"It's probably nothing," Patty decided. "I don't know why I'm even telling you. Especially now. I mean, here you are beaten up and wanting sympathy . . ."

"I don't want sympathy, doll. I just want witnesses. I want somebody to know about it, is all."

"Well, whatever. But this isn't the time to be telling you. I don't know why I said anything." But she did know. She decided to talk to "Mrs. Lump" because she was tall and slim and tan and wore too-tight pants and too-low-cut dresses and exuded sex and even though, granted, Emmy was not the brightest girl in the world, all this added up to the fact that there was something about her that Patty trusted. Good looks and confident chatter, in Patty's mind, meant a kind of instinctual wisdom, a street-smart invincibility that Patty wanted to understand and possess. And seeing Emmy's vulnerability somehow made her even more perfect to confide in. Besides, Emmy was the only real friend Patty had made in the four months she had been in Los Angeles, and right now Patty felt the vague inkling that she needed to talk to a friend.

"It's really nothing," Patty said.

"Well, tell me anyway," Emmy responded. "Even if it's nothing. I've said everything I intend to say about my little misfortune."

"There's nothing specific. But he's been different. Alex, I mean, of course. Ever since his parents were . . . uh . . . died."

"What's he been, real depressed like?"

"No, that's the thing. He hasn't."

"I don't get ya."

Patty sighed. "He *looks* at me different. That's what's wrong. Lately he looks at me different."

"That's it?"

Patty smiled sadly. "And I don't know what he's thinking."

Emmaline Lumpano pointed at the check-out line, indicating she was ready to go.

"Do you still fuck, sweetie?"

Patty turned beet red. Embarrassed that she was so embarrassed, she picked up one last can of soup and nodded.

"Is it still good?"

Still red, Patty nodded again. Her eyes turned soft and vulnerable at the thought of sex with Alex, at the way he liked to lie on top of her, resting, while she stretched out on her stomach, and he would rub his muscular chest over her bare back. She nodded more vehemently.

"Does he hit you?"

The smile disappeared. "God, no."

"The kid?"

"Does he hit Russell?"

Emmy nodded.

"I don't think he's ever even spanked him! No, no. Russell's very special to Alex. They're very close. Alex—"

"Is he late for dinner?"

Patty shook her head.

"Does he ever disappear for days on end? Make you dress up sexy and tease the dicks off his friends? Or call you names and make you feel like shit?"

"No," Patty said.

"Well, whadduz he do?"

"Nothing," Patty admitted. "He's flawless."

Emmy whistled, finished lip-glossing her sweet lips, smiled flirtatiously at the pimply checker, and paid for her groceries.

"Do you think in twos?" Patty asked as they turned onto the road coming out of the parking lot.

"Come again?"

"I think of 'me' as 'us.' I'm two people, me and Alex. We're one person, Alexandpatty."

"That's nice. That's real nice. Like I said, you're lucky," Emmy said, and meant it. "I know the Lump doesn't think like that. I don't even think he can *count* to two."

"I don't think Alex does. He says he does but he doesn't. Not really. He thinks there *is* an Alexandpatty. And an AlexandpattyandRussell. But it's different. He's separate too. He's definitely separate."

"Let's get us some lunch, Patricia. My treat."

"It's not easy bein' married to a ballplayer. They're little boys, only big is all, and they're used to people cheerin' every time they move their little finger."

"I know," Patty said. "But he is one, and I know that's partly what I love about him."

Emmy nodded. "So let's hear some of yours," she said knowingly.

"Some of my what?"

"Bein'-married-to-a-ballplayer stories. Everybody's got 'em."

"I don't . . ."

"Bein' alone when the kid's got the mumps, havin' the hubby forget an anniversary on account of a doubleheader. You know. Bein'-married-to-a-ballplayer stories."

Patty grew silent. She stared ahead at the waitress carrying over her spinach salad. When the greens were put in front of her and the waitress was heading off across the room, Patty lifted her head and spoke quietly to Emmy.

"When Russ was born," she said. "That's my only story. That's my only one. Honest."

"Give."

"We hadn't been married very long. In fact . . ." She blushed again, deeply. "Russ was, uh . . . we had just started to . . ."

"I know how those things are."

"Well. Alex was in Schenectady, his first season in 'A' Ball. And that summer and fall before he left, we had . . . you know."

"I know. Believe me, I know."

Patty didn't know why she was telling these things to Emmy. She had never told these things to anyone and here she was blabbing to a casual friend, a bleached blond shopping companion. But she found that she couldn't stop. Couldn't stop talking, couldn't stop thinking. About that summer and the wonderful, wonderful first time with Alex, and then the sneaking around and all the times when they only had half an hour before they heard a key turn in a locked front door. And how Alex always said it was perfect, *perfect*, and she wanted it to be, she almost willed it to be, and it was, it was for her, but she knew, somehow, there was something that was not right, something was missing. She was sure it was her fault, sure she was doing something wrong, sure that Alex would notice how afraid she was. She loved him God-oh-so-much but maybe that wasn't enough to make up for whatever it was that was wrong, that was her fear.

But they had to be doing something right, because he went off to Schenectady, much closer than North Carolina, and she started feeling funny and thought she was sick, only she was pregnant. So she called him from a phone booth on First Avenue. She didn't say "Hello" or "It's me," she just said, "Alex, I'm going to have a baby. What should I do?" She had to say "Alex?" again before he answered. And he answered slowly, carefully, "I guess we'll get married." She started to cry, right there in this smelly phone booth and he said, "What's the matter? Don't you wanna?" And she said, "Yes, yes, I do. Do you?" And he said, "I do. I really do. You can stop crying, because I love you and I really want to get married, and this is a happy thing, not a sad thing."

So they got married. She was so happy and so in love that nothing else mattered. Not the fact that she was seventeen years old and pregnant, not the fact that they didn't have much money, not even the fact that she couldn't go to college now. None of that was important, because she had Alex. Sweet Alex. Strong Alex. Perfect Alex.

And her fear gradually faded. Things were perfect. Had been, always would be. Except . . . except. Except when Russell was born.

Alex was playing winter ball. In Havana. The Havana Sugar Kings. She had come down for a while and it was wonderful.

The sun and the glory of being on a tiny little island where people spoke Spanish and led horses through the center of town and toasted Americans as they passed by the outdoor cafés. It was splendid! She got fatter and happier and then the baby was due soon. They decided she should go home, back to New York, to stay with her mother; the baby should be born at home. He would come back a week before the due date and be with her, stay for a while, then return to Cuba until the season was over in February. But the baby came early. Two weeks early. Patty was awakened by a terrible pain, *terrible,* scary, and her mother took her to the hospital at three in the morning. They took Russell from her while she screamed and gasped and moaned and cried out for Alex. But he was in Havana, sleeping soundly before going out to play a day game. She thought the pain was going to destroy her, but of course it didn't, and Alex came the next day. He paced in her hospital room and told her how much he loved her, how beautiful their son was, how sorry he was he hadn't been there. It was all right, she told him. She told him it was all right over and over again. To herself she admitted he had let her be separate and that she had had the pain all to herself. But it was still all right. It *was.* It didn't matter. It was all right.

"That's my only story," Patty said to Emmy. "Not much, really. Not his fault, that's for sure. And other than that . . ."

"I know," Emmy said. "Flawless."

"You wanna know why I married the Lump?" Emmy asked. They were back in the car, through with the meal, heading home.

"If I can ask you a question first?"

"Anything."

Patty smiled. "Doesn't it bother you being married to someone you call 'the Lump'?"

"Do you want to know why I married *Walter?*" Emmy asked haughtily.

"Because you love him."

"Well, sure I love him. Sort of. I wouldn't marry someone I

didn't love. But love, that's not the only reason for getting married."

"It isn't?"

Emmy snorted. "What do you see when you look over here?" She spread her hand over herself, tapping her head and waving down toward her feet. Patty shrugged, confused, and Emmy said, "I'll tell you what you see: one hot number. Minus the left eye right now, one hot number, right?"

"Right," Patty agreed.

"Yeah. Most people take a look at this tight little bod and they think, *Well, that's all there is, that's what she is, that's all she'll ever be.*"

"Wrong, right?"

Emmy shook her blond head. "I got something. Something special that most people ain't got."

Patty waited. Finally, when Emmy went no farther, she had to ask, "What?"

Emmy Lumpano nodded solemnly. "I know what I want."

This was, as far as Patty could sense, a great revelation. She almost grinned but sensed this was far too important to her friend to be taken lightly.

"That is," Emmy went on, "the single most important thing in life. To know what you want."

"And what," Patty asked, "do you want?"

Emmy smiled serenely.

"I want to be a TV weathergirl."

Patty rolled down the window on her side of the car. She took a deep breath. She rolled the window back up. Took another breath. The window went down and stayed there.

"Listen," Emmy said. "Here I am married to the best ballplayer in Los Angeles, nothing against Alex, Patty. But the Lump, if the Angels were halfway decent, he'd be in line for the MVP. So when he's up at the plate, people talk about him, *announcers* talk about him. And his attractive wife, Emmaline, they talk about her too. When the game's on TV they show a close-up of his adoring wife, who chews on her nail waiting for her hero to hit a home run. So I'm on TV and then the next step is the magazines, and there I am in my living room looking pretty, like the perfect wife, and I start saying how I love people and spreading good news and *bam* I'm a sensation and local shows start calling me up and I go on, give a few recipes, you know, then the next thing, before you can snap your fingers . . . ta daaaa . . . I'm a weathergirl."

Emmy looked over at her wide-eyed passenger.

"Now, there's a point to that story—I mean, why I'm telling you all this, Patty girl. I love the Lump and all that, and I'm a damn good wife, too, considering what a disgusting slob he is. But the thing is you've gotta know what you want out of your marriage. If he hits me every so often, well, I don't like it much, but it comes with the territory."

"Uh-huh" were the first words Patty could utter.

"So? What is it you want?"

"What do I want?"

"Out of your marriage?"

"Nothing," Patty said. "I don't think I want anything out of it."

"Everybody," Emmy told her, "wants something out of everything."

"I don't know about that," Patty said.

"I do."

"I think I just want," Patty began, "I think I just want everything to be perfect."

"Oh," Emmy said. "Ohhhhh. Is that all?"

The phone was ringing in Alex's hotel room. Alex didn't notice, however. He was too busy watching the Lump throw up.

"Oh, Christ! Jesus, Lump! Holy shit!"

"Bwaaaa . . . bwaaaa . . . bleahhhhh."

"Oh, shit! Lump! Get into the bathroom! Or the fuckin' hallway at least. Oh, my god!"

"Whoooaaahhh . . . oohhh . . . eeeeeyyyeeaaahhhhhh."

"Oh, fuck!"

"Hey," the girl said, "the phone's ringing."

"What?"

"The phone."

Alex watched the puddle of the Lump's vomit curl under his

bed. He turned away, disgusted, and tried to focus on the sexy little girl in the T-shirt who was standing, horrified, in the corner, as far away from the Lump's choking noises as she could. She was pointing to the telephone.

"Oh," Alex said, and picked up the receiver. "Yeah?" he said dourly to whoever was calling.

"Hi," Patty said.

Alex snapped his fingers, hoping that everyone would understand that meant to shut the hell up.

"Hi," he said, and realized he didn't sound too thrilled. So he put some zip on it. *"Hi!"*

"Everything okay?"

"Sure. Sure. Everything's great."

"What's going on there?"

"Whaddya mean?"

"I hear a lot of noise."

"Yeah. Well. Listen," he said, lowering his voice in a strictly confidential whisper. "Lump's here getting sick all over my room. It's kinda ugly."

"Do you want to call me back?"

"No. He'll be throwin' up all night, so it won't make any difference."

The girl guided Lump into the bathroom, much to Alex's relief. He hoped she'd come back out to clean the puke off the carpet.

"I miss you," he told Patty. "Boy, do I miss you."

"You do?"

"Patty . . ."

"Are you shaking your head and smiling?"

"Uh-huh."

"Why?"

"Because I *always* miss you and you're always shocked when I tell you."

"Uh-huh. I'm grinning too."

"Why?" he said, and for the first time in the conversation his voice had that special softness, that little lilting high pitch, that meant he was talking to someone he loved, to his wife.

"I'm grinning because I can tell you want to be annoyed but

you're sitting there thinking I'm too cute for you to get angry at."

"You are pretty cute," he admitted. "Annoying but cute."

"When do you come home?"

"You tell me."

"Wednesday."

"Why do you always ask when you always know?"

"I just like to hear you say it. It sounds more real when you say it."

"Wednesday."

"Oh, good." She was relaxed now, he could tell. When they spoke on the phone she was always uncomfortable, even after all these years, for the first few moments. It was almost as if she was waiting to hear, from the tone of voice, whether he still loved her. Now that she was sure he did, she could ask whatever questions she wanted to ask. She did. "So what's happening with the Lump?"

"Look," Alex said into the phone, "you know what goes on on the road."

"I know. It makes me nervous."

"Well, it doesn't have to, 'cause it doesn't have anything to do with me." He lowered his voice just a little. "But the Lump has some Annie and he's been drinkin' like crazy and he just got sick."

"Oh, God. I just had lunch with Emmy today."

"Don't say anything to her."

"No, no. I wouldn't. But . . ."

"But what?"

"It just seems so . . . sleazy."

"It is."

"Why were they in your room?"

"Patty. 'Cause we're roommates. And 'cause the Lump's an asshole and he wanted to show her off. You know the way he is. They were all rowdy and we were just havin' fun. But then he got sick. Man, did he get sick."

"Alex?"

"What?"

He anticipated her, knew from the way she said his name, got the timing exactly right, so they said, at the same moment, "I love you."

"Don't be so smart," she said. "How did you know that's what I was going to say?"

" 'Cause that's what you always say when you sound all timid and I'm telling you about sex in Baltimore."

"You really don't ever do anything," she told him, "but you can always make me feel better."

"Good," he said, and he thought of Patty in her apron; for some reason he pictured her with a paintbrush in her hand, green paint in her hair, down on her hands and knees painting the kitchen of their first apartment, the one in Schenectady. "I like to make you feel better. That's my job."

"Yes." He listened to her breath on the phone. He could swear he was smelling its familiar sweet odor through the wires. "Do you want to go to sleep?" she asked.

"Got a day game tomorrow. I have to get up early."

"Okay, my love."

"Thank you. I like when you call me that."

"Well, that's what you are."

"Yes."

"Good night."

"Sweet dreams."

They each blew a kiss at the other and Alex hung up the phone. He thought about how much he loved her, needed her, and how he hoped they would be together forever. He turned to the skinny girl, who was just coming out of his bathroom.

"Is everything cleaned up?" he asked.

She nodded.

"How about you?"

"I took a shower. That's why I was in there so long."

"Good."

She twirled her hair and looked confused.

"Well," he said. "It's late."

"So, listen," she said, still twirling her hair. He listened but she didn't say anything.

"What?" he asked finally.

"I don't have anyone to fuck tonight."

"Yeah." Alex nodded sympathetically. "That's rough."

"I was supposed to fuck a ballplayer tonight."

"Your momma must've told you there'd be nights like this."

"Shoot."

He saw the lightbulb go on over her head even before she realized it had lit up.

"*You're* a ballplayer," she said. He nodded. "What's your name?"

"Ruth. Babe Ruth."

"You wanna fuck me?"

He shook his head. She grabbed her T-shirt and, in one jerk, pulled it up over her head and off. She tossed it on the floor as she shook her tiny breasts at him.

"You can fuck me up the ass," she said. "I won't mind."

He thought about it. He really did. But she knew the answer before he opened his mouth.

"You're not gonna do it, are you?"

"Uh . . ."

"You don't wanna, do ya?"

"No." He shook his head. "No. I don't wanna."

"Why not?"

"I'm married."

Her mouth dropped open in astonishment. Alex looked down, partly embarrassed at his own righteousness, partly afraid to look at her because then he might just go ahead and fuck her. Up the ass.

When he did look up at her, finally, he caught the last flash of her tits disappearing under the T-shirt. She stared at him and he thought he saw, in her eyes, a hint of understanding, a touch of respect for his morality. She smiled at him, he was sure with a trace of approval. And she spoke.

"Cripes," is what she said. "You are one flaming asshole."

15

It was the next night. The Orioles had beaten the Angels four to one.

"There he is."

"Where?"

"In the back. Off to the side."

"Where?"

"In the *back.*"

"Oh, yeah. I see 'im. The scum bag."

A gray-haired man in a shiny tuxedo came up to them. He tipped his head forward in a formal greeting. "May I help you, gentlemen?"

"We're with him." The Lump pointed and the maître d' turned.

"Dave Manning," Alex said to clarify.

"Ah," the maître d' said. "Mr. Manning."

"Yeah."

The maître d' led them to Dave Manning's table.

"Ah," the Lump said. "Mr. Manning." He then contemptuously coughed some phlegm into his throat.

"Lump," Manning started to warn.

"Too late," Alex said, as the Lump hocked a giant loogie onto the gleaming wood floor.

"Sit down, would ya," Manning said, annoyed.

"What is this bullshit?" the Lump asked.

"This is a classy restaurant. I come here a lot. They know me here, and believe me, they will not be thrilled that I brought in a new customer who spits snot on the floor."

"Get that guy in the monkey suit to lick it up. He looks like he'd do it for a fin."

Manning laughed. "You're a total jerk-off, but you *are* perceptive." He turned to Alex and said, "It's good to see you."

"*I'm* a jerk-off?" Lump shouted. "What about Alex?"

"What'd he do now?"

"I didn't fuck one of Lump's Annies."

"Sixteen years old, for Chrissake, with nipples the size of that fuckin' ashtray."

"Where were *you?*"

"He was off pukin' his guts out," Alex said.

"Some things never change," Manning said to Alex.

"*Most* things never change," Alex said.

Manning smiled. "Just the way you like it."

Alex nodded. "That's the best thing about baseball. Always different but always the same."

"Hey, fish-breath. If they know you so good, whaddo I have to do to get a fuckin' drink around here?"

Manning waved at the waiter, who came and took their orders. Manning asked for a dry vodka martini, the Lump for a boilermaker, and Alex for a bourbon and soda.

"At least *some* things change." Manning tapped Alex's bourbon when it arrived. "No more milk."

"What's that?" the Lump asked. "That piss they get from cows?"

"*You* drink too much," Manning said.

"Bullshit," the Lump answered.

"Why didn't you play today?"

"Sick."

"Sick from what?"

"Flu."

"Hung over," Alex said. "He could barely make it to the park."

"I coulda pinch hit."

"You *did* pinch hit."

"I did? Oh, yeah." The Lump drank three quarters of the stein of beer in one gulp. "How'd I do?"

"I struck you out," Manning told him.

"Damn! That's right. Shit."

"Three pitches."

"Fuck you!"

"You pitched a helluva game," Alex said.

"I was sharp."

"You're always sharp these days."

Manning nodded. "It's been a good year."

"You guys look like you might go all the way."

"It's a good team."

"We suck," the Lump threw in. "I'm the only decent ball-player on the whole fuckin' team."

"You're not playin' that much, Alex," Manning said, concerned. "What's goin' on?"

"Kids," Alex told him. "They're goin' with the kids."

"I'm in my fuckin' prime, I'll tell ya that!" the Lump mumbled.

Manning had quietly signaled for another round and the drinks arrived. They drank quietly for a minute. Alex broke the silence.

"I heard from Dotty," he told Manning.

"Who?"

"You know. Scott's wife. Ex-wife. Whatever you call her now."

"Oh, yeah."

"She called me."

"How come?"

"Oh, somethin' with his insurance payments. She collects it now."

"Yeah. I always figured that's why she married him. Why else would you marry a—"

"Somebody might as well collect it."

"I guess." Manning shrugged.

"Anyway, the company's tryin' to screw her out of it or they're goin' out of business or something. They missed a coupla payments. She thought maybe I could help. Get her a lawyer or somethin'."

"Did you?"

"I made a few calls. Yeah. I think I helped."

"Why'd she call *you?*"

Alex cracked his knuckles. "He told her to. 'Keep in touch with ol' Alex,' he said. So she keeps in touch." Alex smiled. "I can really hear him saying that, you know."

"Christ," Manning said. "How long's he been dead?"

"Four years."

"Christ," he said again. *"Christ."*

"Dotty," the Lump blurted. "If I remember, she looked like she might also have nipples the size of that fuckin' ashtray."

"Shut up, Lump," Manning said.

"Maybe I have her mixed up with somebody else."

"You guys *really* good enough to get to the Series?" Alex asked Manning.

"Maybe. We're pretty good."

"You got a shot at the Cy Young Award."

"A shot."

"Well, you're certainly takin' it in stride," Alex noted as the Lump ordered another drink.

"We'll see what happens."

"Damn, I'd like to play in a Series!" Alex said.

"Would you?" Manning asked, and Alex had a sudden flash back to Wilson. Manning's voice dripped, for that one quick line, with minor league contempt. There was, suddenly, layer upon layer of that old Dave Manning mystery, of challenge, of that disturbing façade. Alex looked over at Manning, who smiled innocently, questioningly, and Alex felt foolish at his suspicions. Manning was just a fucking cynic and that's all there was to it. No magic, no mystical bullshit. So, shit, he thought, what was it about Dave Manning?

"You probably will, Judge."

"What?"

"Get to play in a Series."

"Oh." Alex nodded. "Damn, I hope so."

"Not with the fuckin' bunch of buttholes we're playin' with

now, I'll tell ya that," the Lump tossed in, and signaled for yet another drink.

"You're drunk again," Alex said.

"Am not."

"You *are*. You're drunk every night."

"Fuck you."

"Always an argument winner," Manning said. Then he turned to Alex, waving a waiter over at the same time. "Let's order. The steaks here are great."

"The steaks suck!" the Lump decided.

Ignoring him, Alex said, "Medium rare with a cold beer for me."

"Exactly the same," Manning said to the waiter. "With some steak fries for the table."

"Steak fries suck!"

"Will you be ordering?" the waiter asked the Lump.

"You suck!" the Lump responded. When the waiter turned and headed back to the kitchen, the Lump jumped up from his seat, staggered over to the waiter, and tackled him. He pinned the man to the floor and sat on his chest and said, "I said you *suck*, buddy. What are you gonna do about it?" When the man didn't respond, silenced mostly by the terror of having a 220-pound animal kneeling on his torso, the Lump screamed, "Where're your fuckin' balls?" He screamed it again, then again, and again, until Manning and Alex were able to wrestle the catcher off to the side of the room.

"Get off me, you fuckin' pigs!" the Lump ordered.

"Jesus, he's strong," Alex muttered.

"Fuck! Fuuuuuuccccckkkkkk! Fuck!"

"Cover his mouth," Manning said.

"Are you crazy? He'll bite my fuckin' hand off!"

"Fuckin' pigs! FUUUUUUUUUCCCCCCCCCKKKKKKKKKK!!"

"Uh-oh," Alex said.

"What's the matter?"

"He's gonna throw up!"

"How can you tell?"

"I live with him. Trust me!"

"FUUUUUUCCCCC . . . oooooooooohhhhhhhhhhh."

They jumped off him in the nick of time. Manning looked at Alex gratefully. They stood above him, looking down at the Lump, who was now quietly curled up in the middle of the restaurant, moaning, face down in his own puke. They both became aware, the same second, that the restaurant was engulfed by a total silence, and that every single person in the room was swiveled around, staring at them.

"Mr. Manning," the maître d' said in an extraordinarily polite tone, "you are a good customer and this is very awkward."

"I think he wants you out," Alex said.

The maître d' nodded and his smile was not really a smile, rather something that seemed tied around his mouth to prevent him from screaming.

"Right," Manning said. And he looked at Alex, touching his shoulder. "I know you're thinking something," he said. "What are you thinking?"

"When we first met," Alex said, "when we were younger, I'm pretty sure I woulda thought this was funny."

"And?"

Alex shook his head. "Maybe gettin' older is thinkin' stuff isn't so funny."

"Maybe gettin' older," Manning said, "is just needing *new* stuff to think is funny. *Bigger* stuff."

"I'll tell ya," Alex said, bending down and grimacing. "I *never* thought I wouldn't think puking on the floor of a fancy restaurant wasn't funny!"

And Alex Justin and Dave Manning started to laugh. They laughed when they got the Lump on his feet, they laughed as they carried his dead weight through the restaurant, and, by the time they got him out on the streets of Baltimore, they were laughing so hard they were crying.

16

He came home on Wednesday, as promised. They didn't make love Wednesday night; he was too tired. They didn't make love Thursday morning; she'd never been really crazy about morning sex. Thursday night he had a game that she went to. They went out to a restaurant for a late-night supper, the Scandia, and he ordered a bottle of champagne. *French* champagne. Now it was two A.M. There was no music in the background, only her soft and happy murmuring.

"Mmmmmmmm," she said. "Mmmmmmmmmm."

Her voice had that same lilt to it, that soothing smoothness, the sense of such innocent passion. He smiled because, even after all this time, she still denied that she ever moaned, much less spoke, during sex. As his hand reached between her legs, he knew she'd compress her lips into that look that could either be pleasure or pain and she'd now go, "Oh. Oh, oh, oh."

"Oh," she said. "Oh, oh, oh."

She was dry, almost crusty, and even though his fingers were right on her favorite spot, twisting and massaging with pinpoint precision, she was not getting wet. He could feel her tense. Even though they had probably made love a thousand times, whenever she didn't get wet right away she viewed it as her own inadequacy. He put his hand farther inside her, massaged a bit harder, and when he pinched too hard he knew her eyes

would open and she would reach down to move his hand back
to where it had just been.

When her eyes closed again, he kissed her again. They still
kissed well together, although they didn't really do it too often
anymore, not *real* kissing. They pecked now—on the lips, on the
cheek, each other's hands, gently on a closed eyelid, on the top
of the head. They used to love real kissing. Now they only did it
when they had sex. He opened his mouth wide, her tongue
automatically went round the inside of his lips. When his tongue
penetrated deeply, reaching back to the roof of her mouth, she
nibbled gently, holding it prisoner, releasing it, snatching it
again, letting it go. He realized, as his lips now grazed downward along her chest, that she tasted so familiar, her breath was
no longer a new infusion of energy. It was as if they breathed as
one. There were no new positions for their lips. He couldn't
remember when they had surprised each other with a bite or
the withholding of a tongue tip.

His hand passed over the tiny mole on her breast. It used to
be an interesting aberration, one he would play with; now it was
just her breast.

He kissed her left nipple, wrapping it with his teeth, licking it
at the same time, and he knew she would now roll her head
back and say, "The other one."

He shifted his head and kissed her right breast, circled the
nipple with his kisses, bit down until she gently pulled his hair
with both hands and guided his head down toward her legs.

He went right for the cunt, as he knew she wanted him to. He
liked to lick her stomach, kiss her thighs, but she'd never enjoyed that. She was self-conscious about her stretch marks, and
the few tiny jiggles in her upper thighs. She was still in good
shape but, she felt, not good enough. She also got embarrassed
because she sometimes got tiny, blotchy red pimples on her
thighs and ass. She didn't like the spontaneity and lack of structure his tongue could have playing with her whole body. She
liked him to have a target, a goal. She loved oral sex, and so now
his tongue plunged right in and he licked and chewed and
pressed in and out until she suddenly twisted her body over his,
rolled him onto his back, and reciprocated.

She didn't massage his penis with her fingers, she never did that. She just took it right in her mouth and began sucking. Alex closed his eyes; Patty's head bobbed up and down, as a few quiet slurping noises came from her mouth.

.He thought of a girl he'd seen at the ballpark two days before.

And he got harder.

The fantasies started right after the plane crash.

He had sucked in his gut and suppressed his agony as best he could, rubbed dirt on the wound, and gone right back in the game. The night after the crash Patty had let him collapse and sleep. The night after that she lay next to him for as long as she could before, frustrated by the separateness of his grief, she decided to share it. She decided to ease her own pain by trying to ease his, which he did not want eased. She touched him.

When he turned away, over on his side, she moved with him, her body wrapping around and clinging to him.

She kissed him in between his shoulder blades. Rubbed his back tentatively, too carefully. Her fingers were too respectful of his injuries as they scratched through his hair.

She reached down and touched his penis, gently caressing it as if this would somehow restore what he had lost.

He was empty, drained, she didn't exist for him—he was alone. But he felt her need and he loved her and he *was* a performer. So he turned and kissed her. But he fantasized he was kissing someone else. He was shocked, but there it was. He tried to shut off his brain, but curiosity got the best of him and he let himself be carried off by his fantasy. It was almost as good as turning the lights off and making love in the pitch dark to Teddy Wilson's "Liza."

At first this someone was faceless. She was beautiful but she had no features. Then, as Patty kissed him, stroked him, guided him inside her, the image took form. Her hair turned dark and began to swirl around her head in beckoning wisps. She was young, firm—he felt her for the first time, touched her shyly—smooth. She wore a cream-colored dress that magically fell from her shoulders. Her thighs were muscular, they quivered as he parted them. That was all he saw before he came inside Patty and the image faded. She disappeared and he couldn't dredge her back up as he turned over again to go to sleep, Patty's quiet breaths pleasantly warm on his neck.

She came back the next night, when Patty again took the initiative in their lovemaking. This erotic specter sprouted sexy, pouting lips, a flared nose, a flat, muscular stomach, and small breasts that looked as if they had been sculpted. Alex came, groaning and thrusting and jerking wildly, and the vision again faded. Patty smiled, satisfied, and stroked his hair.

Two nights later Alex reached for Patty—he wanted to bring his dream back to life. He did. He also realized that he *knew* her. He had seen her. She was real. But he didn't know *how* he knew her. Or where he'd seen her. Or whether she was, indeed, flesh and blood.

Three weeks and much sex later, he remembered.

She was a girl he had seen in Central Park when he was a kid. The details were fuzzy: he was not sure exactly when it had been or how he had first spotted her. He had not thought of her in years, did not know why he was thinking of her now. He had never talked to her, did not even know her name. And yet here she was, replacing his own wife in his bed.

He made love to this girl for several more weeks. And remembered more about her—the way he had followed her, that she had been barefoot, that he had been young and sweaty and innocent. One night, he remembered that he had seen her only moments before he had met Patty one day at his favorite spot. He wondered why he had pulled this girl from the recesses of his brain. Why, when he touched the woman he loved, did he dream of his youth, return to an adolescent longing? He had no answer. Patty moaned with pleasure, the girl from the park beckoned and Alex shook his head. That night, before falling asleep, before he could remember anything else, Alex decided he would never think of her again.

He didn't—for a while. He thought of others.

He recreated Katie for the first time since he had left her in Wilson. When he got bored with Katie, he flashed on her waitress friend, oh, God, he couldn't even think of her name for three nights. And then it came to him: Louisa. In his dreams he fucked Louisa, at long last. And then he mauled this girl he had met in Cuba, she was Latin with the sexiest walk he had ever seen. And then tens and maybe even hundreds of girls threw themselves in front of him as he kissed Patty, fingered her, made her come with his tongue.

He had never had a fantasy life before. Playing ball had managed to merge fantasy and reality. He sometimes wondered what had changed. He sometimes wondered whether these fantasies were a good thing or a bad thing. He sometimes wondered whether Patty could ever tell he was not making love to her. After months passed and she'd said nothing, he was sure she could not. So he stopped wondering about the other things.

They were through now. He had come in her mouth. She liked that, he knew. She said his come tasted nice and salty.

They snuggled together. Without a word being said, they moved in perfect rhythm: he turned on his left side, legs bent; her right arm threw itself over his back to wrap around his chest; her face burrowed into the back of his neck; her right leg curled over his at the ankle.

They had slept this way every night, for years. They had even given it a name, referred to it as their "Sleeping Position." Gradually that got shortened to simply SP. "Time for SP," Patty would say happily when the TV was turned off late at night. If he had an injury—had to sleep on his back or even in another bed—she stayed awake all night tossing and turning. "I can't sleep without SP," she'd say, embarrassed. "I need it."

He was tired from the sex, comfortable in their SP. He looked at her hand on his chest, recognized the redness of her knuckles, the thinness of her wrist, the tiny patch of straight hair on her arm.

"I love you," he said.

"I love *you*," she said, and he knew she was smiling sleepily.

"Happy anniversary," she whispered.

"Happy anniversary," he said.

17

The Saturday after their anniversary Alex stood on the back steps overlooking their yard. The sun was hot and birds were chirping. He grinned at the shrill peeps.

"Look at him," Alex said to Patty as Russell crawled along the grass on his stomach. "What do you think he's thinking?"

"I don't know," she said, and smiled. "What is he thinking?"

"He's on the moon," Alex decided. "That's my guess. He's on the moon and the air in his helmet is running out and he's got to break into the palace and kill the evil emperor."

"I hope he gets back in time for lunch," Patty said.

"Maybe he's on a mission in the Alps. That could be it. He's been sent to kill a spy who's holding out in the snow caves."

"Uh-huh."

"Look at him."

"I'm looking."

"Didn't you ever do that when you were a kid? Play like that? Make-believe?"

"No," Patty said. "I never thought about moon men or snow caves. I was a girl."

"Look, look at him."

Russell had gotten up and was charging a large oak tree. Before he got there, however, he clutched his side, staggered a few steps, and dropped to the ground, obviously in great pain.

"Uh-oh," Alex said. "He's been shot."

"Bad?"

"Ray gun. He'll pull through."

His son valiantly struggled to his feet, limped to the tree, and ducked behind it.

"Ppphhheeeww," Alex said. "He made it."

"Thank God."

"Alex?"

"Yes?" Watching Russ had put him in a good mood and his "Yes?" came out sounding playfully like the Great Gildersleeve's.

"I am not a nagging wife. True or false?"

"Ummm . . ."

She gave him a karate chop in the neck.

"True," he said. "I was going to say true all along."

"So I can get away with asking a nagging question?"

"Nag to your heart's content."

"What's *wrong?*" she asked quietly, seriously.

He started to say, *What do you mean?* but he knew that look in her eyes, and for that matter he also knew what she meant. So he told her everything he had figured out.

"I don't know," he said. "I have no idea."

"But something *is?*"

"Wrong?"

"Mmmmmmm."

"No," he said. "It's just . . ." He trailed off.

"Just?"

"It's weird sometimes. I just find myself *wanting* something. I turn around and I expect something to be there. Only it's not."

"What is it you're expecting?"

"I don't know. If I did, I guess I'd go out and get it."

"That *is* your way."

"I guess that's what's wrong. That's all. Nothing important."

"Funny," Patty said.

"Funny?"

"When I had lunch with Emmy the other day, she said sort of the same thing. She said you just have to know what it is you want. She made it sound as if once you do that, it comes to you pretty easily."

"Huh," Alex said. "I never thought of it quite that way."

"You believe that?" she asked.

"I'm not sure."

"Well, do me a favor," Patty said.

"What?"

"When you figure out what it is you're expecting, let me be the first to know."

"You know what I always wanted my whole life," he said.

"Yes."

"I still want that."

"To be a great ballplayer."

"No, more than that, really. Not to *be* great. To *do* something great. To do the greatest thing anyone's ever done."

"You'll do it," she said.

"Do you believe that?"

"Yes," she said without even a moment's hesitation. "You know I do."

"And you always will, won't you?"

"Yes."

"I have so many other things I want, though. It used to be that *all* I wanted was that. Now it's different. There's you. And Russ. I don't know, maybe I want too much. Maybe I want everything."

"Alex," Patty said.

"What?"

"I feel like I *have* everything. I just want you to know that."

Alex smiled and turned back to Russell, who was now on his belly under a green bush. "I bet that's where the beautiful maiden is being kept."

"What beautiful maiden?"

"The one who's being tortured. The one he's gotta save."

"Oh," Patty said.

"So he can be a hero."

"Russell!" she called. "Lunch is ready."

The boy crawled out from behind the tree and stood up. He tried to brush the grass stain from the right knee of his jeans,

realizing it was going to be there forever. He frowned then ran
over to his parents.

"What were you doing?" Patty asked him, brushing a twig
from his dirty-blond hair.

"Just playin'," the boy said.

He looked at his dad and smiled. His dad smiled back.

"Dad?" Russell said later that day. They were cruising around
L.A., just the two of them. They had gone to a small makeshift
amusement park on Beverly Boulevard—it had a mini–roller
coaster and a pretty good whip and bumper cars. Then they
went to Pink's for a chili dog with onions and hot peppers, only
after Alex made his son swear that news of this postlunch snack
would never reach his mother's ears. They were now on their
way to meet Patty at May's on the Miracle Mile to look at a
couch.

"What?" Alex said.

"Are you good?"

"Good?"

"Yeah."

"A good *person,* you mean?"

"Ballplayer. Are you a good ballplayer?"

"Sure I am. Of course I am. I'm a *real* good ballplayer. Why?"

"Kids in school."

"What'd they say?"

"You know."

"No, I don't."

"They said you stink."

"They *did?*"

Russell nodded glumly. Alex almost drove the car through a
red light straight into a small truck carrying about ten thousand
oranges. As a pedestrian gave him an Italian salute, a thought
flashed through Alex's mind: *I never used to lose my concentration like that. I wonder if I do that playing ball?*

While they waited for the light to change, Alex composed
himself. *Stink?* Christ, they were just little kids. He shouldn't be
so stunned. They were saying it to annoy Russell. He didn't
stink. Okay, .254 wasn't fantastic, and he wasn't driving in a lot

of runs, but he wasn't playing much either. Not *great* for the moment. But not *stink.*

"Listen," Alex said to Russ. "At least they didn't say that *you* stink."

"Yeah," Russell said, not taking any great consolation from that fact.

"I feel pretty bad about it, too, you know."

"You do?"

"Sure. I don't like people sayin' I stink."

"They weren't people, dad! It was just Arnie and Paul."

"Well," Alex said, "what do *you* think?"

"I don't know. I can't really tell. You seem like you're pretty good."

"Russ," Alex said, "your dad is the best baseball player in the world."

"You are?"

Alex put a big grin on his face. It wasn't easy, but it stayed there. And the longer it stayed the easier it got.

"The very best. Mays, Mantle, Kaline, Aaron, you name it."

"I *knew* you were good. That's what I told 'em."

"Good!"

"I said you just had a bad year. Everybody has a bad year."

"Wait till Arnie and Paul have theirs. They'll find out."

"Mom said you were good."

"Did you tell her?"

"Uh-huh. I told her and she said they were crazy."

"She did?"

"Yup. She said, 'When your father makes up his mind, he can do anything he wants.' "

Alex smiled.

"Is that true?" Russ asked.

"What do you think?"

"I think it's true. You can do anything you want."

"And so can you, kid."

"I can?"

"Anything."

"Wow!"

"You wanna go to the game tomorrow night?"

"A night game?"

"Yup."

"Can I?"

"I think so." Alex winked. "I'll put in a good word with your mother."

"Oh, yeah! Neat!"

They drove another block before Russell shyly said, "Dad? Will you hit a home run?"

"What?"

"Tomorrow night. If I bring Arnie and Paul. Will you hit a home run?"

Alex hesitated, but not long enough, because he was pretty damn surprised to hear himself say, "Sure."

"You *will?"*

"A home run. Over the left field wall." He made an arc with the palm of his hand. *"Beeyooooooommmm.* A home run."

"Wow."

Alex grinned happily. "Sure. Didn't your mom say I could do anything I wanted to?"

"Yeah!"

"Then let's go tell your mom!"

"Neat."

"We'll tell her I'm gonna hit a home run tomorrow."

"Neat-*o."*

The next night it wasn't until the sixth inning that Alex began to panic that he might not get into the game.

Pasqual was on the mound for the Twins and he was up two runs and his curveball was a sonofabitch tonight and Alex knew that for his career he was two for sixteen against Pasqual. He looked over at Al Dressler, the manager, who was pacing up and down the dugout. Alex wondered if Big Al knew he was two for sixteen against Pasqual and his sonofabitch curveball.

In the seventh inning Alex worked up his nerve to look over at Russell. The kid looked pretty calm, but Patty was a wreck. All the boy had talked about all day was how his dad was going to hit a homer for him. All day. Over and over again. *"Mom, is Dad really gonna hit one tonight?"* And Patty would twist her neck uncomfortably and fiddle with something on the stove and explain to their son that his dad would *try* to hit a homer but that no one could guarantee anything. And Russell's voice would go up an octave, quivering, a touch of panic, and he'd say, *"But he said he'd hit one tonight."* And Patty would nod and say she knew. *"He's going to try, sweetheart."* Then Russ would wait about five minutes. He'd fidget, put on a sweater as if he were going to run outside, take off the sweater and sit, jump up and start playing with the wax apple on the kitchen table. *"Mom,"* he'd say. *"Do you really think Dad's gonna knock one out?"*

As the seventh inning ended, Alex looked over at Russell's two friends, Arnie and Paul. They were grinning and eating hot dogs. The little fuckers, he thought.

Bottom of the eighth.

The crowd cheered when the Lump doubled off the right-field wall. He had to slide into second to barely beat the throw, but he made it safely. The Angels had the tying run at the plate and Brownie Moreno was up. Moreno was called "Brownie" because when he first came to the States from Puerto Rico, brownies were the only food he knew how to order in English. Someone, somewhere, had made him chocolate brownies and taught him the word. When he'd go into a coffee shop he'd always order the only English word he knew: brownie. A lot of times the waitress would nod and say, "No brownie, pal. How 'bout a doughnut?" Brownie would nod and say, "Okay, pal," hoping that somehow he was getting a steak. He told Alex that once he'd eaten nothing but brownies or doughnuts for nine straight days, breakfast, lunch, and dinner. He said that what probably saved his life was when he learned to say, "Ham on rye with mustard."

Brownie fouled the second pitch right down off his ankle. The whole bench could hear him swear and he tried to hobble around behind the plate to walk it off, but after five minutes he still couldn't put any weight on the foot. Big Al tapped Alex on the shoulder. "Hit for him, Judge," Big Al said. And Alex, startled, reached for his bat then sprinted onto the field.

There was a smattering of applause when his name was announced. He had his fans. Alex had been on a decent amount of postgame interviews, had made a number of appearances at clothing stores and supermarket openings at a hundred bucks a pop. He always signed autographs, spoke to kids, was polite. One of the black guys on the Phillies had once said to him, "You're *po*-lite and white. Shee-ittt, you be makin' big bucks 'fo' you through." And he was a good ballplayer. He was. He should've made the All-Star Team three years ago. Everybody thought so.

Alex heard the Lump yell something from second base as he stepped up to the plate. It sounded like "Knock me fuckin' in, douche bag."

The count was 1 and 1 on Brownie when he went down, so Alex knew he only had two swings. After the first pitch, a fastball by Pasqual that caught Alex by surprise, he only had one swing. The fastball was right down the center of the plate and it was now 1 and 2.

Alex stepped out of the batter's box. He didn't look over at his wife and child. He no longer knew they were there. They didn't exist any longer. Not in this enclosed universe. Alex was concentrating on one thing only: *Pasqual gets me out with his curveball, he just threw a fastball, I should be expecting a curve, he knows that, knows I'll be waiting for the curve, he'll try to sneak another smoker by me, only this one won't be over the middle of the plate, this one'll be bait, just an inch outside, if I can just crowd the plate, be a few inches closer to the outside corner, I can hit it.*

It was perfectly clear to him and so he waited confidently, inching up on the plate. Pasqual wound up—he wasn't worried about the Lump stealing third—and threw. Alex waited for the fastball, knowing he was right.

Alex was wrong. He got the sonofabitch curve. Only it was a bad one. It bounced in the dirt, got away from the Twins' catcher, and the Lump lumbered into third.

2 and 2.

Now Alex figured curve. Gotta be. Curve with a little taken off it. Pasqual would figure he'd be overanxious. Yup. Slow curve.

The fastball came inside and almost took Alex's head off,

sending him sprawling. When he stood up, he stared hard at Pasqual, trying to figure out if the knockdown was intentional or if Pasqual had just let one slip away from him. It didn't really matter, but the stare might unnerve the pitcher just a drop, at least let him know he wasn't dealing with any kind of pussy.

Okay. Now the slow curve. Gotta, gotta be. Throw it. The slow curve. Please. Throw it.

Pasqual threw it. Alex watched it all the way, saw the spin the moment the Cuban threw the ball. He had his eye on the stitching almost from the instant of release and his eye was still on it when he swung and hit the home run.

For one second he thought he'd gotten too far under it. But then he knew he'd really done it. The left fielder backed up against the wall and jumped, but it was a halfhearted effort. The ball was in the eighth row.

When Alex trotted past first base, Patty was looking at him in a way she hadn't looked at him for a long, long time. Her glow was so obvious, she looked as if she were going to melt away between the cracks in her box seat. He smiled at her, cool. She grinned when he touched his fingers to his cap. He wouldn't tip it now, he was too old for that, and besides, this was still a last-place team he had just hit for. But she remembered the way he used to do it for her on the sandlots. She remembered and she grinned. Russell was going berserk, screaming, jumping up and down, pounding his two excited buddies on their backs. Their eyes met—Alex and Russ's—and Alex was almost scared by the worshipful expression on his son's face. But that twinge of confusion disappeared as quickly as it had struck when Alex realized that, goddamn, he'd done it, he'd really done it. And he suddenly realized that's what he was screaming as his eyes met Russell's. "I did it! I did it! I really did it!" Everyone was cheering now, as if the whole crowd somehow realized he'd done more than just hit a simple potential game-winner. While Pasqual was being taken out of the game, Alex's teammates were slapping him on the ass in the dugout. Even Big Al nodded to him in appreciation.

The Angels lost the game in the tenth inning, but Alex didn't really care.

He'd done what he was supposed to.

As he always had.

And, he knew now, as he sat down at his place on the bench, he somehow always would.

18

It was mid-August and Alex was in the shower trying to cool off. The famed Los Angeles breeze had disappeared, replaced by pure heat and hazy, choking smog.

"They'll be here in fifteen minutes," Patty called in. As always, her singsong voice, the way her voice raised that slight pitch when she spoke only to him, brought a reflexive smile to his face.

"The Lump's always late," Alex called back.

"Emmy's always early."

"I'll be ready," Alex said, although he wasn't really sure that was true. The Girl from the Park was asking if she could join him in the shower.

"I wonder why they were so insistent on seeing us?"

"Don't know," Alex mumbled. He had talked to Emmy Lumpano when she'd called that morning. She was excited, she had to come see her best friends, she said; she and the Lump wanted to see Alex and Patty for dinner. Alex had invited them over for an early barbecue. A few dogs and some homemade slaw under the streaked sky of twilight.

A quick blowjob, the Girl from the Park pleaded. *Come onnnnn.*

No, Alex said silently. *I've gotta get ready.*

Let me suck on it for a few seconds, she said.

No! Alex got angry at himself for his erection. This was not the time for a major-league boner. Especially over her. He hadn't even seen her in a couple of months. Since his big home run, he realized. He hadn't missed her.

He turned the water off, hopped out of the tub, and quickly dried himself. Alex wiped his forehead with the back of his hand. He wasn't feeling any cooler.

"Can I come in?" Patty tapped at the door.

"Sure."

She stepped into the bathroom, playfully nudging him out of the way so she could get to the medicine cabinet. He was sure she noticed his hard-on but she didn't acknowledge it. Just as well. He wondered what she'd do if he said to her, *Honey, could you just shoot me off before the guests arrive?* Probably she'd do it. Patty was not a prude, not at all. He just insisted on treating her like one. No, it wasn't even that. She was his wife and he respected her. There weren't too many people, deep down, that he respected, and he didn't ever want to chance losing that feeling he had for her. He didn't want to put her in a position where he might have to say to himself, *She is not what I thought, she is not what I need, she is not what I want.*

Alex was not a contemptuous person. But he was not automatically respectful. That was something that had to be earned and earned by performance. His respect, for almost anyone but Patty, was an annoyingly temporary response. If a pitcher struck him out, he had his respect. If he hung a slider and Alex laced a double, that respect disappeared. It could be recaptured, but never in the same way. Never with the same fear.

With respect, it seemed, at least for him, came a kind of fear. A tension. Restrictions. When he was young, he never felt restricted. When he was sixteen he never altered his swing, even if some phenom fireballer struck him out three times in a row. He went with what he had, and that was usually good enough. Now, it was *he* who changed. When beaten, he adjusted. *Adjustments,* he thought. *Restrictions.* Those were *old* words. Words that were unknown to youth. With a shock it suddenly occurred to him that he was no longer young. It was absolutely the first time such a thought had struck him. And strike him it did. He was not old, not yet, Christ, not at twenty-nine. But he was not young. Then, with even a bigger shock, he realized that in all their years together, Patty had never given him a handjob.

He had never in his *life* had a handjob!

Why was that? He didn't know. Suddenly, though, more than anything in the world, he wanted to be in some dark restaurant with drip candles flickering on the tables, Ella crooning on the jukebox, and a sexy babe choking his chicken under the curtain of a red-and-white checked tablecloth.

Holy shit, he thought. Where the hell is *this* coming from? And then he thought, that's an easy one to answer. It's coming from a shitty batting average, over six weeks without a home run, and that waitress three days ago who really wanted to fuck him, *really* wanted to. But he hadn't. Wouldn't.

Why?

He looked up to watch Patty as she dabbed at her face with some strange, fluffy beige pad.

That's why. Because he liked being married to her and he knew if he started fucking waitresses he wouldn't be married to her any longer.

She smiled at him. Whenever she smiled at him he was glad he didn't fuck waitresses.

Restrictions, he thought.

"Makeup?" he said, to turn himself away from his thoughts.

"Uh-huh."

"For the Lump?"

"For *me.*" She squinted at the mirror. "I need it."

"Oh, yeah."

"I'm getting old."

She frowned when she said it, a mock frown meant to be cute and funny, but she meant it. He patted her on the back, left his damp palm there for a moment, a gesture of familiar affection. She might never have given him a handjob, but they *were* on the same wavelength.

"Twenty-eight," he said. "I'm surprised you can get around without your wheelchair." He squirted some shaving cream onto his fingers and then nudged her back so he could share the mirror while he shaved. He still liked to shave in front of her.

Silly, but what could you do? He remembered the first time she had ever watched him slide a razor over his blond stubble, and ever since then it always made him feel like a seventeen-year-old trying to be grown up. There was something oddly warming in the sensation. He knew she liked it, too, although she'd never mentioned it. It was an unspoken ritual that, whenever possible, he would shave at the same time she washed her face or now, at age twenty-eight, applied makeup.

"My body's changing." She slapped at her thighs. "And look at this." She ran her fingers around the edge of her eyes. "Wrinkles. Crow's-feet!"

"Disgusting. It's like something out of *House of Wax.*"

She scrunched up her nose at him.

"You want me to tell you something?" he asked.

She did. "What?"

He pecked her on the cheek, leaving a dot of shaving cream on her chin. He was feeling affectionate. Thoughts of other women tended to bring out overt affection.

"A few days ago . . . last weekend, I think . . . when we drove out to the stadium together?"

"Uh-huh?"

"Well, when you got outta the car, I was lookin' at you. And it was as if, for a second, I didn't know you. You know, the angle was just right so for one split second you looked like someone new, someone I didn't recognize. And I thought how pretty you looked. Really pretty. And nice. So if I didn't know you, I'd *want* to. Then you moved or I moved and you looked like you again. And I thought how pretty you looked when you looked like you. How you haven't changed much, how you still looked so, I dunno, you just looked like you, and I realized how much I still liked you."

"Ahem, ahem," she said.

"Yes, yes," he said. "I also *love* you. But this was different. I mean, of course I love you. But it's nice that we're such good friends."

"It is, isn't it?"

"Uh-huh."

"I don't know *why* you like me so much."

"I know you don't. That's probably why I like you so much."

"Even though I look like me, I'm sure I'm not as pretty as some of the Annies who throw themselves at you. And I never say anything funny. I mean, I'm not a laugh a minute."

"Hey, listen. I just meant to say something nice. You know, a husband to wife bit of intimacy. I didn't expect a whole history of your faults."

"And I still cry for no reason and I get all insecure when you're away and I still don't know all that much about baseball."

"Anything else?"

"I don't think I'm a really good mother, I'm not that great in bed, and I don't *do* anything, so I can't be all that interesting."

Alex shaved over his Adam's Apple very slowly.

"I never realized all this before," he said. "I better leave you."

She threw a towel that landed over his head, covering his face.

"Alex?"

"What?" he said from under the towel.

"I want to go back to school."

That surprised him. He took the towel off his face.

"You do?"

"Yes."

"Why?"

She shrugged.

"Patty," he said, "it's not that I don't believe you when you shrug like that, but I *have* known you for a while, and I don't think I've ever seen you do anything without a reason."

"Then for all the reasons I just said: I'm starting to feel like I need something."

"Ah," he said. "Like my mysterious expectation?"

"I don't think so," she said. "I don't think I'm nearly as mysterious as you are. But when you said that, it made me nervous. I thought, *Well, why am I so content if he's got all these needs?*"

"I don't have all these—"

"And I thought I should find something to do. To *want*, like you and Emmy. And this is something I used to want quite a bit. I'm starting to miss the fact that I never went."

"What about . . ." He didn't know what he was asking about.

But his instinct was to ask about something. He felt very odd about this request of hers. "What about Russ?"

"He's in school all day. I'll work my schedule around his."

"I don't know," he said.

"Why not?" The thing about Patty was that she never whined. She was really interested to know why he was hesitating, not so much because it affected her future as because it was more insight into him.

"I don't know," he said, "why I don't know."

"I want to. I really want to. And I can get into UCLA. It's not even very expensive."

Alex finished towel-drying his hair. While he rubbed he said nothing.

"Alex?" she said.

"What?"

"I have a real reason too."

He grinned. "I know you do." She hesitated. "What is it?"

"I need possibility."

"Come again?"

"I need to feel that something new could happen to me. I need to feel . . ."

"Possibility."

"Yes. That's the reason."

He shook his head.

"You're confused," Patty said.

"You want things to change?"

She smiled. "Never. Never with you."

"I don't get it."

"I don't want change. I want the *possibility* of change. Is that nuts?"

"Yes."

"It's like flirting."

"It is?"

"I like to flirt. But that's as far as I'd take it."

"So?"

"So it's time for me to do something different. To expand."

"But not change."

"Never. And I don't want *you* to ever change."

"I think it's weird," Alex said.

"It's just not you, is all. You don't flirt. With you, it's all or none. It's do or don't. It's win or lose."

"Yeah," he said.

"This isn't like that. This is just . . ."

"I know. Possibility. It seems risky to me."

"What does?"

"Flirting. You flirt, there's the definite *possibility* you get fucked."

"I won't do it if you tell me not to," she said.

She looked so sweet, so sincere. So vulnerable. As if he might either laugh or get angry and either would be like poison to her system.

"Okay," he said, very slowly. "Okay. It's a good idea."

"Even if you don't get it?"

"If it makes you happy, it's a good idea," he said, and he meant that.

She smiled, one of her specials. They kissed.

I'll blow you later, the Girl from the Park said. *Tonight.*

Okay, Alex told her. *Until tonight.*

"This is fabulous!" Patty exclaimed. She clapped her hands together in pleasure and excitement.

"No shit," the Lump proudly shared her sentiments.

"I can't really believe it," Emmy said modestly.

"Sure you can," Patty told her. "You can believe it 'cause you made it happen."

"It just hasn't sunk in yet."

"Let's hear it from the beginning," Alex said.

"Lemme have another beer first."

"You finished the first one?" Patty asked, surprised. She had never felt comfortable with the Lump since she'd learned about his hitting Emmy. Emmy's bruise had disappeared, with the help of a little makeup, and so, apparently, had her resentment and fear. But not Patty's. She had not told Alex what had happened because Emmy had asked her not to. If she *had* told him, she'd probably never let the Lump in their house. As it stood, she had to, because she didn't have an official reason not to let him in.

"He's like me with cigarettes," Emmy said. She pointed to herself. "Chain-smoker." She pointed to the Lump. "Chain-*drinker.*"

"I'll get it," Alex said and headed to the kitchen.

"I never saw anybody drink so quickly. I didn't even see you swallow."

"He sort of sucks it down more than he actually swallows," Emmy said.

"Oh."

"It's kind of endearing once you get used to it."

"Kind of gross until then."

"Okay," Alex said, returning with three beers, one for him, two for his teammate. "Let's hear."

"Well," Emmy started. "Two weeks ago, I got a call from this agent."

"Agent?" Patty asked.

"Yeah. You know, talent agent. He represents actors and stuff like that."

"Wow."

"Yeah. So he calls me and he says he saw me when I and Walter were on that talk show, the Granger show, remember that afternoon?"

"Sure."

"So he says I was great on the show. Real pretty and smart and that I was a natural."

"For what?" Alex asked.

"For show biz, honey. For show biz!"

Patty grinned a secret grin at Alex, using only her eyes. Alex returned it with a barely discernible nod.

"So get to the good stuff al-fuckin'-ready," Lump said.

"Okay. So he says he wants to represent me. And that we should meet."

The Lump belched. "C'mon," he said impatiently.

"Let her tell it, Lump. This is exciting." Patty turned to Emmy. "Go on."

"I'll cut it short. But, brother, this guy is somethin'!"

"What's his name?"

"Kapstein. Daniel Kapstein."

"What's he like?"

"Smooth. Boy, is he smooth. He took me out to lunch. To the Brown Derby!"

"Big fuckin' deal."

"Lump!"

"Anyways. He winds up sendin' me over to KRLX, you know, Channel Ten. 'Cause guess what?"

"They're looking for a weathergirl!"

"Are they ever! They gave me a script, told me to study it . . ."

"I can't believe you didn't say anything to me!"

"I didn't wanna jinx it. But now I can't, 'cause I got it!"

"This is so great, Emmy," Patty said. "It's really great."

"I did a tape, in front of a camera and everything, right on the set as if it was the real thing. That was last week. And today they called and said I got it!"

"Amazing," Alex said slowly. So slowly that Patty turned to look at him to see if anything was wrong.

"A-fuckin'-mazin'," the Lump agreed. "But tell 'em the good part."

"Lump!"

"Well, you left out the best fuckin' part of the story!"

"Walter, sometimes you are an insensitive human being," Emmy said.

"*Sometimes?*" Alex asked.

"The best fuckin' part o' this is she's pullin' in fourteen grand a year. That ain't nothin' to shit on."

"Christ." Emmy shook her head disdainfully.

Patty reached over and touched Emmy on the arm.

"It's wonderful," she said. "It really and truly is wonderful."

"Ain't it?" Emmy said, then got a pained expression on her face. "Excuse me. I mean, 'isn't it?' "

"That's another thing," the Lump said, a note of disgust apparent. "She's gotta start watchin' what she says."

"When do you start work?" Patty asked.

"Two weeks."

"Can I get another drink?" the Lump growled.

"You finished both of those?" Patty stared at him, shocked.

"What are you, the F-fuckin'-BI?"

"I'm gettin' it," Alex said. "Should I start the barbecue while I'm up?"

Patty was still looking at Lump curiously, squinting at him as if surprised by what she saw.

"I'll help," she said to Alex, but she was still staring at the Lump.

She probably is surprised, Alex thought. And he liked her all the more for it. When he stood up, he kissed her on top of the head.

"What was that for?" Patty asked as she walked with him to set up the hot dogs.

"For being you," he replied. "For thinking you're wrinkled and old and for being so happy for Emmy and for not ever realizing what a revolting slob the Lump really is."

"Well, for that I should get a kiss on the lips, don't you think?"

"Tongue?" he asked.

"Maybe," she replied, doing her best to look coy.

"Okay. Here goes."

They kissed and their tongues met. It was a good kiss and they held each other for a pleasurably long moment. It had been a long time since they had kissed like that.

"You really don't mind?" Patty asked him, leaning her head against his chest.

"About school?"

She nodded.

"One thing I've learned from playin' ball. With two outs in the ninth inning, a runner on third, and a four-hundred-foot fly to dead center, you don't bother to try to throw the runner out at home."

"Wanna run that by me again, Slugger?"

"Only crazy people and rookies try to stop the inevitable."

"What does that have to do with my going back to school?"

"It means that things move on, that's all. And I ain't crazy."

"And you're certainly no rookie." She grinned.

"But," he said very seriously, "something you said *is* bothering me."

Panic showed in her voice and she frowned in concern. "What?"

"You said you're not a laugh a minute. I think you're funny."

She waved at him, relieved. Then she slapped his arm to show him that he might be a celebrity, but for scaring her like that he was still a jerk. "Sure," she said. "But you think I can *sing* too."

"No, I don't. That's a blatant lie. I said I just like your singing voice."

"What's the diff?"

"*Big* diff," he said.

"That's how I know you love me. When the love goes, it's gonna hit you like a sledgehammer that I have a *terrible* voice."

"I know you have a terrible voice," he insisted. "But I like it anyway."

She clucked her tongue at him in mock despair at his indiscriminate affection for her. Then she smiled at just the right moment, in just the right way, so there was no chance he'd think she didn't appreciate, no, *need*, no, *long for* that same affection.

"Will you do something very important for me?" Patty asked.

"Anything."

"Anything, my *dah*-ling?" She flicked an imaginary cigarette holder.

"Anything."

"Good," Patty said. "Tell Russ dinner'll be ready soon."

The door to Russell's room was closed. But the music was loud, even in the hall. Rock and roll. Russell loved it, was mesmerized by it. He could sit all day in his room with the hi-fi turned up full blast listening to the Beatles and the Stones. It seemed to have a sensual hold on him. Alex thought rock and roll seemed, at times, to possess Russ much the way jazz sometimes possessed him.

Alex remembered the first time he had heard Charlie Parker, *really* heard him, all by himself. He had listened to the Bird but never heard him before. It was after he'd gotten back from Wilson. He'd been walking down Twenty-second Street and he heard this music coming out of the ground-floor window of a dilapidated brownstone. Alex had stopped short on the street, frozen. He stood there for two hours, oblivious to passersby, oblivious to everything but the magical sounds of the saxes and the bass and the piano.

He was hooked right there. He had been learning from Willie, he'd been on his way, but he had never before encountered a force so much stronger than himself.

Alex thought that Russell, too, was being overpowered by an outside force, but whereas he trusted jazz, he didn't completely trust his son's music. As much as he liked it and felt its power, it seemed too violent, too angry, too full of turmoil. Where jazz glided, this snapped. Where jazz was beautiful and wise, this said, *Here! Fuck you!* We're *dishin' it out now!*

Alex pounded on Russell's door, then opened it.

"Don't you think that's a little loud?"

Russell rubbed his eyes sleepily, as if coming out of a trance. "What?"

"TURN IT DOWN!"

Russ slowly walked to the cheap, gray hi-fi in his room and lifted the needle off the record.

But he can't be a man 'cause he doesn't smoke the same—

The silence was startling.

Father and son stared at each other. Alex clenched and unclenched his fists. He hadn't realized how tense the music had been making him. How intrusive it was. He took a deep breath and felt a little foolish. He'd been all set to yell at his son; he'd been all worked up over a little bit of too-loud music.

Alex took a deep breath, his little boy looking up at him, confused.

"Don't you think it was a little loud?" Alex asked as patiently as he could.

"Loud?"

"Yeah."

"You *gotta* play it loud."

"You do?"

Russell nodded importantly. "It's rock and roll, Dad."

Alex grinned and nodded back. "You really like it, don't you?"

"Sure."

"What do you like about it?"

"Everything. It's great."

Alex shook his head. "Can you take time out from this great music to eat dinner?"

"I'm starved!"

"Well, let's go!"

And then, perhaps as a residue of the clinging force of the Rolling Stones, as if the music had ripped open a tiny part of him, drastically exposing him, Alex had a surging rush of anxiety. He was at the mercy of outside forces: young pitchers with ninety-five-mile-per-hour fastballs; his low paycheck; the mortgage payment on his house; his wife's abstract search for possibility; the Stones and the Who and the Animals; the waitress who wanted to sit on his face; the Girl from the Park, firm breasts beckoning.

It was like a flash of white lights, blinding him, freezing him in place. It was a wave of panic that tasted as sour as vomit in his throat.

"Dad?" Alex heard Russell say.

"Hon?" Patty called from the backyard. "The coals are hot."

He looked down at Russell, patted him reassuringly on the head, took both hands and mussed up Russ's hair, and, when the boy squealed, practically smothered him with a hug.

Then he winked at his son and pointed the way down the hallway, as if there were miles and miles of green carpet stretching before them.

Alex swung an imaginary bat, a level swing, smooth and easy, and he and Russell watched a nonexistent ball fly high, higher, out over every left-field wall in every park Alex had ever played in.

"Hey, asshole!" the Lump yelled. "I need about three more fuckin' beers!"

Alex pushed all the thoughts away, shoved the images viciously aside, and he smiled as the ball flew out of the stadium, bounced in the parking lot. The anxiety faded. He nodded confidently, took his son's hand, and the Judge sauntered to the back door to toss a couple of franks on the white-hot barbecue.

It all got put in motion because Alex was longing for simpler times.

He was longing for simpler times because he'd just gone zero-for-four in a day game against Baltimore. He'd gone zero-for-four because the Orioles had brought up this nineteen-year-old kid pitcher, Grayson, to help them in their stretch run for the pennant. Grayson had a fastball that jumped a foot as it crossed the plate, right at the last possible second, and Alex just couldn't hit it. He couldn't see it, couldn't time it, could not hit it. Eldew Washington put it quite succinctly when Alex returned to the bench: "He made you look like dog crappola, bro."

It was the next to last day of the season. The Angels were in last place, thirty-four and a half games out, and all the Birds had to do was win their last two games to clinch the pennant. They sure won this one, as Grayson came out of the bullpen to strike Alex out with two on in the ninth. Three fastballs, three strikes. Alex hadn't thought there was a pitcher in this or any other world who could throw a fastball right by him when he was looking for one. Now he knew he was wrong.

So because this kid threw bullets, Alex was already unhappy when he got home at six o'clock. He wasn't cheered up when he read the note from Patty.

Alex,

Sorry, sorry, sorry. I forgot to tell you I had a night class tonight. Psych 101 (the prof said he's reading my paper to the class—I got an A). It's only from six to eight but I won't be here when you get home. If you want to hold off on dinner till I get back, it would make a repentant wife very happy. If not, I won't mind. That's how easy *I* am! See you later.

Love, love, love.
Your brainy wife

P.S.—Don't feel bad about the game! Your family adores you.

P.P.S.—Russ is at his friend Glen's house for dinner. I said it was okay. I'll pick him up on the way home.

xxxxxooooo

P.P.P.S.—If I miss Dave tonight, say hi.

Dave Manning read the note over Alex's shoulder.

"School?" he asked.

"Yeah," Alex said.

"Well, good for Patty," Manning added.

"Yeah," Alex said again, clearly his last word on the subject.

"So what should we do?" Manning asked. "This is your burg."

"Before we do anything, I have to make a phone call."

"Go right ahead."

Alex picked up the kitchen phone and dialed the operator. "What's the area code for"—he checked a list on a yellow pad pinned on a corkboard by the phone—"Denver?" When the operator told him, Alex dialed ten numbers. "Hello," he said next to the person who answered in Denver. "I'd like to know if you have a listing for a Dan Cappollo. C-A-Double P-O-Double L-O." He waited. "No? Okay. Thank you very much."

When he'd hung up, Manning said, "What was that all about?"

Alex shook his head, as if to clear it. "You remember my friend Danny?"

Manning shrugged.

"He came down to see me one weekend in Baltimore. When we played you guys in May?" Manning looked blank. "You renember. Emmy was visiting her mother or somebody so she was in town, too, and we all went out to dinner? You, me, Lump, Emmy, and my friend Danny."

"Oh, yeah, yeah. The advertising guy, right?"

"Yup."

"Right. I remember. Really funny guy."

"The thing is, Danny's my best friend. Has been forever, right? He's the one who told me, you know, about my parents. And he's the one who sort of keeps tabs on Elliot, my little brother."

"Jesus, you guys still haven't talked?"

Alex didn't answer. Instead, he said, "So, anyway, I call Danny up about, I don't know, six weeks ago. 'Cause I hadn't heard from him in a while, a couple of months. And his number's been disconnected. I thought that was weird so I call information in New York. Not listed anymore. My best friend, right? I call his mother, she still lives in Stuyvesant Town. I said hello, she said hello, then I said, 'Where's Dan? I'm trying to reach him.' There's this long pause and then she says, 'I don't know.' Then she says, 'You better call Brenda.' 'Who's Brenda?' I said, and she says, 'His fiancée.' Now, this is my best friend in the whole world, and I say, '*What* fiancée?' Anyway, to cut this whole thing short, I called up this girl, Brenda, who lives in Nyack, outside of the city. Are you ready for this? She and Danny'd been goin' out for a year. A year! My best friend! The guy I know better than anyone in the world and they were gonna be *married* and I'd never even *heard* of her!"

"Maybe he's just a closed-mouthed kind of guy," Manning suggested.

"Listen. This girl Brenda turns out to be rich. Her parents are rich, anyway. And they're plannin' on gettin' married and then one day Danny tells her he thinks they should live in California. He says his company offered him a great job out there—here, in L.A. She thought it was a great idea, so they worked out this plan: He'd take her car, an expensive car, I forget what kind, and take a bunch of their stuff and move it out here. He'd get settled, come back for her, they'd get married, and their honeymoon would be their drive back here together. Great. So about four months ago he takes her car and drives off. Three days later she gets a telegram—a *telegram*—that says, *Sorry, the wedding's off. As soon as I can, I'll send you the money for the car.* That's it. She never heard from him again. No one has. She called his office and he didn't get transferred. He'd quit. And so now he's disappeared."

"That the end of the story?" Manning asked.

"Yeah."

"Why were you calling him in Denver?"

"I've been callin' a different city every day. Alphabetically. I called everywhere in California and can't find him, so I'm tryin' the rest of the country. I mean, he's gotta be *somewhere.*"

"Sounds like he doesn't want to be found."

"I'm his best friend!"

"Yeah," Manning said. "So you said."

And so because he'd struck out and because Patty was off studying psychology and because his best friend had disappeared off the face of the earth, Alex decided he didn't want to wait for dinner. He wanted to get out of his house and go someplace where life was simple.

"Let's go to the T-Bone," Alex said. "I'm sure a bunch of the guys'll be there. Let's get outta here and get some prime ribs and some milk."

"Sounds good to me," Dave Manning said. Then he stopped short and said, "Milk?"

"Uh-huh. I've got," said Alex Justin, "a real craving for milk."

At the T-Bone a few of the Angels were hanging out at the bar, waiting for the better-looking Annies to come along so they could do some serious clamming.

Alex took the usual gentle, subtle, ballplayer ribbing for his strikeout.

"Hey, dick-brain! What were you doin', swingin' with your cock?"

"Heyyyyy, Babe Ruth! Nice goin', Babe. No kiddin', you really reminded me of the old Babe out there today. Why don't you buy me a drink, Babe?"

"Hey, lay off, lay off. The Judge has had a hard day. Right, you shit-bag strikeout artist?"

Alex took it all with an ulcer-inducing grin. He was surprised, however, at the genuine respect that Manning was greeted with. He'd have thought that, as the next day's opposing pitcher, Manning would be assaulted; but when they strode past to get to their table, the Angels turned shy, mumbling quiet greetings, halfhearted barbs.

"Hey, Manning. We'll get you tomorrow, or somethin'."

"Big Dave. Big Dave, Big Dave, Big Dave."

"Hope we beat you, but if you get to the Series, well, good luck."

Alex was impressed and said so, as the two friends were seated. "I guess they've never seen a Cy Young winner close-up."

"I haven't won it yet" was Manning's quiet response.

"Yeah," Alex said, unconvinced at Manning's modesty. "We got a pool in the clubhouse. MVP, Cy Young, and Rookie. You're even money. Definitely the fave."

"I'm flattered."

"I bet on you."

"You're just a sentimental guy." Manning smiled and suddenly Alex remembered, so vividly, the first time he'd ever seen Dave Manning, lording over the Tob clubhouse with that knowledgeable leer. Manning was still as dazzling a figure, maybe even more so. He still had his looks, and he still had that confidence and aura of success. And he still, Alex was positive, had that secret locked way down inside him. And he, Alex, was still no closer to discovering whatever the hell that secret was.

The waiter came over with their drinks. He set a beer in front of Manning. Then he turned to Alex. "The bartender says to tell you the cow juice is on the house, Mr. Justin. He says you're the first person over the age of twelve he's ever served it to."

Alex smiled over at Fred, the bartender, and flipped him the bird.

"I guess it's true," Manning said. "The more things change, the more they remain the same."

"So, listen," Alex said suddenly. "What is it you want to do? I mean, what's the one thing, more than anything in the world, that you want?"

Manning stroked his upper lip, à la Bogie. "What's it to ya?"

"Here's the thing. I'm startin' to see this pattern and I want to know what you think."

"Lay it on me."

"Take Emmy, for instance. It's stupid, but what does she want out of life—to be on TV. That's it, that's what she wants, now she's got it. Patty, she only wanted to be married to me. I don't wanna make it sound like I'm so great, but that's what she wanted, what she still wants. We're married. It's terrific, we have a perfect marriage. But that's what she wanted. Now she wants to go back to school. I guess she's, uh, secure enough to want two things. Maybe when one thing works, you can go after something else. But anyway, she wants school, plain and simple, so she's back in school. Danny, my friend Danny, all he ever wanted, I swear to God, was to fool people, to prove to everybody that they were nothin' but assholes. Who the fuck knows where he is, but that's sure the hell what he's done." Alex was speaking faster now. His hands were on the table in front of him, palms down, his fingertips seemingly propelling his body forward. "And the more I think about it, even poor old Scotty. Shit, he never cared about zip other than, you know, meetin' up with his 'glorious maker' and all that shit. So what happens? He gets himself killed and he speeds right on up to heaven. You know what I'm talkin' about?"

"I know what you're talking about," Manning said evenly.

"So what do *you* want?" Alex said seriously. "The Cy Young Award?"

"No," Manning said.

"Come on, it's the greatest thing that can happen to a pitcher!"

"I don't give a shit about the Cy Young Award."

"The pennant? The Series? You wanna be a champion?"

"No," Manning said.

"Money?"

Manning shook his head.

"Family? Religion? Two-on-one sex? What the hell is there?"

"What is it *you* want?" Manning asked.

Alex leaned back, now relaxed. He tipped the chair back so it balanced on its back two legs. He chewed his lip before answering.

"Here's maybe where the problem comes in," Alex said. I want *everything.*"

"Some people think you *have* everything."

"That's true," Alex agreed. "The thing is, I do. I mean, I love Patty. I love my kid. I *love* my kid. Nothing really makes me as happy as watching him grow up. I'm playin' ball. I had a good season. Not fantastic, but I had a good year. Played the whole last two months, did a good job." Manning nodded in agreement. "I got a house, I make my payments, I buy the clothes I need." He tapped the wooden table. "I can take my friends out for roast beef when I want."

"So?"

"So it's not *great!* It's just not . . . *great.* It's all . . ."

"Dull."

"Damn. It isn't even that. It's just . . ."

"The same. The same as everybody else."

Alex nodded slowly, pondering the implications of agreeing.

"Yeah," he said. "Yeah. That's part of it. And goddammit, I wanna do something great. That's really what I always wanted. Always. More than clothes or a house or roast beef or . . . or a wife."

"Why?" Dave Manning asked.

"What?"

"Why," Manning asked once again, "do you want to do something great?"

"Are you kidding?"

"Uh-uh."

" 'Cause that's what it's all about. That's, shit, I don't wanna start soundin' like a nut, but that's what we're here to do, isn't it?"

"Is it?"

"What else?"

Manning shrugged, then smiled that faraway smile. "Maybe we're here to just be like everybody else."

Alex thought about that. "No," he said, finally. "I've done that. I've got all that. It's not enough."

Fred, the bartender, passed by and slapped Alex a friendly slap on the back. Manning grabbed him before he could disappear into the kitchen.

"Fred," Manning said. "We've got a philosophical question to ask you."

"Shoot," Fred said. "Plato's my fuckin' middle name."

"The question is," said Manning, "what do you do if you've got everything you've always wanted, only it's not enough?"

"That's an easy one," the bartender answered. "Hardly worth the stopover. You get drunk or you get laid or you kill yourself. That's what man's been doin' for three million years or however fuckin' long we been on this fuckin' planet. Can I go get the crushed ice now?"

Manning nodded as Fred disappeared. "There you have it," he said to Alex.

"Maybe," Alex said quietly, boring in on an emerging truth, "I got diluted. Is that the right word?"

"Could be."

"Maybe I've been wanting too many things, working at too many different things. Do you think that's possible?"

Manning didn't answer.

"Maybe I've been doin' things I shouldn't do, not doin' things I should."

"Like?"

"I'm a ballplayer. That's what I *am*. It's been a long time since I just let myself *be* a ballplayer, let everything else go, just, you know, concentrated on that."

"So, Alex. After all this, what is it you want?"

"To do the greatest thing a ballplayer can do. I wanna make the greatest play in the history of the World Series. I wanna do the greatest thing in the history of baseball. That's what I want."

"And after that?"

"Then I can die happy."

"Hallelujah."

Alex grinned. "So, am I right?"

"Does desire equal result equal happiness?"

"Yeah."

"You wanna get drunk tonight?" Manning asked.

"That your answer?"

"What's yours?"

"I've never been drunk."

"You heard Fred, didn't you? You got three choices. I never pegged you for the third, I know from experience the second is out, so that leaves the joy of destroying our livers."

"Even Willie," Alex said suddenly.

"Willie? What about him?"

"Even Willie. I don't know where the hell he is, but I bet he's off somewhere tryin' to get blue."

"Willie's dead is my guess, Alex."

"Why do you say that?"

"I just think it. I think they cut out his heart down there in Wilson, and I don't think Willie's the kind of guy who could go on livin' without his heart."

"I don't think so," Alex said. "I think he's doin' what he wants to do. Same as everybody else."

"We'll never know, though, will we?"

"He might pop up."

"Yeah, but even if he does, he won't be able to *tell* us what the hell he's been doin'." Manning smiled and shrugged. The shrug was supposed to be an apology for the smile.

"*You* do all right livin' without a heart," Alex said.

"Sure. But I never had one in the first place."

"Okay." Alex sighed. "Let's *do* it." He signaled the waiter to come over so they could get drunk.

They didn't do it, however. Alex, in fact, came close to never doing anything ever again.

Before they could even order their drinks, there was a crashing noise at the bar. It sounded as if a truck had driven through the wall and into the restaurant.

"It's the Lump," Alex said. "Gotta be."

"I'd recognize that graceful entrance anywhere."

They stood up and moved toward the noise. They both knew what the Lump was like when this smashed; they both had plenty of experience getting him the hell out of places like the

T-Bone. But when they got close to the bar, they were both shocked. Scared. Not scared because of any physical menace. Scared because of the naked image revealed on the Lump's distorted face.

Walter Lumpano looked like a monster.

A wild man.

His hair snaked out in all directions, standing on end as if charged with electricity. His right cheek was slashed, cut open so it looked like there was a small pouch in the middle of his face, dried blood caked on top of it. His clothes were clinging to him, not just from sticky sweat but, it seemed, for protection from his waving arms and lurching body. His shirt rode halfway up his back. Alex was shocked to notice, for the first time, a huge roll of fat around the Lump's middle. The Lump had always been one solid mass of muscle, radiating strength, an immovable object. Even though Alex saw him naked practically every day, somehow he hadn't realized how that muscle had dissipated. Loose flesh now seemed to roll grotesquely all over the catcher.

And his eyes. The Lump had always had mean eyes, but that meanness had always been benign, inherent but buried. Now, though, now those eyes shone with a violent, nasty intensity. They looked like eyes that could kill. That would enjoy killing.

"Lump," Alex said, as he'd said a hundred times before in similar situations. But his voice had none of the usual calming influence. Walter Lumpano just turned to his teammate, staring at him with a hungry look. They faced each other, a questioning expression on Alex's face. The restaurant was silent as Alex stepped forward, hand extended toward the Lump in a gesture of support. The silence was broken when, like a rabid dog, the catcher growled, an eerie noise from the gutter, and charged. He leapt upon Alex, knocking him to the ground, and savagely went for his throat.

It took six men to pull them apart. By the time Manning had kicked the Lump in the nuts, doubling him over, blood was gushing out of a wound in Alex's neck; his forehead was already purple from the Lump's having slammed it repeatedly into the

wood floor; and his back was on fire at the point where the
Lump's knee had driven in, again and again, like a jackhammer.

Manning helped Alex stand. Alex stared down at the fallen
figure, now stunned and sick, face down. As Manning relaxed
his grip, Alex bellowed and dived to attack the maniac. He felt
his kick connect viciously to the Lump's head, but the beast
didn't stir. He was down and out. Still, Alex kicked and
screamed and spit until Manning grabbed him again, in a fierce
bear hug, and then, suddenly, Alex was spent, too weak to resist
the restraint. He crumpled onto a chair, noticed through a haze
the stares of the curious and horrified patrons. He closed his
eyes as the police arrived.

Two and a half hours later, after police questioning, a doctor's
swabbing and patching, and a call home to Patty, Dave Manning pulled Alex's car into Alex's driveway. He moved to help
Alex out of the passenger's seat but Alex wearily waved him
away.

Patty stood by the open front door, framed by the inside light.
She looked as if she had been standing there, unmoving, since
the phone call an hour before. She ran over to her husband and,
asking no questions, let him lean on her for support. He hesitated, unused to leaning on anyone, but he relaxed and let her
lead him inside to the living-room couch. It was five minutes
before he nodded that it was all right to speak, that he was ready
to talk.

Before she talked to Alex, though, Patty turned to Dave Manning. "Thank you," she said.

"I didn't do a thing."

"Uh," Alex croaked.

"You're all right?" she asked tenderly.

"Yeah." He coughed, his voice raw. "My throat hurts. He
tried to strangle me."

"I think he would've killed you," Manning said.

"Why?" Alex asked. "Why?"

"He's crazy," Patty said. "He's a crazy and sick person."

"You don't know the half of it," Manning said.

"Yeah," Alex said. "You don't know what he did to Emmy."

"Yes, I do," Patty told him. "I know more than the half of it."

Alex cocked his head. He'd been aware from the moment he'd seen her that she was waiting to tell him something. If he weren't so tired and sore and confused, he'd have smiled affectionately at her and her transparency. "How do you know?" he asked.

"Emmy's here. She's in Russ's room."

"Get her outta here."

"Alex—"

"Come on. Out. Get her outta here."

"If you'll—"

"Patty, get her the fuck outta here! I don't want her in my house!"

Patty didn't answer. She knew he didn't mean it, that he would never turn out her friend, that it was just the last outburst of pain from the Lump's assault. And when she didn't answer, he just nodded, giving in and acknowledging the fact that she knew him too goddamn well.

"What did he actually do?" Manning wanted to know. "The cops just told us he beat the shit out of her."

"It looks worse than it is, really," Patty said. "He ripped out a clump of her hair." She shivered. "Punched her in the eye. Her eye looks really awful. He broke two of her ribs."

"The doctor with her now?"

"No. That's all been done."

"Patty," Alex asked suddenly, "whose car's in the driveway?"

Patty didn't answer.

"Who do we know who owns an MG?"

"Alex," she said. "I've got a real shocker to spring on you."

"What?"

"This is extremely complicated and I only just learned it an hour ago."

"Whose car?" Alex asked again.

"Mine," Danny Cappollo said, and stepped into the room. "Patty," he said next, "I think I better handle this one."

"Daniel Kapstein?"

"Yeah."

"You're as crazy as the fuckin' Lump," Alex said.

"I know it sounds a little weird."

"*Weird?*"

"But it makes sense."

"You're a fucking lunatic!"

"Alex. There are three things that count in Hollywood: money, power, and connections. The first step is the connections."

"I don't believe this."

"Every successful agent in this town is a short, pushy Jew. I'm five six and aggressive as hell, but that's only two outta three. And since every producer and network executive and studio head also seems to fast on the High Holy Days, I figure, what's the harm in a little . . . deception? They'll never know and it'll just make my life easier if I can throw my arm around the head of MGM and say, 'Believe me, J.B. *Emmis.*' "

"*Emmis?*"

"That's Jewish. It sorta means 'trust me.' "

"You've been studying?"

Danny nodded humbly. "I've picked up a few phrases. I've got a good ear."

"I think you're *crazier* than the fuckin' Lump!"

"Come on, come on."

"I mean it!"

"Blame it on love."

"Bullshit!"

Danny shrugged.

"What about, uh, Brenda?" Patty asked. "Speaking of love."

"Oh. That."

"Yeah. *That.*" Alex didn't even try to hide his disgust.

"Okay. That was pretty ugly. I admit it."

"Give," Alex told him.

"She was rich. She was rich and she had a face like a foot. You know me, you know the kind of girls—"

"I know.'

"So I went out with her for a while."

"Yeah. The way I heard it is you were gonna get married."

"Now, that's a matter of opinion. I never actually agreed to specifics."

"Christ!"

"Okay, it was a shitty thing to do. I admit it. But her parents knew a lot of people. And the more I met them the more I knew I should get the hell out of advertising and get out here."

"An *agent?*"

"It's the wave of the future! I'm tellin' you that every ball-player in the country is gonna have an agent pretty soon. The money in entertainment hasn't been touched! Not as far as I'm concerned. TV, movies, sports. Christ, suppose I'm handling you and next year you hit three hundred with thirty-five home runs. Well, you think I'm gonna let you sign for a ten-percent raise? Bullshit. Especially out here. The first thing I do is get you some kind of TV or radio deal."

"What do I know about—"

"What's the diff? The Angels gotta make a TV deal for their away games, right? So, say they make the deal with Channel Five. Well, I go to the Angels and say, sure we'll sign. But my boy wants a TV deal. We want to be the weekend sportscaster in the off season at thirty G's per. The Angels go to Five and say, if you want the rights, Justin's gotta have his own spot. There's big bucks out there, and it's a pretty easy business as long as you've got some balls. I've already done pretty well with Emmy."

"So we've heard."

"Well, you know how important that is? Since I got her that job, I've had three, four clients come my way. One of whom I think's got a legit chance at bein' a biggie one of these days! Plus, I figure with your help, I've got a decent share at a few ballplayers. And—"

"Danny," Alex said. But he didn't say anything past that because he didn't have anything else to say. He just held up his hand so his oldest pal would stop talking.

"How did you get involved with Emmy?" Patty asked quietly.

"That was an accident." He looked over at Alex. "I came down to see you in Baltimore, remember? And we just, uh, hit it off. I mean, there she was with this big jerk and she was clearly unhappy. . . ."

"You always did have a good eye."

"For?"

"For pickin' up stuff like unhappiness."

"Well, it was obvious. And I liked her. And I thought she was great looking. I mean, Jesus, she *is* great looking. So that sort of set things in motion. I knew this was the direction I wanted to move in. I'd already had some ad guys set me up with agents in New York so I could learn the lay of the land, so to speak. It made perfect sense to have Emmy as my first client. Hey, listen," he said suddenly. "This isn't as totally sleazy as it sounds. I mean, we're gonna get married as soon as she gets divorced from that asshole."

"How is she now?" Patty asked. "Should I go sit with her?"

Danny shook his head. "She's asleep. It's the best thing."

"Tell me what happened from the beginning," Alex said with a quiet sigh. "I wanna know why that bastard almost strangled me to death."

"She wanted to tell him alone. Tell him that she was leaving him."

"Jesus!" That was the first word Dave Manning had said since the conversation started. When they all jerked their heads around to stare at him, he said, "Sorry. I was just overwhelmed by the stupidity of telling something like that to the Lump all alone."

"Look, I knew that," Danny said. "I told her. But it *is* her husband. She wanted to do it."

"Go on," Alex said, rubbing his neck at the place where his throat was really starting to burn.

"She said she'd call in about an hour, when it was all over. I gave her two hours and then called. When there was no answer, I drove over to her house. Just a hunch that there was something bad going on."

"Good hunch."

"Yeah. Well, the lights were on and the door was wide open, so I went in. Apparently, Lumpano was drunk when he got home, real drunk, and when she tried to tell him, he hit her. He went crazy. She told him it was me, that I was your friend—"

"Christ."

"Yeah. He figured you knew all about it. That's probably why he went berserk when he saw you."

"Yeah," Alex said. "That's a solid guess."

"The only thing that doesn't fit is that Emmy really didn't think he'd take it so hard. The way she talked, women were just so many sides of beef to him. He fucked around all the time, he didn't really care about Emmy. I mean, as a person. That's what doesn't figure. He didn't really care, so why'd he go so crazy?"

"I don't know," Alex said. "You're right. It doesn't figure."

"Yes, it does," Manning said. "Sure it does." His eyes met Alex's and Alex looked at him searchingly. "There," Manning told him, "you have the danger of going after what you want. You just paid the price of failed expectations."

"Anyway," Danny went on as Alex shivered and turned away from Manning's stare, "I took her to the hospital. She was pretty beat up, but it wasn't anything too damaging. Mostly shock and the fact that it hurts like hell. When the doctor was done, I couldn't bring her back to her place. And I knew this was all gonna come out now, I mean, that you'd now know it was me. So I thought we should come here." Danny Cappollo/Kapstein shrugged. "That's it. *Emmis.*"

Alex exhaled a long, slow breath and leaned back against Patty on the couch. "Man," he said. "Do you have any idea how the shit's gonna hit the fan over this one?"

"The Lump'll be suspended," Manning noted. "Unless the team decides to keep it quiet."

"They won't be able to," Danny said. "Emmy's somewhat of a celebrity herself now. That makes it a story, not just another drunk ballplayer getting in trouble."

"The Angels can keep it quiet."

"I won't let them," Danny challenged.

"What?"

"It's good publicity," Danny said quietly. "People'll turn to watch Emmy after this if it's played right. She'll be front-page news. In a sick sort of way, I grant you that, this is gonna turn out to be good for her. Good for her, good for me."

"You broke it already," Alex said, not a question. Not at all a question.

Danny nodded. "From the hospital."

"Goddamn," Manning said, whistling through his teeth. "Goddamn! This guy's right. He's gonna make a shitload of money in this town."

"Everybody gets what he wants when he wants it bad enough," Alex said.

Patty shook her head. "Except the Lump."

"We'll see," Alex told her. "We'll see."

Dave Manning stood up suddenly. "I've gotta go," he said to nobody in particular.

"Good luck," Alex said. "I never rooted against my own team before, but good luck."

"I don't need luck now," Dave Manning said, and smiled. "I know what I want and I want it enough to do it." He did a not bad two-step on his way out the front door. "Thanks, everybody."

20

Patty drove Alex to the game late the next morning. Russell sat in the backseat, excited that he was going to the last game of the season, equally excited that his dad would now be home for the next six months. Russell loved the off season when his dad would have catches with him, take him for long rides in search of the perfect pastrami-and-egg sandwich, talk to him in warm, relaxed tones about growing up, about honor and trust, about the way things would be. He was hoping that his dad would also talk about the really cool stuff that had happened the night before. His mom had made him go over to Glen Waggoner's house when Mrs. Lump had come over all bandaged up. He hadn't figured out exactly what had happened, but he did have a sense of the violence that had taken place. Strangely, he hadn't been scared by it. He had been drawn to it, curious. Lying awake in Glen's room, in the extra bed, he was excited thinking about it. He had the same buzz that he got from rock and roll. He felt electrified.

"Listen to this," Alex said to Patty. "This one's even worse." He folded back the *L.A. Times* on his knee and read: " 'Walter Lumpano, star catcher for the Los Angeles Angels baseball team, was arrested last night on two counts of assault.' " Alex looked up at Patty. "Then, blah, blah, blah, two paragraphs of the same stuff as the other articles, then: 'One team official, who

vished to remain anonymous, said that Mr. Lumpano had long
been suspected of being an alcoholic.' "

"You know," Patty said, "I knew he was always drunk,
but . . ."

"Yeah. I know," Alex agreed before she finished.

"It's so weird. I mean, of *course* he's an alcoholic. How could
we not . . ." She trailed off.

"Listen: 'Doctors confirmed that tests showed strong traces of
amphetamines in the catcher's blood and urine.' Boy. I would
not wanna be the one to give the Lump a urine test."

"Amphetamines?" Patty asked.

"The guy's always poppin' somethin'. Speed, usually." At Patty's shocked expression Alex said, "A lot of guys do it."

"You?" Patty asked, incredulous.

Alex was hurt. "Noooo! I would never touch that stuff. You
know that." He rustled the paper. "Geez, this is gonna all come
out now. Bad for the game. Bad for the game." He turned his
eyes back to the paper. "Oh, God." He groaned. "Catch this
one: 'Mrs. Lumpano's theatrical agent and admitted paramour'
—*paramour?*—'Daniel Kapstein, said that "Walter Lumpano is
a dangerous member of society's criminal element. He is a
violent alcoholic and now, we discover, a drug addict as well.
He should be behind bars and I intend to see him put there." '
I'm tellin' ya, Danny's gonna make this stay on the front page
for a week. He's gonna come outta this a bigger star than anybody else."

"Lᴏᴠᴇ Aɢᴇɴᴛ Iɴ Vɪᴏʟᴇɴᴛ Tʀɪᴀɴɢʟᴇ!" Patty envisioned.

"Yeah."

"Dɪᴅ Iᴛ Fᴏʀ Lᴏᴠᴇ—Aɴᴅ Tᴇɴ Pᴇʀᴄᴇɴᴛ!"

"You got it."

"Daddy," Russell said, "is there any more good stuff about
your fight?"

"Yeah," Alex mumbled. "But I don't wanna read any more of
it, okay?"

"Sure," Russ said, disappointed.

"How's your throat?" Patty touched Alex's arm sympathetically.

"Better."

"Back?"

"Okay."

"What happens to the Lump now?" Patty wondered.

"He's suspended for sure. The commissioner already said that. They're not sure for how long, though. My guess is for all of next year with no pay."

"Then?"

"Then, he's lucky if he doesn't go to jail. I don't think he will, though. I'm not gonna press charges, I decided."

"I figured."

"You think I should?"

"No," Patty said. She patted her husband on the thigh.

"How did you know I wouldn't?"

" 'Cause it's over. 'Cause I know how you think. Yesterday's loss is just that: yesterday's. You're not like me. You don't hold a grudge."

"Mmmmm," he murmured.

"We're here!" Russell shouted.

Patty drove into the stadium parking lot. The guard nodded at Alex and waved them through.

"Listen to this one," Alex said. "Murray Lansing's column." He read: " 'He was strong enough to carry the entire team on his back for weeks at a time. But even Walter Lumpano couldn't handle the monkey when it jumped on the bandwagon. The Lump is courageous enough to catch a doubleheader with two broken fingers. But even he couldn't last the distance against the loneliness of the road, the pressure of the game, the hundreds of beers gulped in hotel bars waiting for the jukebox to play that favorite song. That song, for Walter Lumpano, catcher extraordinaire, turned out to be a desperate cry for help.' A little much, don't you think?"

"I feel sorry for him," Patty said. "In a way. I can't help it."

"You got your tickets?" he asked as the car pulled into his space. Patty reached into the pocket of her red-and-white checked cowboy shirt and pulled out two green tickets. He nodded, satisfied.

"Good seats, Dad?" Russ asked.

"Do I ever give you bad seats?"

"No."

"So what are you asking for?"

"There's always a first time."

Alex and Patty both laughed.

"They're good seats. The usual."

"Oh, boy."

"Oh, boy," Patty echoed.

The Angel clubhouse was eerily quiet. Everyone knew about the Lump's arrest and his attacks on Emmy and Alex. Everyone was depressed as hell.

Not only was the Lump the best player on the team, but he was a member of the family. He was an insider. Sure he could outcrude anybody on a good day, sure he went a little nuts sometimes with the booze and pills. But the consensus was that really all the Lump had done was break the great silent law of all ballplayers used to being able to live by their own rules: It don't matter none what you do, just don't get your ass caught.

No one said very much to Alex. He was getting a lot of stares, though. A few of the players were still busy reading all the various stories on the Lump in the papers. Most of the guys had read them earlier.

Al Dressler, the Angels' manager, strolled over to Alex, patted him an encouraging pat on the ass, and said, "How ya doin', Judge?" Big Al wasn't much of a talker. In fact, he rarely spoke at all. When he did, he always sounded rusty, out of practice. His "How ya doin', Judge?" came out "Owyuhdoonjuh." It had taken Alex three weeks of being with the team before he felt reasonably sure he understood whatever Big Al was trying to say. As he was greeted now, Alex felt pretty good—he'd definitely gotten the message that Big Al was saying hello.

"How ya feelin'?" the manager asked. *Owyuhfiln?*

"Okay," Alex said.

"That was shitty about the Lump." *Shittybowluh.*

Alex just nodded. No one had said anything to him, but it was clear that somehow, for some reason, he was being blamed for the Lump's downfall. It was as if he only hadn't interfered, the

Lump would be there now, slurping beer, belching, and farting in his favorite corner of the clubhouse.

"Friend of yours, that agent fella, huh?" *Frennayers, thagenfelluh?*

"Yeah."

Big Al shook his head. "Asshole." *Asshole.*

Alex shrugged.

"Fuckin' around with the Lump's wife, huh?" *Fuhkrown-withLumswifhuh?*

Alex shrugged again.

"You up to playin' today?" *Yuptaplaynday?*

Alex nodded.

"Maybe you should take a rest today. Your throat an' all." *Mebbeyewshdtakaresday. Yerthronall.*

Alex shrugged. "I'm okay."

"Yeah. Take a rest today, Judge." *Yetakarestdayjuh.*

Alex nodded.

Right before the national anthem, as the Angels paced and stretched and gabbed and chewed in the dugout, Big Al Dressler called for silence.

"I ain't big on no pregame pep talks. But, fuck, it's the last game o' the year. The best we can do is be spoilers. We can ruin their season if we win this game, knock 'em right outta the pennant. That ain't much, but at least we'll be remembered by somebody."

Big Al's words were the most prophetic he'd ever uttered. In the bottom half of the first, as the Angels came to bat, Dave Manning made sure they were remembered by everybody for this game.

As Eddie Fox tapped the dirt off his shoes and stood at the plate to lead off, Dave Manning placed the baseball firmly into the pocket of the seven-year-old glove on his left hand. Then he slipped the glove off his hand and laid it gently on the pitcher's mound, directly on the rubber. He looked over to the Angel bench until he found Alex. At first Alex was paying no attention; he was simply staring down at the concrete floor and his own spiked shoes. Then, as if indeed he felt the heat of the stare all the way from the mound, his head jerked up. He found Manning staring at him, that same damn insolent stare that as much as said: *Look, I'm tryin' to show you something, why the hell don't you pay attention!* Alex paid attention as Manning held his gaze momentarily, then turned to leisurely scan the stadium: the press box, the left-field stands, the bleachers, the right-field fans, the bullpens, the box seats along both baselines, his own dugout.

It looked as if Dave Manning was simply enjoying a perfect summer day, but his enjoyment was lingering a bit too long. The umpire took one step toward the mound, waving his hand, a signal for the pitcher to begin. Spud Wallach, the Orioles' manager, stood on the top step of the dugout. He said nothing, only looked out curiously at the passive figure of the ace of his pitching staff.

Satisfied, finding whatever it was he hoped to find with his long, three-hundred-and-sixty-degree gaze, Dave Manning, in front of 38,472 paying customers, quit the game of baseball. He gave out a huge, carefree, relieved-as-hell smile, stepped off the mound, and walked back to his own dugout.

No one knew what was going on. Not the people in the stands, not the announcers, who kept saying things like "If he has a blister or some such thing, it's difficult to ascertain why he looks so happy," not the Angels or the Orioles.

No one except Alex, who now stood, rigid, his muscles locked in an unbearable tension. He watched the Orioles' manager meet Manning halfway to the dugout on the first-base line. There were low, questioning murmurs from Spud, a moment of confused silence, then sputtering. Then came the eruption. An explosion of disbelieving profanity and wild, jerky body movements. The curious first baseman was the first to intrude on the scene, followed only a split second later by the catcher. They, too, exploded in a fury. The catcher started for Manning, fists cocked, but Manning didn't move. There was no tension in the pitcher's body or face. He would not have hit back, he would have taken whatever was dished out, and the passivity of it all froze the catcher into a raging stillness.

The whole Oriole team now slowly made its way onto the field. No one had quite pieced things together yet. It was total chaos, but a remote, dreamlike chaos. Everyone seemed to be lumbering in slow motion. Gradually, Alex began to hear, to focus on, the bits and pieces of hysterical explanation.

"He won't pitch!"

"What?"

"Hurt?"

"He quit."

"What?"

"He quit! He quit!"

"This is the pennant!"

"He said he wants out."

"This is the whole goddamn season!"

The manager still hovered around Manning, poking at him, screaming, kicking dirt, slapping his face, hard, twice. Manning never acknowledged his presence, just calmly made his way to the dugout. The word was now filtering around the stadium. Dave Manning, the ace of the Baltimore Oriole staff, possibly the best pitcher in baseball, had just refused to pitch the most important game of the Orioles' season. If he won—and he was going against the worst team in the league—he could give them the pennant and lock up a pitcher's most treasured award. It was a foregone conclusion: Manning would surely beat the Angels and the season would end in triumph. He could be a hero, a baseball immortal. He could be rich and famous, he could achieve it all.

And he quit.

There was practically a riot going on now. The Angels were shocked into near silence on the bench, but the fans were booing, screaming, stamping their feet, throwing things onto the field. An alternate pitcher was frenziedly warming up in the bullpen. The Orioles' Latin second baseman walked side by side with Manning, spitting on him with every step he took. The Angel announcer was hollering into his mike.

"I don't see how this is possible! This is the ugliest day in the history of professional sports! This is a scandal, a cheat! Ladies and gentlemen, in twenty years of broadcasting baseball I have never seen—never thought I would see—anything as nasty and unpleasant as this. Dave Manning of the Baltimore Orioles, with a chance to pitch his team into the World Series, has walked off the field! Has quit the team!"

Even the Angels were getting angry. The smug looks on their faces were turning to scowls. Sure, Manning was the enemy, but he had violated their ethics of battle. He was making a mockery of their lives.

"Bastard." This was said quietly.

"Chickenshit!" This was said louder, spoken for the entire dugout.

"Cocksucker!" This was hurled onto the field, a loud empty challenge picked up by no one.

Alex stood frozen on the infield grass, silent, straining to see what was going on. As Manning finally reached his own dugout, he turned back to search the field one last time.

The noise was deafening. Garbage—hot dogs, cups of soda, beer, cardboard carrying-cartons, programs, peanuts—filled the air. The ballplayers were all shaking their fists in Manning's direction, swearing, spitting.

The pitcher found Alex, the object of his search. Dave Manning smiled as Alex looked on in horror. Manning raised his arms in triumph before disappearing down the dugout steps, mustard from a thrown hot dog splattered on his left arm, his uniform covered in beer.

21

"You shouldn't have brought the letter," Patty said.

Alex was distracted. He didn't hear her. "What?"

"You shouldn't have brought the letter," she said, a little more gently this time.

"I know. It's just that . . . Jesus!"

Alex looked down at the letter—handwritten in pen in a childish, overly large slant—and reread it:

Alex Justin,

I red you are a frend of that communist David Manning. Your probably a commie too. You will both go to hell. I hope you die.

Unsigned American

"Jesus," he said again, and shook his head, not so much in bitterness as wonder.

"Alex, we're going on this trip to relax, to forget about all this. Look, look down." Alex followed her fluttering hands and peered out the window of the airplane. Fifteen thousand feet below them was the Atlantic Ocean. "Look. Water as far as the eye can see. No baseball teams. No Lump, no Dave Manning. No agents or newspapers. Just water. Lots of water and me."

Alex grinned, if a bit weakly. "That is a pretty good combo."

"Me and water. It's almost as good as Surf 'n Turf."

"When do you think this kind of stuff will stop? I mean, it's been, what, five months?" he asked.

"What difference does it make? They're all from cranks. You didn't have anything to do with what Dave did. And even if you did, what's so terrible?"

He cocked his head at her.

"I mean, *really?*" she insisted. "All the papers made it sound as if he were a worse villain than the Lump!"

"He is, to most people."

"I don't see how that's possible."

"Trust me on this one. The Lump'll be out of baseball maybe a year. Then, not only will he come back a hero, he'll have licked his problem and he'll be starting all over, and I guarantee you every columnist in the country'll be calling him the most courageous battler of all time."

"And Dave?"

"Christ, Dave is probably the biggest social outcast this country's had since Benedict Arnold. He'll *never* be able to get back into baseball—he'll be a hundred years old before they invite him to an old-timers' game. He'll be lucky if he can even get into a stadium to *watch* a game. Not only that, wait until he goes out and gets a real job! Who's gonna hire him? The guy's a fuckin'—excuse me—the guy's a menace to society. That's how he's gonna be seen. That's gonna follow him around for the rest of his life."

"You can say *fuckin'* in front of me, you know."

"I know, I know." He made a face at her for changing the topic.

"I'm sorry Dave did it," she said in response to his scowl, "because I know he's your friend and I know it upsets you. But you've got to forget it. It's over and done with, isn't that your motto? And it doesn't have anything to do with you."

"Why?" Alex said, almost pleadingly. "Why did he do it?"

"We've discussed this a million times. Dave is clearly somewhat of a masochist, a bit of an exhibitionist. He's obviously not at peace with himself and is rebelling to try to find something, some part of himself he thinks is missing. But he didn't hurt anybody. He didn't almost kill his wife and best friend. That's a lot worse."

"Mmmmm."

"It drives me crazy," Patty said, "that you don't believe that."

"I don't *not* believe it, Patty. I'm just not sure. What the Lump did, that *is* over. I'm all right. Emmy's okay. No more pain or anything, no scars. But Manning. That's gonna last a long time. That's something that . . . changes things."

"What does it change?" she asked gently. She knew this was a sensitive area for him.

"It changes . . ." He hesitated. "It changes who you can trust. It changes what you can hold on to. It changes what you can believe in."

"Is that worse than committing a criminal act?"

"Patty," he said, and he took her hand as if his touch would help to emphasize his words. "He *quit*. He could've done what everybody in this whole country dreams of doing—making it all the way to the top—and he quit! He just fuckin' *quit!*"

"A lot of people quit before they get to the top. They just do it more quietly and they don't do it on national television. It's called 'fear of success.' "

"You do a paper on it?"

"Yes, as a matter of fact." She paused, hesitated, then they both said at exactly the same moment, "Got an A." They smiled at each other.

When the smile faded, Alex clutched her hand tighter. "Manning's not afraid of anything," he continued. "I'm telling you, not anything. What he did was 'contempt' of success.' Not fear. What would he have to be afraid of?"

"I don't know," she said. "Do you?"

He looked up at her, surprised. He wondered if that was just a casual question or if she were even more insightful than he gave her credit for being.

He didn't know what there was to be afraid of. But Alex knew that since that last game of the season, since he'd seen that goddamn smile on Dave Manning's face, he'd been afraid. He'd been ready to burst, to explode. He didn't know why. He didn't even know what it was that was on fire inside him, what it was that was growing, forcing its way out. He didn't know how much longer he could—or would want to—fight this thing back.

"No," he said—with an even tone, he hoped. "I don't know."

Patty lowered her voice. Her lips softened into a tender smile and she put her hand on his thigh. She spoke sincerely and lovingly. "This vacation is for you," she said. "You've had a really bad year. . . ."

"I've noticed."

"You have. And I just want you to relax for a week. We'll sit in the sun, we'll drink, we'll get all romantic. We'll talk. Things'll be like they used to be. You need that."

"I do."

"Spring training doesn't start for three more weeks. I don't want you to even think about baseball. Or anything. It'll be like a second honeymoon."

"We never had our first one."

"So it'll be like our first honeymoon. But this is to let yourself go. Isn't that what you're always talking about? You don't have to worry about coaches or managers or pinch hitting or Russell playing his music too loud or picking me up at school. None of that. I just want you to be *you* for this trip. And everything'll be perfect, okay?"

"Okay," he said. And felt that thing growing inside him. He wondered if that was the *him* that Patty wanted. He hoped so. "I love you very much."

Patty smiled. "You better," she said. "I've got a lot of grocery money riding on this trip."

Alex took her hand; it fit, as always, perfectly inside his. He leaned back in his chair, put his stereo headphones on, and contentedly listened to the airplane's jazz station for the entire next two hours, until their plane landed in Port au Prince, Haiti.

The hour-and-a-half drive to their hotel was a bumpy one, but pleasurable. The eager-to-please black cabdriver took them on a brief tour of the city before heading out to their beach destination. They saw the tiny hovels in the ghetto, crammed with families of naked babies and pregnant women. They drove past the huge mountaintop open-air market with its cages of live chickens strung up and carried by sturdy women on their heads as if they were living Easter hats; its stalls of artists, painting their brightly colored primitive portraits and junglescapes, jewelers weaving stained glass beads that sparkled like diamonds, sculptors whittling away on their wooden totems; its urchins, running alongside the car, pleading for coins, candy, and cigarettes; its rows upon rows of fresh fruits and vegetables—mango and papaya and coconuts and yellow seas of bananas and pineapple; its crates packed with ice, topped with oysters and clams and mussels and crabs, still alive, still squirming under the rays of the bright sun. They drove through green, green forests, passed fried-food stands, black men with their shirts off swinging scythes at huge stalks of sugar cane, and minibuses painted with jungle murals and dragging teenage daredevils clinging to the outsides of the backs. They passed a huge American-owned sugar factory, its chimneys spewing gray smoke into the air that glistened from a recent downpour. When they finally pulled up to the hotel, Alex and Patty were laughing and poking each other, bubbling over with: "Oooh, did you see that?" "Oh, my God, look at that!" "Look, look, look!"

They were checked in quickly. The owner—a brittle little woman who looked to be two hundred years old—said she spoke only French, although Alex was sure she understood what he was saying. Finally, he showed her a piece of paper from the travel agent explaining all the details, and they were led away to their cabin.

"It's perfect," Patty said, swinging her arms around the room. "Isn't it perfect?"

Alex looked around the one-bedroom hut. He plucked a straw from a corner of the inside of the thatched roof and pulled a switch that started a brass ceiling fan twirling. From the front window they could see and hear the Caribbean, and from the various others they saw birds and fruit trees and black waiters scurrying with drinks to the beach.

"I gotta admit," he said. "Perfect."

They threw off their sweaty clothes. Patty had the top of her new bikini almost fastened when Alex took her hand and led her to the bed. They had the best sex they'd had in a long time, passionate and hard and strong, and it wasn't until right before he came that the Girl from the Park slipped in and replaced Patty beneath him and the thing inside him began, once again, begging to get out.

The first night they ate dinner under an umbrella at a round table on the beach, oblivious to the chattering German, French, and American tourists surrounding them. They held hands in between courses and danced close together when the small four-piece band came out. Alex even got a little high on a bottle of chilled Chablis.

Patty asked him questions: about Manning, about Lump, about the possibility of a trade, about Danny, about a reconciliation with Elliot. Alex—though he felt a little too much like a subject for one of her classes—answered. He knew how much it meant to her to understand him, to feel that nothing was escaping her perceptions, that nothing was coming between them. So he answered her questions: He still hadn't really sorted out Manning's actions. He didn't know what they meant, but he absolutely felt the message had been for him, that it had been another of Manning's obscure challenges. He was no longer angry about the Lump; he honestly hoped he'd get help and play ball again. He was, unfortunately, expecting a trade—he didn't want to leave L.A., but they'd moved before and could do it again; besides, he wouldn't mind being on a good team, one with a real shot at a pennant. Yes, he still felt close to Danny, in a funny way he trusted him more than ever—he knew him so well, knew the crooked side of him so intimately, that he could never really be surprised. No, he wouldn't call Elliot—he didn't think it was possible to force someone to feel something he didn't naturally feel, and his brother's silence made it clear that he was not yet over the pain that Alex somehow was causing him and had caused him for so long. Then he asked her. He pretty much knew all the answers, but he could tell she wanted to hear the questions and give her own responses: Her classes were becoming more and more important to her, she felt she was learning, rethinking things, growing. She had never felt entirely comfortable with the passion of emotions and she was in her world there—controlling the directions of the mind. She didn't want another child, she'd been thinking about this a lot— she felt ridiculous, but the pain of Russ's birth had made her too afraid and she had never been able to tolerate pain. She was glad when Alex assured her one child was enough—Russell gave him plenty of pleasure, he looked forward to watching the boy turn into a man, was content to channel all his efforts into that one growth. She felt that, sometimes, she was not close enough to Russ, that she loved him but worried that she was making mistakes while helping him to grow up. She loved him, Alex, very much—that love had never lessened, never changed—it was the one constant in her life and it was the one thing, the only thing, she really and truly trusted. Perhaps she did under-stand his obsession with Manning's betrayal, she said—it would be how she would feel if he betrayed their love.

The bottle was empty and they were both all talked out. They tried swimming in the sea but found themselves swarmed over by tiny jellyfish, so they ran back to safety, not stopping at the beach but continuing on to their thatched haven. There they showered to get the salt off and washed each other's hair. Ex-hausted, they fell asleep—without making love but wrapped together under a single sheet.

The next few days blurred together in a haze of sun and strolls and laughs and fresh fruit and touristy voodoo ceremonies and sailing and snorkeling and blundered French and dancing and deep, restful sleep.

Patty was happy. Glowing. She was tanned and beautiful and she was all alone with Alex. SP every night, snuggling so close as to almost be climbing inside him; relaxed talk over meals, silent touching on the beach; tender and loving sex, gentle, slow, with lots of kissing and smiling and caressing. Yes, Patty was very, very happy.

Alex was ready to explode.

Literally, he felt, physically explode.

He'd been right on the edge like this since the last day of the season, when his body had gone rigid as he watched Manning leave the field. That rigidity hadn't disappeared; rather he'd been getting tighter. His skin felt as if it were going to burst;

with every movement he made, he felt himself become stiffer, heavier, more weighed down. He was sure that with one sudden movement, his skin would tear. And like Pandora's box, Alex Justin would rip open and . . .

And what?

What was it that would come pouring out of him? And why was he suddenly so sure it would be so terrible?

He didn't know, though he had thought about little else since they'd arrived in Haiti. The feeling was so overpowering that at times he couldn't breathe—he had to stop and hide the panicky expression on his face and close his eyes and breathe in, out, deeply, slowly, until the pain in his chest subsided.

No, he didn't know what it was, but one thing kept coming back to him: the last conversation he'd been having with Manning before the Lump went berserk. He had everything, that's what he'd told Manning. And it was true. He certainly had Patty. One thing this vacation had proven: they were still very much in love. He delighted in her delight, took comfort in their comfortableness; he couldn't imagine life without her. In fact, over the past few days, he'd tried to do just that, imagine. He envisioned driving her to the airport—she was off to visit her mother—and he saw a plane crash, saw her lost to him forever. Even knowing this was strictly a morbid imagination playing, testing, his eyes welled up with tears as he sat in his lounge chair, hiding behind his paperback best-seller, and he stayed saddened until Patty tapped him on the shoulder, coaxing him into a swim. No, he loved his wife. He didn't understand why he sometimes made her disappear in favor of strangers, but he did love her. His kid too. The perfect kid. Sweet, smart, nice. A joy. It still surprised Alex, in fact, how much pleasure he derived from Russell. And he expected that pleasure to spiral, to grow as the boy grew. He was looking forward to developing his son, to teaching him, to showing the direction that might keep his life joy-filled and pain-free.

Okay. One: his family. Perfect. Two: friends. Ahead of the game here. Teammates, lifelong friends. He wasn't lacking. Three: money. Fine. Not great, not rich, but fine. No complaints for the time being. Four: his health. He was getting a little rickety, but nothing worse than the usual wear and tear from nearly twenty years of sliding and banging and stretching his body to its absolute limits. Five: career. Couldn't knock it. Eight years in the majors, a .275 batting average, a good rep. Fine. Good. Solid.

What else was there?

Nothing. He'd covered all the bases.

Except . . . he wanted greatness. The kind of rush he'd gotten when he'd fucked Katie's brains out on the floor, in the sink, on the kitchen table. Only more permanent. The rush he was sure Charlie Parker and Miles Davis and Max Roach and Tommy Potter and Louis Jordan got when they finished the last song at the Massey Hall concert.

He wanted what Manning refused to touch, what the Lump lost when Emmy dumped him. He wanted that connection to perfection.

Getting blue.

He wished Willie were there to talk to.

What had he said to Manning that night? "Maybe I'm diluted." *Maybe I'm not trying hard enough. Maybe I'm trying too hard to do, to be, other things. Maybe I'm being tied to earth by all the "perfect" things I've acquired over the years.*

Maybe the real me, what I am, has never even seen the light of day.

For one brief, horrible moment Alex thought he was having a heart attack. The pounding in his chest made him gasp and fall back against his beach chair.

"Are you all right?" Patty asked him.

Alex didn't answer right away. He took a deep breath, then another. Then he reached over and oh-so-gently touched her cheek with the calloused fingertips of his right hand.

"I'm fine," he said. "Just being myself."

That night was their last in Haiti.

"Come," Madame Chaumont, the tiny owner of the hotel, said to them. "It is the first night of Mardi Gras. I take a car into the city. I take the four Germans, the fat ones. You come. You can fit in the car."

Alex hesitated.

"Oh, we've gotta go!" Patty said. "It's Mardi Gras!"

Alex looked at her sadly, a look she missed in her excitement. "Yeah," he agreed. "We've gotta."

An hour later they parked in some back alley. Their hostess made them all write down the name of the street in case they got separated.

"Midnights," she said. "We meet at midnights."

Alex and Patty immediately strolled away from the main street. She wanted to see what was going on behind the scenes. Alex had a lousy sense of direction, but he trusted her to get them back to where they'd started. They passed little children putting the last touches on their makeup and costumes. They passed floats on their way to meet up with the parade. Bands tuned up, plugging in their electric guitars to outdoor amps. Dogs roamed the streets, yelping and jumping and chasing. Lovers kissed. Parents yelled. They wandered left and right and circled around and then, to Alex's amazement, they were back on the main drag.

The colors were staggering. They splashed all over the city, all combinations, all hues and tones. A red papier-mâché bull danced in front of Alex's nose. Black skin and blond hair and glistening white sweat filled every inch of the city.

Noise filtered in from everywhere. Laughing, crying, screaming. Music—festive and electric, alive with the beat of the soul of the island. Trucks whirring by carrying soldiers with machine guns. The clop-clop of horses, a city-blockful of horses. Radios blaring commercials. Policemen issuing orders. Whores offering their bodies.

Beef sizzled on skewers over trash-can fires. Spoiled garbage mixed in the air with expensive perfume. Sweaty bodies, exhaust fumes, ripe coconut, and spilled puddles of alcohol dominated the hundreds of thousands of dancing, joyous participants.

"Isn't this incredible?" Patty yelled.

"Incredible!" Alex yelled back.

It *was* incredible. And he was lifted immediately into the

atmosphere, the spirit, the pulse. They drank. Soon, Alex had the pineapple ice of a piña colada dripping down his face and onto his collar. Patty laughed and he grabbed two more drinks from a passing vendor. He was soaring, he was as one with the celebration. He looked at Patty and she smiled, but she seemed distant, removed from what was happening around them. Her foot was tapping in time to the music of the parade, but the rest of her was still, stiff and awkward.

A truck now puttered by. On it were five black musicians. A guitar, a bass, a xylophone, and two conga drums. The five boys, teenagers, were grinning outrageously happy grins. Their rhythm sliced through the crowd and zeroed in on Alex. He dropped Patty's hand to clap along with the congas. She laughed and whooped. He whooped back. He grabbed another drink and downed it, throwing the empty cup way up into the air. His feet were stamping, leaping in frenzied spasms of excitement.

Somehow, he and Patty had separated. The crowd had come between them, pushing them apart. For a moment, he couldn't find her. She was gone. No, there she was! Just a few feet away, shoved aside by a woman trying to grab her wandering child. He laughed. Patty didn't laugh. She looked frightened.

He couldn't get close to her. A crowd of costumed young girls swarmed between them. Patty was nowhere in sight. Alex grabbed another drink, realized he was still stomping his feet to the sound of the conga band. The faster they played, the faster he stomped, the more his blood raced with excitement.

He turned again to look for Patty and his drink spilled, knocked out of his hand. He spun around, apologizing, laughing, to the person next to him: a woman, a black woman with a thin, short, low-cut dress. Her legs were thick, strong, and she wore no shoes. One tooth was missing, he saw when she smiled at him. The drink had poured onto her breasts, her huge breasts. The icy slush outlined her nipples and trailed down to her ribs. She laughed, too, now, a deep laugh that came from her stomach and made her head jerk backward. She stuck her fingers down the top of her dress and took out a ball of slush. She popped it into her mouth, licking her lips like a vision of satis-

fied lust. She reached back in when she saw his stare, pulled out
a small bit of ice. With one hand she opened his mouth, her
fingers prying his lips apart, and with the other she fed him, let
him taste the flavor of the pineapple, the alcohol, the scent of
her nipple, the salt of the sweat on her fingers.

The crowd surged again and he felt himself being pulled
along now by this woman. He laughed and clapped his hands,
and she did too. He thought to take one look behind him to see
where Patty was. For an instant he was sure he spotted her, but
the woman he saw disappeared, perhaps around a corner, or
maybe it just wasn't Patty. Maybe it was just another stranger.
So, drawn as if to a sexual magnet, he followed this black woman
with the strong legs.

They turned into an alley, still dancing. She whirled and
pushed him against the wall, yanking her dress down. Stunned,
he watched her rub both breasts with her own hands, watched
her enjoy their sudden freedom. Hungrily, he lunged for her,
took first one breast, then the other, into his mouth. He sucked
off the last of his cold drink, then kissed her nipples, hard,
harder, till he was biting them and she had to grab his head with
her large hands.

"Ten dollars, mon," she said. "Ten dollars for fuckee-boom-
boom."

"Fuckee-boom-boom?" he said.

"Ten dollars."

"Fuckee-boom-boom!"

Alex reached into his pocket, took out the first bunch of paper
money he found, and threw the crumpled bills at the whore.
She snatched them up, then pushed him farther back into the
shadows of the alley.

She let her dress fall to the ground and stepped completely
out of it. Alex lunged again, desperate to get her breasts back
into his mouth. She let him suck, then she climbed on top of
him, opened the zipper of his pants, placed him inside her, and
rocked back and forth, her breasts dangling over his face, her
stomach dripping hot sweat onto his stomach, until he came.

The violent spasm over, the whore immediately climbed off

him, grinned her toothless grin, pulled her dress on over her head, and disappeared.

Alex, propped up against the brick wall of the alleyway, groaned. He stood up, brushed himself off, and took a deep breath. He ran his hands through his hair, looked down at the torn knee of his pants, looked back up again. Patty stood there. Half a block away, standing still, rigid, staring. He started to call her, to reach out to her, but he didn't. He looked back down, and when he raised his eyes again, she was gone, as he knew she would be.

He knew he had done something bad, something horrible, perhaps irreversible. He knew the damage had been done. But as he stood there, he wanted to smile. He wanted to jump into the air and swing his fist in celebration and then fall back again in blessed relief.

The pounding had disappeared.

For the first time in five months the pressure was gone. His body felt normal, his muscles were loose, his head was not bursting.

He looked around, disoriented, then looked at his watch. It was midnight. He stumbled back to the main street. He ran for two blocks, recognizing nothing, and, now beginning to panic, ran four blocks in the other direction. He thought he remembered seeing this one restaurant, and, walking behind it, saw the Cadillac. He took two steps toward it and realized what he looked like.

Alex started to tuck in his shirt, to put himself back together.

"Mr. Justins," he heard Madame Chaumont call.

He looked up. There were Madame Chaumont and the four Germans. There was Patty, standing beside them, not looking at him.

He walked over. Saying nothing, they all piled into the car. About five minutes out of the city he had to say something to Patty, had to, tried to do it by touching her arm, but she shrank back as if his touch were poisoned.

As the Germans chattered happily away, Alex and Patty said not a word all the way back to the hotel. Not a word as they walked into the bungalow. Not a word until he stepped naked out of the shower and prepared to get into bed beside her. Not until he said, "Look, there was this thing inside me, this thing I've wanted to tell you about forever. This—"

Her movement interrupted him. It was so precise. She turned to him and quietly, whispering, said, "I'll never forgive you."

He said nothing. Their eyes met, and hers had no love in them. No, that was not true, Alex realized. Love could not be destroyed so quickly. But it could be transformed. And in Patty's eyes, he saw the transformation: fear, distrust, a throbbing pain, defeat, and hate.

"Never," she said.

Around the Horne
by
Ed Horne

... It will forever be known simply and deservedly as the Play.

Who knows what he heard, what he saw, what he thought. Ballplayers are not thinkers, they are men of action. They are doers. They are not watchers; they are meant to be watched. They are not poets; they are meant to be poeticized. Unfortunately, Alex Justin will probably never be able to tell us what it is that one feels when one achieves greatness, other than the usual clichés. Nor will he be able to tell us how it feels when greatness collides head-on with tragedy.

As time passes, the greatness of the moment will surely override the pain. And just as surely that's the way it should be. But let's not forget that greatness and pain are inextricably entwined.

Of course, who *could* forget after seeing the Play? ...

PART THREE
1970s

One never knows, does one,
The moment or the place?

—"One Never Knows"

22

Alex Justin shrugged. He was in the locker room talking to a nineteen-year-old boy wonder, wondering what the hell he was doing having a conversation with somebody so young.

"I mean, am I right, Judge, or what? Women don't know what they want."

Alex didn't answer. He was staring at his open locker.

"Hey, Judge. All of a sudden I get the feelin' you're not really listenin' to me. Judge?"

"What?"

"Are you listenin' to me?"

"No."

"Why not?"

"My wife knows what she wants," Alex said.

"Huh?"

"My wife. She's a woman. And she knows what she wants."

"What's the matter, Judge? Somethin' botherin' you?"

"Bothering me? Why would you think that?"

"I dunno. You just look like somethin's makin' you uptight. Like somethin's wrong."

"Hell, what could possibly be wrong? I'm thirty-seven years old, I've been playin' ball for twenty years, and this is my first World Series. It's all tied up three–three, tomorrow's the last game, win or lose, this is one of the most exciting Series in the

history of baseball, and I haven't played one inning. You thin
I'm upset 'cause I'm the only player on either team except fo
two flake relief pitchers who hasn't gotten into one game fo
even one shitty pitch? You think that's enough to get me a littl
pissed off? Pissed off so I don't really give a shit about how man
girls you're fuckin' on the side?"

"Yeah. Stupid of me, huh? I thought all that might b
botherin' you. I mean, especially with this whole Patty thin;
. . . I guess I shouldn'ta been mouthin' off about clam."

Alex looked at his roommate on the New York Yankees. Ron
nie Benson was twenty-two years old, in his second season c
pro ball. He was a very talented third baseman, and he'd hi
.280 with power all year. He had a perfect body, no hint of an
flab around the middle. He had more women than he coul
count and a lucrative commercial deal with Yamoto motorcy
cles. He wasn't in the least intimidated by this, his first Serie
appearance; in fact, if the Yankees won, he'd probably be th
MVP, because he was fielding like Brooks Robinson and had tw
game-winning hits.

"Don't be so fuckin' perceptive. You're too young."

"Stop tellin' me how young I am all the time."

"I've got *bats* older than you."

"Does this mean you're tiring of my company?"

"Yes."

"Then I'm goin'." Just for good measure Ronnie Benso
added a "Gramps" and slid out the clubhouse door into the nov
quiet players' tunnel. Alex sat in the clubhouse for five minutes
not moving. He knew he was already late to meet Patty bu
knew he needed five more minutes. When the five minute
were up, he needed five more but didn't take them. Patty
would understand if he was late, but he didn't want her under
standing. He was almost as tired of her understanding as he wa
of *needing* her understanding.

He stood and stretched his arms up toward the ceiling unti
he could feel the strain in his armpits. Then he picked up hi
gym bag and headed off to the parking lot to meet his wife.

*   *   *

Alex loved Patty.

It was amazing to him that after all these years he still loved her as much as he did.

Back when they were both teenagers, she'd once said that she'd always love him. She had also said she'd never forgive him after Haiti. And she hadn't. He was equally sure of that. A stalemate. Equal parts love and hurt. It added up to years of a politely caring marriage which, now that Russ was through with school and about to go out on his own, was going to end in a polite and very caring way.

He knew that divorce was the right thing to do. There was no longer a reason for them to be together. Neither love nor hurt was a strong enough force to keep them as one any longer.

He was going to miss her terribly. Her company, her quirks. Her touch. He was going to miss making love to her.

Their sex life was still fun, consistent in quality if irregular in quantity. They would often go as long as three or four weeks without making love. But when they did it was always nice, comfortable. Never exciting. But reassuring.

They didn't have sex for six months after that time in Haiti. And in that six months Alex never once cheated. His explosion had left him drained, desire free. He was also convinced that abstinence could clean the ugly blot off his past.

After six months, though, the pressure began to build again. He could feel himself swelling. So, apparently, could Patty, for one night, as he was almost asleep, she kissed him, she slid over into his arms and he held her for a while, saying nothing; then they made love. It was surprisingly passionate and kind love-making; they touched, they kissed, they smiled, they moaned. When they were done, he was like a happy puppy, kissing her, licking her, giggling, and smothering her with affection. Patty pushed him away after a while, not vindictively, quite warmly really, and said, "Have you been fooling around over the last six months?"

"No," he said. "I swear it. Not once!"

"You can," she told him.

"I can what?"

"You can have affairs. You can do whatever it is you feel you have to do, or want to do." He started to protest but she held up her hand to quiet him. "I love you. I still love you," she said, "and that was nice just now, the sex. But it's not the same anymore. We'll stay married and we'll probably have as much sex as we've always had. Everything'll stay about as it's been, I'd say. We'll probably be pretty happy. But you can do what you want."

"I don't want to do anything," he said urgently.

"You will," she said with no urgency. "And you can. It just isn't the same anymore."

Alex went another month before having a one-night stand. Two more weeks passed and he had a two-night stand. Those first two flings were deliberate, cautious choices. After that, though, he just played it by ear. He never became the fuck-anybody-at-any-cost type, not like the Lump used to be or a lot of the guys in the game whose main goal in life was to get as many sexually related diseases as possible. If he was in Cleveland and he was horny and an attractive stewardess was sitting at the hotel bar, he'd make a pass. If he'd just gotten off the phone with Patty and he wasn't in the mood to sweet-talk a stranger, he'd leave it alone. When he returned home, Patty didn't question him like an inquisitor, nor, as time passed, did she avoid the issue entirely. This was a new aspect of his life and she, as always, was curious about it.

As their marriage patched itself up gradually, like a wound healing itself, he felt her withdrawing, protecting herself. It was the only way she could stay with him. She devoted her time to her classes, got her degree in psychology, went on to graduate school. It was about a year ago, Alex realized, that she'd gotten a counseling license. Patty was now a psychologist with her own small practice. Alex was very proud of her. She specialized in treating women who were having marital problems.

His career had gone the way of his marriage, Alex thought—it had lasted. He had been a major-league ballplayer for nineteen years. Currently the third oldest player in the league, he had been consistent, never rising to spectacular heights, never sink-ing to demoralizing lows. His lifetime average was .268. He had 219 home runs, 750 RBIs, and 120 stolen bases. He played the outfield as well as anyone and, the past few seasons, had done a passable job noodling around first base when called upon. He had played for six teams before being traded to the Yankees at the start of the season. They thought they had a pennant winner and decided they needed a veteran right-handed hitter, someone who could also shore up the defense when needed and be a good influence on the kids. Enter the Judge.

He was glad to be back in New York, even though it was in exchange for a washed-up middle reliever and two kids down on the farm with absolutely no futures. Even before he'd been traded back, he and Patty had bought a little house in New Rochelle. They'd bought it after he was traded from the Cardinals, who'd gotten him from the Angels, to the Braves. They wanted a permanent home, particularly for Russell. Patty had her own office in the house, Alex had his yard, from which he could drive Wiffle golfballs.

His career, also like his marriage, was winding down now. He'd done his job for the Yankees; they'd made it to the Series and he'd helped. He was in excellent shape; his weight was down, his legs were strong. Still, he could feel the strain. He knew it was getting tougher, not easier, and he'd thought about making this his last season. He hadn't decided yet. But it was a possibility. If it *was* to be his last season, then there was only one game to go. Tomorrow could be his last chance. His final opportunity, at long last, to do what he had always wanted to do. To be a winner, to go down in history. To be a hero. To achieve that ultimate moment that justified all the tinier moments.

He wanted to play in that game tomorrow so badly that it physically hurt.

Well, he thought, *perhaps with Russ back. Maybe that's a good omen. My son will return and so will my glory.*

Alex had not been entirely comfortable the whole summer while Russ had been in Europe. There were stretches of over a week at a time when neither Alex nor Patty knew where their boy was, and Alex hated those days with a passion. Then a postcard would come with a picture of the red light district in Amsterdam. On the back would be Russell's scrawl:

Dear Old Folks,

How come you never told me this kind of stuff was over here? I would've come after grammar school, not waited until I was all the way through college and practically over the hill. Anyway, have no fear. Helga and Katja are swell gals. They want to meet you. Oh, yeah, I nearly forgot. Please wire me $8,000 so I can buy drugs. Try me next at Am. Ex. in Florence. Or Stockholm.

Patty wrote the letters back to him. Alex never felt the need. What would he say to his own son in a one-page note?

Dear Russ,

Life is pretty much more difficult than you imagine. Please, please be careful. Don't make the same mistakes I've made. I will help you. I will make sure your life proceeds smoothly. I will make sure you discover the answers I have not yet uncovered. I will do everything I can to help you "get blue." Enjoy Paris.

Dad.

Patty had never understood about getting blue. She did not believe things *moved*. Things were or weren't.

Russell had always understood.

Alex remembered the day he had first mentioned it to his son.

Patty was off at a class. The boy came home from high school, had walked in the door as Alex was on the living-room couch listening to "Rainbow Mist."

"Looks like you're enjoyin' the song," Russ had said.

Alex nodded. Russ sat and listened. But by the time the song ended, Alex saw he was restless.

"Don't you like it?" he asked.

"Yeah. It's good."

"Coleman Hawkins."

"It's just too *slow* for me."

"Slow?"

"Yeah."

"You're a pain in the ass."

"This won't make any sense to you, I'm sure, but it doesn't have any *life*. It doesn't have movement, action. It doesn't psych me up. It doesn't *tell* me anything. Or make me wanna *do* anything."

"Who makes you want to *do* something?"

"That's right."

"What?"

"No. Who." Russell grinned.

"Hold it, hold it," Alex said. "We're having a major failure to communicate."

"I'm sorry, Dad. I was just pullin' your leg. Doin' a little 'Who's on First' routine. You know, *Who* makes me want to do something? *The* Who. Pete Townsend, Daltrey. You said, 'Who makes me?' I said, 'That's right.' Get it?"

"Yeah," Alex said. "You've got your mother's superb sense of humor."

"Anyway. To answer your question . . . the Stones, the Who. Lou Reed. The Dead. Dylan, when he's on. Beatles, Lennon, more than anybody, when he's right. There's a lot."

"And what is it," Alex asked, "they make you want to do?"

"Well, there's the catch," Russell said calmly. "They whip you up into a frenzy, they can make you crazy, but then they leave you on your own. It's like they don't have any answers . . . No, that's not right. It's like they *do* have the answers but they won't give 'em to you. They make you feel all the . . . all the . . ."

"All the *what?*" Alex said, leaning forward.

Russ shook his head. "I don't know. They make you feel *everything*, but they don't tell you what to do about it. It's like they're saying, *Just go farther. The answer's around the corner. One more step. A little closer.*" Russell laughed. "Sounds crazy, huh?" He rolled his eyes. "But that's rock and roll for ya."

It was then that Alex told Russell his theory about getting blue. Russ was interested. And he *got* it.

"Yeah," he said. "I see it. It's sorta the same thing. Only Jagger's sayin' to me, *Step right up and take it. Grab for it, over and over again. Keep doin' it over, not just once.*" He laughed again. "Boogie till you puke. That's my new motto."

"Very nice," Alex said. "Very mature and very constructive."

"Don't worry, Dad. We're both getting blue. I just don'
wanna wait till it hits me. I wanna grab *it* first."

Alex wished he knew exactly what *it* was. Not just for his sake
but for Russell's.

He knew that he was overprotective of Russ. Not that he'd
ever stopped him from doing things. Just the opposite. He was
never afraid that Russ would break a leg or get in trouble or any
of the little things parents were supposed to worry about. Alex
worried about Russell's life.

They had a bond, a very special bond, one that Alex never
wanted to lose. He believed that it had sprung up that night
long ago in Los Angeles when he had hit the home run on
Russell's command. Ever since, his son had had that look in his
eye: the gleam, the hint that his father could do anything he
wanted. Even as mediocrity set in—as career, marriage, money,
life-style, all settled into a decidedly nonheroic rhythm—deep
down Russell felt that if Alex really wanted to change things, he
could. And every time son looked at father, son felt that hope.
Every time father looked at son, father felt that strength. It was
a strength Alex valued more and more the older he got.

Russell had gone through a lot of stages. But the bond had
endured, had, in fact, gotten tighter and stronger. Now Russ
was out of college and Alex was not looking forward to the next
stage. He still did not completely like surprises. And he, unhap-
pily, had been sensing a change in Russ for quite some time. A
change he found disturbing, if hard to define.

His boy was restless.

Russell's fingers moved at all times. His legs tapped. He stared
out the window, seeing or hearing something beckoning in the
distance. He wore restless clothes—jeans and T-shirts that could
be discarded at a moment's notice. His girlfriends were also
temporary attachments—plentiful but temporary.

He listened to restless music.

Hard rock. Electric. Acid rock.

Alex often wondered if Russ was into drugs. He thought not.
Surely he smoked dope. Even Patty kept a little grass around
the house—a sign of the times. Alex figured Russ had probably
experimented a little with harder drugs. Coke—which a lot of

the guys on the team snorted as casually as popping aspirin. Psychedelics? Maybe, Alex thought. Probably. A few times.

He thought Russ was the kind of person to do *anything* once or twice. The boy was smart, real smart, and real smart people usually got curious. Patty was like that. Only Patty wanted to hear about things, not experience them. Yes, Russell's curiosity came from Patty. But he was half Alex too. So he'd go out and *do.* Patty was curious about everything but wanted to do very little. Alex was curious about little and wanted to do only one thing: be a great ballplayer. The natural product was Russ: curiosity and action. It seemed like a good combination. A little dangerous, but the possibilities were infinite.

And to Russ, above all the possibilities was the music. Russ was going to make rock and roll fit into his real life as Alex had made baseball fit into his. Danny, old pal Danny, now ran one of the most successful and powerful entertainment agencies in the business. He handled sports celebrities, Alex included, actors and actresses, writers, directors, and had recently absorbed a smaller agency that specialized in the music business. Booking rock acts, negotiating record contracts, finding new talent to develop. And Danny had offered Russ a job in the talent division. A scout, in essence. A restless person to travel and find restless talent.

Alex was glad for his son because something was beginning and it was something that Russell liked. He was also wary because Alex knew the power of music and he was a little frightened of the language of rock and roll. He wasn't sure what it was telling his son, what it was going to make him do.

As soon as Alex stepped out onto the parking lot, he heard the familiar toot from the horn of Patty's car. One quick beep, that was all that was necessary.

He got behind the wheel of the car to drive, and even before he was out of the lot her left hand had crept over and settled lightly on his right thigh. She squeezed it supportively.

"Thank you," he said, and she didn't have to ask why he was thanking her.

"Russell's plane lands in three hours," she told him. "Do you think we should go home or just drive out to the airport?"

"I guess the airport. We'll have a couple hours to kill, though."

"You hungry?"

"A little."

"We can pick a crummy coffee shop and have a bad Patty Melt."

"Oooh. That *does* sound pretty good."

They smiled at each other. They had been married twenty-one years and were comfortable eating and liking bad Patty Melts in each other's presence. She squeezed his thigh a little tighter. His eyes watered.

"Don't," she said softly. "Please."

"No, no. Don't worry. I won't. I'm just feeling a little sad."

"Me too. I'm feeling a lot sad."

"Look, Patty, maybe—"

He stopped when he saw her look and the tilt of her head. There were no maybes about it.

"Do we have to tell Russ tonight?" he asked.

"I think we should."

"Why don't we wait till after the last game? It'll be better. We'll all fly to Cincinnati tomorrow, then after the last game we'll come back here. Let him get a couple days of being back home. Then we'll tell him."

"Okay," Patty said, after hesitating a fraction of an instant. "You wanna tell him tonight."

"I do," she confirmed. "But I can wait till after the Series. I don't mind."

"What's he gonna do, you think?"

"About what?"

"Living. You know. Where's he gonna stay, stuff like that?"

"I hope he'll stay with me for a while. But I'm sure he'll start looking for his own place as soon as he can."

"In Manhattan?"

"Wouldn't you if you were twenty-one?"

"Hell, I am and I'm thirty-eight."

"Thirty-eight," she said. "That doesn't seem possible."

"Frightening, isn't it?"

"A little."

"Especially 'cause that means *you're* up to twenty-six."

She laughed and her long hair shook down around her shoulders. "I have an idea," she said. "Maybe you two can share a place."

"I thought about it."

"Alex, I was just kidding."

"Well, I didn't think about it all that seriously. But it did cross my mind." He scratched underneath his chin. "We'd probably kill each other in a week."

"You could probably meet a lot of nice young chicks."

"Patty," Alex said sadly. There was no point in continuing with a real sentence. The sadness was his only point in speaking.

"You think he knows?" she asked finally, breaking the pall of silence.

"What, that we're . . ." He trailed off.

"Getting a divorce. You might as well say it."

"I can say it all right." He was a little annoyed at her tone. "I'm just not crazy about thinkin' it."

"I'm sorry," she told him. "I didn't mean to sound like a . . . whatever I was sounding like."

"You sounded like you were a psychologist and I was your patient. I'm *not* your patient, Patty. Not yet, anyway. I'm still your husband."

"I know." She waited, then spoke like a wife. "Does he know?" she asked again.

"I'll bet he does. You know kids."

"He's not such a kid."

"I'm *playin'* with twenty-one-year-olds. They're kids."

"We were an old married couple at twenty-one."

"We were *definitely* kids."

"I guess. I didn't feel like one, though."

"That's how you know you're a kid. Now that I finally *feel* like a kid, I know I'm an adult."

She nodded and smiled.

"You think he'll still want a job with Danny?" Alex asked.

"I think so. I think he's already doing a little scouting at that music festival in Denmark or someplace like that." She shrugged. "Our son the music agent."

"You can make real megabucks."

"I suppose."

"I'm glad he'll be back for the last game. He's always wanted to see me in a Series."

"Mmmmm . . ."

"You're drifting off, Pat. What are you thinking about?"

"Ohhh . . . everything. Us. Regrets. Russ. I wonder if he'll be different when he comes back."

"Three months in Europe, backpacking with his best friend? He'll be different."

"All I ever wanted was for everyone to stay the same," Patty said.

Alex took his right hand off the wheel and touched her hand on his thigh. Their fingers curled together. Patty leaned over and kissed him gently on the neck.

Patty touched his hand. She squeezed it, excited.

"There he is!"

Russell stepped through the customs gate and waved, and Alex lit up with pleasure. He looked at Patty, who was beaming, grinning from ear to ear. Sometimes he selfishly thought of Russ as *his*. But he was very much Patty's too.

Patty and Russell were hugging now. The boy looked exhausted. A little haggard, too thin. He had two or three days' growth of beard and his hair was too long, longer than Alex had ever seen it. He was burning with intensity, that Alex could tell. Well, why not? He'd probably seen things he'd never imagined, done things that had changed his life. Encountered moments of goodness and experienced things wicked. He'd been man and boy. Russell had changed, there was no question about that. He looked as if he were on fire. Alex couldn't put his finger on it, but there was now something dangerous about his son. Maybe it was just because he was now an adult. He was no longer controllable.

Alex knew that late that night, after Patty was asleep, Russ would talk to him. He'd get all the details, the impressions—at least those that were safe to tell a father. And that was okay with Alex. He wasn't in this fathering business for vicarious thrills. He just wanted a sense of what his son was becoming. He just wanted to make sure he was on the right path. That he was getting blue.

It was his turn now to hug and be hugged. Russell's scraggly beard scratched Alex's chin.

"So what have you learned?" Alex said with a smile.

"I dunno. A lot. Nothing. I think I learned that we don't learn. We just get older and we know."

"So what do you know?"

Russell shrugged. "That life's too short to spend a lot of time thinking about it. You just gotta *do* somethin' about it."

Alex rubbed his hand across his son's beard.

"The final game," Russell said as they began walking to the baggage area. "Do I have a ticket?"

"Of course," Alex said. "We all fly there tomorrow."

"You gonna hit a homer?" Russ asked.

"I'll do somethin'," Alex said. He hugged his son again. He was glad Russ was home. Glad but strangely disturbed. Russell was still restless. Europe hadn't changed that. And maybe angrier. Alex saw it in the eyes. But at least he was home, where Alex could protect him. "I'll do somethin'."

23

He wasn't starting. That was for damn sure. But he hadn't expected to, even though he *had* checked the lineup card. What the hell, he thought. There was always a chance.

So before he went out into the field at Riverfront Stadium to stretch and shag flies and take batting practice, he went to Fred "Spider" Frederickson, his manager—Christ, he'd sure as hell been through a lot of managers—and humbled himself. He was desperate.

"Look, Fred," he said. "I'm sure this, uh, this isn't your main worry right now, but this could be my last chance at playin' in a Series. And, uh, it'd sure mean a lot to me if I could get into this game. A real lot. I mean, I *gotta* play. Pinch-hit, somethin'. I *gotta*."

"Well, Judge, I'll tell ya." Fred Frederickson was only four years older than Alex but he talked like he was an old man and Alex a child. "I'll put ya in if I can. You can count on that. But I ain't gonna do somethin'—I mean, like for sentimental sakes—that might lose this game."

"Fred, I'm not askin' ya to lose the game. I'm just tellin' ya I wanna play."

"I'll keep it in mind, Judge."

"Listen, Fred. I'll be frank here. I'll fuckin' suck dick to get in this game. I'll be honest with ya on that one. I been waitin' twenty fuckin' years! And my kid's out there! I'm tellin' ya with my kid there—"

"Judge!"

Alex stopped short. He took a deep breath and nodded at the manager. Jesus. He hadn't meant to get so carried away.

"I'll do what I can, Judge. I'm glad to see you wanna play so bad, but the best I can say is I'll do what I can."

"Right," Alex said. "Do what you can."

There weren't too many people in the stands yet, when Alex headed to the outfield to shag a few. He still loved this part of the game, the early practice: it was lazy, professional, systematized. It always filled him with the unbeatable excitement that, in a few short hours, *anything* could happen.

The field was fairly empty too. A few infielders were just starting to play pepper. Some of the national media and a few of the local boys were already doing their print and TV interviews. Daniel Kapstein, agent extraordinaire, was one of the few civilians allowed on the field. He was meeting with Teddy Shore, the Yanks' ace starter, about a major deal with one of the networks. Danny's long-range plan had been pretty accurate. TV made sports big business. Free agency turned players into conglomerates. Among other things, Danny'd been as responsible as anyone else for the high-paid jock color-commentator on TV. He'd definitely pegged things right.

Danny waved to Alex and trotted out to right field. They talked as Alex limbered up.

"I'm surprised the Skipper let you out here today," Alex said.

"Still a few hours to game time. Besides, he's a new client of the office."

"You're kidding? You signed Spider?"

"Yeah."

"To do what?"

Danny shrugged. "We'll get him a local commercial. A clothing store or something."

"Boy, you don't miss a trick."

"Not if I can help it, *boychick.*"

"Don't call me *boychick,* Danny. It drives me crazy when you talk Hebe."

"Sorry. Hey. How do you get a nun pregnant?"

"I don't know."

"You fuck her."

Alex tried not to laugh but he couldn't help it. Danny had

made him laugh for over thirty years; Alex couldn't change the habits of a lifetime just because his career was ending and his marriage was over. So he laughed.

"I can tell you this one because it's on my own people. What's the difference between a Jewish-American princess and a plate of spaghetti?"

Alex was already laughing. "What?"

"Spaghetti wiggles when you eat it."

"Oh, Jesus!" Alex threw his hands up in disgust but laughed again.

"Russ come home?"

Alex nodded. "Last night. He and Patty flew in with me."

"Good time?"

"I'd say perfect."

"He ready to go to work?"

"I guess."

"Alex, old pal?"

"What?"

"Now that you're in a good mood from my fabulous sense of humor, I got a question to ask you."

"Go ahead."

"Why do I get the distinct feeling you're not ecstatic about Russ's coming to work for me?"

"What makes you say that?"

"Hey. I've known you only, what, all my life? What's up?"

"Everybody in my whole fuckin' family's gonna be workin' for you."

"What are you talkin' about?"

"What do you think?"

"Two. That's all. Elliot and now Russ."

"Two. That's almost all I got."

"But it's worked out, hasn't it? Didn't I get you back together with your brother?"

"Sort of."

"Look, you don't have to be best friends, but you talk now, don't you?"

"We talk."

"Don't I handle you for free?"

"Yup."

"Have I ever once taken a commission?"

"Never." Before Danny could remind him of any more favors, Alex asked, "Is Elliot a good lawyer?"

"The best in the music business. Negotiates a contract better than anyone has a right to. And, hey." Danny was back on the favor track, Alex could tell. "I offered *you* a job, didn't I? When you retire?"

"Yeah."

"You turned me down."

"I remember. What's the point here, of reminding me of all the great things you've done for me?"

"Look. You're my best friend. You helped me get into this business. I couldn't've done this kinda sports biz without your connections early on. This is just my way of tryin' to pay you back."

"I guess I'm just wary of people paying me back. I think you taught me that. It usually means they want something else."

"My, my, you're getting a tad cynical."

"I know. It's my age. My roomie was just tellin' me how nasty I was getting."

"Ronnie?"

"Yup."

"Good kid. I just got him a great deal with Panasonic."

"You wanna pay me back, Danny? Get *me* a great deal with Panasonic. You can even take your commission."

"Hey, pal, it's not like I'm not tryin'."

"I know, I know. Stars."

"That's what they want. You gotta produce if you wanna reap the benefits."

"Thanks for reminding me."

"Now, if you can hit a home run and win the game today, we can clean up in endorsements during the off season."

"Well, I'll try. I'll do my best."

"Hey," Danny said. "You watch *Good Morning, World* today?"

"No. Why, you got a new client? . . . Shit. I completely forgot!"

"Asshole."

"Emmy took over as host today? Damn!"

"Not only that. You know who her first interview was with?"

"No."

"My newest client."

"How was Emmy?"

"She was great. Don't you wanna know who my newest client is?"

"Sure," Alex said.

"The third-base coach for the Reds."

"What?"

"Uh-huh."

Alex, who'd been catching fly balls all during the last part of their conversation, let the next fly sail over his head. He never even moved an inch to chase it.

"You signed up the Lump?" Alex asked incredulously.

"And his first interview, under my guidance, was this morning—with Emmy."

Alex stared at Danny, dumbfounded.

"I can't believe this."

"Here he comes. Ask him."

Alex turned and, sure enough, walking toward him was Walter Lumpano.

As third-base coach of the opposing team, the Lump was in full Reds uniform. The uniform did not fit him as well as it had in the prime of his playing days. The Lump had gained an easy fifty pounds since retiring six years earlier. The muscle was gone, turned to flab. His hair was mostly missing also, except for a few strands combed badly over the rest of his balding dome. But the most noticeable aspect of the Lump's physical makeup that was missing was the fire in his eyes. That had turned to born-again Christian blandness.

The Lump was the most famous person to be born again since Jimmy Carter had hit the campaign trail. He had told his story to a ghostwriter, a reporter for the *Christian News*, and the book was now popping up on best-seller lists around the country. The book, titled *From Behind the Plate to Behind the Lord*, detailed the entire fascinating story of the Lump's rise from the ashes: from suspended alcoholic to a resurgence as the Angels' starting catcher to breaking his hand in the All-Star Game making a game-saving tag, which ended his catching career, to a skid back to the dread booze to the discovery that Jesus was with him.

Alex had not seen the Lump very often since "the incident," as it was called in *Behind the Lord*. Their paths hadn't crossed with great frequency. When they did, as before the first game of the Series when the Lump had come over to say hello and preach a little gospel, Alex realized he harbored no grudge, had no dislike for the man. On the other hand, he had no nostalgia for the good old days, no remnant of affection for a broken friendship.

Patty's relationship with Emmy had also slowly dissipated. After "the incident," Emmy just started appearing around their home with less regularity. Alex was sure it was because they had seen her broken—with blood, bandages, and uncoiffed hair—and that vulnerability was something she couldn't handle. Patty thought rather it was because Danny had become a fixture in the Justin household.

Emmy and Danny never got around to getting married. Somehow "the incident" had come between them too. Once they each had used it to their maximum advantage, there seemed no reason for them to be a couple anymore. Emmy began dating the head of her news department. Danny began to see what seemed like every sexy starlet in Los Angeles. The last Alex had heard, Danny was going out with the owner of one of the major movie studios and working on getting rid of wife number three.

"Alex," the Lump greeted him. He stuck out his fleshy hand and they shook. The Lump tried to put as much Christian sincerity into the handshake as he could muster.

"Lump. How ya doin'?"

"Fine, Alex. I'm doing just fine." The Lump looked him straight in the eye and smiled ingenuously. "I think about you a lot."

"Yeah? I think about you every once in a while," Alex said. *Every couple of years or so,* he thought.

"How'd the interview go, Walter?" Danny asked.

"Fine, fine. Emmy was wonderful."

Alex realized that he wasn't recognizing the Lump's voice. It had none of that nasty, gravelly tone Alex was so used to. This voice was smooth, serene. Vocal cords by the Lord, Alex thought.

"She even brought up 'the incident,' " the Lump continued. "She did it tastefully and with a sense of humor."

"Yeah, I remember it as a lot of laughs," Alex said, and as soon as he did he was sorry he'd spoken. The Lump turned on him with those sincere eyes.

As if wounded, the ex-catcher said, "You know, Alex, I'm glad you said that."

"You are?"

"Yes. Because it reminds me that you're the one person I never apologized to. I've never said to you, from the bottom of my heart, how truly and deeply sorry I am."

" 'S okay," Alex mumbled. "I don't hold a grudge."

"It's *not* okay," the Lump insisted. "But I'm trying to make up for my past transgressions. I'm trying the only way I know how, by obeying Jesus."

"That's good enough for me," Alex said, wondering how in hell the Lump knew enough to use the word *transgressions*. He wondered if Jesus had told him about dictionaries.

"Me too," Danny said quickly.

"You would be as wise to forgive as I have," the Lump said to Alex, nonaccusingly accusing.

"Who do I have to forgive?" Alex asked. "I told you, I don't hold a grudge."

"Not against me. But how about Dave Manning?" the Lump intoned.

"Manning? I haven't even seen him since . . . well, since . . ."

"He's here."

"At the game?"

"I got him tickets."

"He asked *you?*" Alex was beginning to wonder what the hell the world was coming to.

"We've kept in touch. I've always felt somewhat responsible, in the, uh, larger sense, for what he did in his final game."

"Yeah," Alex said. "Well. There might be something to that."

"He's in the box seats over the first-base dugout. Why don't you go see him?"

Alex said nothing.

"Listen, Lump," Danny spoke up. "I think you'd better get back to your dugout. Fraternization and all that."

"We're all brothers in the eyes of the Lord."

"Yeah," Alex said. "But not in the eyes of George Steinbrenner."

The Lump shook Danny's hand, then clasped Alex's hand with both of his own.

"Alex," the Lump said. Sincerely, of course.

"Yes?" Alex tried to outsincere him, but it was impossible.

"I'm doing something very important. And I'd like your help."

"What are you doing, Lump, that's so important?"

"I'm having a golf tournament."

"What?"

"I'm having a golf tournament. My own celebrity golf tournament. Billy Graham's coming. Sinatra's coming."

"*Frank* Sinatra?"

"We got friendly when I was with the Angels. After you left."

"Sure," Alex said. "I always thought you were a natural for the Rat Pack."

"I'm starting my own foundation. For the victims of drug and alcohol abuse. The Walter Lumpano Christian Aid Society. The WLCAS."

"Got a nice ring to it," Alex said. "Catchy."

Alex looked at Danny. Danny nodded and said, "We might even have our own telethon this year."

"Can we count on you, Alex?"

"Lump?" Alex said.

"What?"

"I don't know how I'm going to tell you this. But I don't know how to play golf. I never played a fuckin' round of golf in my life."

"Oh."

"Maybe as color commentator," Danny suggested. "I might be able to set that up."

"I'll let you know. How's that?"

"That'll be fine, Alex. Jesus be with you."

With that the Lump trotted back from whence he had come.

"I liked him better the old way," Alex said to Danny.

"He's worth a lot more money this way."

"Right." Alex looked Danny over from head to foot. Perfectly layered hair, a gold chain around his neck. Designer jeans. Gucci loafers. "Everyone's got their own god, I guess."

"Smartest thing you've said in years."

"I'm gonna go see Manning," Alex said to his lifelong friend. "Take good care of my son."

"So," Dave Manning said, leaning over the home-team dugout, hand extended. "So."

"My feelings exactly," Alex said, taking Manning's hand. "Walk to the aisle so we can talk."

Manning ambled over to the railing while Alex watched. He looked the same. Alex was sure he *was* the same. The same goddamn Manning.

"You never returned my calls," Manning said.

"You stopped calling," Alex retorted.

"Well, it got to be several years," Manning said. "I do have my pride, you know."

"You do?"

"Not really. But I finally figured, what's the point?"

"Yeah," Alex said. Then he said, "You called the *Lump* for tickets?"

"He's a religious fanatic now. I figured he'd have to get 'em for me or everyone would doubt his sincerity."

"I just talked to him. No one's gonna doubt his sincerity. Christ, Dave. Who woulda thought the Lump would wind up a Jesus freak?"

"Doesn't surprise me. When somebody's as crazy as he is deep down, the craziness can take a lot of different forms."

"You speaking from experience?"

"As an observer only." Manning lit up a cigarette.

"When'd you start smoking?" Alex asked, surprised. Then he realized how silly he sounded. He hadn't seen Dave Manning for ten years—smoking was probably the least of his changes.

"As soon as I quit the game."

"You look like you're still in good shape," Alex observed.

"Not a pound over playing weight. I work out three days a week. Run every morning. Swim."

"I'm impressed."

"This is the first game I've been to, you know."

"Since you . . ."

"Yup. Since I walked out. This is my first game."

"What brought you out of your retirement?"

"You. I figured this was your last game."

"Not necessarily."

"True. But probably. The Yanks gonna pick you up?"

"Doubtful."

"So I figured it was worth the trip."

"From where?"

"Michigan. I'm back in Ann Arbor, where I started."

"Me, too, sort of. I'm moving back into the city."

"I know."

"You do? How?"

"Patty. *She* returned my phone calls."

"Son of a bitch."

"I just wanted to keep track of you, Judge."

"Manning, I swear to God, I don't know what the hell you want, but keeping track sure as shit isn't it."

Manning smiled and there it was. It hadn't changed. The smile was still the same; still so beautiful, still so elusive.

"What is it?" Alex asked suddenly. He was sure it was his imagination, but it seemed like the whole stadium quieted down. "What the hell *do* you want?"

"I told you once before, Judge. Nothing."

"I didn't believe you then and I don't believe you now. And the reason I never returned your phone calls is probably because I realized I'd never really find out."

Manning laughed. An easy laugh, relaxed. "I'm a doctor now. I've got my own practice."

"I'm still a ballplayer."

"See that woman there? The one with the short, dark hair?" Manning pointed and Alex nodded as the woman smiled over at them. "That's my wife. Anna. Those are our two kids with her. Debbie and Len. Seven and five."

"Congratulations."

"Yup. I'm a doctor with a family and two cars and a country-club membership. I'm the perfect husband, a damn good doctor, and I can whip any dad in Ann Arbor on the tennis court."

"Made in the shade, sounds like."

"I couldn't've put it better myself. Made in the shade."

"Well," Alex said as the two men stared at each other in awkward silence. "I've got a game to play, maybe."

"Judge?"

"What?"

"You honestly don't know what I wanted? You never got it?"

"Manning, I swear to you. I've wanted to know since the day I saw you in that goddamn locker room in Wilson. I wanted to know when you walked off the mound in L.A. I bet there hasn't been a day gone by since we met that I haven't thought about what the hell you want and whether you'd ever get it."

"Never," Manning said. "No chance."

"Is this the revelation?" Alex asked.

"It's a simple one. I've always wanted to be you."

"Come again?"

"I've wanted what you've wanted from the very beginning." Manning stared hard at Alex. There was no smile on his face now, and its disappearance somehow made him look naked. "I wanted that moment you've always talked about. I wanted it so bad it ate me up inside. I tried everything to get it too. Sex, drugs. Shit, I wanted that high. I wanted that moment. Any way I could get it."

"But you had it. You had it right in your hand and you let it go!"

"I was afraid."

"Bullshit."

"No bullshit, pal."

"Afraid of what? Afraid of *what?* A moment?"

"Afraid of what would come after. Shit, I was twenty-eight years old when I quit. I didn't wanna have to spend the next fifty years livin' off a memory. I didn't wanna hafta spend the rest of my life lookin' back, remembering a moment, a day, an instant. Uh-uh. I didn't want people sayin', *God, you look old,* 'cause I didn't want them remembering what the hell I looked like at all. I didn't want anybody sayin', *Hey, I was there that*

day, or *What are you up to now, old-timer?* So finally my fear
got so bad that all I wanted was out. I just wanted to be normal.
Left alone. I wanted what I have now: a perfectly boring life.
Nothing to look back on, nothing to look forward to."

"I think," Alex said, "I'd kill myself first."

Dave Manning rolled up the sleeves of his shirt. He thrust out
his wrists toward Alex. On the wrists were two jagged scars.

"I tried to," Manning said as Alex tried to hide his shock. "It's
a shitty thing to do. It hurts like hell and doesn't accomplish a
damn thing."

"Shit," Alex said, and wiped sweat off his forehead.

"It *is* a good thing to drop into the conversation on about the
third date, though. Good for a lot of sympathy and usually at
least a blowjob."

"So what the hell," Alex said after a long pause, "are you
doing here?"

"I came to see whether you're gonna do what I couldn't.
Wouldn't."

"Manning, I haven't even *played* in this fuckin' Series."

"I have faith."

"You and the Lump."

"You were right, Alex. Dead-on accurate. As long as you're
white, middle class, and don't have brain damage, everybody
gets what they want in the end. You ran down the list before and
it still applies. Danny, Emmy, Scott, Lump."

"Lump?"

"You know how much Bible Belt pussy there is on the born-
again circuit? As soon as the Lump comes down a little bit, he'll
be back up to his ass in the same stuff he was always up to his ass
in. He'll just be richer and he probably won't puke as often. At
least not publicly."

"Patty?"

"What about her?"

"She didn't get what she wanted. We're getting a divorce."

"I'm sorry. What happened?"

"Hell, there's a dumb question. What *hasn't* happened?" Alex
watched Manning light another cigarette. "Well . . . wants
change, I guess."

"Maybe. I always thought what she wanted was to be safe, to

be protected. She thought you were the person to do that. Now
maybe it turns out she'd be better off doing it herself."

"You *have* been thinkin' about all this."

"There's not much else to do all day in Ann Arbor. I gotta
think of *somethin'* while I have my finger up some little seven-
year-old's asshole."

"You still have all the answers."

"Except one."

"Me?"

Manning nodded.

"Whether I'm gonna get what I want?"

"You're not paying attention, Judge. I told you—I have faith.
You'll get what you want, one way or the other. I wanna find out
what it is and what happens after you get it."

There was not much left to say between them. Manning
turned and waved to his wife and kids that he'd be back in a
second.

"You know," Alex said, "I once said to my dad that the hardest
thing in life is to find out that people aren't what you thought
they were. He said the hardest thing is to find out that *you're*
not what you think *you* are."

"He's right. Only most people don't ever get the chance to
find that out. You gotta be pretty good to find that out."

"I *am* pretty good."

"Yeah," Manning agreed. "You always were."

"Manning?" Alex said.

"Yeah?"

"All this bullshit you've been throwing at me. Is this another
pose? I can't tell anymore with you. Is this just another one of
your games?"

"That's the problem with games," Manning said. "We usually
never know we're playin' 'em till they're over. But I *did* come
all the way from Ann Arbor, didn't I?"

"Like a vulture."

Manning stuck out his hand again. And again Alex took it.

"Guess I'll be seein' you," Alex told him.

"Good luck, Judge."

"Hell," Alex "the Judge" Justin said. "I don't need luck. I
know what I want."

24

He had no premonition, as was written later, no sense that greatness lay only moments ahead. He was merely watching; carefully of course, but no more keenly than usual. Not considering that this was a bit *un*usual. This was the bottom of the ninth inning of probably the most exciting World Series game ever played. This was the Yankees leading seven to six. This was the bases loaded with two outs and the Reds' clean-up hitter at the plate. This was Alex Justin being inserted as a defensive replacement in right field two batters earlier when Eddie White snapped his Achilles tendon. This was the Judge's last chance.

Something—instinct, twenty years' experience, his crooked right fingers, his faintly graying sideburns—made him instantly understand that the curve was hanging over the outside corner; then, that the bat was reaching, stretching slightly, an extension of its wielder's tension. So he leaned toward the right-field line and, even before the swing powered forward, was moving. Only after two vicious strides did he hear what he was listening for: in his slow-moving reality, more a muffled thud than a mighty crunch.

His eyes were with it from the beginning. They never lost the arc of the seemingly structured flight. As he raced, a wind touched his lips, perhaps his own heavy breathing, and he smelled the usual: dirt, body, and the odor he could identify only as the game itself.

He hadn't moved like this in years. *Years.* He was aware of every muscle straining, heaving, steeling, of the blood pounding, swirling, and of each single drop of sweat from his forehead under his arms, soaking his stomach.

The noise of the crowd was neither a help nor a hindrance, only a proper swell, a portion of the total movement. He had never heard a roar like this. Had never imagined, in his wildest dreams, any sound so enveloping. It was like the greatest music ever created.

He knew exactly where he was: ten feet from the line, one step onto the warning track, slicing at a forty-five-degree angle into the bleachers.

As he coiled, he saw not only the floating white but a strangely lucid line of red shirts, blue caps, green and yellow relish, open mouths, flaring nostrils. He knew it was impossible, knew it had to be a hallucination, but he saw Patty. She was young and looking at him the way she looked at him when she was young. Then she disappeared and there was Russell. This was more real; there was Russell, cheering, standing, pumping his arms up into the air in a loving exhortation. Then he, too, was gone.

And then he saw . . . no, it was impossible. He saw Willie Trotty. By the foul pole, in the cheapest seats. Everyone was standing, straining to see, but Willie sat calmly, barely looking at the play, as if the outcome was a foregone conclusion. There was Willie, and Alex wanted to rush over to him, grab him, but he couldn't because Willie was swallowed up by the crowd, hidden by clapping hands and craning necks, and it was time to act, it was time to make the play.

Alex leapt up into the sky. One foot, eighteen inches, two, then three extraordinary feet, higher and higher as if gravity had, momentarily, blessed him with relief from its rigid laws. His glove scraped the top of the walls, his left wrist bent back at an inhuman angle. The spinning sphere, a sure home run, landed right in the center of the webbing, sending vibrations through his fingers, shock waves into his palm. The leather closed around it, protective, enveloping. His back and hip and then his thigh crashed into the wall. His head rocked, his eyes closed, but he held on. It was almost over, it was near to triumph. He saw Manning, grinning.

Ready now to slither to the ground and receive his hero's welcome, he started his slide back to the world, mitt and horsehide outstretched still. But his right foot caught in a strand of brown ivy. A noise like an imagined cannon shot from somewhere, from out of his very being. The crowds were chanting, "Judge, Judge, Judge." Then, "Justin, Justin, Justin." Hysterical victory surrounded him, swarmed, dwarfing him. For a lingering moment there was glory, then came the excruciating pain.

Then, as he writhed on the grass, face smothering in dirt, hands clawing at invisible relief, a flat southern accent softly filtering from the heavens above, an angelic proclamation in the form of the second-base umpire: "Gol-damn! His leg's torn up for shit!"

And as Alex Justin's brain clouded over with the pain, he did manage to think: *I did it. I did it, Willie. I did it.*

The Moment.

What I want.

As the stretcher carried him off the field, one of the attendants heard Alex Justin moan aloud: *"Getting blue."*

Around the Horne
by
Ed Horne

. . . To Alex Justin, professional baseball player, perhaps the only thing that matters is that he made the play. The Play. Perhaps the years of mediocrity no longer matter. Perhaps the shattered ankle will heal. Scars do fade. Glory masks a lot of disappointment. Perhaps all that matters, all that *should* matter, is the great and magnificent achievement that took place in right field yesterday afternoon. According to everyone who knows him, it is an achievement that Justin has craved his entire life. Well, the moment is his. And it is a moment that will be remembered and talked about for years to come. It is a moment that made a man a hero.

The question I hope Alex Justin is prepared to face is: What happens when a hero becomes a man?

The country is screaming for heroes, and for today, Alex Justin is the most famous hero we've got. Let that be enough. Let the moment be enough.

Let Alex Justin not have to answer the question, "What next?"

PART FOUR
1980s

There's a change in the ocean
A change in the deep blue sea
I tell ya now, there ain't no changin' me.

—"Crazy Blues"

25

It was so stiflingly hot inside his apartment that the sweat on his palms made him almost drop the can of beer he was casually holding a crooked arm's length in front of him. His left eye was closed, for no real reason except that this was his fifth Bud, while his right eye concentrated on the label's red-and-blue lettering, carefully documenting every swirl and dip. The can slipped about an inch but his whole body swooped straight down with it, paralleling the exact angle of the can, knees bent. He gripped tightly, fingers wrapped around the aluminum, and stayed perfectly still. Overly pleased with himself, he held his breath, but he held it just a split second too long, because he began to feel silly. His lip curled up to the right, an awkward grin attempting to convince the flat white walls he had just been fooling around. He stood without moving for another few moments, trying halfheartedly for a little solitary dignity, then his left eye opened, squinted, reopened, and his arm brought the beer can in closer to his body. It was steady and he nodded, ultimately satisfied. He hadn't spilled a drop.

Standing in the middle of the living room of his fourteenth-floor West Side apartment, Alex Justin thought about putting a record on, then decided the time was not right for music. He wasn't sure of the effect it would have on him, so, as was becoming his frequent choice these days, he opted for ubiquitous silence over disruptive risk. A rumbling within told him that it was not the time for precarious symphonies.

Instead, Alex snapped on the TV. Television was unimportant company, familiar noise; when necessary, it provided enough of a presence to let him make an easy transition from being lonely to being alone. He stood by the nineteen-inch color set and didn't move while he drank his beer in seven or eight long, gentle gulps. The whole room seemed to sag with the heat; the lines of the furniture were wavy in his vision. He rolled the can against his forehead but most of the refrigerator chill was gone. Outside the window it was 102 degrees. A New York City July. The paved backdrop was sizzling. His apartment was not high enough to reduce the people on the streets to insect size. They looked more like little dolls or puppets, funny little midgets. From his vantage point the people in the real world looked unhappy and Alex couldn't blame them. With his air conditioner broken he felt very much as if he were paying $950 a month for the privilege of living in hell.

A faint breeze actually stirred the curtains, a minor miracle. He used them to mop the sweat off his forehead and hands, but both were instantly wet again. He was just about to let loose with a quiet "Shit!" when he suddenly realized what was going on on his TV. Snared without warning, he was suddenly helpless to do anything but turn his head, squint his eyes, and pay attention.

A great singer was on the screen, a fat babe who'd been around for years, and Alex was one of the few people who knew who she was and what she'd done and knew that she was one of the very best. The camera was in tight on her, too close, almost, for comfort. She, also, was sweating—on her upper lip over the light strands of a moustache—and her blue eye-makeup was smeared. The stage lights turned slowly from blue to green to red, kept a rainbow effect briefly, before easing back to normal white light. She was singing "Lush Life," accompanied only by a clear, untrembling sax. Alex stirred, a mild attempt to avoid her spell, but the song sliced into him, took him somewhere far away. He didn't really know where he was, nor did he particularly care to find out. Just the traveling was enough, especially right now with this dame paying for his trip. She was going crazy. Her fat freckled arms were right up against her body; five meaty fingers held a hand mike that kept brushing up over her caked-red lips. Her huge breasts were thrust out, exposed, glistening. Her voice was deep, smooth, and from the way she lingered over certain phrases, syllables, sounds, he was aware that she knew a lot of things he could only vaguely feel, never express. Because he was fairly drunk, the realization pleased him. Only when he had a little alcohol in him did he enjoy his inarticulateness. Sober or when he was *too* drunk, his own flaws never delighted him. Lately, they persistently, ominously, had kept him from peace.

Part of that unease, he knew, came from the club. Something was going on, but he didn't know what. At first, of course, it had been a godsend, a dream come true. But the place had never quite lived up to his expectations—he had never gotten everything he had hoped to get from it—though he was not ready to stop searching. Something was changing there. Danny was up to something. And Alex knew that when Danny had a new plan, someone got fucked.

After the accident—"the Play," it was now called in baseball lore—he had signed a deal with Handler Sporting Goods. The Play had made him famous. He'd won the World Series for the Yankees and the New York media made him a celebrity. They magically transformed his years of mediocrity into a lifetime of workmanlike craft pointing toward the ultimate moment. His brushes with notoriety—"the incident" with Lump, the friendship with Manning—became fascinating bits of color. His marriage to a local girl was the stuff of New York folk-heroism. His divorce, so soon after the Play, took on tragic and epic proportions. So he got a good deal with Handler, and, out of baseball for the first time in over twenty-five years, he was thrilled just to be in a world that made sense to him. He liked going into stores and sniffing the leather gloves as if they were oxygen masks. And he would pick up a bat, give the owner or some kid a pro tip. "Choke up a bit, you'll be more comfortable. No, put your right foot here, uh-huh, and lift your elbow, yeah, to here." They'd talk about who was gonna win the batting crown, compare the new Dodgers to the old Dodgers, remember Mays when he was the best. He'd tell them what Durocher once said to him about the DH rule: "Being a designated hitter is like fuckin' a whore. You might hit a home run, but ya got nothin' to be proud of." It was okay. For a while. Then he started to feel less and less like a pro and more and more like a sporting-goods salesman. Which he wasn't, technically. He was a rep, a roving goodwill ambassador for horsehide, pigskin, and leather. And even that wasn't so bad, for a while. The money was good, remarkable considering how easy the job was. He got his name on a glove too. All over the country weekend players were hugging softballs into their stomachs with Alex Justin "the Play" Specials.

But slowly, over months, a year, two years, it began to disturb him. Gradually. They'd ask if he was gonna make a comeback. They'd ask about the accident, some of them even wanted to see the leg. They'd gab about it; almost everybody swore they'd seen the Play in person, that they had been at the park. Then they'd make jokes about his being out of shape (he wasn't; he wasn't a pound over his playing weight, 173). The worst was when they started to talk as if he were from a different era.

The first time he'd gone into a store and the assistant manager didn't recognize his name, that was the worst. After a half hour the kid (kid! He was probably twenty-six) had looked up and said, "Wait a second, aren't you that guy? In the World Series?"

That guy.

Most of the salesmen were ex-jocks, college or high school stars. Most of the buyers too. Serious fans. Coached Little League, took the high school hotshots out to fish-fry dinners. They drank too much, went on real binges every couple of months, got laid sometimes, even paid for it when really necessary. They prayed for white guys to get back into basketball while their wives went to church and prayed for their salvation. They had peaked and they had fallen. Their best shot was not nearly what his had been; they hadn't flown as high. But they were down and they knew it, most of them, and they were waiting for him to follow. And not just to follow, to go farther, to keep on going past them. Alex didn't like it, not one bit. He hadn't fallen yet and he didn't want to. No. Alex "the Judge" Justin wanted to go higher.

He was pretty surprised that he wanted to.

Needed to.

He'd miscalculated. He'd gotten blue. On the ball field. Now he found he had to do it in real life.

Damn!

He'd been thirty-eight years old when he achieved his moment of perfection but he had, he hoped, another forty years to live. After the Play he thought it was going to be forty years of relative ease, basking in the glory of past heroics, satisfied forever for what he'd *done*, not worrying about what he'd yet have to do.

Wrong.

So after a while he came up with a plan. If the bunt goes foul and there are two strikes, you change tactics. You hit and run. So he decided that maybe the Play was only Stage One. Maybe getting blue involved a Stage Two.

That's why he accepted Danny's offer. It seemed perfect. At least it seemed better than sucking dick for Handler Sporting Goods.

Danny Kapstein wanted to open a small club. A jazz club. A little music, some simple food, drinks.

"You can't turn it down," Danny said.

"Why do you need me?"

"Look, *bubbie*, I don't need you, I *want* you. No, hold that. If you want pride, I *do* need you. You're a celeb, especially for somethin' like this. Everybody likes to go to clubs run by jocks. You're still big stuff in this town. You're a good gimmick."

"I don't know."

"Also, pal, you know more about jazz than anyone. Shit, I thought you'd be jumping for joy! You've wanted to do this ever since I've known you. Your own club! You pick the acts, you tell me how you want it to look, you get your own regular table with your regular drink right by Stan Getz or whoever the hell you want it by. I thought you'd kill for this."

"It does sound pretty good," Alex said slowly. "Am I an investor?"

"*Schmuck!* You don't have to put in a penny. You're getting your own free jazz club! No strings attached. I need you, I don't expect you to pay, I don't expect you to work for free. You're a partner, you get a percentage."

"I don't put up any dough and I'm your partner?"

"Not *my* partner exactly. I'm getting investors. You'll get a full share without putting up what they put up. They're *silent* partners. You've never been silent in your life."

"And what about you?"

"I won't officially be, uh, connected."

"Why not?"

"Well, hell, it's a little tricky if my company owns a club and my company's also booking the acts *into* that club."

"Ah."

"So it's your club."

"But you book the acts."

"Not all of 'em, not all of 'em. I don't handle Getz, but you want Getz, you book Getz. All it means is I got someone who I think is gonna be hot, I come to you and say, 'Put him on on a slow coupla days.' What's the big deal?"

"I . . ."

"Alex." Danny put both hands on his shoulders. "This is a piece of cake for you. You're the front man. You can do what you wanna do and not do what you don't wanna do. I certainly don't expect you to run the restaurant or negotiate with agents or shit like that."

"I'm the front man."

"It's perfect."

Alex said nothing.

"Our lawyers'll meet and work out the details."

"My lawyer's *your* lawyer," Alex said.

"Yeah," Danny said. "But he's *your* brother. That's okay, though." Danny grinned. "I still trust him."

A year and one week later, Alex Justin was part-owner and manager of Getting Blue.

It had gone just like Danny said. They got a nice, small room on East Sixty-third, did it up so it actually came reasonably close to resembling Bell's, the old club, long gone, where his dad used to play. Danny had quite a bit of clout and they had no trouble booking a lot of the big names: Eckstein, Gillespie, Tormé, Carmen McRae. They got lesser names, too, and Alex began scouting for younger jazz talent. He began paying very close attention to those guys who were beginning their voyage, who were on their way to getting blue. And he began to concentrate very hard on what he'd now have to do to get blue himself. Again.

Alex closed his eyes so he could do nothing but listen to the music coming from his TV. The singer was belting now, and her chest was heaving; he could tell without having to look. She was perfect, and he smiled in fierce anticipation. He knew what was coming next; yes, there was no doubt. He allowed himself to linger gloriously in this first awareness.

He turned over on his side, gently, then, onto his stomach. His chest rubbed lightly, grazingly, over the couch. He lifted himself up, perhaps an inch, with his knees, then slowly back down, his head face down, buried in the fabric. His mouth started working slowly, half kissing, then almost sucking at, the coarse material. There were no sounds except for the slight meeting of skin, clothes, and sofa, and of lip against lip. One leg draped over onto the floor and then his whole body slid, in one long, tantalizing motion, off of the couch and down to the carpet. His arms stretched into the thick, dark strands, twisting luxuriously; his legs went taut, relaxed, then curled. He moved slowly at first, tentatively, as always, but soon with more confidence, more of an appetite. His erection hardened, right on schedule. It was a good one, rigid, firm against his left thigh, not unpleasantly constricted by his jeans. At last the music blended into his motion and he was able to lose himself absolutely in this most important ritual.

Alexander Justin loved to masturbate.

He did it a lot. Never got tired of it. Almost anything could set it off. It might be a woman glimpsed through a window in the building across the way. It might be someone on TV, an actress in a wet T-shirt riding a skateboard. Lately it was Arlene Francis. Alex never failed to get hard when he watched old reruns of *What's My Line?* on cable. His set made Arlene look as if she had the world's largest breasts. She was so proper, so inviting. Plus, she had a sense of humor. Warm, intelligent, not too pushy. Well dressed, if perhaps a bit flashy. There was definitely something about Arlene that made her irresistible—the way she always guessed the mystery guest, the shape of her mammary glands jutting out under her usual sequins. The Judge always looked forward to those nights when he had an early evening alone to handle a six-pack and a half hour of jerking off on Arlene Francis's jugs.

Often it was music and not a woman, not a living thing, that got to him. Made him remember. It was usually the past that jerked him off. He was more and more becoming a man of memory, for it was memory that gave order to his life. He would come moving rhythmically to images of past girlfriends, unchanged in his mind. Where he used to slip away into fantasy while making love to Patty, he now sometimes returned to her in his mind. When he fantasized what sexual acrobatics he'd like performed, Patty's body frequently appeared, though as a slightly refined apparition. He often flashed on friends' wives, lost chances, unknown nymphs glimpsed in elevators or at receptionists' desks and filed permanently, drawn when a sensual vision was needed.

And he still thought way too often of the Girl from the Park.

It amazed him, actually, how real she had become to him. It was as if they'd known each other for years and as intimately as if she were a lifelong mistress. He had created her entire body, her skin, the touch of her fingernails upon his chest, the smell of her hair when her head was buried on his shoulder. He had, in fact, created everything about her, for he had to admit he didn't really remember what she looked like. He had an image, an ideal. Whether her nose had been, in truth, as flared as it was in his masturbatory dreams, he couldn't tell. Whether her hair had really been the dark shade he buried his face in, he just didn't know. He did know, however, that thirty years after he'd first seen her, she was still young. Her breasts remained firm, her bare feet uncalloused, her eyes were ever glancing back at him, inviting him to touch and to play, to love, be loved, get hard, and come. There were times when he thought of her hourly.

Sometimes weeks went by and she didn't make her presence known; other goddesses, perfect limbs, blond straight hair, dominated his dreams. But the girl in off-white—he couldn't ever bring himself to think of her as a woman—always reappeared. Always beckoning him, always promising fulfillment, always satisfying.

Alex Justin moved in quick, simple spasms. His hips rotated, lifted, and returned to the carpet. His penis, now thick and long, was scraping itself raw inside his pants, rubbing hard against the floor. The jerks were faster now, harder. He wanted to come.

Now a mysterious fat woman was crawling over a red satin bedspread. When he tried to grab at her breasts, she smothered him with her whole body. He buried his face in her chest, her thick legs massaged his cock. She spoke dirty.

Lela Finkelstein, an Annie who used to fuck half the team when they hit Detroit, now placed his rapidly swelling penis in her mouth. She squirted Scotch all over his chest, giggled, licked it off, soaked it all back into her own body. While she rolled over him, Patty was there on top of him again, excited to be part of a threesome. Lela suddenly disappeared, and there was Patty's friend and neighbor, Donna Jenkins. Donna, no matter the season, always had a perfect tan. Now, her bathing suit removed, Alex saw two pure white breasts and a pale ass which he immediately attacked.

Both women vanished. His park teenager walked by, stopping long enough to take a seat on his face. His tongue went deep inside her, swirled around, savoring all of her young and sweet fluids.

He was moaning out loud now, in his apartment, ready to burst. His body motions were clearly defined. He was getting higher off the floor, coming down harder, firmer, spending more time and effort on the downward thrust. Moving faster and faster, his head rolling back and forth, his shirt crumpled and thrown off to the side.

His body filled with a thrilling violence, his mind went blank, turned itself away from all images. For one eternal moment he had no links to the outside world. He had one last spasm, a fantastic thrust of power, and then his mind returned, a flash, he

was up on the wall, he was falling, he had won, he was finished
he was rolling on the outfield grass trying to grab his knee and
his ankle, trying to hold back the pain.

He came.

Alex jerked twice more, then collapsed, his head resting on
his outstretched left arm. His breathing was heavy; he slowed it
got it under control. He relaxed, the noises of the room filtered
back into him. The singer on television was not singing, she was
being interviewed by Merv Griffin. Her enormous breasts were
no longer sexy and beckoning. Her husky, inviting voice wasn't
able to salvage her remarkably uninteresting observations.
"Oh, yes?" she was saying. "Then how come you see so many
more old drunks than old doctors?"

Alex couldn't move. He lay there for slow-moving, distorted
seconds. Something was wrong. He wearily moved his arm,
turned his head toward the side. He was face to face with a shoe.
It took him an instant to realize it was a woman's shoe. And then
another instant to realize that there was a foot inside the shoe,
and attached to the foot was a familiar-looking, well-shaped leg.
Above the leg was a blue plaid skirt and farther up, a pale-blue
shirt, the top buttons opened. The exposed neck was white,
perfectly tapered, elegant, strong.

Alex tried to say something to the red hair and hazel eyes, a
name, *anything*, but all that came out was a very small gurgle
and, to add insult to injury, a tiny bubble of spit.

His ex-wife looked at him, the keys to his apartment still
dangling in her hand.

"Please," Patty said. "Don't get up."

26

"Hiya, Judge. You're in early."

Alex touched the waitress lightly on the shoulder. His hand lingered only for a second, then dropped to his side. Patty leaned against the long pine bar, her favorite part of Getting Blue. "Jane," Alex said to the waitress, "you remember my . . . uh . . . my, uh . . ."

"Patty," Patty said, helping him out. All these years, she marveled, and he still can't bring himself to say "ex" about anything he was once connected to. To Alex there were no ex-teams, exwives, or ex-friends. Only blanks or fuzzy memories or something strange that fell in between lies and romantic optimism. Patty shook her head, partly at his constancy, partly at her reaction to it. She had always thought that Alex had been the one to change over the years, and that it was his change that had picked their marriage apart. But looking at him here and now she began to suspect that it was she who had gradually and subtly changed. He was slightly the worse for wear, but she was standing next to the same man she had fallen in love with. She had once marveled at this trait of his, this extraordinary ability to form permanent attachments—no matter the external intrusions—to people, to things, to concepts. When Alex made a commitment, that was it. It could survive sickness or pain or lies or adultery or divorce. It could survive failure, stagnation, si-

lence. She had thought she was like that. She had always wor
ried about his sense of commitment, had always trusted he
own. How wrong she had been. Hers could not survive a harsh
reality. She was now afraid of attachments, cynical of anything
that dared to hint at permanence. When had it happened? And
why hadn't she noticed? It couldn't only have been Haiti
Crazy, she thought. Crazy to have married a man and divorced
him for all the same reasons.

She sat at the bar. Alex went behind it to get them each a
beer, then came and sat next to her. The club wasn't open yet
Jane, the waitress, was setting a few tables. A busboy was scrub
bing the floor. Alex went over, pointed at something in a corner
The busboy nodded.

Watching Alex, in his element, she smiled. He liked bars and
restaurants. He'd always dragged her to old stomping ground
for her approval of the ambience and for the regulars to ap
prove of her, as well as to new hangouts for trial runs at estab
lishing tradition. He was comfortable in these public places
comfortable with their imposing personalities, jostling isolation
ism, and indifferent friendship. She knew he felt much more at
ease at Getting Blue than he did in his own two-bedroom apart
ment. Gazing at the sea of red-checked tablecloths, drip can
dles, and sudsy beer mugs, she wondered if he realized that
there was more of his real self in the darkened corners of the
jazz club than up on West Seventy-ninth Street.

A picture of Alex in a Yankee uniform hung on the wall off to
their right. It was starting to tear at the corner. Sipping her
Dubonnet on the rocks, she remembered one of the first fights
they'd ever had. He'd wanted to hang a team picture in the
living room. It was their first "real" apartment, one full bed
room and an honest-to-God separate living room. Right after
they'd gotten married; they were living in Schenectady and
they were living high, buying furniture they thought they'd
have for years, forever. A fake oak dining table, seascape oil
paintings, a couch that folded out into a lumpy bed. He'd
wanted to hang the photo above the couch, she wanted it to go
in the bathroom. "This is the room for classy things," she had
said firmly. He had responded just as firmly as a young married

breadwinner could: that he was a ballplayer, that the picture was the same as *him;* it had to stay. She cried (she cried more easily in those days), he stood firm, she got angry, he got angry, she cried some more, he apologized. "Huhh-nneyy, it's just that, well, it's important to me. It's the way I make my living. It's paying for all this." He swept his arms over *all this* as if the Schenectady walk-up were Buckingham Palace. She said she was sorry (was she? she didn't remember) and sniffed, wiping her nose. This apartment was just so *serious* to her. He nodded. He knew that. He knew that, so they compromised. The framed photo went in the bedroom over his night table. They made love that night under the glossy black-and-white eyes of the Schenectady Blue Jays.

Patty wondered if he could possibly be remembering the same conversation, the same apartment, the same sex, because he was smiling at her now, a fond smile of years gone by, years that turned fights into amusing anecdotes. They hadn't had many more fights for the rest of their marriage. In fact, she didn't remember *any* other fights. Only over that picture. The team photo was still framed in his apartment, she realized. It was in his bathroom now, along with various other photos and a montage of newspaper clippings. He also kept a scrapbook buried under magazines and Time-Life art books on the coffee table which she had picked out for him when, a year after their divorce, they had fully reached the stage of being best friends.

That was a good time, a binding period that was important to them both after months of total separation. They talked a lot then, actually learned new things about each other. They'd tried sleeping together again and it was nice, secure. They still slept together occasionally, but those occasions were becoming rarer and rarer. They dwindled without any real acknowledgment; the same way they happened. She was the one who had first started talking about her new life. There were no important men—Alex was her one great love and she never thought she would have another—but he heard about the casual ones. Slowly he dropped names, too, and asked her questions about his women, sometimes sought advice or reassurance. Patty even picked out most of the furniture in his apartment. His bed. The living-room pieces. She had gotten him a couple of prints for birthday or Christmas gifts. He acquiesced willingly to her taste. She tried to think if there was anything she hadn't given him or decided for him. The living-room curtains. What was his name? Leslie! She remembered the names of everyone he talked about. Leslie had made those for him. He confessed to her that Leslie thought it would be cute if his curtains matched hers. They had gone out together for a few months; it was his first lengthy affair after the divorce. Alex had told her afterward that Leslie came out of the relationship with a bruised heart and a deeply felt commitment to marry a young dentist instead of an old athlete. Alex had survived with an important introduction to foreign films and white-and-blue flowered drapes.

Donna made his bedroom curtains. And gave him a chest of drawers, a nice antique leftover from her own divorce. Patty was vague on who went with him for his rugs; Sara picked out his kitchen utensils; Felicia bought, potted, and talked to his plants. He himself paid the rent, gave out a key here and there, and personally installed a Magic Fingers shower nozzle.

Patty stared at Alex, hands wrapped around the mug in front of him, and she thought, *His apartment, like his life, is not really his own.*

She had been silent for a few minutes, which was unlike her. She hadn't even mentioned Russ yet. Alex wondered if she was upset by his beat-off fest. Patty always looked good when she was upset. Aggravation went well with her body and with her movements. It made her jut her small breasts out. She looked very appealing at the moment, so he thought she might be upset.

"I think I'm getting over my embarrassment," he said.

"People masturbate," Patty told him evenly, in her best psychologist voice.

"Ah. Thank you for telling me that," he said. "Do a lot of them do it in front of other people?"

"You'd be surprised," she said.

"I probably would be."

"Alex—" she began, but before she could continue, he interrupted.

"You know," he said thoughtfully, "I always hated that you called me Alex."

"What?" She was genuinely caught off guard.

"I never liked that you called me by my real name."

Patty cocked her head, curious, startled. He never used to drift like this. He was always focused. "Why?" she asked. "Why didn't you like it?"

" 'Cause it's what everybody else calls me." He smiled and raised his eyes to the ceiling. "Ever since we were teenagers, I always hoped you'd have some sort of special name for me. But you never did."

"I didn't know."

"No."

"Why didn't you ever tell me?" she asked, and she was liking him so much at this moment she was afraid she was going to cry. They had been married for twenty-one years, divorced for almost nine, and Patty hadn't felt this way about her husband for five. "Why didn't you ever tell me?" she asked again.

He shook his head and put a finger to his lip, pulled at the skin, then moved it off. That was his shrug, she knew, his way of saying he had his reasons but didn't know what they were exactly. "I guess I should've, huh?"

"I guess so," she said.

"I never talked enough, did I?"

"No," she said. "But I talked *too* much, didn't I?"

"Yeah." He smiled. "You always interpreted and analyzed and thought in such a damn complicated manner. It's too bad, 'cause you were always so wonderful at laughing and shrugging and winking and coughing. That stuff was much more effective. I always thought you were smart enough not to have to say much."

"I'll remember that for my future sessions. I'll analyze less and wink more. Tell me about you."

"You know all about me, Patty."

"Is everything all right?"

"All right."

"You're telling me the truth?"

"I almost always tell you the truth." He smiled again.

"You know something?" she said, and shook her head. She sounded half relieved, half disappointed. "I'm still in love with you."

"Sure," he said matter-of-factly.

"What do you mean, 'sure'?"

"That was never the issue."

"It wasn't, was it?"

"Never."

"What *was* the issue?"

"We both just realized that love isn't enough."

"Enough for what?"

"Enough to hold things together. Enough to make things last. Just in general. It's not enough."

"What *does* hold things together?" Patty asked quietly.

"Is this an important and urgent question or just hypothetical?"

"Why?"

"Because usually when you barge in unannounced it means you've got something important to tell me or ask me. Otherwise you call first. So I'm wondering if this question has to do with whatever important thing you haven't mentioned yet."

"I had dinner with Russ last night," Patty said. "He was very nervous."

"Nervous?"

"Uh-huh."

"Are you being a psychologist or a mother now?"

"I'm being both."

"That's a killer combination."

"I'm worried about him."

"I can answer your question," he said. "The answer is, I don't know. I haven't found out what holds things together. At first I thought it was love. Then I thought it was me. Now all I've discovered is that neither of those two things is strong enough."

"Is everything really all right with you?"

"No," he said.

"Tell me." She touched his arm and left two fingers lingering by his wrist.

"I'm getting old."

"Is that it?"

"Maybe."

"It happens to the best of us."

"I know. But I don't like it. I'm not as strong as I used to be. I'm not strong enough for Russell. And I worry about him too."

"Why? What are *you* worried about?"

"I worry because he doesn't have anything to hold things together either."

"Maybe he doesn't *expect* things to hold together."

"No," Alex said. "He expects as much as I do."

"Oh, Alex," Patty told him. "No one expects as much as you do."

"No one?"

She smiled a crooked smile. "No one. I haven't for a long time."

"You always put too much faith in other people, you know that?"

"I only put faith in you."

"Yeah. So did I. I've let us both down."

"No." She shook her head. "I never told you this, but I was wrong to be that hurt. About Haiti. I assume that's what we're talking about." He started to speak, but she cut him off. "I knew it even then. That didn't make it any less painful, but I knew I was wrong."

"That's the thing about knowledge and pain. They don't have anything to do with each other."

"Alex," she started to say, but now he cut her off.

"You wanna know what it is? About me, I mean?" She nodded and he said, "I'm *afraid,* Patty. For the first time in my life I'm really and truly afraid."

"Of what?" she asked very softly.

"It doesn't really matter, does it, once you're afraid?"

Patty smiled sadly and shook her head.

"Well," he said.

"Well," she said, and cleared her throat. They had exhauste
their melancholy. "Call Russell."

"I will."

"I think there's something very wrong."

"You make it sound serious."

"There's something wrong with him, and I don't know what i
is."

"You do like answers, don't you?" He smiled at her, gently
and touched her hand. Her fingers closed over his.

"I *need* answers," she said. "I don't always like them, but
need them."

"I'll talk to Russ. I'll get you an answer."

She slid her hand out of his now. "Is Willie here?"

Alex looked around. "Not yet. Any minute, if you wann
wait."

Patty glanced at her watch. "I can't. But tell him I said hello."

"I'll tell him."

She stood up.

"You know," he said. "I still love you too."

"Sure," she said, and grinned at him the same way she'
grinned at him when he'd first met her almost thirty year
before. "If only that was enough."

Alex waited for Willie Trotty. He wanted to talk to him.

With all the disappointments, with all the ups and downs
with all the barriers, Alex still believed wholeheartedly that h
was on the way to getting blue. The day Willie walked back int
Alex's life Alex knew that the past, indeed, had meaning. Tha
in the past lay the all-important foundation for a satisfying fu
ture.

The club had been open only a few weeks. It was late at night
a weeknight. A few customers straggled at their tables, postpon
ing their return to the outside world. Snow had begun to fal
The door opened and Alex looked up, about to say, *We're gonn*
close in fifteen minutes. Only, when he looked up Willie Trott
was standing in the doorway.

There was no doubt about it. He was older and the skin on hi
face was a little blotchy, almost as if his cheeks had bee

burned, and he was wearing only a thin cloth raincoat and he had gained some weight, not a lot, but he no longer had that lean greyhound look. But it was Willie. After all these years. Alex had stopped searching, but he had never stopped remembering or wondering or hoping. Trembling, Alex had stood up and walked over to the black man.

"Willie?"

Willie looked over at Alex, not surprised, very much at ease, quietly confident. He didn't say a word, didn't nod or in any way acknowledge Alex's question. But somehow the answer was yes. The man's face said, *Yeah. Of course I'm Willie. Who else could I be?* Alex started to ask a million questions; he talked quickly, one question running rapidly into another. "Did you know I was here Where have you been What have you been doing Were you at the Play I thought I saw you Did you know I looked for you for years Did you know . . . ?"

And at that moment Alex realized that Willie didn't speak.

He knew it wasn't just that Willie hadn't yet spoken or even that he didn't want to speak. Willie *didn't* speak. Ever. *Christ,* Alex thought, *the guy has no tongue, of course he doesn't speak.* But it was more than that. Even without his tongue—the sudden image of the knife slashing, blood spurting, practically knocked Alex over—Willie could have made some effort to talk. But he was absolutely silent. No slurred or mumbled words, no grunts or groans. Willie barely even shook or nodded his head. He didn't write notes, didn't use sign language. It was almost a surprise sometimes to hear him breathing.

Without realizing how, Alex had determined that Willie wanted a job. Alex hired him on the spot, made him a bartender. Willie didn't acknowledge the job, didn't make any effort to thank Alex. He simply went out the door and came back the next night and started work behind the bar. He'd been there ever since.

Somehow, despite Willie's silence, you could have a conversation with him. Alex was convinced of that. At first he thought that maybe he was the only one who spoke to Willie, and that maybe he was imagining Willie's responses—the sense that Willie was, in fact, talking back without saying a word. Then he found out that everyone at Getting Blue talked to Willie. Willie hardly so much as moved an eyebrow or changed expression but everyone talked to him and came away satisfied. Alex realized, after a while, that was how Willie had played ball back in Wilson. The ball was hit, no one saw Willie move, Willie was there, the ball was caught. Now, no one heard Willie speak, but somehow something was said.

Maybe it was the way he looked at you. Gently. Innocently. Honestly. Maybe it was just that he listened and let you make up your own answers.

Willie never revealed anything about his past. It made no difference, he seemed to say. He was here now. "Once I was in Boston," Alex would say. "I heard—" And something in Willie's eyes would stop him from going on, from telling Willie that he'd heard he'd gotten married, that he'd heard he'd been in a fight had almost killed someone, that he'd been in jail for a d and d, that he was dead. Alex never found out if Willie was really at the Play. It didn't matter. Willie was at Getting Blue and he would stay late after the club was closed and sit with Alex, listen to him, look at him, be with him.

Alex locked up and Willie was beside him, tying an apron on over his khaki pants.

"I didn't see you come in," Alex said. "I must have been daydreaming."

About what?

"I was thinking about Wilson. 'Bout the Tobs. I gotta call Manning, I haven't talked to him for a while."

I don't want to talk about Wilson.

"You just missed Patty. She left a few minutes ago. She sent her love."

What's the matter?

"She was upset about Russell. There's somethin' goin' on."

What?

"I dunno. But it must be important or Patty'd never ask me to, uh, interfere." He laughed. "She still thinks I can . . . make things right."

Can you?

Alex said nothing. He looked into the eyes of the black man, remembering so many things.

Can you? came the unspoken question again.

Alex still said nothing. Only thought: *I don't know.*

27

Alex rang the doorbell to his son's apartment. He waited, long enough to suspect that no one was home. Then he heard movement from inside, and Russell's voice, a little gravelly, yelled out, "Coming!" *Christ,* Alex thought. *He's fucking somebody.*

Alex waited another thirty seconds and then the door opened. As always, whenever he hadn't seen Russell for a while, he was taken aback at his appearance.

Russ looked good. And Alex smiled because Russ knew he looked good. He had that certain slouching carriage that only someone very confident of his appearance could carry off. With his hand still on the doorknob, Russell flexed his arm just slightly, and Alex saw him glance down so he could watch his muscles tighten and bulge. He wore no shirt or socks and his hair was mussed, drooping over one eye, sticking up in back. He had a terrific body, long and lean. His eyes were piercingly blue. His hair was long and shaggy, his lips were sensually inviting. His face was a little bloated, Alex noticed. And the bags under his eyes seemed particularly deep. *He looks like he's drinkin' too much,* Alex thought. *And staying up too late. Still, he looks pretty good. I have a good-looking son.*

Russell saw his father staring at him and he grinned. "Richard Gere, eat your heart out, huh?"

Alex stepped inside the apartment. They hugged lightly but affectionately and traded kisses on the cheek.

"Sorry for taking so long," Russ said. "We were, uh, dozing."

"Ah," Alex said. "We?"

"I'm real glad you could come by. It's a good time to meet Janice and Didi."

"Janice and Didi?"

"Yeah." Russ turned toward the bedroom. "Come on out," he called.

Before the girls came out, Alex's eyes flitted around the living room. He had the same reaction he always had when he came to Russ's apartment: a strong mix of pride and confusion that his son was much more successful than he was. Russell was rich—he was a sensation in the music business and was getting hotter all the time. Russ was the most important agent in the biz, Danny had said that many times. He had a knack for picking not only sounds but trends. When C&W hit the cities, Russ had been ready with just about every strong bluegrass sideman around already in his stable. When rock went disco he wasn't happy but he convinced several of his agency's biggest groups to cut disco albums and almost every one of them went platinum. He'd made his biggest mark, though, in New Wave rock and roll. It was his greatest love too. He picked the groups, dressed them, developed their sound and their sensibilities. He nurtured the onstage nihilism, the outrageous and cynical violence. Danny once proudly confessed to Alex that Russell was probably more responsible than anyone else in the world for the fact that millions of thirteen-year-olds accepted the fact that the world was one big pile of shit and that they should gleefully dive in, purple hair and pierced noses first, with a flagrant attitude of disdain and unconcern for the results. Alex was not nearly as proud as Danny.

He was prouder when Janice came out of the bedroom.

She came out alone. Alex's immediate impression was that she was one of the loveliest women he'd ever seen. Her hair was light brown and it was long and full and free. She was tall, lanky, coltish. Alex was glad he had the presence of mind not to gasp.

Instead he glanced at his son and raised an eyebrow in appreciation and commendation.

"Janice, this is my father. Dad, J.J."

"Janice Jakes," she said. "Russ calls me J.J." She had an even, husky voice that perfectly matched the rest of her.

"Hi," Alex said.

"You can call me J.J., too, if that's your question."

"Question?"

"You looked like you were going to ask me a question. Must've been in your eyes."

"Sorry," came a smoother, higher-pitched voice behind Janice. "I was in the shower. I'm Didi."

Didi was short as Didis are supposed to be; half a foot shorter than Janice. She had dirty-blond hair, large breasts; she was far less elegant than Janice. Everything about Didi seemed to be spread all over her face. She smiled at Alex but the smile said not so much *I'm glad to meet you* as *I hope you like me.* Alex did. Instantly.

"Well," Russell said.

"Let's go for a walk," Alex told his son.

Whenever Alex's father wanted to have a serious talk, he would take Alex out for a long walk. Those strolls had never settled anything in Alex's mind. Maybe they had made Carl feel better. Alex wondered if the talk he was about to have with Russ was going to make either one of them feel better. Alex's general observation was that talk never really did much for anyone in the long run. Heart-to-heart talks usually turned out to be one-way outbursts of emotion, flat-out lies, or sincere niceties that didn't stand the test of time. Alex wondered if his father used to have these doubts when they had wandered the streets of New York. Then he decided it didn't really make much difference. Carl was long dead and buried. He didn't have any doubts at all anymore.

"They both seem like, uh, nice girls," Alex said.

Russ grinned. "You think it's really sick, don't you?"

"Hey. I was a ballplayer for too long to think *anything* is really sick. But I do think it's a little . . . odd."

"I guess it is. A little."

"You gonna tell me about it or what?"

"What do you wanna know?"

"Russ," Alex said patiently, "there are two things I want to know. What the hell are you doing and are you all right?"

They were on Lexington Avenue and Fifty-third Street, where they had automatically stopped at their favorite egg cream stand, each ordering one chocolate to go. Back on the street again, they stirred the thick chocolate syrup at the bottom of their cups and went right back to the conversation.

"First I started going out with J.J. She's a biologist."

"You're kidding."

"At Columbia. She's actually important up there."

"Where'd you meet her?"

"At her school. I was giving a lecture on the record business and she came. She was going out with the guy who taught the class. But we met and . . ."

"Sparks just flew, huh?"

"Right. So we went out for a while. Couple of months, off and on. I told you about her." Alex nodded, vaguely remembering, and Russ continued. "She's really smart. And really nice. And I was crazy about her right from the start."

"Sounds good."

"Yeah. Except one day I woke up. She'd spent the night. We started to make love in the morning and suddenly I was thinking, *Jesus her breasts are small.* I got pissed at myself because I knew she was great but I realized I had to sleep with someone with larger breasts or I was gonna go crazy. I mean I just had to have . . ."

"More."

"Yeah." Russell's eyes lit up. "Yeah! Did that ever happen to you when you were married to Mom?"

Alex didn't answer.

"Dad?"

"What?"

"Do you understand what I'm saying here?"

"I understand."

"I mean, suddenly, all I could think about was missed opportunities. I started walking down the street and I'd think, *Whooo, how do I meet* her or, *Jesus,* that's *a hot one.* You know?"

"I know. Missed opportunities."

"So I met Didi. She's a secretary at the agency. Wants to get into show biz. I started going out with her at the same time I was going out with J.J. You know, one on Thursday, one on Saturday. Whatever. And the more I saw them both, the more I realized they were complete opposites. Complete! Tall and short, blonde and dark. J.J. likes nothing better than doing research in a lab; Didi's into *Wheel of Fortune,* if you know what I mean. She's not stupid, but"—Russ searched for the right word— "she's sensual. She thinks with her body. So I started thinking, this is great. I basically had everything I wanted. Between the two of them I had the perfect woman."

"Perfect."

"Yeah. Until one time Janice decided she wanted to see me on a Friday and I was seein' Didi. She decided she didn't want to be a part-time mistress. She didn't mind being a mistress but she didn't like bein' a part-timer."

"Everybody's got her limits, pal."

"We talked about it and I finally told her I wasn't gonna commit to anything. So we split up. I felt shitty, but . . ." There was no need to qualify the *but.* "Anyway, about two weeks later, I'm out with Didi and we run into Janice. We were all seeing the same movie, it was the afternoon, Janice was alone. It was awkward, but we all started talking. We sat together. We went for a drink. We all had dinner. We all went back to my place. When it was time for one of them to leave, nobody knew which one."

"So they both stayed?"

Russell grinned, embarrassed just a bit—this was his father— and shrugged and nodded.

"I don't know what to say," Alex told his son.

"I do."

"What?"

Russ took an expensive cigar from his pocket. He clipped off the end with a sterling silver cigar cutter from Tiffany. He lit it slowly and with great pleasure.

"Dad." Russ puffed twice more, partially to make sure the

cigar was well lit, partially to punctuate the importance of his sentence. "You always wanted to defeat the world. To beat it like you were in some sort of game—you against it. Well, I *can't* beat the world, not one on one. I don't have the brains, the power, the energy. I don't have the desire. I can't save a World Series game. I don't think I'm ever getting blue. The way I see it, the world's too fuckin' tough. It's too mean, too shitty, and too unfair. It's too damn big and too damn overwhelming to try to take it on."

"Russ . . ."

"*You* take it on. You try to beat it. What I'm gonna do is create my own world." Another puff of the cigar. "I'm makin' a shitload of money. Megabucks. I have a new group that's playin' the Garden tomorrow night and if they do what I expect, they're gonna be the biggest group in the country."

"What's their name?" It was the first coherent statement Alex had come up with in a long time.

"Psycho."

Alex nodded. "Nice touch."

"Dad, do you understand what I'm doing? I'm gonna just do what I *want.* I'm gonna put the world outside where they can't reach in and fuck things up. If Psycho hits, I'm gonna just pick up and move to the south of France. I'm gonna eat till I get fat, I'm gonna fuck these two women till none of us can move, and unless there's a nuclear holocaust I've got no more problems. I'll buy a boat, take a carton of great books, listen to music. Do you understand what I'm talkin' about?"

Alex looked at Russell, who was now sweating, nervously waiting for an answer, for approval. "When did"—Alex swallowed—"when did you change?"

"What?"

"When did this happen?" Alex waved his hand over his son. "All of this."

"It's been happening a long time. A long time."

"Why?"

"Because I don't like what I see when I look around me." Russell put his hand out, placed it on his father's chest, and stopped him from speaking. Then he just turned a 360-degree circle and pointed to the world as he turned. "Don't you see it?" he asked quietly.

Alex took a deep breath, exhaled slowly, and nodded. "I see it."

"There you go."

Russell started to walk, but this time Alex stopped him.

"I can beat it," Alex said. "I always have."

"I can't. So I'll pull out. It's easy."

"Is it?"

"I'll send you a postcard and let you know."

Alex nodded slowly and they began walking again.

"It's not really that weird, Dad. People do it all the time. They have families, they come home, they shut out reality. The only thing different here is that I've got two women to come home to."

"No. That's not the only difference."

"What else?"

Alex coughed, rubbed his throat. "It's so *important* to you, that's the difference. I tell you, Russ, I haven't learned that much in my lifetime, but one thing I have learned: It's the things that are important to you that get fucked up."

"Don't worry, Dad." Russell smiled now, a relaxed and confident smile. "As long as you're strong enough to beat 'em back, I'm strong enough to hide from 'em."

28

The next morning at nine-fifteen Alex got a phone call from Danny Kapstein.

"Hey, *boychick.* I wake you?"

"Had to get up to answer the phone anyway."

"You always were a witty guy."

"What's up?"

"You free?"

"When?"

"Now."

"I can be in an hour or so."

"Come on up to the office."

"Sure. What's goin' on?"

"Just a few things I want to run down. But I don't wanna let them slide."

"Just have some hot coffee waiting and I'll be there soon."

When Alex walked into Danny's office an hour later, the hot coffee was waiting. So were Alex's brother, Elliot, and Danny Kapstein né Cappollo.

Elliot stood up and the two brothers shook hands, Alex putting one hand on Elliot's shoulder in a restrained gesture of affection. Elliot responded with a tight-lipped smile, a slight hunching of shoulders that might have been a lean toward a hug, then a stiffening. He sat back down, his bad leg extending stiffly in front of him, his strong arms guiding him into the seat.

"So what's so important?" Alex asked.

"Nothing urgent," Danny said. "We just have some stuff to go over about the club. We didn't want to settle anything without you."

"Good."

"Did you hear about the gay fortune teller?"

"No."

"He reads fists."

"Shit!" Alex laughed.

Elliot nodded, as if to say, *Yes, okay, that's funny*. But he didn't laugh.

"So what about Getting Blue?" Alex said, breathing out one small last laugh.

"We wanna start booking a couple of rock acts."

"What?"

"Rock. We've got a couple of small groups, it's the perfect place for them. People'll take 'em a little more seriously if they play there. Plus we'll get a younger crowd, maybe they'll come back for the jazz."

"How many acts?"

"Hmmmm?"

Alex sat up straight in the chair. He was not laughing now and his voice was very soft and very even. "How many rock acts do you want to book?"

"A few."

"I want the number."

"Whenever they come up. We've got three or four now; we'll have more later. It's no big deal. It'll be a real help for record contracts."

"Let me think about it."

"There are a few more things," Elliot spoke up.

There was something strangely menacing in his tone. Challenging. Alex squinted at his brother, perplexed. "Such as?"

"We're thinking of moving," Elliot said.

"The club?"

Danny nodded and took over again. "It's too small. If we're going to be bringing in more rock, we want to expand."

"No."

"Look, Alex . . ."

"The club is perfect, Danny. It's the right size, it books the right acts, it's the best jazz club in town."

"The menu's too small."

"The menu's *perfect*. People don't want food to get in the way of the music, they want it to be simple and good and stay in the background."

"The club's not making enough money, Alex."

Alex paused. He bit down on his lip before answering. "It *is* making money, Danny."

"But not enough."

"What's enough?"

"There's *never* enough. But it's stopped growing."

"Maybe it's found the right level."

"Once you stop getting bigger you're as good as dead. You're a failure."

"You hit three hundred you're still not hittin' seven outta ten times. But people are pretty happy to hit three hundred."

"Come on, Alex. Don't give me the baseball bullshit. We're talkin' real life here. In real life you keep goin' till you hit a thousand."

"Can I have some more coffee?"

Danny buzzed his secretary, who came in, took Alex's mug, and returned a minute later with hot coffee in a new mug.

"Where do I stand legally? I mean, do I have enough control to stop you from doing this?"

"No," Elliot said. His face betrayed no emotion, not pleasure, not regret.

"It's already been taken care of, Alex. It's already being done. We've got a new site all picked out; we've already got Russ workin' on booking a few of the acts."

Alex leaned casually against the wall of Danny's office. These revelations had knocked the wind out of him. He felt a little panicky. But he didn't want to let on. When hit by a pitch, don't rub it, he knew. Make them think their fastball's not hard enough to hurt you. "Why," he asked as unemotionally as he could, "did you make me get out of bed for this meeting?"

" 'Cause I want to convince you not to quit."

"Why?"

" 'Cause you're my best friend," Danny said.

Alex nodded.

"After the Play," Danny went on, "how much money did you make, you know, from personal appearances, ads, stuff like that? In the first year?"

"Fifty grand, maybe. Maybe a little more."

"You made more. Plus the sporting-goods deal."

"Yeah."

"They still pay you pretty good money?"

"They do."

"Plus you're makin' good bucks at the club."

"Very good."

"How much of that you think you'd have made, total, if I wasn't handling you?"

"A quarter," Alex said. "Half, tops."

"*Tops.* Which is my whole point. You've still got a sweet deal. The club'll still be yours—it'll just be a little different. It won't be perfect, but that's life."

"That *is* life," Elliot said.

Alex said nothing. He drank his coffee calmly.

"Seems to me you're takin' this pretty well," Danny said.

"I can't win, so what's the use of fighting?"

"This isn't a matter of winning or losing, Alex."

"*Everything's* a matter of winning or losing."

"Maybe you're right."

"Russell know about this?"

"No," Danny said. "He just knew we were gonna be booking some rock into the city. Maybe for Getting Blue. He knew we had to talk to you first."

"Okay," Alex said. "You talked to me."

"You gonna stay?"

"I don't know. I doubt it."

"Stay. At least think it over. Don't just walk out."

Alex said nothing. He stood up to leave. He nodded, he

smiled, but when Danny extended his hand, Alex didn't shake it. He stared at his oldest friend until Danny's hand dropped to his side.

"I told you," Danny said as Alex moved to the door. "I've been tellin' you since we were nine years old." Alex took another step. "Why the hell didn't you become a sports agent when I gave you the chance? You could've made a lot of money and I never would've had to fuck you."

Alex stopped and turned. "You were always gonna quit when you hit forty. That was your goal since we were little kids."

"Yeah."

"You shoulda done it. You shoulda quit."

"Hey," Danny said. He smiled and shrugged. "I like my work too much."

"I'll call you for dinner," Elliot said to his brother. "Let's have dinner. Maybe next week."

"Maybe," Alex Justin said, shaking his head. "Maybe next week."

The bass hummed into Alex's consciousness. The deep, rich vibrations lifted his eyes to the small stage. The bass player—Lester Tunis, the world's greatest bass player—smiled over at Alex's table. Alex raised his drink in a toast to perfection. He then downed the bourbon in the toasting glass. It was his fifth toast of the set and his fifth double bourbon on the rocks.

When the set was over, the great bass player sat down with Alex. The huge, fat black man settled into a chair and used a white handkerchief to mop sweat off his face.

"Very nice set," Alex told him, slurring his speech.

"Nice is as nice do."

"That's so true."

"This club don't look like it's goin' round," Lester Tunis said.

"Come again?"

"It ain't swingin'."

"I know. You can't have everything."

"Everything is nothing."

"Right, Les."

"All is none."

"Uh-huh."

"One is two."

"You're on a roll now," Alex slurred. He *loved* the way Les Tunis played the bass. The four-hundred-pound musician was a genius, a poet, a musical philosopher. It bothered Alex tremendously that the man spoke no known language. His nickname among musicians was Aristotle because he was the person least likely ever to string together a coherent sentence. Alex wondered how in hell one would ever find out all the great things that were inside Lester's head, the things that made the music. The music was enough, Alex supposed; at least that was all Lester was going to give. Through his drunken stupor Alex looked at the hand-lettered sign hanging outside the tinted glass wall of the club.

GETTING BLUE.

"Cats don't fly," Lester said.

"I know, man. I know."

"London, England. London, *England!*"

"A good place." Alex wondered what the hell London, England, had to do with anything. "Never been there."

"Home is away."

"I think Eddie wants you." Alex looked over at Lester Tunis's drummer, who was signaling for Les to come and get his share of the coke he'd just bought from one of Alex's waiters.

"Know everything," Lester said, and struggled to rise from his seat. His mammoth, calloused hands lay on the table, supporting his weight. For a moment Alex thought the whole thing would collapse, but Lester made it to a standing position with a huff and a wheeze. He lumbered over to the stage for his conference.

GETTING BLUE. The sign seemed a little faded. Blurry. Alex wondered whether it was the sign or his eyes that were getting fuzzy. Another drink might help him decide, so he signaled for his cute little brunette waitress, the one who wanted to be a dancer, to bring him another Jack Daniel's. Danny had fucked the waitress, Alex knew. Danny had told him that she liked to be tied up and that she screamed the word *yes* as loud as she could when she had an orgasm.

"Are you sure you should have another one?" the waitress asked handing Alex his drink.

"Are you sure you want to work here?" Alex asked back.

"Excuse me for trying to do you a favor."

Alex's eyes lit on a woman sitting alone at the bar. She was not great, he could tell that, but she looked sad and drunk and available. Perfect, he thought, and smiled at her. She nodded back an it's-about-time nod. That was fair, Alex decided. It *was* about time. It was after one in the morning.

Before he could get the dancing waitress to send a drink over to the woman at the bar, Russell came bouncing through the door. He was very hyper, a bundle of nerves. His body seemed to be going in every direction at once and he practically ran over to his father when he spotted him.

"Dad, how ya doin'?" Russell's fingers played with the smoky air of the club. His knee jiggled, his toes tapped against the butt-littered floor.

"Great," Alex said.

"You don't look great," Russell said.

"Well, I am." Alex tried, not successfully, to sit up straighter.

"You look drunk."

"I am that too. How was the concert?"

"Un-fuckin'-believable! France, here I come!"

"Good." Alex started to tip over in his chair. He caught himself just in time and managed to wink at the woman at the bar as he righted himself.

"They were incredible. Great! It was probably the best show I've ever done." He looked down at his hands. "I'm still sort of shaking from the whole thing. I mean, they really just brought things to life. It was like the birth of a major—"

"Where are the girls? The two girls."

"Right outside. They bumped into someone they . . . here they are." Russ stood up and waved at Didi and Janice as they came in. They headed straight for Alex's table.

"Hi, Mr. Justin. How are you?"

"Drunk. How're you?"

"Stoned."

"Have a seat."

They sat and Alex gave another reassuring look to the woman at the bar, who did not look happy being peripherally involved with a family reunion.

"Dad," Russell said, "I heard about what happened today."

"What happened?"

"With the club."

"Oh."

"I don't know what to say."

"What *did* happen?"

"You got fucked, that's what happened."

"Oh, yeah. That's right."

"What are you gonna do?"

"Do?"

"Yeah. What are you gonna do?"

"Have another drink. Help yourselves," he said to the two women.

"No, I mean what are you gonna do about Danny? How are you gonna stop 'em?"

"Can't. Who *told* you?"

"Elliot. He was at the show tonight. Hey," Russ said as he peered curiously at his father. "When did you start wearing glasses?"

"What?"

Russell stared at Alex's conservative tortoiseshell eyeglasses. "When did that happen?"

"Coupla weeks ago."

"Why?"

"I couldn't see."

"They make you look . . ."

"They make me look what?"

Russell lowered his voice. "Old." He spoke that one word with a sense of wonder and bewilderment.

"He *would* tell you, wouldn't he?" Alex said suddenly.

"Huh?"

"Elliot. What was he doing there?"

"Dad, we're partners, remember? I mean, basically he's Psycho's lawyer."

"Was he happy when he told you?"

"No."

"Shit."

"He said he was just doin' his job."

"Yeah," Alex said. "And he's good at it."

"You gonna quit?"

"Quit?"

"Yeah."

"Too much money."

"*What's* too much money?"

"They *pay* me too much money."

"You're *not* gonna quit?"

Alex shook his head. The movement made him feel a little nauseous.

"I was gonna. I was gonna say fuck you. I was gonna quit. I was even gonna hit him."

"Why didn't you?"

"I didn't know what would happen."

"I don't . . ."

"Usually, when I do something, I know what'll happen afterward. But it's like things were backward today. It was like hittin' a home run and being called out."

"I'm kinda surprised," Russell said, letting out a deep breath and slowing down for the first time since entering the jazz club.

"Are you all right?" Didi asked.

"Which one of us?" Alex wanted to know.

"Either one," J.J. said.

"Judge!" a voice boomed out. "Holy shit! It's the fuckin' Judge!"

The booming voice sounded, to Alex's liquor-soaked ears, about as subtle as a cannon explosion. The sound popped his eyes open but he didn't yet recognize it. When he turned to see who was greeting him so effusively, he saw a little man, around sixty or older, wearing a madras sport jacket and brown polyester pants that were at least an inch too short. The man's face was gaunt and his day's growth of white stubble beard looked as if it would be impossible to erase. The guy looked vaguely familiar to Alex. All he could really remember, though, was that he didn't like him.

"Judge, how the fuck are you?"

"I'm the fuck fine. How are you?"

The forgotten old pal lasciviously eyed the two young women at Alex's table. "I see you're doin' fine! What are you, grabbin' all the wool for yourself without sharin' with an old pal?" The man smiled at Didi and Janice. He ignored Russell, who didn't seem to notice. Russ was still staring, somewhat wide eyed, at his father. "Hi, ladies. I've been admiring your shapes for quite some time before I realized you were here with my old friend the Judge. As soon as I realized that, why, I knew it was my duty to come over and give you the chance of a lifetime. My name is Enos J. Farrell. Perhaps you've heard of me."

"Yes," said Didi. "Aren't you a famous asshole?"

Enos J. Farrell blinked his eyes, then roared with laughter. The laugh turned into a sour cough but that didn't slow Enos down one bit. He pounded the table with his hand, laughing and coughing.

"Tell 'em, Judge. Tell 'em who I am."

It was Alex's turn to stare now. And he was staring at Enos Farrell, this old man.

"Tell 'em, Judge, for fuck's sake!"

Alex turned to Didi and Janice. "Enos J. Farrell," he said wondrously, "was one of the best ballplayers I ever saw. He was a twenty-year man when I was a rookie with the Phillies. Over the hill but still a great shortstop."

"The greatest," Enos said none too modestly.

"When I was tryin' to make the club in spring training, when I was trying to break into the big leagues, this guy made my life a living hell."

Alex's voice had turned suddenly icy. Enos noticed, because he turned from the girls to squint at Alex. "Come on, now, Judge. Those was fun old days."

"Every time," Alex said to Russ's women, "I slid into second base, this cocksucker made sure he did his best to knock my teeth out with the tag."

"I did too," Enos cackled. "That ain't no lie."

"He'd trip me when I was running—"

"Tryin' to toughen ya up."

"—and spit on me if I'd double and slide in safe to second."

Enos coughed out a fond laugh. He enjoyed the memory.

"He did his best to make sure I didn't make it. Rode me unbelievably all day long. Sneered, spit, spiked."

"You was a rookie. We rode all the rookies."

"They once put me at second base in a spring training game, just foolin' around to see if I could help out in other spots."

"Biiiig mistake," Enos Farrell said, and grinned.

"Enos here singled and then tried to steal second. When I tried to tag him, he came in and spiked me. Went two feet out of the baseline to take me down."

"That's what the game was all about."

"Twenty-three stitches I had to take."

"Just a cut."

Alex turned to look Enos in the eye. "You used to sharpen your spikes, didn't you, Enos?"

"Yup. You betcha."

"He used to sharpen 'em so if anybody got in his way they damn sure paid for it."

"And they damn sure did too," Enos agreed. "Lemme buy you a drink, Judge."

"I hated your guts."

"That weren't my problem, boy. My problem was to keep playin' as long as I could so I kept gettin' my paycheck."

"You were a real scum bag."

"I still am. But lemme buy you a drink."

"You're twenny years too late, Enos. Get the fuck out of my restaurant."

Alex tried to stand, but all the alcohol he'd consumed made him very wobbly. One bourbon he didn't get to consume was the one right in front of him—because before Alex could get up, Enos J. Farrell picked up the glass and threw the drink all over him. The ice cubes stung his cheek and the liquid splattered his face and dripped down to Alex's shirt. Stunned, Alex plopped back down into his chair, frozen.

"Dad," Russell said urgently, "aren't you gonna do anything?"

Alex didn't move. Enos crouched like an arthritic panther

ready to pounce, but Alex acted as if his old tormentor weren't even in the room.

"Dad," Russell almost pleaded, "hit him or something."

Alex didn't move.

"Hit him!" Russell said louder. His fists clenched and un- clenched, his head cocked to the side, questioning his father's lack of movement. "Hit him, Dad! *Hit him!*"

"You were a pussy then and you're a pussy now," Enos spit out. "And I wouldn't buy you a drink even if these two babes sat on my face till the cows came home."

That was the last thing Enos J. Farrell said for quite some time. Alex stood up. His rage made him instantly sober. But before he could even take one step, Russell had slammed the old ballplayer up against the wall. His first punch was to the old man's stomach; it doubled him up and made him gag. The second punch was to the side of the head. It broke two knuckles on Russell's right hand and made a sickening sound against Enos's skull. No one expected a third punch, but Russell threw one that caught the old shortstop in the right eye. By that time Janice was able to grab Russell and yell at him to stop. He stopped. She sagged with relief. Alex saw the expression on his son's face and it terrified him. He started to call out a warning but it was too late because Russell had whirled and slapped Janice across the face. She fell backward over a chair and a sliver of blood appeared on her forehead over her left eye. Russell snarled at her and would have hit her again, but two waiters had him now. They held him until he nodded that the fury was gone.

Someone took Enos into the bathroom. At the table Janice stood shakily, one hand on the back of a chair. Didi stood at her side. Russell looked at the two of them. His face did not show the relief of escaped rage; it expressed contempt and satisfac- tion and amazement.

Alex, who hadn't moved one inch during the entire scuffle, turned away from his son. He had nothing to offer him in the way of comfort or explanation.

Russell moved to Didi and Janice, said nothing, just waited. When they were ready, they both turned toward the door, as one. Russell followed them as they left. He never once looked back at his father.

Alex stayed slumped in his chair. He stayed like that while the waiters cleared the last dishes off the tables. He stayed while the band packed up and cleared out. He stayed while the woman at the bar made one last attempt to go home with him, strolling past his table and smiling at him. He stayed while the dancing waitress locked up and the last employees left at three-thirty in the morning. Willie was the last one to leave. Before going out the door he turned to Alex and looked at him. *Do you want me to stay?* the look said. Alex shook his head and Willie left.

Alex stayed slumped in his chair until he fell asleep, head down, arms cushioning him from the round hardwood table. His last thought before he fell asleep was that maybe he would just wait there forever or until whatever he was waiting for decided to reveal itself.

The last thing he saw before his eyes closed was the sign outside the club. The first ray of the morning light streaked across the scratched black lettering and dirty white background.

GETTING BLUE.

29

The call came one month later. Alex had almost expected it.

"Alex. This is Elliot."

Alex heard the catch in his younger brother's throat.

"I'm at Russell's. I think you'd better come over."

"What's wrong?"

"Don't—don't—don't—" Elliot began stuttering, "don't worry. But I think you should come here right away."

His brother sounded just as he had the day they'd talked on the phone when their parents had died. Alex barely managed to say okay before hanging up the phone.

Rush hour made the taxi ride interminable. Alex had nothing to do but stare out the dirt-streaked window and think about his son.

They hadn't seen each other much since that drunken night at Getting Blue. He'd call Russ and the boy would respond in monosyllables. They'd had dinner one night, but Russell had left early, before dessert, saying he had business. Alex knew there was no business. His son just didn't want to be around him.

He heard from Patty that Russ was even more hyper, and always angry. Alex had been around enough people like Walter Lumpano—like himself—to recognize the signs.

He'd heard a few days ago from Danny—and tried not to

sound surprised—that Russ had bought a house in the south of France. Alex had taken that as a good sign, although he was hurt his son hadn't told him about it. A retreat sounded good to Alex. He wasn't at all sure it was possible to keep the world at bay, but it was an effort that seemed more and more worth making.

The first thing Alex saw as he stepped into Russell's apartment, the first thing to be forever implanted as a frozen picture dangling in his memory, was his brother. Elliot was standing in a corner of the living room. He wore a light-blue long-sleeve shirt and dark-blue pants. He wore a tie that was askew and loose. His dark-blue sport jacket was crumpled and lay like a pile of rags in the corner. Elliot was leaning on his cane. He was so pale and his darting eyes were so full of desperation that the cane appeared to support not only his weight but his very life. Alex thought, as he took in the sweat stains under Elliot's arms and his curling, sweaty hair, that if he kicked Elliot's cane out from under him his brother might never get up.

Alex turned his head with distaste.

At the far end of the living room, in front of the spotless bay windows, stood Russell.

He wore faded jeans and a white T-shirt, no shoes or socks. The sunlight glistened off the windows and cast an angelic glow around him. Russ was calm, serene. He looked as relaxed as Alex had seen him in years.

In his left hand Russell held a rolled-up magazine. In his right hand he held a gun.

"Dad," Russell said, and bobbed his head by way of a greeting.

"Russ," Alex greeted in return, though the word had a lot of trouble getting past the cold, harsh lump in Alex's chest and throat.

"Tell him," Elliot said. His voice was weak, shaky. It didn't have its usual accusatory tone. It was the voice of a frightened animal.

Russell said nothing.

"Tell me what?" Alex asked as gently as he could.

"I'm in trouble," his son said.

"Tell him," Elliot said again, and then to Alex, "Maybe you can do something."

"No." Russell shook his head. "There's nothing he can do."

"Tell me," Alex said.

"I was in Didi's apartment today. We were going to pack up her things. For France. Janice was going to meet us there, at the apartment." Russell's voice was a dull monotone. "We started to sort through things, her things, and we kept touching each other, brushing up against each other, and we both got incredibly horny. We had to make love. So we did. Right there on the floor of the living room." Russell's lips curled into a grin at the memory. "It was . . . perfect."

"What happened?" Alex asked.

"She touched me when it was over, took my hand, told me she wasn't going to come to France. She didn't want to go. I asked her why not. I mean, I was kinda stunned." He half turned to face the sun, then swiveled back to his father. "She didn't know. She just didn't want it anymore."

"What did you do, Russ?" Alex whispered.

"I killed her," Russell said matter-of-factly.

Alex wanted to laugh. But the expression on his son's face and the oppressive silence in the room stopped him. He waited.

"I strangled her. I mean, the whole point was for the three of us to go. Then we could have created our own little world. But without Didi . . . I don't know. . . . We couldn't've. The point was so it would be perfect."

"So you *killed* her?" Alex asked incredulously.

"I couldn't go to France anymore. I didn't want to. I didn't want to stay here with Janice and Didi either. I didn't want things to stay the same."

"What *did* you want?" Alex asked cautiously.

"Well, that's the thing. I asked myself the same question. What did I want. And you know what?" Alex shook his head. The motion was so tight it was as if he were being pulled taut by an invisible puppet-master. "I didn't want anything," Russell said. "I thought about what I'd done, and I'd done a lot. I've traveled and I've had women and I've been really successful in business. I've pretty much done everything that anybody could do. Drugs, kicks, scenes. Money." He smiled. An inner smile that made Alex shudder. "I thought about all those things I'd already done and I thought, *Do I want to do any of them again?* and the answer was no. So then I thought, *Well, what* haven't *I done?* I mean, what could I do that might . . . that might . . ."

"*Mean* something," Alex finished.

Russ smiled, a broad smile this time, and shook his head. "Give me a jolt," he said. "I don't care about meaning. I just wanted a bigger jolt."

"A jolt."

"You know about jolts," Russell said evenly. "All I wanted was for something to make me feel like I hit a home run to win a game."

"Jesus," Alex said. "Jesus Christ."

"Are you sure she's dead?" Elliot asked. "I just realized, sometimes . . ."

"I thought she was dead after a few minutes, but she wasn't. She scared the shit out of me because she was still alive and she started crawling. But she was pretty close to dying." He pointed toward the door of his apartment. "She got almost to her front door and then she stopped and died."

Nobody said anything for a long time. Alex tried to absorb what his son had just told him in his long, passionless monotone.

"Where do you come in?" Alex turned to Elliot and addressed him for the first time. His brother's color had not returned. He looked like a zombie and didn't respond to Alex's question.

"He came by," Russ said, "because I called him. After I got home. About an hour after I killed her. We were supposed to have a business meeting anyway."

"What were you doing," Alex asked, "in the hour before he came by?"

"Nothing. I was just sitting, thinking. Nothing."

"Where'd you get the gun, Russ?" He almost called him "baby." That was what he used to call the boy when he was first born. For the first few months of Russ's life Alex had called him "baby." It was a term of love, of awe over the infant's vulnerability and innate trust. Now, this was the most vulnerable he had seen his son since those early months of life. Now, again, he

was naked and vulnerable. The only thing that was missing was
the trust.

Russell nodded over at Elliot and Alex didn't react. He was
not surprised.

"When?"

Russ didn't answer. Alex turned to his brother. He didn't ask
the question again. He just waited.

"Now," Elliot said, choking out the words. "I gave it to him
when I came over. Now."

"That was our business meeting," Russell said. "I wanted a
gun so I could kill myself."

"No," Alex said. He shook his head and found that his whole
body was already shaking.

Russell raised the gun slowly and put the end of the barrel
into the curve of his ear.

"You gave him the gun?" Alex said to Elliot. His mouth barely
opened; his words spit past his clenched teeth. "You came here,
saw him, and you gave him the gun?" On the word *gun* Alex's
voice broke and his body trembled, one hard twitchy shiver.

Elliot, whose body was almost doubled over, cramped, managed a curt nod.

"Why? Why'd you give it to him?"

"Can you speak louder?" Russ asked. "I've got a gun in my
ear."

"*Why?*" Alex realized that his shirt was sopping. It clung to
him, sticking to the hair on his chest, shoulders and back. His
palms and his face were drenched in sweat.

"You'll never understand this kind of pain," Elliot said.
"You've never felt it. *I* know. I understand." He pointed toward
Russell and the gun. "Because I've wanted to do the same thing
for thirty years."

Alex faced his son. "He's wrong," he said. "It doesn't have to
be that way."

"Not for you," Elliot said. "For us. For the cripples."

"He *likes* the pain," Alex said to Russell. "He likes it. I swear
to God, he thrives on it. Right from the start, he liked it."

"This is for me," Elliot said. "You told me years and years ago
that sooner or later you have to decide that *you're* the point. You

have to do things because it's what you are. Well, this is for me.
This is the point. This is what I am."

"Christ, look at him!" Alex screamed and turned and waved
broadly at his brother. "Look at you. You hardly even limp
anymore! But you're still a cripple. You made yourself into a
cripple!" To Russell he said, as urgently as he'd ever said anything in his life, "He never fought back! He won't fight back!
But it doesn't have to be that way."

"I'm ready," Russell said.

"No," Alex told him. "No. You can't."

"Give me a reason," Russ said calmly. "I *don't* like the pain. I
can't live with it. That's why I asked Elliot to call you. To give
me a reason."

"Because you can't! That's . . . that's the reason." Alex's
hands were clenched. He realized that one of his fingernails was
dug so deeply into his own palm, it was drawing blood.

"Will things get better? Will I be happy? What's the point?"
Russell paused. "Will I ever be closer to getting blue?"

Alex said nothing.

"You used to tell me," Russell said, "that life was like a baseball game. All the subtleties, all the nuances. All the options
with which you could control your own destiny."

Alex nodded, remembering. And he listened to the eerie
calm of his boy's voice.

"You were wrong. And, boy, imagine my surprise. I mean,
there you were, always there, hitting home runs to win games,
making an unbelievable catch to win the World Series. So I
always thought . . . well, it doesn't matter what I always
thought. But what I found out is that it doesn't make any difference how many home runs you hit, how many catches you
make. 'Cause they always come right back and load the bases."

Russell raised the gun again. He put it inside his ear.

Alex heard a click. He turned, realizing it was the sound of a
door being opened.

Almost before any of it could register, before he could begin
to understand what he was seeing, Janice walked into the living
room. The smile on her face turned into a gasp and she dropped

the Bloomingdale's bag she was carrying. Makeup rolled along the hardwood floor.

Elliot began choking, wheezing. Alex's eyes flickered to his brother, then back to the door.

Didi stepped inside.

She, too, had a shopping bag and, until she saw Russell, a smile.

Alex whirled back toward his son. He said nothing. He didn't have to.

"Because I *would* have done it," Russell said to his father. "Once I thought it, I would have done it."

Russ smiled, a broad, relaxed smile and, as if for the first time, noticed the rolled-up magazine in his left hand. "You'll be proud of me," he said. "I made the cover of *Time* magazine. Look."

He tossed the magazine onto the floor in front of Alex, who looked down. Peering up from the cover was a photo of Russell. He looked young and handsome and successful. Underneath his photo were the words: HAVING IT ALL: THE MOST IMPORTANT MAN IN THE MUSIC BUSINESS.

Didi and Janice were both screaming, Elliot was making more choking noises, and Alex was staring down at the triumphant face of the perfect young man on the cover of *Time* magazine when Russell pulled the trigger.

It was still that night. God, could it really be the very same night? And Alex was sitting at the bar. All the lights were off; the place was closed. Willie Trotty stood behind the bar, practically invisible in the dark. It was after the shooting and after the cops and after Patty, who was at last asleep with the help of several sleeping pills, and after the reporters. It was after everything.

"So tell me," Alex said to Willie. "I never once asked you, but now I am. Speak to me. Tell me something that makes sense. Tell me where you were for twenty years. Tell me why that guy cut out your tongue. Tell me what you're thinking. Tell me about getting blue. Tell me *anything* that makes sense, Willie. Please."

Alex heard how desperate his *please* sounded. He didn't care. All he cared about was getting an answer.

Of course, he got no answer. No words came from Willie's lips. No sound. No attempt.

Alex looked into Willie's eyes to see what *they* told him. They, too, were silent.

30

The plane hummed as it soared thirty thousand feet over the Pacific Ocean. The monotonous drone did its best to lull Alex to sleep, but it wasn't working. He was awake. Awake and thinking.

As usual, he realized, he was thinking about the past. He thought very little these days about the present. Not at all about the future. Mostly he remembered. The good times. The painful moments. The sex. The violence. The love. It was the love that was the hardest to recall. It was the love that had resulted in the most pain. In the tragedies.

The little tragedies.

Someone in his past had called them that. Life as a series of little tragedies. Who was it? He couldn't remember. Oh, well. It never really mattered who said things. Only that they were said. And remembered.

At least this time, Alex thought, he was drifting off into the *recent* past. Only hours ago.

He was with Dave Manning. He hadn't seen Manning in maybe a year. But he came through New York and called, and they'd spent a couple of nice evenings together. Dinner, drinks, some time at the club. Manning liked Getting Blue.

"We're moving," Alex told him. "In another couple of weeks."

"Same kind of place?"

"No. Bigger. Newer. Less intimate. More . . ." Alex waved his hands.

"Just more."

"Yeah." Alex nodded.

"Too bad," Manning said, looking around. "I like this joint."

"I used to," Alex said. "Now I don't really care."

They reminisced. About baseball, about the players. Surprisingly, Manning had stayed on top of what had become of their old compatriots. This one was a beer distributor. That one sold cars. This one had a ranch. That one was a drunk. Manning had even seen the Lump. He was now a very successful color commentator for one of the networks. He'd been passing through Ann Arbor covering a team on its way to the College World Series. He'd called Manning and they'd had a drink.

"He basically wanted to know if I could get him some pussy," Manning told Alex.

"Did you?"

"Judge, first of all I'm a happily married man and I don't *know* any single pussy except for two eighty-two-year-old twin sisters who come see me for monthly checkups. Second of all, if I did, I don't think they'd be too thrilled to meet a three-hundred-and-fifty-pound born-again sex maniac who's mainly interested in doing weird things with spurs and lime Jell-O."

"God," Alex said. "That stuff all seems so long ago."

"Does it?"

"Doesn't it?"

"Not to me. It's all right there at my fingertips." Manning snapped his fingers. "It flashes right in front of me just like that. The Tobs, the Bigs, Lump, you."

"Sometimes," Alex said. "Sometimes it does for me too. Mostly not, though. I gotta work at it if I wanna bring it back."

"So," Manning said seriously after their second dinner and fifteenth beer together, "did you ever find it?"

"What?" Alex asked, though he knew what his friend meant.

"The Moment."

Alex laughed. "Do I sound like I have?"

"I don't know. Maybe you found it and it's just not as great as

you thought. Maybe you got it on the field but it doesn't trans
late to real life. Maybe this is it."

"No," Alex said. "I haven't found it."

"Are you sure?"

Alex shook his head. "I'm not sure about anything."

"Are you still looking?"

Alex didn't answer.

"Judge?"

"What?"

"You look kind of pale all of a sudden."

"I'm getting *my*"—Alex snapped his fingers—"*flash* into the
past. That's all."

"I guess it's not a good one, is it?"

"No. No it isn't."

"How's Patty?"

"Okay. We haven't really talked much since Russ . . ."

"She holding up okay, though?"

"She always holds up. I think she's just refusing to let herself
feel this. I think she's just not letting herself feel things in
general."

"Maybe she's got the right idea."

"Maybe." He sat quietly, chin in his left hand. "He looked me
right in the eye, Dave. And his eyes said, *Give me an answer.
Give me the answer you've always said is there.*" Alex shook his
head. "I didn't have it. I did not have the answer for my son."

"I'd like to see him, Judge."

"There's not much to see."

"Do you go often?"

"Sometimes. Not very often. Patty goes, though. Every day, I
think. And when we do speak she tells me about him. He
doesn't know if anybody's there. He doesn't know who he is. His
brain's gone, the doctors say." Alex sipped from his beer. "She
has to see it before she can accept it. I guess she has to see it over
and over again. Me, I've already seen it."

"Why don't you turn the machines off?"

"Because he's alive." Alex shrugged. " 'Cause I sit around all
day for the last three months hoping for a miracle."

"That was never your style."

"Styles do change, you know." Alex grinned weakly.

"Maybe," Manning said seriously. "Although I've never seen it happen."

"I'll be a pioneer," Alex said, and tried another grin.

"I've thought about it a lot, what happened to Russ. I've thought about what I'd do if it happened to one of my kids. I can't conceive of it."

"No," Alex said. "It's not something we should conceive of."

"How bad is it?" Manning touched Alex lightly on the arm.

"There's nothing to compare it to. When it hurts it's unbearable. When it doesn't hurt it's worse, 'cause it means there's something wrong with you 'cause it *should* hurt."

"I'm sorry, Judge. I don't know how these things happen."

"Hell, we've seen a lot of it, haven't we? Death, pain, hate, maiming, cripples."

"We just move in a fun crowd, I guess."

"Go to the hospital tomorrow," Alex said. "I'm sure Patty's going. You can see her."

"I'd like that. Will you come?"

Alex shook his head. "Nope." He blew out a long sigh. "Tomorrow I am on my way to Hawaii."

"You're kidding."

"A Handler Sporting Goods convention. I'm their gladhander."

"Very nice. A week in the sun."

"Yeah."

"Ever been?"

"Never wanted to go."

"Oh, Christ! I forgot."

Alex smiled. "Who knows? Maybe it's fitting." He leaned back to emphasize the sardonic tone of his voice. "Maybe I'll hit the land of my parents' dreams and discover the great secret I've been searching for."

"Why not, Judge? Why not? Hawaii's as good a place as any."

"Okay." Alex pushed his chair back and stood up. "I'm off."

"In the words of the great Walter Lumpano, so-fuckin'-long and have a great-fuckin'-trip."

"Will-fuckin'-do," Alex said, and watched Dave Manning head out the door.

Sitting on the plane over the Pacific Ocean, Alex remembered Manning's turn at the doorway.

"Let me know," he said. "If you find it. I'd truly like to know. I won't ever do anything about it, but I'd sure like to know."

Looking around the plane, Alex didn't think this group of people was going to help him find anything.

He was flying to Hawaii on the same flight as about twenty of the regional Handler managers and sales force. They were all quite excited about this little jaunt and Alex thought they were more than ready for the lampshade-on-the-head turn and the fake-handcuff trick. He hoped they would leave him alone for at least a few more minutes. He was ready to have to think about Hawaii, what this trip meant to him, about how this was indeed a kind of pilgrimage for his parents, for his mother really, about how somewhere deep down he really was hoping for some kind of answer. That's why he was going, why he'd accepted the invitation from the head of Handler sales. Because he was out of answers, out of places in which to seek them, and he thought maybe, somehow, he might still calm this great force that was forever driving him forward.

It had disappeared for a while, the force. Forever, he'd thought. But though he thought his pain had snuffed it out, the thing about pain, like love, he realized, it was never as permanent as it seemed when it was new.

He began to get used to it and it became a part of him. He absorbed it like a sponge. And he could live with it. When the pain had diminished enough to allow him to function, to be normal, he missed some of that agony. Somehow, it made everything more important. Without it he was just a part of . . . of a little tragedy.

To his surprise, when the head of Handler called about the Hawaii trip, he was ready. The thing inside that made him *him* had begun to regenerate. He was relieved but he was also afraid that he was hearing that inner music once again.

He had seen too much innocent destruction to be entirely comfortable moving in the real world again. He was not used to living with doubt and fear, and he did not know how well he would come to like it. But he knew it was time to find out.

Alex sat in his cramped airplane seat and wondered what the hell was going to happen to him. He wondered where the music would lead him now.

It led him back to the past.

"Hello," a woman said politely, and slid into the seat next to him. She looked to be in her forties. Her hair was very short, stylish, her face was lined, more weather beaten than aged. She wore jeans and boots that showed her to be in good shape, and a shirt that fell softly and delicately over small breasts. "You may not remember me," she told him, "but we used to fuck each other's brains out."

"Oh, my God!" Alex said. "Katie!"

"Alex Justin," she said, and smiled a bit devilishly, as if she had just discovered a long lost wad of money in an old cookie jar. "As I live and breathe, how y'all doin'?"

"Katie Gray."

"I'm flattered. Last name and everything."

"Katie, I can't . . . I mean . . . What . . ."

"Still got a way with words, huh?"

"What are you doing here?"

"I'm on my way to Hawaii for Handler S.G., same as you."

"But—"

"I'll tell you all about it, honey, if you have dinner with me tonight."

"I—"

"We don't start work till morn. This is a free night, as they say in the convention biz."

"I'd like to have dinner," Alex said. "I'd love to have dinner."

"Well, good."

"Yeah. Good."

"Well, whaddya know."

They were whisked through the Honolulu airport by a chubby guy wearing a Hawaiian shirt, loud orange shorts, and two leis.

The hotel, tall, all glass, modern, unthreatening, was a quick twenty-minute drive in the chartered bus.

Alex unpacked slowly. He liked unpacking in hotels and motels. He had spent most of his life on the road, and tucking a shirt away in a cardboard-thin drawer somehow made him feel like things were going along okay. When he was done, he took a long shower. Although he had never allowed himself consciously to think it, he'd been nervous about the flight. After all, his parents hadn't survived it. As soon as he stepped under the hot stream of water, he realized how nervous he'd been. The water stung his strength away. He stood for a long time, ten minutes maybe, before bothering to soap himself. When he turned the water off he felt exhausted. Drained. He took a deep breath, stepped out of the tub onto a white bath mat, and began getting ready for his evening.

At eight o'clock there was a knock at his door. He opened and Katie breezed into the room. She'd changed into a light shift, vaguely native-looking. She wore no makeup, no jewelry. Unadorned, he thought.

"You look nice," he told her.

"Old but nice."

"Yeah." He grinned.

"Well, that's always the way it'll be with you. What were you when I led you down the wayward path, nine?"

"No, I think I was at least eleven."

"Well, you look like you've stayed fit, at least."

"You too."

"I've heard about you sometimes. Read about you. Sounds like you've had your ups and downs."

"That's pretty accurate."

"We gonna stand here all night or what? I'm too damn hungry and tired to gab in your doorway."

He took her arm at the elbow and guided her through the door back into the hallway. They took the elevator up to the rooftop Luau Room. They were ushered to a table in the corner. From the tall glass tower they could see the beach. The ocean blended into the dark night.

"So," Katie said when they were seated. "Tell me about your ups and downs."

"No," Alex replied. "Tell me about you first."

"Have you thought about me a lot?"

He thought for a second then shook his head. "No."

"You always were a flatterer."

"I'm glad to see you, though."

"Hell, we don't even know each other. For all you know, I've become a mass murderer."

"We know each other."

"Would you like something to drink?" the waiter interrupted. Like everyone else in the hotel he wore a lei over a Hawaiian shirt.

"A mai tai for me," Katie said. She looked at Alex. "When in Rome, you know, honey."

"Two mai tais?" the waiter asked.

"One," Alex said quickly. So quickly that Katie noticed and cocked her head at him questioningly. "I'll have a, uh, what else is there?"

"A piña colada?"

"Great. I'll have one of those."

"You have a thing against mai tais?" Katie asked when the waiter left.

"Yeah," Alex said. "No. I mean no. I'm just not ready for one yet."

"Anyway," she said. "This is my life, Katie Gray."

"I'm listening."

"When you last saw me, there I was, bitter and pissed as all get-out, standin' in mah little bare feet in mah little bare apartment. I decided you were maybe the worst guy on the face of the earth and that life was no oil painting for a southern girl like myself." Alex smiled and Katie went on. "But then when you were gone, I started thinkin'. *The thing about that goddamned kid*, I thought, *is he sure did like what he was doin'.* He sure did think that stupid game of baseball was important."

"I did, didn't I?"

"Hell, yes. So believe it or not, I started goin' to ball games. Me! I went a few times to see the Tobs. I went alone, sat alone, didn't talk. I watched. I didn't see much the first coupla times and I started to think, *Oh well, that boy was just another crazy dream machine*. But I kept goin' for some reason and pretty soon I started to see things. I started to like it. I started to learn things. Pretty soon, I knew every damn thing there was to know about baseball. I mean, I wasn't just followin' the Tobs, I was checkin' the major league box scores, I was followin' teams in the papers, I was havin' favorite players. I'd've like to died for Willie Mays."

"Good choice."

"So what I did was"—she sipped her drink—"I thought to myself, all this brand spankin' new appreciation of a game is not takin' me out of the waitress biz and into the world of high finance where I belong."

"So . . ."

"So I went out and got myself a job in a sporting-goods store."

"In Wilson?"

"No. Hell, no. I took a big plunge and drove on up to Raleigh. Well, I can't tell you how impressed the manager of this store was when I started talkin' Bobby Shantz and Mel Parnell, an', shoot, he didn't have a chance."

Alex laughed.

"He hired me as a salesgirl and I been sellin' ever since. About ten years ago I went to work for Maloney Sporting Goods and they eventually made me Southeast regional sales manager. Then about three months ago I got hired by Handler. And here I am."

"What about . . ."

"A husband?"

"Yeah."

"The guy who hired me in Raleigh? At the store?"

"Yeah?"

"I married him."

"Good for you."

"He was a damn nice guy, and for me it was a pretty easy way to get a promotion. And for him, well, there I was danglin' in front of him every day. I wasn't a real beauty, but nobody'd been beatin' me over the head with an ugly stick either."

"You still married, Katie?"

She hesitated, taking a long swallow of mai tai before shaking her head and saying, "No. Divorced. Long ago."

"Me too."

"From that girl? The wonderful sweet, perfect girl in *New York City?*"

Alex nodded and grinned. "Uh-huh. You have kids?"

"Never wanted any."

"I did."

"I heard, honey," Katie said sadly. "I heard. Now just fill in the gaps for me."

He did. He went a long way back and brought her up to the present. He started hesitantly, but he soon relaxed, and his whole life came pouring out of him remarkably easily. He began to enjoy telling her about himself. He enjoyed reliving the triumphs and the laughs and the sadness. He was surprised how simple it was to recap his life. Some things she knew—she'd followed his career, she'd seen the Play on television, she'd read about Russell—others she didn't. Some things surprised her greatly, others made her smile and nod as if she'd thought about what would happen to him and those events had been anticipated.

She did not smile when he told her about his parents and why he hadn't drunk the mai tai; nor when he told her about his marriage, about Haiti; she did not smile when he told her the details about Russell. She did not smile when he told her about getting blue, nor when he told her the reason he'd really come to Hawaii.

When he was done, when he was all talked out, she smiled again. There was not much humor to the expression, rather warmth tinged with regret.

"You used to be . . . you used to be . . ." She trailed off, confused.

"I used to be a lot of things. I still am a lot of things."

"You used to have an unlimited amount of passion."

"I think I used up my allotted amount."

"I'm a little drunk," Katie said suddenly. "And before we have coffee or any sort of pineapple dessert, I think we should go back to your room. I haven't seen you in thirty years, Alex, honey, and I'd like to find out how much passion y'all have left."

They began tentatively, slowly, unsure of what was to come. Fully dressed, they kissed, standing up by the foot of the bed. Her tongue swept through his mouth and after all the years it was a familiar taste and smell. She was leaner than she had been. As his arms clutched her firmly to him, she felt smaller than he remembered, harder.

They broke apart after their first long kiss. She took a step backward and peered up at his face, searching. She stepped back into him and he went to kiss her again, but at the last moment she averted her mouth and bit his neck. Her teeth dug into his flesh. He yelled in pain and she grabbed the back of his hair and kissed him. She bit his lip until he pushed her away, hard. She tumbled over onto the bed.

"Fuck me," she told him. "I want you to fuck me the way you did when we were both young."

He didn't move.

"Katie," he said.

"What?"

"I . . ."

"What are you waitin' for, Alex?"

"Nothing." His throat was dry. "I'm afraid."

"Of sex? My, my, my. What *has* happened to you over the years?"

"Katie, everything I do . . . everything I touch . . ." He looked down at the beige-carpeted floor. "I'm always on the lookout for tragedy now. And that makes me afraid."

Katie was quiet for quite a while. She didn't make any move, however, to shift from her inviting pose on the bed. "Alex, honey," she said finally, softly but with a surprising firmness, "when you left me that dark day long ago, I thought, *Well, goddamn, I'm destroyed.* And I remember standin' there, then sittin' on that old ragged couch and waitin' to just die or disappear or whatever the hell was supposed to happen to you when you were destroyed. And you know what? Nothin' happened. I wasn't destroyed. I didn't disappear. Imagine my surprise."

"I can imagine."

"You can only destroy yourself, Alex. Nobody can do it for you. Life does its best to push you over the edge, but you're the one's gotta do the jumpin'. Your momma coulda been drinkin' those damn mai tais all her life. You didn't destroy your boy, your dreams didn't destroy your boy. He's the only one who pulled that trigger."

"I don't like to think, somehow, that we're that alone. I don't know if that's any better."

"Well, there ain't no teams, not in real life. Maybe when we all get up to heaven, but not here and now."

"Well, what *is* here and now?"

"Me," she said.

Alex took a small step toward the bed. Katie cocked her head up at him, her eyes glowing. She gently took his hand and pulled him on top of her.

They kissed. Their lips began, their tongues more ravenously intervened. They sucked and licked with a desperate pleasure. Then their hands began to explore. Alex felt Katie's fingers groping his back. He sensed she was pleased that he was still so firm. He flashed on Patty, then on one of the stewardesses who had given him a big smile when he'd boarded the plane earlier that day. Katie's nails ran down his spine and Alex arched his back and neck at the wonderful sensation. They had both kicked off their shoes and now Alex removed her dress. She was skinny and her breasts were small. He fingered her nipples. He saw the nipple of the Girl from the Park, was going to lean down to kiss it, but then Katie's hands were on his chest, trying to scrape their way down to his heart. The Girl from the Park disappeared. Alex's hand reached between Katie's legs and shot up inside her. She gasped. His other hand pushed her backward and he brought his mouth to her cunt. She grabbed his hair while he licked, bit, chewed, until she was wet and dripping all over him. He licked her asshole and then, as she lay on her stomach, face buried in the pillow, he climbed on top of her. He licked the small of her back, worked his way up to her shoulders, her neck, bit her ear. The Girl from the Park arched *her* shoulders, her graceful swanlike shoulders, but Katie suddenly

flipped herself over. Suddenly he was looking into her eyes, int
Katie's eyes. She kissed him, kissed his face, licked him clean
and then with one sudden motion he was inside her. Her hand
were outstretched and he was pulling at them, practically rip
ping her apart. Her feet were kicking wildly at his back, diggin
into him like spurs. They moved like this for a long time, neithe
saying one word, until sweat began pouring down his face and
he could see the veins on her neck sticking out and they both
began thrashing like fish on a hook. The Girl from the Par
grabbed him, then Patty, then the hands of thousands of strang
ers tried to rip him off of Katie. He shook them off, swinging hi
head back and forth until they all had gone, until only Katie wa
left. Katie, who was groaning and gasping and clutching him

He came. And she came, too, screaming as she did, really
screaming, and then he just collapsed on top of her. She tried to
move, to get one last bit of hardness from him, but he clamped
his arms around her and held her absolutely still. When she
stopped resisting, he relaxed. All that could be heard was the
sound of their breathing, heavy and thick. They weren't looking
at each other; there was no need. Alex's hand went to his face
and as he patted at his wet and matted hair, he rolled off Katie

"Did it do it for you?" Katie asked.

"What?"

"Did it make you forget everything that's happened in the
past and hopeful for everything that'll happen in the future?'

"No," he said.

"Too bad." She laughed.

"It used to," Alex said. "With you, it used to."

"Well," she said, "you were a lot younger then. A lot less had
happened in your past and your future . . . well . . ."

"It was a lot less knowable."

Katie laughed again. "That is one of the things about gettin'
older. The gap between the future and the present becomes a
lot less mysterious."

"I haven't," Alex said slowly, not so much to Katie as just to
say it out loud, "made love to anyone since Russell shot himself."

"Lucky for both of us," she said, "that passion wasn't gone, ust warehoused for a while."

He leaned in to her, covering her with his body. "It's a strange thing, Katie," he said, his words muffled in her hair.

"Hold it, honey. Are you gettin' serious?"

"Maybe."

"Okay. Wait. I wanna change positions." She moved him off of her, sat up cross legged, and put a hand on his chest. "One of my little idiosyncrasies now. I like to be comfortable when I gotta get serious."

"Are you comfortable?"

She smiled. "Very. Now shoot. Tell Katie what's so strange that you're not lyin' here simply goin' *Whoo-eeee, that was the best damn thing that's happened to me in a long damn time!*"

He put his hand on top of her head. "I've done some great things," he said. "Perfect things."

"Such as?"

"The Play. That was perfect. That was *perfect*. And sometimes so was being in love with Patty. Once with Russ, when he was a boy, I took him to this dive for a pastrami-and-egg sandwich, and I'm tellin' you it was *perfect*. He knew it, I knew it, the short-order cook knew it. And sex," he went on. "Sex with you. Thirty years ago. And now. Perfect." He cleared his throat. "It's strange," he said.

"What is?" Katie asked softly.

"It all fades. It all fades. Except in the mind. Except in memory."

"It fades quickly too."

"How do you keep it? How do you have great sex every day? How do you make a great play every day? All I've wanted in my life is something that lasts. How do you make something *last?*"

"You don't," Katie said without hesitation. "Life doesn't last," the naked woman told him, pulling at a hair on his chest, "why should anything *within* life last?"

"Then what matters? What's the point?"

She didn't answer. He could tell she was thinking about it, though.

"How do I see you again?" he asked. "I don't mean in Hawaii I mean in the real world." She still didn't answer. "Katie?"

"You don't, honey." Katie looked down at the floor as Alex cocked his head. "I got a couple things to tell you."

"Uh-huh."

"I told you a little fib during the course of the evening."

"What was that?"

"My divorced husband?"

"Yeah?"

"You can scratch that 'divorced' part. We've been married twenty-three years. Happy as a couple of goddamn lovebirds. I also got me some kids. The oldest one's a goddamn beautiful boy. Alex we named him."

"Why didn't you tell me?"

"I thought you might've had some scruples about sleeping with a married lady."

"Well, goddamn," Alex said. But he smiled.

"I have somethin' else to tell you too," Katie said, and her voice was now almost a whisper. "Nobody knows this. It'll be our little secret."

Still smiling, he nodded.

"I'm dyin'," Katie told him.

"What?"

"I'm dyin'." Her voice was louder now, and remarkably calm. She pointed to a thin hairline scar on her breast. "The Big C for Katie."

"No," he said. "No. It can't be."

"Hey. Don't go feelin' sorry for *your*self. It ain't happenin' to you. It's happenin' to me."

"Christ," he croaked. "I'm sorry."

"And don't apologize neither. I noticed this seems to be a pretty common occurrence. The survivors take it harder than we dyin' ones. It's like they're bein' punished and we lucky folks just get to fade away."

"Katie," Alex said. "It's not that. It's just . . ." He actually laughed. Not much of a laugh, but a laugh. "I'm startin' to feel a little jinxed."

She laughed, too, now, though she had to wipe a tear from her eye to keep it from rolling down her cheek.

"I'll tell you somethin', Alex. I had to pull a lotta strings to get on your damn plane and work this whole thing out."

"What?"

"You think this is just a coincidence, my bein' here naked on your bed?"

He rolled his eyes. "I guess it seems kinda stupid, but yeah, I did."

"No, no, no, sonny. A lotta work went into this."

"Why?"

"Now you're lookin' for flattery."

"No, I'm not. I really want to know why, I mean after all these years."

"Wanna hear a story?"

"Sure."

"When I knew you, honey, way back when, you weren't much for personal details."

"Yeah, but—"

"Hey, hey. You were young and interested in one thing and one thing only. This isn't a criticism. I'm just tellin' you that you don't know too much about my background."

"No, that's true."

"Very true. The point is, my dear sweet momma is a crazy woman. Not like nuthouse crazy, but crazy neurotic. We never got along. She always thought I was a slut, which I was, and I always thought she was a witch, which she is. So somethin' happened, I don't even remember what, it was when I was around fourteen or fifteen, and I left home. And I told her I'd never speak to her again. Ever. Now, I know this is hard to believe, 'cause I've always been so svelte since you knew me, but at one time I was a regular chubbo. I mean, when I left home my hips were out to here and I wore these funny glasses and my hair looked like, whoooo, I don't even like to think about my hair." The more Katie talked about the old days, the more her accent sneaked into the story.

"But when I left home, part of it was leavin' that whole side o' me behind too. I stopped eatin' and I worked out and I fixed my hair up some. I looked a lot different, I guess, a lot better. And that part of my life was over as far as I was concerned. All of this is just by way of saying I never did speak to my darling mother again."

"You're kidding. Never?"

"She tried. Believe me. The worst was when her mother died. She called me—I guess one of my sisters gave her my phone number—and she said my grandmother had had a heart attack and was dead and she needed me at home."

"You didn't go."

"I didn't. It might seem a tad cruel, but that woman, once she had her hooks in, it was damn hard to yank 'em out again. It was bad for me to go, it woulda hurt me. I was better off away. And I never spoke to her again."

Katie took a deep breath, and Alex thought the story was over; but it wasn't. After a second breath Katie went on. "So some years ago—Christ, maybe seven, maybe ten—I'm sittin' in a bar, havin' a drink with a girlfriend. I'm on the road in a little town, a little southern town. And I turn around and who's sittin' in the booth next to mine but my mother. She's there with some guy, a date. I mean, she's no spring chicken, but she's lookin' pretty good. I figure, before she sees me and starts a scene, I better say somethin'. So I stand up, go up right in front of her, an' I say hi. Well, there was the damndest pause. And my momma looked at me and looked at me and pretty soon I realized she had no idea who I was. I mean *none*. So I said somethin' like 'Oh, I'm real sorry. I thought you were somebody else.' She laughed and that was the end of it. Except I can't tell you how creepy it was to have your own mother not know who you are. I wanted to get away from my past, but I didn't want it to *die*, you know." Another deep breath, then a slow smile. "Anyway, sugar, I think this is kinda the reason I wanted to see you. I had this life that I left behind, and now that I ain't gonna be around for too much longer, I wanted to see someone who knew me the way I used to be. I'm dyin', Alex, and one of the things when you're dyin' is you get this weird urge to try to make sure your life was *real*." She laughed and ran her hand over the scattered sheets. "I'm tellin' ya, it was real then and it's real now."

"Potential," Alex said.

"I beg your pardon?"

"*Po*-tential. That's the way they used to say it down in Wilson."

"What *are* you talkin' about now?"

"I've been lookin' for *po*-tential all my life when it doesn't even exist."

"Oh, no," Katie said. "There's always potential. That's what makes life so nice. You just can't worry about it, is all."

"I saw Dave Manning before I left. He'd agree with you, I think. He says he stopped looking, stopped searching. But it didn't make him happy."

"Then he shouldn'ta stopped. There's only one thing that's important in life, Alex. That's doin' what makes you happy."

"That's what you always wanted, wasn't it? Just plain happiness."

"What else is there?"

"I wanted a lot of other things. They don't seem so important, though, now."

"It's 'cause they're not real."

"And Manning?"

"Who knows? Who knows what makes people unhappy? Sure he gave up this great search. But maybe he doesn't have any moments of his own to be happy with."

"Maybe. He was always afraid of those moments."

"I wish I had the answers for you, honey. I really do. Maybe I'll get 'em before I go to the Great Sporting Goods Store in the sky."

He kissed her. They made love one more time. No one beckoned to Alex during it; no images filled his head; no musical strains called him into the past. Alex made love to Katie and then she lay in his arms until two in the morning.

"Well," she said at two, "I should be gettin' back to my room." She winked. "Before people talk."

"How long, Katie?" Alex asked quietly.

"Six months, tops."

"I—"

"No," she interrupted. "I won't see you again." He nodded. "But I tell you what I will do," Katie said. "I'll leave you somethin' in my will. How's that?"

"I'd like something of yours."

"Well, I got a *real* good idea. That'll be another of our little secrets. When you get a gift and a little note from me, you'll know that old Katie is livin' on a cloud somewhere."

She put on her shoes and moved to the door. She stopped before opening it and turned back to Alex.

"You know," she said. "This business of things lasting, the things that you want. I don't know if it's so all-fired important. I wanted *you*. And shit and goddamn, I *had* you. I had you thirty years ago when you were in your *prime.*" She opened the door. "Thanks for my moment."

"You're welcome," Alex said.

Katie stepped out into the hallway and closed the door behind her.

31

"Happy birthday to you. Happy birthday to yooo. Happy *birth-day*, dear Alexxxx"—Alex heard a few voices stretch out the word *Juh-uhdge* instead of *Alex*—"Happy birthday to yoooooo."

Everyone applauded. A couple of people whistled apprecia-tively. You could tell that the whistlers knew it was uncouth to whistle but they did it anyway, a joking, friendly punctuation to the surprise.

Alex *was* surprised. He thought he'd be having a nice, quiet dinner with Patty to celebrate a birthday he didn't much feel like celebrating. She suggested a drink at Getting Blue to begin the evening and, without much effort, convinced him to make the stop there. One of the waitresses asked him to step into the back room and the next thing he knew everyone was singing and clapping their hands.

He looked around at the group gathered for his party. He was glad Patty was there. They had seen a lot of each other the last few months. They had talked, they had touched. They hadn't made love, but they were perhaps closer than they had ever been in their lives. There was, at long last, a level of honesty between them that had never existed, a degree of truth. It added up to a confusing yet permanent kind of love and he was very glad for it.

Manning had come in for the party. Alex watched him, glass of bourbon casually held in his hand, lounging against a corner of the room, the ever-present smile on his face. Alex felt a strong and strange kind of love for Manning too. Their sparring relationship had endured. With something of a shock Alex realized he was at the age where endurance was enough to engender importance. And caring.

Danny was there, with his new wife. Alex didn't remember her name and he figured he probably didn't have to, since Danny was already flirting with one of the pretty waitresses, telling her a joke, charming her. Now he came over and kissed Alex on the cheek.

"Jews kiss," Danny said. "Happy birthday, *boychick*."

"Thank you," Alex said, and smiled. A genuine smile. He clapped Danny on the shoulder. "Thank you."

To Alex's surprise Walter Lumpano came up to him.

"Danny invited me, Alex. I was in his office when Patty called," the Lump said. "I hope it's all right."

"It's all right, Lump," Alex told him. "I'm glad to see you."

"Happy birthday. God bless and happy-fuckin'-birthday."

He watched the Lump's three hundred and fifty pounds waddle off to the makeshift bar in the corner.

"Your whole past is here," Patty said to him.

"Yeah." He nodded. "Kind of strange that this is what I've accumulated."

Now it was Patty's turn to smile. "Who would've thunk it, huh?"

He kissed her on the cheek and she squeezed his hand.

"I'm going to bring Willie over," Patty said.

"He won't come."

"Well, I'll try, anyway."

He watched as she walked firmly over to the pine bar and tried to tug Willie Trotty from behind it. But he wouldn't budge. He didn't shake his head as Patty argued; he didn't respond. Finally, she shrugged and returned to the party.

"Maybe he'll come later," she said.

"Maybe," Alex said back.

And now others were converging on him. Some of Getting

Blue's regular customers. Peripheral friends of his, a few women friends of Patty's. The waiters and waitresses. Alex had a few drinks, chatted, hugged, kissed, ate, opened gifts. He had a good time and was surprised when people started to slip away, saying it was late. It *was* late. After midnight now.

The Lump came over and said good-bye, and for a moment past and present melded together. The Lump was young again. Two hundred and twenty pounds of raw, crude muscle. And Manning was an arrogant, vibrant phenom. And Willie a talkative thing of beauty, Patty an innocent, wonderful creature, unhurt and unspoiled. He himself was young too. Strong and dedicated. So sure of what he was doing, of where he was headed. Certain of his own importance. Alex shook his head. His youth vanished and he wondered if it had always been an illusion. Had Walter Lumpano ever been as imposing as he remembered? Had Manning been as impenetrable? Had Patty *ever* been as pure?

Danny and his wife came over.

"I got a new scheme," he said. "And I want you involved."

"I think I'll pass this time," Alex said.

"We'll talk."

"Good night, Dan. Thanks for comin'."

"My office. Wednesday. Ten-thirty."

Alex shook his head.

"Talk to him, Patty," Danny said. "This could be a big one."

"Night, Dan," she said softly. She and Alex smiled at each other, secure in their own small stand, in their mutual support.

"I want to talk to you," Alex said to Patty. "I really want to talk to you."

"Okay."

"Now."

"That's okay too," she said, still smiling.

He started to speak, but before a word came out there was a faint tug at his sleeve.

Alex turned and looked into Willie's eyes. He wondered what Willie would do, what he'd communicate for his birthday greeting, but the black man simply turned away, looked down at the floor. He handed Alex a telegram.

Dear Alex, it read. *When you receive this, I'll be in the Great Sporting Goods Store in the sky. Don't weep, please. I've had my share and then some, and I got no complaints. But I promised you something, and this is it.*

I got three things to say. My farewell address, so to speak.

1) You said life is too damn complicated. Wrong. Facing death, you realize life is too damn simple. People *are too damn complicated.*

2) Don't be afraid. There ain't nothing to be afraid of. So maybe love's not enough to mean *anything. But it's enough to live on.*

3) Thanks again for my moment. That, too, is enough.

I told you I'd send you a gift too. It'll be there in a minute. I hope it's everything you thought it was going to be.

I'll be seeing you.

Centered at the bottom of the telegram, it just said, *Katie*.

Alex slowly folded the piece of paper in half, then in half again, then one more time. He put it in the back pocket of his pants.

"What is it, Alex?" Patty asked. "Is it bad news?"

"No," he said after a fairly long pause. "It's just news." He did his best to look reassuringly at his ex-wife.

The remaining stragglers came out and wished him happy birthday, then headed out onto the streets of the city. Manning lingered still, off to the side, nursing his bourbon. Willie went back behind the bar.

"What did you want to talk to me about?" Patty asked him gently.

Alex rubbed his eyes with his left hand as if to wake himself up.

"I want to tell you something very important," he said. "I want to tell you that I love you."

"This is nothing new," she said, but clearly she was as moved and touched as when he'd first told her.

"It is," he told her. "I want to marry you again."

She said nothing.

"I think this may be the first time I ever shocked you," he said.

"Can we sit down?"

They sat.

"So whaddya say?" he asked.

"I bumped into your brother," she said, out of the blue. "On the street. Yesterday. To tell you the truth, I think he'd been following me."

"Why?" Alex said, his voice suddenly dry and hoarse.

"He wanted to apologize."

"Christ!" Alex said and slapped the table, a short, violent slap.

"I accepted it."

"Patty . . ."

"I accepted his apology, Alex. I didn't hate him anymore."

"I do," Alex said.

"Good. Good for you. I think, to tell you the truth, Elliot deserves hating."

"Patty. I know you very well."

"Yes, my love."

"I figure all this is a way of telling me you won't marry me again."

She almost smiled, but couldn't quite manage. "It is."

"Why not?"

"I don't have any hate in me anymore, Alex. And I'm afraid I can't risk love again. Not the kind of love you're talking about, anyway. I just can't."

"I—"

"Yes," she said. "*Yes.* I *know* you can. I don't know *how* you can, I swear to God I don't. But I can't. If I get married again, it'll be to someone with gray hair who's very nice and very safe."

"I'm sorry, Patty," Alex whispered.

"You don't understand. It's *me.* It's not you. It's not what you've done or haven't done. Alex, I'm glad that you're what you are. And I don't want to get in the way. Not again. Keep going. Please. Yes, I love you, sure. But not the right kind of love. Not the kind of love that'll help you . . ."

"Get blue," he quietly finished when she trailed off.

"Yes," she said. "*Yes.*"

They sat in silence. Then she kissed him.

"Just go," she said. "Go get it. Whatever it is, whatever it brings, go get it."

"I'll have gray hair one of these days."

"I know you will."

"Maybe it'll make me very nice and very safe."

"Maybe."

They smiled at each other and she kissed him again.

Dave Manning came over to the table.

"Willie has a present for you. It came with the telegram."

"Bring it," Alex said, and Willie was right there, with a tray. On the tray was a drink. One drink.

"What is it?" Alex asked.

"It's a mai tai," Manning said. "Willie got instructions in a note."

As if it were a bomb, Alex gently lifted it off the tray and placed it on the table in front of him. "Sit," he said, and Manning sat. "You, too, Willie." Willie hesitated but took the fourth seat at the table.

"So?" Manning said.

"So this was a good birthday."

"You look different, Judge. You look sorta happy."

"I do?"

"Yeah."

"Maybe I am."

"Is there something I should know?" Manning asked, with that trace of hopeful sarcasm. "Have you suddenly found your answers?"

"Maybe," Alex said. "Maybe."

"You gonna keep us in suspense?"

"I don't know."

"Will it do me any good?"

Alex shook his head. "I don't think so."

"Ah," Manning said, and shrugged. "Then don't bother."

"Make a toast, Alex," Patty said.

He looked at the mai tai in front of him, a long, challenging look. He picked it up.

"Aloha," he said to the group, and took a long drink. The cold made his teeth tingle and the liquor warmed his tired body.

"How is it?" Manning asked, as seriously as Alex had ever heard Manning ask anything.

"Shitty," Alex said with a huge grin. "Way too sweet."

Patty sighed. It sounded like a sigh of relief. Or maybe disappointment. Alex couldn't tell. Willie stood up, ready to go back behind the bar. A customer put some money in the jukebox and some nice easy jazz took over the background.

"Aloha, buddy," Dave Manning said.

"Aloha," said Alex Justin, and took another sip of the terrible drink. "Alo-fuckin'-ha."